A BREAK IN THE CLOUDS

Prickly Hawthorn Village #3

KAREN DEAN BENSON

A BREAK IN THE CLOUDS
Copyright © 2021 by Karen Dean Benson

ISBN: 978-1-955784-07-8

Published by Satin Romance
An Imprint of Melange Books, LLC
White Bear Lake, MN 55110
www.satinromance.com

Published in the United States of America.

Cover Design by Ashley Redbird Designs

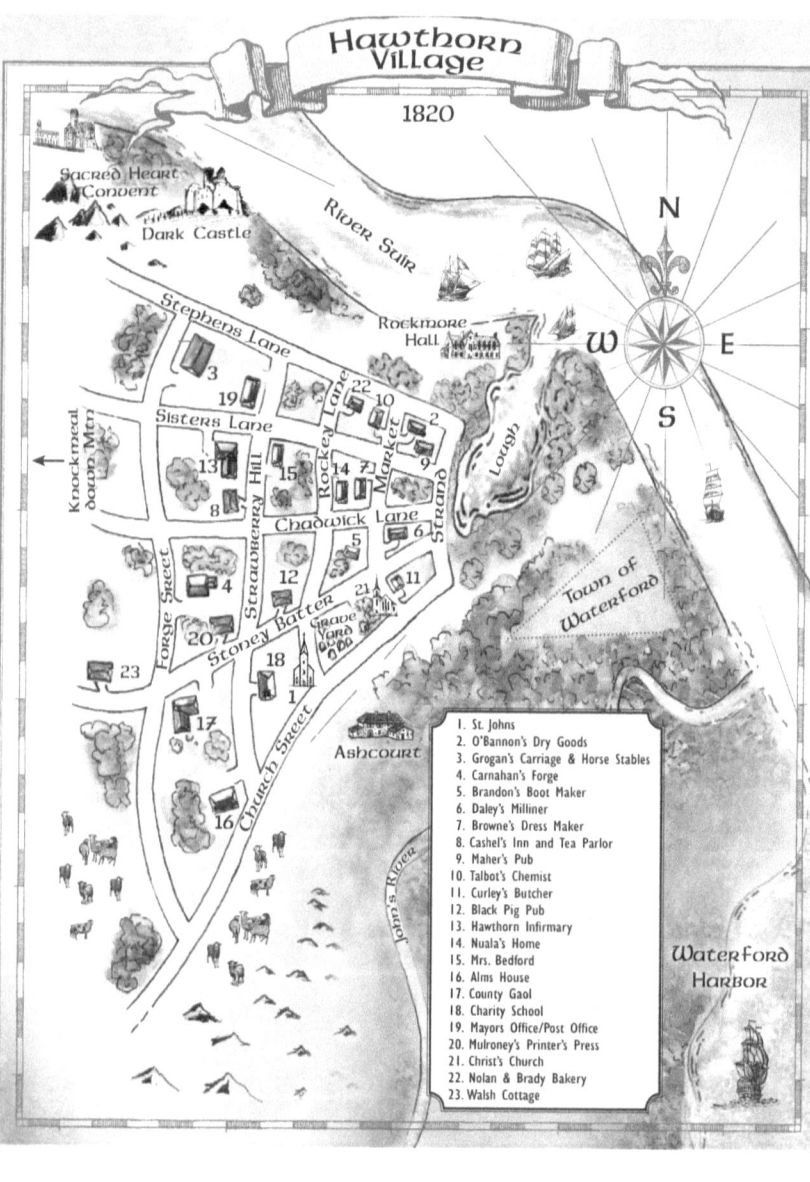

Hawthorn Village
1820

Sacred Heart Convent
Dark Castle
River Suir
Rockmore Hall
Stephens Lane
Sisters Lane
Rockey Lane
Market
Strand
Chadwick Lane
Strawberry Hill
Stoney Batter
Forge Street
Grave Yard
Church Street
Ashcourt
Knockmeal down Mtn
Lough
Town of Waterford
Waterford Harbor
John's River

N
W   E
S

1. St. Johns
2. O'Bannon's Dry Goods
3. Grogan's Carriage & Horse Stables
4. Carnahan's Forge
5. Brandon's Boot Maker
6. Daley's Milliner
7. Browne's Dress Maker
8. Cashel's Inn and Tea Parlor
9. Maher's Pub
10. Talbot's Chemist
11. Curley's Butcher
12. Black Pig Pub
13. Hawthorn Infirmary
14. Nuala's Home
15. Mrs. Bedford
16. Alms House
17. County Gaol
18. Charity School
19. Mayors Office/Post Office
20. Mulroney's Printer's Press
21. Christ's Church
22. Nolan & Brady Bakery
23. Walsh Cottage

Dear Reader,

A strange thing happened on the way to writing this story. My husband, Charlie, and I decided to sell our Michigan home and our Florida condo and build ONE new home in Florida. We intended to uncomplicate our lives.

The universe had other plans. For the most part, I had already laid out the plot for this 3rd book in my series and felt confident I could write *and* make decisions about our new build. Then the pandemic crept into our lives. Now you might think quarantining is a writer's magic cure-all. But with all the distractions accompanying the building of our forever home and the unforgettable disturbance of the coronavirus, well, *A Break in the Clouds* suffered.

I am thankful for the guidance and patience of my publishers, Nancy Schumacher, and Caroline Andrus.

My critique partners Karen Auriti and Doris Lemcke—you know how I feel about YOU!

Kathy Lyles' support was a blessing. I am also deeply grateful for Mr. Benji and his knowledge of the game of Cricket. My daughter Mary Margaret, son Kevin, neighbor Kim, and all of my readers whose encouragement and insightfulness helped bring this story through a house build and a pandemic—I am most grateful for you all.

Happy reading—Karen

County Waterford, Ireland
Hawthorn Village - May 1840

Mim met Brianna at the back door. The housekeeper reached for the drawing pad and satchel the lass carried. "Your first morning home and you were up and out early. I can see you've still got your love of sketching that dilapidated old manor."

Brianna untangled the scarf from about her neck and hung it and her sunhat on a peg. "That *old ruin* as you refer to Ashcourt was on my mind almost every day since I've been gone. I couldn't wait another day."

"For the life of me, lass, I can't see what you like about a place filled with banshees."

"Since when did you start believing in myths?" She hugged Mim. "I missed your teasing. It's nice to know some things never changed. You haven't mellowed one bit."

"Livin' with the rich and haughty as you've done these past three years. Don't think we'll be pampering you now that you're here to stay."

Brianna laughed. "You do know I was one of the staff at the

Reynold's home? I took all my meals in the kitchen like the rest of the workers."

Her aunt's cheerful sounds carried from the front parlor. "I'm in the parlor waiting on you, my dear."

Brianna did not roll her eyes, the love she felt for her aunt was more likely to raise a chuckle. "She must feel better. Thanks for setting my painting gear out of the way." Brianna felt blest to come home to her aunt. And though Mim was the housekeeper, she has been part of the household since before Brianna was born.

Mim set a bowl and whisk on the table, preparing to make something delicious, no doubt. "You're welcome. Now scat."

Brianna hustled into the parlor and leaned over, planting a kiss on her dear aunt's forehead. The lace of her cap tickled Brianna's nose, and she held a sneeze in the nick of time, then sank onto the adjoining sofa. "How is your ankle today? I see you are relying on a shillelagh."

"Mim found it in the attic. It suits simply fine."

Brianna picked at a thistle tangled on her hem and twisted the stem about her finger. "It's grand to be home." The flowered wallpaper and lacy curtains were the essence of her dainty aunt and the sweetness in her heart.

"You haven't been here a full day yet. You must have been out the door before you ate?"

"I packed an apple and a biscuit. I wanted to sketch the early morning sunrise with charcoal. I intend going back this afternoon." She hadn't much time to herself with so many Reynolds children to keep after. Though school hours were normally morning until mid-afternoon, with luncheon served in the schoolroom. After class, the daughters always seemed to want private conversations, or a walk in the garden, or visiting an exhibit or other. Brianna found little time to indulge her painting. And most often was exhausted by the end of the day.

Aunt Natty's fingers were plying knitting needles. She made blankets and caps and booties for expectant mothers. The hospital in Waterford and the Curran Infirmary in Hawthorn Village were her usual recipients. "Mim and I lived a quiet and orderly existence without you and all your comings and goings. It's a great relief to have you returned. Maybe now life will perk up. You were missed, my darling." Aunt Natty swiped at something in her eye.

Brianna swallowed a lump and batted her eyes to keep from tearing up.

Being an assistant governess for a family of six children mostly presented an exciting experience. Her gaze swept about the parlor, but there is something to be said about home.

Brianna's love for her aunt made for a boundless and extraordinary bond. Two souls brought together under quite unusual circumstances twenty-three years ago, Brianna being a wee infant, and Natty eager to become an aunt and love that babe.

Aunt Natty let out a length of yarn as she continued to knit. "Now, I wish to bring up a subject you reflected on last night before we retired."

"Do you refer to the Reynolds family, or the journey?"

"No, no. I've enough about the *ton* and all their grandness. You mentioned a person on the coach. A man you pegged as dreadful?" Aunt Natty set her needles down and sipped her tea. "He didn't give you any trouble, did he? You could have complained to the coachman."

Brianna dropped the thistle on the tray, brushed off her hands, and took up her tea. "He seemed to take dislike of Mrs. Hammond, a passenger, and her two young daughters as they harmonized. She taught them lyrics as a way of passing time.

"He scowled a lot. Mumbled something about privacy. Which rendered him absurd when you consider there is no privacy. Seven days of travel is bound to bring out a snit or two. I would have thought he had the means to own a coach. He was high in the instep. An elegant dresser somewhat similar to Mr. Reynolds."

Huffed up with her explanation, she waited a moment then continued her description. "He wore the finest black leather shoes. And every hair in place. Furthermore, I'm quite sure he hasn't children, otherwise he would have exhibited sympathy toward the mother attempting to keep her little ones occupied." Thinking of his odious behavior raised her hackles and she sipped the cooling tea to calm herself.

Aunt Natty's bright blue eyes peered over the rim of her cup. "It sounds like the attention you paid him gave you an understanding of the gentleman. So, tell me, what did you do next, my darling?" She smiled at her niece, obviously anticipating a quip.

Brianna set the cup down, frustrated, thinking about the five of them cooped up and the coach's pitching and rolling as it sped along the countryside. The need to defend herself bothersome she did so anyway. "I pointed out his impolite judgment of the mother and her daughters. That poor woman already besieged with fidgeting children her face blotched with humiliation no doubt brought on by his boorish attitude.

"Thankfully, her daughters were young enough they didn't appear to take notice. Though I must say, their harmony could have used an adjustment for the better. There were times I would have rather gone into my daydreaming than listen to them sing one more time."

Her aunt grinned. "Are you going to tell me? I've longed for your entertaining tales."

Brianna firmed up her chin. "You are certain I embarrassed myself?"

Her aunt's eyebrows lifted as if to say *and when have you not.* "I'm waiting."

"As any decent person would, I explained to him they were rather young and as children often are, overly friendly. I might also have mentioned that his churlishness came dangerously close to hurting tender feelings."

"Begorrah, lass. Did he put you in your place?"

Brianna's lips pursed as she recalled the entire scene. "We were stopped at an inn to change the horses out and get a bite to eat. I wanted to be as discreet as possible and not say anything in front of the mother—I had to react."

She huffed. "But what did that horrid man *do*? He stalked toward the table where they sat. I knew exactly what he planned from the way he grudgingly stomped his way across the floorboards, and I wanted to put the kybosh on him. His eyes narrowed like chips of green glass as he fixed on the mother and her two daughters and calmly said, *Please accept my apology for being short with you. It was not my intention by any means.* He then tipped his hat and retired to a private corner and sat."

Aunt Natty clapped her hands. "Then, what did *you* say?"

"Aunt Natty, please, I am not a monster. His behavior drew out beyond necessary. Somebody needed to shake him. The mother's cheeks blistered red with mortification." She shifted in her seat and glanced at her hands.

"Don't stop now. What happened next?"

"We were another four hours in the coach with no harmonizing. Thankfully, we stopped at Bennetsbridge for the night."

"That would put you two days from home." She sped on. "It must have been a relief to get away from the cramped coach."

"As it turned out, the mother and daughters stayed at the inn that night then transferred the next day to Kilkenny. The *gentleman* didn't dine that evening, nor did we suffer his presence the next day. Good riddance, I say."

Pussycat trotted into the parlor purring loudly, her yellow-eyed scan swept from Brianna to Aunt Natty. Decision made, she jumped on the sofa, snuggling on Brianna's lap. Her fluffy reddish tail flagged with pleasure.

Brianna teased, "Missed me, did you?"

Aunt Natty reported, "I have something of interest for you. Mrs. Teaberry has been waiting for your return. She has an offer to make you."

Curious, Brianna prodded, "I wonder what that might be?"

"She has need of a part-time assistant sorting mail and tending the window. I can't recall if I wrote about Mrs. Teaberry as our postmistress and that her husband is no longer mayor and now the post office has been fitted into the front rooms of their home."

"Isn't that a bit cumbersome? Will the coach deliver packages there, too?"

"Oh, my yes. Mrs. Teaberry wanted it no other way." She fiddled with her handkerchief, expecting to quell a sneeze, but nothing came of it. "I'll never understand why she gave over her lovely home. A bit of tattle is that she gets paid to use her home, otherwise the General Post Office would have to rent space somewhere else, and it would cost more."

Pussycat must have heard Mim dropping tidbits into her bowl. She pushed off Brianna's lap and dashed down the corridor.

"I shall see her first thing tomorrow then."

☙❧

It was mid-afternoon, and Brianna was intent on painting her beloved Ashcourt. A black and yellow bumblebee, pollen stuck to its hairy legs, fluttered between Brianna's nose and the canvas. The buzzing distracted her focus on what would eventually be a mighty oak with its lofty dense canopy of green spreading toward the ruin of Ashcourt Manor.

As she turned to swoosh the insect away with her left hand, she inadvertently swept her right hand, that held her paint brush, across the image on the canvas. The bee floated on its merry way, leaving her with a mess.

Returning the brush to the sill on the easel, she stood and arched her back, hands at her waist. She glanced at the cerulean sky dotted with wisps of white that gave the appearance of gauze floating in the wind. A light breeze ruffled the pond.

She decided to call it a day and began gathering up her paints and folding the easel. Something about the dappled sunlight in the trees and curled dead leaves skittering across the unkempt drive caused her heart to catch. Over the years, she had been drawn to this sad, lonely place. Many years actually, with the exception of the last three.

Until a few weeks ago, she had been an assistant governess to a family with six daughters, all of whom were little more than two years apart. The Reynolds' huge estate north of Dublin, Dundalk to be precise, overlooked the Irish Sea. Aged out of the schoolroom and ready for advanced learning, one by one the daughters emptied the quaint schoolroom to the point where Brianna had been relieved of her position.

She had known the time would come when her position would cease. The Reynold's daughters were lovely colleens, and quite different. Strong-minded Annette; Jill-Ann sweet as apple pie; Mary, definitely an intellectual; Kristen who always had her nose in a book; Emma quiet and, it was obvious, their father's treasured; and the youngest, Sarah, who with her remarkable beauty, attracted attention whenever she traipsed into a room.

Brianna looked forward to returning to her own life and bid them all fond farewell with a dribble of tears amongst lingering hugs and promises to write.

Having returned to Hawthorn Village and their cozy cottage off the corner of Stoney Batter and Forge, she began picking up the pieces of her life, amongst them her painting visits to Ashcourt Manor. Its weather-worn exterior had been sorely missed.

Like an old friend, she held deep affection for the decaying place.

Ashcourt had been rejected long ago, the same as Brianna had been as an infant. Her empathy for this crumbling edifice knew no bounds. She equated the manor's neglect with her own and always painted the home with something alive. A face in the window, a patch of wildflowers, bunnies scampering about, or a red bloom clinging stubbornly to the crumbling arbor gate.

Brianna stooped toward her box of paints and closed the lid. She should repaint the dark slash that marred the scene. But an ominous cloud, most likely filled with rain, slowly moved in from the east. She finished packing and made for home.

Aunt Natty had suffered an accident two days previous to Brianna's return from Dundalk. She twisted her ankle on her way to the milliners and fallen in the lane. A stranger, a well-dressed gentleman as her aunt explained, came to her rescue, and took her to the infirmary.

Her aunt almost swooned when talking about the stranger. She prattled on in a dither because she forgot to ask his name. A bit of blood from her scrape and her ankle painfully swelling, her manners escaped her, and she didn't thank him. He had been kind and quite considerate.

Hawthorn Village's doctor, Mr. Curran, kept her overnight in the infirmary. In the morning, Aunt Natty insisted she go home. Her niece was arriving after an absence of three long years, and it would not do to be gone when the coach arrived.

Brianna smiled, thinking of Aunt Natty ordering the doctor to take her home. Some things never change. As it happened, Aunt Natty arrived home less than an hour before Brianna arrived with her trunk and satchel. The coach would have been an hour or so earlier, but they were forced to wait for a rider to check in and take his seat.

Upon learning about her aunt's accident, Brianna had considered the coach might have been waiting for the rude gentleman who had gotten off at Bennetsbridge. But was greatly relieved to learn otherwise when an elder gentleman took the seat next to her, though he never offered an explanation as to why he held up the coach for an hour. She could only surmise he either owned the coaching company or paid a great deal of money because the policy did not allow for the postillion to wait on people.

She and Aunt Natty had spent last evening catching up. Though their letters had been frequent, she yearned for their evenings together when they nestled in comfortable chairs with a cozy fire, sipping tea, and sharing the day's events.

A surprising interview

The next day in the early-morning, Brianna readied for her interview with the postmistress of Hawthorn Village.

It wasn't her way to be idle, especially now that she returned home. A soft breeze stirred the leaves and the sweet scent of scythed grass felt like freedom as she made her way to the post office. Last night's rain left a few puddles to be avoided. Crossing over Chadwick Lane the road widened, and she continued until once again on dry ground.

Several folks were queued up in front of the post office waiting for it to open; hours were from nine until three. She checked her watch pinned to the jacket of her day dress. It was 8:28. She had two minutes.

Mrs. Teaberry, on the lookout for her, opened the front door to a gush of questions from the folks standing in line.

"Earlier than usual ain'tcha, mistress?" Suspicion scratching the man's words.

"All's I need are to get these sent off, Mrs. Teaberry," begged a woman, wrapped in a shawl, her arms full of packages.

Mrs. Teaberry's strident tone set the crowd back. "It's not nine. You'll just have to wait." She beckoned to Brianna. "This way, Miss Walsh."

Challenged by several larger men in front of her, Brianna squished past them into the slight opening. Which immediately shut and locked by Mrs. Teaberry to a chorus of disgruntled folks.

"They think the moment the door opens I'm available. I take it your aunt explained why I wanted to talk to you?"

Mrs. Teaberry led them through a corridor and into a large room where the business of the post office took place. Brianna had been on the other side of the half wall numerous times. It looked well organized and should be easy to navigate through a day's work.

Brianna nodded. "Yes, ma'am. She mentioned sorting mail."

Mrs. Teaberry's eyes narrowed. "Well, that will be one of your duties. I believe you will catch on rather quickly. I've known you since you were a sprite. You were an impressive lass and forthright about your objectives."

Mrs. Teaberry's unusual compliment eased Brianna's nerves.

The postmistress asked, "It's necessary for you to be tested in writing and arithmetic. Seeing as how you've been an assistant governess these past years, I see no reason to test you. Can you start this morning? I'll be near if you have questions. Your position will be as clerk."

Brianna loosened the ribbon on her bonnet and began taking off her gloves. "Yes, ma'am. That will be fine."

"Pegs for your use are on that wall." She inclined her head toward the corner of the room. "There is an apron on the other hook, and sleeve guards in the drawer. You'll need them to protect your gown." She checked her watch. "We've fifteen minutes for me to acquaint you with the window."

They returned to the foyer that had been transformed into a lobby with a wall built across the middle space. A wide window casing in the wall, no doubt for accepting out-going mail and payments. Cubby holes lined the backwall where incoming mail would be filed for pickup.

Mrs. Teaberry pointed out. "As you can see, this is our worktable where we weigh packages to determine the cost of mailing them." She tapped a big black book. "And this ledger is where we make note of money received and expenses incurred. You must always do this immediately upon receipt in order for our debits and credits to balance."

She pointed to a tin box under the counter. "All money received will go in there. I do the accounting every evening."

Mrs. Teaberry further explained, "The post office closes at three each day, and tea breaks are taken at that time. Saturday is a half day. We are closed Sundays, and holidays. At 3:30, if the coach is on time, newly arrived mail needs to be filed in the cubbies. That brings the workday to an end at 5:00. But, of course, you won't be involved in the afternoon work of the post office."

As Mrs. Teaberry finished with Brianna's quick tour, Lionel Murphy, the rural messenger, entered the foyer from the kitchen area. He trod the same route each day, delivering mail to villagers living more than two miles out of town.

Mrs. Teaberry, on the verge of introducing them, when Lionel spoke up. "We know each other from church, ma'am." He gave Brianna a nod.

"Miss Walsh is to be one of us now. She'll work at the window three mornings a week."

Lionel's long thin face and bushy eyebrows bunched up into a smile of sorts. "Welcome to the General Post Office of the United Kingdom, established in one form or another almost two hundred—"

"That's enough Lionel. We are due to open the front door in four minutes and I am still familiarizing Miss Walsh to her duties."

He nodded and returned to the kitchen.

Mrs. Teaberry whispered. "He likes to quote the history of the United Kingdom's postal services to anyone who will stand still for a moment."

Mrs. Teaberry glanced at her watch and said, "Two minutes yet. You and your aunt have mailed back and forth, so you know about the Uniform Penny Post that started in January of this year. The charge is *1d* for a prepaid letter and *2d* if the fee is collected from the recipient. And I'm sure you know about Penny Black. Our allotment of stamps hasn't arrived yet. I'm assured they will be soon in coming.

"But until they arrive, you will need to stamp each post with this…" she reached over Brianna and pulled out a stamp pad of ink and a stamp with a wooden knob on the top. "This one is for prepaid, and the other is for the post to be paid by the recipient." She turned it upside down. "See the *payment due?*"

At Brianna's nod, she replaced the pad and the wooden stamps.

She glanced at her watch and said, "Here we go."

Brianna felt as if a dam was about to open.

Mrs. Teaberry unlatched the front door, and Brianna girded herself for her first customer. The postmistress stood to the side of the window allowing Brianna to stand at the opening for customers.

The man with the scratchy vocal cords asked, "How long will it take for a letter to reach my son in Scotland, Edinburgh."

Mrs. Teaberry pulled out a sheet of paper with numbers on it and handed it to Brianna putting her fingertip on the approximate time it would take to arrive in Scotland.

Brianna answered the man, "It looks like it will take seven to ten days, sir."

He nearly asked his next question when Mrs. Teaberry poked her head in front of the window and said, "Are you all set, Mr. Simmons?"

Startled at her head popping out the window, he blinked. "Um, yes. Well, no. Is it *1d* to go all the way to Edinburgh?"

"One penny now, or two pence when delivered. As long as it doesn't exceed a half ounce." Her arm snaked out the window and snapped up the letter and pushed it at Brianna to weigh it.

He impatiently tapped his fingers on the sill. Brianna returned with the post. "Just a fraction under, ma'am."

Mrs. Teaberry moved back from the window. "Well then, get on with the transaction."

The rest of the morning came in quick succession with lulls and then several customers at once. Two women, friends of Aunt Natty's, knew Brianna had newly arrived home after several years. They were curious about Dundalk and the family for whom she worked. Brianna gently pried them away from questions about her last three years before Mrs. Teaberry popped her head in front of the window again and ordered them to get on with business or leave.

It was going to take Mrs. Teaberry some time to feel comfortable with her handling the window. The woman certainly ran an efficient office and challenged idle gossip, and most likely had answered the same questions hundreds of times.

So far, she hadn't erred. But the morning was just begun. She drew in a determined breath. Demonstrating her capabilities and her worth was important.

M im opened the door to a tall gentleman with a bouquet of flowers in hand. "Faith and begorrah," she had no warning to stifle the gush over the lovely blooms.

The handsome gentleman asked, "Is Miss Walsh at home?"

"The elder or the younger, sir?"

He gave the question a moment of consideration. "I would say the elder."

Struck by his vivid green eyes, she asked, "And whom shall I say is calling?"

"Inform her it's the gentleman who assisted her several days ago. Finbarr is the name."

"Ah. Do come in. We are grateful for your attention to our dear Miss Walsh. She is most precious to us."

Visiting the disabled and more

He was led into a small parlor and his attention went immediately to the extraordinary western view out a bay of windows. In the distance and through a fine mist, the upper parts of the Knockmealdowns were majestic. He turned toward the entrance when he heard the tap of a cane.

"Mr. Finbarr is it, then?" Miss Natty Walsh's eyes twinkled. She must be feeling much better since the accident.

He handed the housekeeper the lilies and lilacs mixed with bright-yellow spurge. "These are meant to brighten your day, Miss Walsh."

She gave him a delightful smile. "I prefer Natty. Have you time to visit?" Without waiting for him to answer, she nodded to Mim. 'Biscuits and tea. And put this lovely bouquet in a vase."

Waiting for her to choose a seat, then he sat. "Several days of rest have done you well, Miss Natty. I'm surprised your doctor permits walking."

He perceived a tsk-tsk from the housekeeper as she left the room.

Settled in her chair, Natty ignored his statement saying instead, "I must apologize I didn't ask your name when we first met. Finbarr. A fine Irish name. Though I've not heard the likes of it as a surname?" She gave him a flinty side glimpse.

He said, "I prefer being known as Fin or Finbarr if it's all the same."

"Secrets have we. Well, I enjoy your company and won't challenge your decision, young man. Now, tell me what brings you to Hawthorn Village."

The housekeeper brought in a tray of small cakes and steaming tea then gently closed the door to the parlor on her way out.

"I lived here many years ago. Recently I decided to return and…" he shrugged his shoulder, "…see how Hawthorn Village has developed in the years since. And check on family property."

He disliked being evasive with this charming elder, but he saw no need to get personal. He wasn't sure how long he intended to stay in Hawthorn.

"What is your line of work? You don't impress me as a man who enjoys a desk day in and day out."

He chuckled at her quick perception. "You would be right in that. I am…was…in the mining business in Wales."

"Begorrah, not at all what I expected to hear. How did you ever come by choosing such a vigorous way to earn a living?" She opened a napkin and laid it on her lap, then asked if he would pass the tray. Choosing a biscuit, he set the tray on the table.

He wondered how did he decide? No one had ever asked him before. "I suppose I'd have to say it chose me. While at Eton a friend, Tommy, invited me home for term break. His family lived in Swansea Wales. His father owned a mine, several in fact, and the talk centered around metals, especially copper, and mining.

"Tommy's mother, Mrs. Benford, involved herself in the discussion of metals and the process of mining. She fascinated me with her knowledge and interest, as her husband and son listened."

Fin continued, "Talking through dinner was forbidden in our home. The Benford meals were lively with crosstalk and quips. Fortunately for me, Tommy invited me again at the next school break."

He paused a moment thinking of how many years had passed and chuckled. "My excitement was such that I had my bags packed two days before we left for Swansea."

He grinned at Miss Natty's attempt at interest—involving her brows flexing up and down. "I do apologize. It's a topic I could discuss for hours, and I dislike boring you. Suffice to say Mr. Benford created an internship especially for me. I began living with the family and working for him when I turned sixteen. It's been my interest ever since."

He set his empty cup down and drew his large hands over his knees. "I didn't intend to overstay my welcome."

"Don't hurry off, young man. I would like to know if you have family in the area?"

"You remind me of my mother, always needing to know the story behind the person. My parents are deceased, and my two sisters moved out of the area about the same time I was sent to boarding school."

She airily gushed, "Where you are staying? I would like to have you to supper some evening. I'll send a note."

Quite pleased at her offer, he said, "I would enjoy an invitation. I've taken up at Cashel's Inn. If I'm gone, leave your note at the desk for O'Bannon."

"So, you do have a sur name?" She granted him a warm smile. "Any relation to Nuala O'Bannon, also known as Lady Rutledge?"

"My cousin. It's been many years since I've seen her."

"Well, then, dear lad, you probably need to change that. And you can count on an invitation to dinner, Mr. Finbarr O'Bannon."

A low breath escaped, and he admitted, "Returning to Hawthorn Village has been a challenge. The memories for the most part, are formidable. But a larger sense of duty tugs at me to inspect the family home and see to perhaps selling it or demolishing it and selling off the land."

"And that is why you were reluctant to announce yourself as O'Bannon."

"Forgive me, ma'am. Sometimes I try to be too careful. I apologize for my churlish attempt to hide my identity, especially from you."

"I like intrigue. And getting to the bottom of it. You have a great many secrets I suspect. Rest assured they are safe with me." She wiggled to stand.

"Don't get up, stay comfortable. I will see my way out. Thank you for listening to me, Miss Natty. I sincerely look forward to supper some evening."

Two steps toward the foyer he spied a picture on the wall. It sparked an unsettling recognition of a familiar place, Ashcourt Manor, though the artist depicted it as a ruin. His memory included a stately and well-kept home. This was a shock.

The artist had taken liberty with the oils by inserting a mischievous elfin face in an upstairs window. Not much surprised him, but seeing this oil did just that, regardless the face peeking out of the window.

Miss Natty turned in her chair and called from her seat. "What do you think of it?"

"It churns up memories." He kept to himself the shock of seeing his childhood home where so much misery took place.

"Really? My niece painted it."

"She must have quite the imagination."

She chortled. "She is a firm-minded young woman. And a tongue to match. No doubt about it."

His astonishment was genuine. "Why would she paint Ashcourt?"

He instantly recalled the misery of living there. His father's cold indifference and dismissal of him as a person. His mother's total inability to change her life, and in so doing, change his.

Seized with a rush of anger, Finbarr pushed the sudden emotion down. *This* is why he was so reluctant to return. Now that he had, he needed to follow through. He ran the tips of his fingers across the painting, the massive park leading up to the front door. The past hurtled its way into his psychic, and he inhaled deep regret.

A silent promise to himself, that this too shall pass.

Miss Natty apologized. "She's the light in my life, I shouldn't have blurted that out."

For a moment, Fin's pondering slipped into a deep well of an unforgiving past. "You were saying your niece is strong minded and now wish you hadn't said that?" Miss Natty gave him reason to chuckle and it released the tension in his shoulders.

"'Tis what she is, but as lovely as they come. Born with a mind of her own, it's what I should have said."

"I won't tell a soul." He couldn't help but grin at her.

"As to why she paints Ashcourt. She's been fascinated with the place since a child."

He said, "Ah, well I am relieved that you are up and about, Miss Natty. I hope you continue to do as the good doctor ordered."

The housekeeper *tsked* as she handed him is belongings and bid him good day.

On his hike back to Cashel's, he smiled at being called *dear lad* and was fairly certain no one had *ever* called him that.

The Post Office shock

Brianna's third morning working at the post office began with settling into the routine. Mrs. Teaberry had set her up for Monday, Wednesday, and Friday mornings. She sorted through packages that arrived the day before when the bellpush rang.

"Good morning, wha—" Dumbstruck, Brianna looked at the intolerable man in the coach, the one she berated for rude behavior.

He didn't act as though he recognized her, and she managed to croak out, "What can I do for you, sir?"

"I need a post box. The name is O'Bannon. Finbarr O'Bannon."

She stooped down, pulling out a tray and began leafing through cards and found the one for new addresses. "Fill this out and return it to the window. I'll open a cubby for you."

She slipped the card through the window. "You will find pen and ink on the shelf in the corner." Breathing a sigh of relief, she hoped he would soon be out the door before he recalled when they met.

He took the card and the next person in line stepped up to the window and asked, "Any mail for me? Alice Cavendish."

Brianna turned to the cubbies against the far wall, found one item for the Cavendish household. "Will that be all, ma'am?"

She nodded and left. Next in line, Mr. Winter wanted his mail. Brianna recalled him from earlier and had retrieved his posts as he came through the door. "Here you go, Mr. Winter. Anything else I can do for you?"

"No, thank you. Just give your aunt my regards."

"I will, and good day to you, Mr. Winter."

Regrettably, Mr. O'Bannon stepped up. He slipped the card across the window opening. His writing hand proved to be one of the finest she had ever seen. He then handed her several packets. "What do I owe for the mailing of these?"

She looked up at him. "It will take me a minute to weigh them, then I'll give you the total." He still did not seem to recognize her—she experienced a puff of gratitude. She would hate for him to tell Mrs. Teaberry that sometimes she said more than she should. *Sometimes? Ha!*

She slid the bill across the counter, and he pulled out a small purse, setting down the coinage, snapped the leather pouch shut, then said in his distinct baritone, "I'm relieved to know you are capable of a civil tongue. I did wonder how you might get on in social situations."

She gaped at him as he tipped his hat and left the lobby, his broad shoulders barely missing the doorframe. He might think better of her because of his observation, but she certainly wouldn't change her opinion of *him*.

Furthermore, what was it that would have him residing in Hawthorn Village? Tasked with setting up a mailbox for Mr. O'Bannon, now she would have to deal with him on occasion.

Done with her morning, Brianna headed to Brown's Dress Makers to pick up a yard of ribbon and have a chat with the proprietor, Diane. Her mother passed a year ago, leaving Diane everything. They had been fast playmates as children.

Diane climbed down a ladder just as Brianna entered the millinery shop. "As I live and breathe, is that really you Brianna Walsh?" She stepped off the lowest rung.

"You are just the person I wanted to see." Brianna hugged her old friend. "You must be in your element, surrounded with feathers, ribbons, and hats just like your mother."

Diane sighed. "I miss her terribly, but this place keeps me remarkably busy. Probably just the way my mother would have wanted it."

"Don't tell me you are also doing the sewing and mending?"

Diana folded a length of tulle and laid it on the shelf. "I hired a local colleen. Mother had an exceptionally large clientele. It takes both of us to keep up."

Brianna patted Diane's hand. "I think it's wonderful you are carrying on in her footsteps. She was a dear lady."

"Can I help you with something?" Diana folded her hands as her eyes darted about the store.

"I don't want to distract you. I do need a yard of pink ribbon. If it has embroidered edges all the better."

"I might have." She turned to the shelving behind the counter and ran a finger along the row of ribbons. "Aha." She handed the bolt of pink ribbon to her.

"It's exactly what I need." Opening her reticule, she drew out a pouch.

Diana's bright eyes glistened. "It's nice to see you. You've been on my mind. I saw your aunt a week or so ago and she said any day now. So, I've been waiting."

"It's so good to be back. You seem to have settled into this change quite nicely."

The bell rang as the door opened admitting two women. Brianna finished paying and hugged Diane. "We need to get together when you have time."

Diane's focus already on the customers, she said, "Good Day Mrs. Smythe and Mrs. Wagner."

Brianna whispered to her old friend. "See you soon."

A gentleman's right to privacy

The desk clerk at Cashel's Inn, a thin man with a mustache that spread to the bottom of his chin, asked Mr. O'Bannon's length of stay. When he stated, an unlimited amount of time, several months at the least, the mustache spread into toothy appreciation.

Finbarr reclined in a cane-back rocker, enjoying the midafternoon summer breeze observing the comings and goings of the local inhabitants. He had taken the bull by the horns and hauled himself to this village. Now what?

Seventeen years of avoidance seemed long enough. Memories, good or bad, it was up to him to decide what to do with the family property bequeathed to him. The jarring encounter with a painting of Ashcourt on Miss Natty's parlor wall increased his curiosity. Though he had hardly recognized his childhood home, considering the artist's rendition of it as a ruin.

He did realize that the responsibility to keep it up over the years belonged to him. He pled immersion in his business in Swansea as the reason he hadn't. He began a mental list of what he would need over time. A carriage was an essential if he planned to keep Ashcourt Manor. But did he?

His mother passed when he was eight and he was immediately sent off to boarding school. His father passed nearly eight years later. His sister, Vivian, sent a short account of their father's demise and burial that took place in Dublin. Marion, his other sister, left when Fin was quite young. Other than she had dark brown hair, he didn't recall her.

His father's solicitor, Mr. Boyle, at Blackhall Place, Dublin, followed up soon after his father's demise, apprising Fin he had been named conservator of the estate until Finbarr O'Bannon reached the age of twenty.

As a lad, Finbarr had no interest in Ashcourt. Mr. Boyle sent him a monthly allowance and paid all his bills and tuition. When he followed his dream to work in the mines, his allowance was forwarded to Lloyds Bank in Swansea. When Fin turned twenty, he ordered Boyle to transfer the monetary part of his inheritance to Lloyds and told him to file the papers until such a time as Finbarr would meet with him.

Approaching his mid-thirties and leaving his mining properties in Swansea in the hands of an overseer, he forced himself to think of Ashcourt Manor and Hawthorn Village. And subsequently Mr. Boyle, whose responsibility it had been for the protection and management of the minor's financial estate until he turned twenty.

Clearly at loose ends thinking of his obligations and asking himself what the devil he was doing in this quaint village, he sighed and considered he'd retired far too early.

He pondered his responsibility toward what must be a ruin if the picture on Miss Natty's parlor wall was accurate.

He again set the rocker in motion as villagers passed Cashel's vast front porch. Somewhat reconciled to visiting the family home, he nevertheless felt a reluctance to dig up old memories that he'd deliberately run from as a youth. Yet, it appeared inevitable if he were to visit the place and go through trunks and drawers.

"Yoo-hoo, Sir O'Bannon, is that you?" Glancing up from musing, his gaze settled on a woman, one hand atop her wide-brimmed bonnet, the other clutching an overlarge satchel, as she approached the steps to the porch. What the dash possessed her to call him Sir O'Bannon?

"Oh, my, I dare say it is you. I can scarce believe my eyes. You are the image of your father. And of course, it couldn't be him now, could it?"

Neither waiting for a response from him, nor allowing him to offer her a chair, she plunked down fanning her lovely features in spite of the wind brewing. "My, it is hot. And, what a wonderful surprise. I came looking for you as I decided yesterday, I had noticed you on the porch. Much as you are today. Enjoying the warmth of the sunshine and our bustling village." She paused to take a breath. "What brings you back to Hawthorn after so many years?"

Finbarr tried to hide his irritation at the loss of a quiet afternoon. He attempted to place her but failed. And how did she know to address him as Sir?

She gained her wind and said, "Surely you haven't forgotten —or mayhap you have. It has been such a long time. You simply must recall Edith Breslin. Though I am Lady Hamerlin now. I am widowed but you might recall Lord Hamerlin?"

He hesitated, wondering if it was his turn to say something, he waited for her to catch her wind again. She smiled at him over the top of her fan. Apparently acknowledging he could now speak.

"You have gained the upper hand, Lady Hamerlin. I am at a loss as to how we know one another. I've been absent from the village for many years and only just returned."

Her fan flirted with him, and he wondered why women would use such a quirky nuisance. Folding the annoying black article, she patted his arm with it. "I've snatched you at the cusp then. Fortunate me. We were first acquainted when you played a prank on your sister and me. I am more of an age with your sister Vivian." She paused to see if he could recall the incident.

"Sorry, I can't bring the occasion to mind."

"You let a rooster lose in her bedchamber."

"My, my, I do not recall the occasion." Though he bit his lip as memory returned. From the point of view of a seven-year-old, it was astoundingly hilarious.

A doubtful quirk in her eyes, she offered, "Vivian and I hid under your bed once planning to jump out and scare you when you returned."

His vision narrowed. "Did I return?"

"No and we tired of the game."

"Well, then. I wouldn't recall, would I?" Admittedly an impatient man, he mused as to how long her game would continue.

The woman dug into her satchel and pulled out a worn newspaper. "What a delicious opportunity. I have been sharing this with friends who remember your family. And when I saw you yesterday, I simply had no choice but to offer my congratulations." She handed him a well-read copy of *The London Courier.*

In big print under the headline, in the left-hand corner, he read the name Sir Finbarr O'Bannon, of Swansea-Wales, owner of five copper mines, knighted and awarded a Baronetcy of the United Kingdom at the behest of Queen Victoria for valor in the saving of lives of many of his men in a disastrous dampfire. The investiture took place 23 April 1840 at Buckingham Castle.

Now, he understood why she felt compelled to call him *Sir.* For a man who liked his privacy, it was decidedly unnerving to have the town-tattle wave this article around Hawthorn Village. When in London he had not bothered to pick up a paper. And here it is in his hand, ready to destroy his privacy.

He supposed *The London Courier* would have made it to Ireland at some point, though he hadn't given it consideration until this moment.

Returning the *Courier* to her, he said, "Thank you. Now if you will excuse me, Lady—"

"You cannot run off this quickly, Sir O'Bannon. We've been friends since childhood. Let us at least have a chat about the years between. I insist."

Her dress a dull gray with a bit of lace peeking out from under her chin made him think her mourning might be in its second year. She must have eagerly stepped away from the black imposed by etiquette, the color wouldn't have suited her.

"Lady Hamerlin, I can't recall ever meeting you. It's far too many years to recall when Vivian had playmates over. I was eight when I was sent to boarding school and sixteen when I left for good. It would be impossible for us to be in a friendship all this time. I dislike leaving you to fret over your predicament about the years gone by, but I have an engagement for which I do not intend to arrive late.

"It's been interesting meeting you. Thank you for allowing me to read the article in the *Courier*." He stood, nodded, and left her standing on the porch of Chelsea's Inn and Tea Parlor.

Finbarr almost skipped every second tread on the stairs to his suite. Collins remarked when he entered, "Have you been running?"

"Yes," he barked.

"Should I be concerned?"

Finbarr turned a quizzical expression on his valet. "Only if Lady Hamerlin shows up on this doorstep."

He turned to Collins. "And the cat is out of the bag."

Collins had been arranging clothing in the closet. Several shirts were draped over his one arm and two pair of trousers on the other. "I'm afraid I don't understand, sir."

"I brought it on myself. I had hoped there wouldn't be any attention drawn to the dampfire. Nor the title of Sir. Lady Hamerlin, a woman acquainted with my eldest sister, stopped by this morning. I might characterize her approach as on the hunt for me waving the *London Courier*."

Collins summarized, "Ah, Lady Hamerlin let the cat out of the bag."

He nodded, hands on his waist, lips pursed. "So much for anonymity."

Mumbling came from the closet.

Finbarr barked. "What?"

Collins poked his head out of the closet. "Did you say something?"

"No. You did." Fin's brow furrowed. "What was it?"

"Nothing." He pulled out a hanger, ready to slip a shirt over it.

"Humor me. You obviously have an opinion."

Collins had the look of surrender on his face. "Why is it you prefer no one know about the dampfire or the baronetcy, or the knighting? It's a noteworthy honor. People are going to find out. The more one protests, the more intrigue."

Finbarr narrowed his eyes. Thinking. "You are right, of course. I can't seem to rid myself of an edgy feeling. It's hard to explain it. As if opening myself up for ridicule."

Collins replaced the hanger and took down an empty one. "Your night dreams reflect the same logic. Maybe it's time for you to talk to another professional?"

He glanced at his faithful valet and let out a puff of air. "I'll heretofore be known as Sir Finbarr O'Bannon. Will that do?" He deliberately made no comment about seeing a professional.

Collins pursed his lips, muffling. "If that's the best to be expected, that will do, for now."

"I heard that."

⚜

Aunt Natty, in fine fettle when Brianna returned from her morning at the post office, called out, "Come here, I've wonderful news. Simply grand."

Brianna entered the parlor bringing with her the scent of fresh air and peeked over her aunt's shoulder. "An invitation? To what? It is beautifully decorated. What is the occasion?"

She hung her bonnet on the peg, pulled off her gloves, then returned to glance over her elder's shoulder again.

Practically breathless, Aunt Natty gushed, "His lordship is celebrating his eighty-seventh birthday with a garden party." She handed the invitation to Brianna. "I heard rumors last time I visited the Hall. Cook couldn't hide her excitement over the prospect. But she fretted his lordship wouldn't agree to the party. It seems her ladyship wanted the celebration, and he did not."

Brianna inspected the delicate penmanship. The perfect script, painted flowers, and vines decorating the summons were worthy of framing. "It is lovely."

"I would assume Lady Tremaine created them. Did I ever tell you the Mother Abbess found her on a convent step in a basket? Years later Lord Darnley discovered proof she was his granddaughter. But, before the proof was found, she lived at the convent and the abbess taught her to illuminate manuscripts. A grand artist she is and that would be her delicate hand creating the invitations."

Brianna returned the card to her aunt. "Did Mrs. Atkinson ask you to help in the kitchen again?"

"Yes, and she sent along the invitation to the birthday party because she knows how much I enjoy seeing them." She turned it over. "It really is lovely."

She handed the note to Brianna. "Mrs. Atkinson hoped you would be able to lend a hand as well."

Brianna gave her aunt a sly look. "How would she have learned I've returned?"

"The day of my accident I was on my way home from a visit with Annie Bates. I had knitted booties for Annie's daughter who delivered twins and I wanted to give them to her. And, of course, I had to announce your return home. My friends all think the world of you, sweet." She cast a glowing smile at Brianna.

"With all the fuss over my ankle, I completely forgot about

Lord Darnley's birthday party. The kitchen staff reminded me of geese running about. We will have a grand time, you, and I, my dear. Just think of the food preparations and flowers to arrange. A garden party…" Her aunt's face lit with joy at the prospect of being part of such a grand event.

"How nice for us we can celebrate on the fringes, so to speak. Do we need to inform Mrs. Atkinson we agree to help?"

With a glint in her eye, her aunt blissfully declared, "I told her I would talk to you, but that I believed we would both agree."

Leaving a trail of laughter behind, Brianna excused herself and retreated to her room. There was more to helping out at Ashcourt's garden party than Aunt Natty let on. Always praying that *her darling colleen* might find someone, Brianna supposed her aunt had ideas that a male staff person at Rockmore Hall might catch her eye. Such a man would not do for her.

If she were to consider anyone, it would have to be an independent man. Like a tradesman of some kind, or a teacher. Someone with the ability to create his own destiny. As far as she was concerned, there wasn't a single man in Hawthorn Village who measured up.

༼ঃ༽

In the parlor, Natty rang the bell and the day maid, Jane, appeared.

"I've a note to write, bring my lap desk to me. I'll be done quickly and want you to run it to Cashel's Inn and give it to the person at the desk. And say nothing about it, do you hear?"

"Yes, mum.

"To anyone, Jane." Her brows knitted as she gave the girl an ominous glare. "Not a word to anyone."

"Yes, mum."

Having written her note regarding supper tomorrow evening she folded the missive, sealed it, addressed the front, and handed it to the day maid, saying, "Deliver it to the desk at Cashel's. Off you go then."

⚜

Later that evening, after one of Mim's specialties, chicken, dumplings, and gravy Brianna enjoyed the picture of Pussycat curled on Aunt Natty's lap purring contentedly. A fire crackled in the hearth as the patter of rain struck the panes.

Brianna missed their cozy evenings the most. Wind brushed the branches of rhododendron against the house. A light blue wool shawl warmed her aunt's shoulders, her eyeglasses reflected the flickering candles. Sprigs of graying hair poked out from her mob cap. Brianna's heart warmed with love.

She admitted, "This is so right, being home. I missed you most in the evenings. But I didn't want to write about that. I worried you might be concerned."

"Should I have been?" Her soft blue eyes peered over the top of her spectacles.

"The Reynolds are lovely people. They had scraps between them, but never with me. It made me wonder what life would have been like with siblings. Especially with sisters. I could tell, some days Mr. and Mrs. Reynolds had their fill of their daughters."

"I am grateful I have you, sweeting. But six of you?" A slanted smile crossed her face. "Personally, I wonder how Mr. and Mrs. Reynolds will survive until their daughters marry and they become the responsibility of their husbands."

Brianna kicked off her slippers and tucked her feet up under her skirt settling into the cushions of the settee. "Is that how you see me as shedding off responsibility to my husband?"

Aunt Natty looked over the rim of her glasses. "You, my darling, will bring a wealth of excitement and living to the household you command."

"Do you see me marrying?"

Aunt Natty pushed her glasses up her nose and eyed her. "Now where did that come from? Of course, you will marry. Every lass worthy of consideration does, and you've got so much more to offer."

A real story, not some fairy tale

"Would you mind terribly telling me of that day, again?"

A moment passed, and Aunt Natty shifted in her rocker, Pussycat slipped from her lap, stretched, yawned, and jumped on the settee, gingerly making her way to Brianna's lap.

"The story won't change, sweeting. I will surely tell you what I know. After all, the whole of it changed my life forever and gave me a gift I would not otherwise have." She swept at a crumb on her bodice.

Brianna combed her palm over Pussycat's fur and settled in for the story of how she came to live with her aunt.

"I tramped along Rockey Lane then turned up Stephen's, the weather lovely with the scent of rain to come. By the time I passed Forge Street and turned south on my way home, I had wandered in the trees and brushes, no set path to it. I heard children's playful laughter and such. Like they were playing catch-me-if-you-can. When I arrived where they played, it was as I thought. A peddler's wagon under a shade tree came into view.

"Five children in all that I could see right then, two in a tree, the others running about. The wagon as I could see, because at this point, I had stopped to take in the whole of it, was bright blue. The two windows were bordered in yellow, and red flowers were painted willy-nilly about the sides. The words *Rejuvenating Elixir for hair, teeth, and eyes* written in bold black letters on the side.

"As I moved closer, I saw a woman lying on the sweet grass warmed by the sun. It looked like she slept what with all those active children, when I spotted a man pacing with an infant in his arms.

"I turned about, thinking I had indeed imposed upon their privacy when he shouted to me. 'Miss, miss.'"

"So, I turned back. 'Yes?'"

"Help me. I am in need."

"Then I considered perchance the woman wasn't as I first assumed, but mayhap in distress."

"He asked almost like begging, 'Will you hold the infant? I think my wife is dying.'"

"Well, my heart almost flipped. And I ran to him and took you up in my arms. Your eyes were open wide. I cuddled you close. You were pink faced sucking your knuckle. Your beautiful gray eyes even then turning a blueish color as you eyed me. Inspecting me, you were. As if to say, 'Who is this stranger?' Your worried papa entirely frantic and lamenting, fanning his wife, lightly slapping her face. I began to wonder if her problem might be more than hunger. The children gathered and I wondered if they were all hungry. They looked as if they were.

"So, I offered to get milk and bread and bring it to them. The husband said that would be wonderful. Perchance something to eat might revive his wife. I did wonder if she could be dying, how he would think she might be helped.

"I remember saying 'Take your infant and I will go quickly and return.' But he stomped his boot with frustration. 'You take her so I can tend my wife. Please, good lady,' he said. 'I need to be with her, and the infant takes my time.'"

Brianna buried her face in Pussycat's fur—as if she were the one holding that infant.

Aunt Natty sipped her tea, then took up where she left off. "So, I took you with me and ran home. I fed you with a rag soaked in milk until you had your fill. You were so weary you fell asleep sucking. I pinned a clean linen on your little backside, cleaning you up as best I could. Packed up biscuits I had baked the day before, and a jug of milk in a little cart I had in the shed and carried you in my arm. We trudged toward the spinney bushes, me singing an off-key lullaby to you." She swiped at a tear before it got away from her and shyly peeked at Brianna.

"Does it bother you to tell me?" asked Brianna.

"Not at all. I get emotional thinking of that day, is all. I can't help it, sweeting. But for the next few minutes of my life at that time, I realized what I missed in my life and understood I had to return you to your rightful family. Shocked to see the wagon gone and no sight of anyone, I worried I had gone to the wrong place. But I saw their fire ring, and the ruts from the wagon wheels that had bent the grass as it drove off. I knew I stood in the right spot.

"Of course, Mim, beside herself with joy that we had a babe to care for, took great delight in feeding you. We took turns during the night. For months and months. That is when the fear began to seep in. We worried about the possible loss of you. Could we call you ours? Give you a name?

"A knock at the door caused us both to fret. Could that be your papa? Perchance he had figured out a way to keep you, after all. Your mother mayhap returned to health. Your siblings looking for you as they got older."

Her hands clasped, and she realized they clutched white at the knuckles. This small story served as all Brianna had of her past. That alone struck Natty hard when Brianna asked to hear it. Natty wished she could have told a much different story, but the truth was needed, not some fairy tale.

Pussycat wiggled from Brianna's arms and jumped off the settee, leaving Brianna with a distant vague look as a notion came to her.

Finally, Brianna said, "Both our lives changed that day. Mine for the better I've no doubt. I love you, Aunt Natty, as if you were truly my mother."

A bed of lies

Dervila Murdock lay on the bed, weary eyes closed. She could hear the screech of the gulls as they landed on the roof overlooking the harbor in Bristol. Her husband, Niall, moved about the one-room flat where they lived above a pub.

She kept her eyes shut—no trouble at all with the left one smarting where he had planted his fist.

She lay lifeless, as he swept his palm up her leg, pinching her and chuckling to himself. He finished packing his bag, readying for a month or more aboard the *Blackwind*.

She paid for his absence by allowing him to slap her. She grudgingly endured the pain.

As his fingers clenched her upper thigh, he warned, "Ye stay true to me, lass, or it'll go worse next time."

He trailed a finger down her leg, leaving her skirt flipped over the upper part of her thigh when he flung her on the bed. She waited until she heard the familiar sounds of lifting his gear and slamming a drawer shut.

With a spurt of moxie and devil-may-care, she warned, "I might be gone when you return."

He turned in his tracks, mean as the devil. "You leave me, and I'll hunt you to the end of the world."

His breathing hard, she could feel his eyes on her as she lay on the bed.

She opened her eyes and glared back. "I hate this place. It's time to go back to Ireland, to Hawthorn."

His meanness didn't scare her anymore. Seventeen when they married, his weaknesses, what he liked and didn't like had become automatic, etched into her mind.

He growled, "When I'm good and ready, we'll go back. Not before." His eyes raked over her, and then she heard the pounding of his boots on the stairs as he left.

They grew up in Tramore, County Waterford. A small village where near half the occupants are related to either Niall or herself. But with so many years passed since they lived there, she really didn't think he would see his way to return. Besides, he loved the water, as much a part of him as home. No, her chances of Niall returning to Ireland were next to nothing.

Sometime later, Dervila awakened feeling tired and weary. Streetlamps cast a muted glow. The putrid odor of dead fish and salt water drifted through the open window. The faint chink of dories hitting the docks as they rocked in the waves gave her a sense of Hawthorn Village.

The night people were beginning to move about. Their bibble-babble and the sound of brogues on the cobbles rolled on the breeze and into her one-room flat. Her legs were cold, and she drew the covers up, wishing she could lapse into sleep again but knew she wouldn't.

Instead, she would replay the afternoon spent with Niall. Like all the other afternoons when he readied for the boat. He meant to teach her a lesson about fidelity. That he was the man of the house and what he commanded must be obeyed. Short of running away, she saw no way out of the misery of being his wife. It was years since she cried, having dried up long ago and now her penance for an earlier sin was all she had.

An atonement she endured because men fancied her and she them. What could she do? Her beauty had been acclaimed, a long time ago. And there had been someone. But he had eventually moved on. It gave her satisfaction to think of him now. She had been so careful and always hoped Niall never discovered her fiery affair. When he was aroused, she took refuge in the memory of that other time so long ago.

Niall, toxic with jealousy, wouldn't be missed when he left for the boat.

She rolled over and watched the moon rising over Bristol's Channel. Her cousin came to mind. Natty, younger by a year, and naive as a babe. What Natty lacked in knowledge about men, Dervila more than made up for. Their shared rivalry over Niall and his choosing her didn't measure up to her misery now. She had felt like a queen when he chose her over her mousy cousin.

Dervila had made absolutely certain she would win him by allowing him his pleasure when she knew her cousin would *never* do such a thing before vows were taken.

And win she did, using a method as old as Eve. She told him she carried his child and he cut off his promise to Natty and married her within a few days. She hoped she would get pregnant, but when she didn't, Niall realized she had lied.

Dervila had never rued the loss of Natty's friendship. Her cousin always a bit too nice, a bit too soft. They were opposites in nature. And there were times in their young years when Natty seemed a nuisance accompanying Dervila. The lads would tease Natty, yet all the while their eyes roamed over her. Her skin prickled in response.

What Dervila missed was a certain young man who had adored her in her younger years. She had been beautiful, and men fancied her and she them.

It wasn't just that she liked him and his wild nature, she also liked that he came from a wealthy family. The combination had been hard to resist.

Niall returned in three weeks full of energy and a pocket full of money. He never told her how he earned it or how much he made, but she had her suspicions.

"Pack up yer gear, I've got us a sail for Ireland. We leave at the tide tonight."

Barefoot, she spun around gleefully. Her skirts filthy from the dirty wooden planks. "Tonight?" She jumped at him her arms about his hard waist.

He grabbed her thick hair and pulled her head back, his mouth inches from hers. His dark gaze roamed over her features. "You owe me for pulling up here before I'm ready."

"Owe you what?" Her arms drew back from his waist, and she stepped back putting space between them.

He jerked her back, his mouth came down on hers and for the next hour she paid for her dream of returning to Ireland.

What the past reminds us of

Finbarr purchased a spirited, bold chestnut during his layover in London. The famed stable, Melvin's, celebrated for its fine horseflesh, had been his first choice to find what he sought. He wanted a blood horse with length of leg and proud stature. Jupiter's large forehead, and clear eyes set out on the head and large nostrils, indicated intelligence.

He shipped the stallion to Hawthorn Village, Cashel's Inn and Stable.

The roan's shoulders looked strong and high, and the foreleg was not tied in under the knee, something that happens to blood cattle. Though Ireland was known for its pure breeds, Jupiter, a proud animal, and fleet of foot, allowed him to make the decision to purchase from Melvin's Stables rather than take a chance in small Hawthorn Village.

A month to the day, he received notification the roan arrived and had been delivered to Cashel's. A lad of about twelve was brushing the newly arrived Jupiter as Sir Finbarr entered the stable yard.

Paddy Cashel, chewing on a strand of hay, quirked, "Gotcha a grand piece of horseflesh, there, Sir O'Bannon."

He nodded as he ran his hand over Jupiter's flank. "I'm in the market for a curricle with a folding hood and a tiger. Do you think you can help me out?"

Paddy Cashel, a solid rock of a man, shorter than Sir Finbarr by a head, owned the stable and inn; a bargaining man if ever there was one.

"A fellow I know came onto hard times and needs to sell. It's in the back." He nodded toward the livery.

His gaze drifted past Paddy into the depth of the stable. "Back there?"

Paddy stiffly moved forward. "Follow me."

He opened a back panel, allowing a shaft of light into the stable. A low set phaeton on four wheels with a jump seat in the rear would need two ponies. With a little paint on the wheels and a good cleaning, it should serve his purpose.

Sir Fin walked around the phaeton and ran a finger over a cushion, making him think this buggy had been here a long time. "What is your friend asking?"

Paddy named the figure and Sir Finbarr mentally tallied the sum total of his purchases thus far. "I'll pay ten percent less. Get with your friend and keep me informed. I'll want the buggy painted and the fittings new."

When he headed for the door, Paddy dropped the charge half as much as his going rate for shelter, grooming and feed.

Sir Fin shook on the agreement and Paddy said, "Give me a week. The wheels will shine, and I'll replace the rigging and upholstery."

Paddy ran his hand over the haunch of Sir O'Bannon's new mount. "You've got yerself a fine horse, sir."

The chestnut stood fifteen and a half hands a comfortable height for Sir Finbarr. Even the stallion's name set well. The purchase reminded him he needed to talk to Abernathy about rebuilding the stables at Ashcourt.

❦

Ten months ago, Finbarr received a letter from Queen Victoria stating he was to be knighted in a ceremony April 1840 for bravery above and beyond saving the lives of many of the miners in the dampfire at The Westend Copper Mine.

That date put into motion his travels from Swansea-Wales to Hawthorn Village-Ireland.

He gave himself a month after leaving Swansea, to repose in London. He enjoyed reading biographies, dined at some of the best restaurants, traveled the countryside, and caught up with friends he had played cricket with when last in London.

He indulged his strong desire to avoid returning to his birth home. And, as a ruse to delay the journey, gave Collins time with family and friends in London. Considering they would be in Ireland for a lengthy stay it seemed the right thing to do.

The ceremony with Queen Victoria had been a great honor and one that didn't allow him to forsake.

He did suggest, ever so humbly to her Majesty, that she refrain from mentioning his actions of that fateful day. He preferred she honor those who died, and Queen Victoria did just that. She mentioned to the gathering under the dome in the Cathedral that forty-nine souls died the previous March of 1839 in the disastrous dampfire.

❦

Queen Victoria looked majestic in a red velvet robe and tiara studded with sparkling diamonds, the Royal Garter pinned to her gown signifying the occasion. Though the Queen was short of stature, as he knelt on the red velvet knighting stool their gaze met.

Her gentle smile eased his discomfort as she placed the sword on his right shoulder, raised it up just over his head, then flipped it counterclockwise so that the same side of the blade came in contact with his body as she placed it on his left shoulder. He did wonder if the heft of the blade was too much for her small hands and arms, having to use both to lift it up and over him for the ceremonial anointing.

Immediately thereafter, a page took the sword from her and indicated he should stand. In her regal manner, the Queen pronounced him Sir Finbarr O'Bannon and much to his shock also awarded him a Baronetcy of the United Kingdom for his bravery.

He barely kept his feelings in check. Nothing in his life had prepared him for this honor, and for some freakish reason an image of his father appeared.

Humbled beyond belief as they stood amongst a number of well-wishers the Queen announced to the crowd, "Sir Finbarr O'Bannon narrowly escaped his own near-death experience entering the mine and carrying a dozen men from the horror of last March until he was forced by others to not enter the mine again. His heroic deed certainly earns the Crown's mention."

☙❧

Nine months have passed since his knighting and baronetcy.

He kneed Jupiter to a run. More than three weeks into his arrival in the village, he ran out of excuses to ignore Ashcourt Manor. Riding south toward the home he turned his back on in 1823, he breathed deeply. Salty air stirred in from the Celtic Sea. Memories of that time so long ago swirled in his mind.

The garden's limestone wall was crumbling. The manor's park in a ruinous state and littered with rotten limbs. The grass-weed mixture reached Jupiter's shoulders as he continued toward the manor. Off to his left the stable doors were none-existent as was the hayloft above. The inside of the stable staggered the imagination. Through the generations O'Bannon's bred cattle ribbon winners in this stable.

He was about eight when he began sleeping in the hayloft that now sagged toward the floor. He had come to treasure the nights with the stars, and how the cattle settled in their stalls—the rhythm of late evening closing in. The sounds of nature quieting become a comfort. One he'd not realized until forced to endure the sleeping arrangement.

The stablemaster, Colby, had a hard time adjusting to his employer's treatment of the young heir. It had been Finbarr the lad who comforted Colby, not the other way around.

Sir Fin drew Jupiter to a stand and leaned on the pummel taking in the whole of his ancestral acreage. The beautiful rolling hills, the Knockmealdowns far off in the west, crowns of white topping them off. He could never tire of the view. The wide-open expanse of emerald-green terrain Shepard dogs darting about keeping the sheep in a cluster. Stands of mighty Hawthorns, Oaks, and Elms dotted the landscape. An eagle in search of a meal. To the East, the River Suir was partially visible as it wound in and out of the shoreline.

The first home built on this land was in 1638 by Robert O'Bannon, a Roman Catholic. His descendants converted to the Church of Ireland and prospered.

This was his now. To do with as he wanted. To hurry its descent into Ireland's loam or renew the place. If he could discern his father's inner workings, he would most likely take his revenge in doing the opposite. But he had no way of understanding the man's cruelty toward a child.

Finbarr guided his mount along the west side of the ruin moving in and out of the overgrown hedges. The foundation itself looked solid, but he would need an inspection to be sure. The roof line of Ashcourt's turrets came into view from where he sat astride his mount, low shrubby bushes dotted the heath as far as the eye could see.

He turned the manor's corner and to the west saw the O'Bannon cemetery where his ancestors resided. His mother was there. Seeing as how his father died in Dublin, Fin wasn't certain where he was buried. If not for a spire atop one of the graves he wouldn't have recognized the place. Overgrown vines curling about the iron fencing boxed the cemetery from view. A pair of emperor moths, black spots like eyes on their wings fluttered above stalks of heather.

Inhaling a well of regret, he turned Jupiter left and continued circling his inheritance.

The structure was colonized by ivy, and stone rubble from the roof slates that had broken off and now dotted the drive curving in front of the manor.

The main portion appeared intact centered by an arched doorway and large windows on each side, overgrown ivy everywhere.

The vines would need careful removal for the restoration to take place and a full survey of the entire home, cellar to attic.

He decided to wait another day to investigate the inside which he pictured covered in dust and cobwebs. This wouldn't be a pleasant task, it brought too many memories he had buried, to the forefront. Ready to quit the grounds, he turned Jupiter to the east and something red flashed in his peripheral vision.

Squinting his eyes against the bright sunlight he waited. After a moment, curiosity got the best of him. The red flash drew him toward a grove of beech and ash. He remembered playing in the park as a child.

He came upon the density of wood and low overlying branches and vines, and dismounting, he trekked through the darkened wood into the sunshine. Twenty yards or so ahead sat a woman surrounded with painting materials, an easel, stool, and paints. She wore a red shawl about her head apparently to secure her sunbonnet.

He watched her delicate brush strokes and how she cocked her head to look at Ashcourt before wetting her brush again. Immediately the painting in Miss Natty's parlor came to mind. A smile eased his face. He might be about to meet the niece of whom she fondly talked.

He ambled through the long grass toward the woman with

Jupiter interested in chewing on some grass. He was within a yard of her when she turned abruptly and gasped as if being snuck up upon. He moved forward as her eyes widened and mouth gaped. She stepped back and her easel collapsed with the force of her hand that held the brush. As the canvas flew off, he noted a blue swipe across it—made with her paintbrush.

As she staggered backward, he grabbed her arm and clutched her before she fell on the easel. "I apologize if I startled you."

"You!" She jerked her arm free and in so doing lost her balance again.

This time he reached out with both hands catching her about the waist in a most ungraceful lunge. Their faces inches from each other, he looked into a pair of beautiful gray eyes. In the moment, he also recognized she was furious.

Her breath came swift with the shock of almost falling. Her eyes squinted with malice.

"How dare you sneak upon me. Who do you think you are, sir? That you creep about and scare the wits out of me?"

He loosened his hold on her waist and stepped back. His hands dangled at his sides, fisting and un-fisting. "I apologize for startling you. I was in the area and saw something red and wondered." He quickly realized she absolutely was the woman in the coach...and the woman in the post office...and most likely Miss Natty's niece.

Her motions were jerky as she untied her scarf and took off her straw hat bunching the scarf inside the bowl of the bonnet and placed it on her stool. She grabbed up the paintbrush that dropped and that is when she saw the blue streak smeared across the canvas.

"Look at this mess! Oh, you horrid man. You certainly have a way about you. Grouchy with children, sneak about like a thief on property that isn't yours."

He cleared his throat and prudently decided to say nothing. Though he wondered why she allowed herself to come here when she felt he could not.

She sounded exactly as she did at the coach stop when she gave him a good scolding. Her edgy tone grated. Quite unlike the tone she used with her customers in the post office.

Inflamed with ire, she glared at him as if he were the devil. "You are undefendable, sir. Precisely what I would expect from you. Your failure to act civilized was certainly obvious in the coach and now this…" She pointed at the fallen easel and her smeared canvas on the ground. Stomping her foot, she mumbled, "You and bees."

Her voice hit hard on the word *you*.

"I do apologize, miss. It was unintentional. Allow me to help you." He started forward and she turned on him.

Fists at her waist, her chin raised defiantly, and now her gray eyes the chilliest he had seen fixed on him. "You can take your apology and leave." She used a civil tone, but as her jaw was clenched, he knew it was with great effort.

Not wishing to disturb her any more than he already had, he tipped his hat and gathering Jupiter's lines jumped into the saddle and pranced them back toward the wood. He didn't think it judicious to tell her he had more reason to be on this land than she did.

With the misfortune of causing her upset, he still hadn't discovered if she was Miss Natty's niece. Though by all accounts, it appeared she was. And likely it was only a matter of time before he would know for certain.

He rode toward the village and the Inn. His tiger was waiting, and he handed the lines over inquiring if the lad had eaten.

"A right tasty meal, gov'."

"Glad you are being fed. You need to eat well. And I won't be needing the rig after all." When his tiger nodded in affirmation, Sir Finbarr bounded up the steps to the inn. Inwardly, he squirmed thinking about the encounter at Ashcourt with that saucy upstart of a young woman.

Mrs. Cashel called out to him as he entered. "These came for you, Mr. O'Bannon. Er, sorry, Sir O'Bannon."

He received the two letters and glanced at her with a quizzed brow.

She stammered, "Lady Hamerlin informed me of your true address Sir, seeing as you've been knighted by Queen Victoria herself."

That blasted woman. He wouldn't take his displeasure out on Mrs. Cashel and merely shook his head and marched up the stairs to his room. He supposed it would be the way of address for him now that Lady Hamerlin had seen fit to inform Hawthorn Village in its entirety.

Collins greeted him and took his hat, helped him off with his coat, following him around as he discarded his cravat, and waistcoat.

"A black tie for tonight, sir?"

Fin poured himself a finger of port and stood at the window overlooking the street below. "No, I'll eat in the dining room tonight." He sipped his drink. That chit of a young woman unnerved him. She clearly found him distasteful to say the least. If his assumption is correct and she is Miss Natty's niece, he would have to suffer her presence on occasion. He didn't relish a case of indigestion.

Having downed his port, he broke the seal on one of the letters, an invitation to Lord Darnley's 87th birthday, a garden party. He couldn't recall if he had ever been to a birthday party and was delighted at the prospect. His parents had known the Darnley family in his early years, at a time when Ashcourt Manor thrived. How his lordship was aware he arrived in the village was a puzzle, until he remembered the tattle-monger, Lady Hamerlin. No doubt, she felt it her duty to inform.

It would be interesting to possibly meet someone he knew from back then. Though he had been gone basically from the age of eight, and home on breaks from school for a few years, then never again. Until now.

He broke the seal on the second letter and, unfolding it, discovered Miss Natty's neat penmanship, inviting him to dinner tomorrow evening. Poor Natty, has she a clue how her niece is perceived? Her shrewish and opinionated nature would make her an unsavory dinner companion.

He had no desire to disappoint Miss Natty and therefore he planned to attend. If his earlier assumption is correct, her niece might prefer to avoid the supper. He mumbled to himself as he considered she probably avoided many situations where her disagreeable nature would be obvious.

He felt his brow raise at thought of her sitting across from him. Sparring seemed to be her specialty. Perchance she used a different persona in company with her aunt. He mused it was more likely he would see angels sing than the niece would be sweet and refined.

6

A Gentleman's gentleman

Collins finished with Sir Finbarr's half-dress, and asked, "The laundress asked me to inquire if she is using too much starch."

He turned an arched brow on his valet. "Really?" He squared his shoulders and said, "It seems the same as it's always been."

Finbarr scooped his arms through the vest Collins held for him and glanced at his reflection in the mirror, a high-collared shirt, kerseymere trousers, and black patent shoes.

The evening's entertainment might possibly be filled with drama, if perchance he discovers the painter of Ashcourt Manor is Miss Natty's niece.

Finished knotting the cravat, Collins assisted his master into a tailcoat of dark blue worsted.

He inquired of his valet, "What have you found for entertainment this evening? You need to get out and explore the village? Dressing me should not be the highlight of your day."

A bright flush reddened Collins's face and his gaze searched the room in hopes of landing anywhere but on his employer, dismay clearly etched on his features.

Sir Fin laughed. "You willingly came with me wanting to see the world."

"I did, sir."

"Then why don't you?"

"This is my first trip to Ireland." Collins stood straight and looked his employer in the eye.

"Well, then, take advantage of the sights, get out and stroll about the village. Enjoy yourself before you get to an age when you can't. Eat in the dining room, who knows someone might strike up a conversation with you."

Collins' chin tightened. "Yes, sir."

Sir Fin scooped up the white gloves that Collins had laid out. then grabbed his walking stick and top hat. "Well, then maybe we'll have tales to trade when I return."

Collins, rigid by nature, and hired on a whim one day when Sir Fin purchased his second copper mine and felt in need of some organization in his home life. Both men were of a similar age. Collins came recommended because of his dedication to detail. Unused to having a male servant, Sir Fin recognized how much easier it was with help. Collins pays the marketing bills, checks on his horse daily, assists him in dressing, and sees to meals when dining in.

It was Collins who had arranged a month in advance to secure several rooms for them. They arrived to discover they were given one bedroom, a major mix up. By the time Fin returned from a hard run with a mare from Cashel's stables, Collins had secured two large suites. He somehow had gotten his way with the woman because he also created a small den from a third bedchamber. He was a miracle worker.

Over the last ten years, their relationship evolved. Sometimes he felt as if he lost control of anything to do with the personal side of his life. Which suited him.

Sir Finbarr could imagine Collins having a bout of apoplexy when he strode into the one-bed room assigned to them. He imagined Collins looking down his nose at the woman and in no uncertain terms demanded her best suites available.

The first evening in their rooms, Sir Finbarr congratulated Collins on finding a bottle of Jameson Whiskey. Collins quickly acknowledged, "Mrs. Cashel regretted putting you out with the room arrangement and offered a bottle of Jameson by way of apology."

Collins had made it happen. He was a treasure.

Entering the front parlor she shared with her aunt, Brianna noticed her elder wearing a white poppy worked into the bun at her nape. "What is the occasion?"

"I feel festive. And happy you are back where you belong." She smoothed a wrinkle on her skirt. "What have you been up to today?"

"For starters, I had the pleasure of following Mrs. Teaberry all morning. She is quite the taskmaster." Glancing quickly at her aunt, she continued, "I enjoy the occupation. But, if I sit for even a moment, she seems to appear and instruct. Almost as if she peeks about waiting for me to take a second breath."

The doorbell rang and Mim rushed past the parlor door on her way to answer. The sound of a man's deep timber sifted along the corridor.

Brianna recognized her aunt's mischievous countenance as it spread into an extremely broad smile. She was up to something.

Mim announced, "Sir O'Bannon, ma'am."

Brianna's breath held. She had absolutely no time to slither out of the parlor and pasted a dour look on her face. What was he doing here? How did he know where she lived?

He was dressed handsomely in an elegant navy-blue waistcoat and snowy white cravat. She didn't dare look at him and set her eyes on her aunt, who pinkened when he bent over her hand, saying, "Thank you for having me to supper. Your invitation is the highlight of my day."

Brianna's mind twirled. What? Aunt Natty invited him to dinner?

Aunt Natty tittered, "I don't believe you've met my niece, Miss Brianna Walsh."

He glanced at her, with a slight lift of his brows. "I have already had the pleasure." He nodded politely, his eyes twinkled with mischief, and of course, now she understood the white poppy in her aunt's bun. And the delicious scent of Mim's favorite company dish, ham slices swimming in raspberry raisin sauce.

Brianna narrowed her eyes. "Sir O'Bannon was a passenger on the coach that brought me home." She hoped her aunt recognized the underlying situation with this person she'd invited into their parlor.

Her aunt's puckered regard slid from Brianna to him. "I'm pleased that you are already acquainted. Do sit, sir. Ease the strain in my neck from having to look up at you. Oh, but before you sit, make yourself a drink at the sideboard." She waved her arm in the direction of the far corner.

Brianna tried to secretly get her aunt's attention while his back was turned. Aunt Natty's brow furrowed, and she shook her head. "What?"

Brianna groaned and looked away just as Sir O'Bannon turned back to them.

Both women already enjoyed a libation, and with his drink in hand, he took the chair across from them. "I'm savoring a delightful aroma. I can't recall when I've had a meal in a real home with two lovely ladies in attendance." His eyes sparkled with impishness.

Brianna's interest honed on her fingers, twined in a grip of irritation. He certainly retained his superior manner. The difference in his behavior in the coach was the smile he now bore and his pleasant demeanor.

He was slick and sure of himself. Brianna refused to bring up that odious coach debacle and his cantankerous behavior toward those two little lasses, though it was on her mind. Vexed having made mention of the occasion to her aunt, she tried to force a smile. Drat! A miserable evening was ahead of her.

His comment about never before dining with two women had to be a misrepresentation. She eyed him through lowered lashes grudgingly admiring his handsome manner and elegant attire. Surely, he had shared a meal with more women than he could count.

"I first met Sir O'Bannon the day of my accident." Aunt Natty spoke to her about their guest. "Do you recall me telling you about the nice young man who took me to the infirmary and stayed with me until Mr. Curran made a diagnosis. Of course, when we met, I had no idea who he was."

Brianna's gaze shifted a moment from her hands to her aunt. "You never mentioned the name of the gentleman who helped you."

She begrudged every word etiquette demanded she afford him. But the gaze she settled on him wasn't pleasant. "We are most grateful for your care of my dear aunt."

"This scoundrel…" auntie cast a pixie grin at him, "…took off before I acquired his name. He came by a day or two later to see how I felt and introduced himself." She smiled graciously at him, "I want to repay you in some way for your tender care, sir."

"You can begin by calling me Fin, or Finbarr, Miss Natty."

He deliberately glanced at Brianna. "Miss Walsh, may I ask if we could be on a Christian name basis as well?"

Brianna tried not to roll her eyes. His gracious manner a bit overdone for her sensibilities, considering their encounters. "Allow me to think on it."

"As you wish."

Aunt Natty asked, "Might I ask, what are your plans for the coming week?"

He mentioned some paperwork and explained how he was still settling into a temporary living arrangement.

As he answered Aunt Natty's questions, Brianna carefully glanced at him again from lowered lashes, noting though handsome, he wasn't flamboyant like the younger men she saw about the village. He appeared natural and quite at home in conversation with her aunt. And, he was relaxed, not uptight as he'd seemed in the coach.

Mim came into the parlor carrying a large vase filled with incense of lilacs and baby's breath. "Compliments of Sir O'Bannon, ma'am." And placed them on a table. "Supper will be served within minutes."

Brianna's mind swirled with stupefaction. After their altercation, she couldn't fathom he would be any more comfortable than she. Yet, he appeared so. Could he be an interloper cozying up to a spinster and her niece, taking advantage of a household where no man provided protection? Brianna almost shook her head at the notions bombarding her. She understood a thing or two about men like him.

She had read several crime broadsides and a penny dreadful when living in the Reynolds' home. Publications brought in by a footman, no doubt, and never made their way out of the kitchen or into the trash.

As soon as the door shuts behind their guest, she intended to remind her aunt about the insufferably rude boar in the coach. That should settle the matter permanently. Her aunt would never allow him to be familiar with either of them again. Poor Aunt Natty, she had definitely fallen under the spell of a disagreeable man who faked his manners when in the company of ladies.

With all the light bibble-babble of Hawthorn Village taken care of, Aunt Natty inquired of Sir O'Bannon, "At the time you visited me when I came home from the infirmary, you did mention you were acquainted with our village in your younger years. If I do not discomfort you by asking, I'd like to know the circumstance."

Brianna had offered little exchange and attempted to stifle a yawn or two, but her aunt's question piqued her interest.

For some reason he turned his attention to Brianna. "I have some property in the area and wanted to check on it. It's been neglected for years."

Aunt Natty seemed surprised. "So, you are originally from our village?"

He took a deep breath. Brianna skeptical of him, was unprepared to believe anything he had to say.

"Yes, born and raised here until ready for boarding school." He sipped at the red vintage wine he had given to Mim when he arrived.

"You must have been quite young last time you saw your cousin, Nuala?" Aunt Natty's pale blue eyes sparkled.

"Her father and mine were brothers." He glanced at Miss Brianna, "Miss Walsh, are you self-taught with your painting?"

Did he deliberately change the subject? His question peeved her. "Yes, I am. Do you have an opinion about that?" Intending arrogance, she looked down her nose at him.

He chuckled. "Only that I think you have real talent. I was surprised to see a painting of yours on the parlor wall when I visited last. Mostly because you rendered it in a ruinous state, yet I still knew it to be Ashcourt Manor. Would it be correct to say you have somewhat of a fascination for the place? Especially having watched you paint another likeness yesterday."

She glared at him, wondering if he would challenge her right to paint Ashcourt. Fascination indeed! She pulled on her lace cuff, knowing it to be a nervous habit, and quickly brought her hands together. "It is a sad home. Anyone with an ounce of care can see that."

"Is that why you painted a smiling elf in the upstairs window?" His gaze steady on her, and the corner of his mouth lifted in amusement. Or sarcasm? She couldn't define his motive for asking.

Mim entered the parlor announcing supper. Brianna was glad

for the interruption. His question was impertinent, and she had an excuse for ignoring him.

He stood and held his arm for Miss Natty, then looked at her. "Miss Walsh?" while offering his other. She stepped into place for his escort to the dining room.

Aunt Natty chatted as he helped her with her chair. "You might not know Nuala is titled, but prefers to be called Nuala though her formal status is Lady Rutledge?"

He held a chair for Miss Brianna Walsh and then seated himself. "I recall something my sister wrote years ago. Nuala and Lord Rutledge were secretly married? Does that sound right?"

"Yes, they married when she was nineteen, though no one was made aware of their nuptials."

"Wasn't he an heir to the Darnley title?"

Aunt Natty nodded as she shook out her napkin and tucked it in her bodice.

"He met an unfortunate death as I recall. Many years separate me from that era. And I lived in Berkshire attending Eton as a lad until I absconded to Wales."

Brianna passed him a platter of cut ham. "Aunt Natty could be a bibliophile except she collects Darnley memorabilia instead of books."

Aunt Natty tutted. "I'm do…"

"Oh yes you do. Just listen to yourself go on about them all. I grant you they are a lovely family, and treat you like one of them. Well deserved, too. If I say so." She glanced at Sir O'Bannon. "You barely recall Nuala, then?"

He forked two slices to his plate and said, "As with most divisions in families, the O'Bannon's division came when one branch changed from Catholicism to the Church of Ireland, causing a rift. My cousin's family didn't change their religious affiliation." He scooped a ladle of raspberry and raisin sauce over the ham, then forked a lump of potato leaving the women to their silence.

Finally, Aunt Natty offered, "When religion separated many

families it forced people who loved one another to take sides. It all happened so long ago I can't think it still matters to this day. Perchance you will want to visit with her now that time has passed." Her brow cocked as she smiled at him.

Reaching for his goblet, he agreed. "It never was my fight, and you are correct, most of it being before our time. But you rightfully pose that I should remake my acquaintance with her now I've returned."

Brianna inquired, "Where is your property located, if you don't mind my asking?"

His green eyes glistened with merriment. "You are acquainted with it far more so than I."

He watched her puzzle it out, not taking his inspection from her. Until the moment she realized to what he referred.

"*You*—Ashcourt Manor is your family home?" She coughed and quickly put a napkin to her lips.

Aunt Natty's delight was apparent. "What a surprising revelation. How quaint. She has been in love with the place since a lass. Nearly the same time you were gone, and your father abandoned it."

"Aunt Natty…" She coughed and scratched out, "I…I wouldn't say I'm in *love* with the place."

"If not *in* love with it…" inquired Sir O'Bannon, "…what then?" He seemed to enjoy her embarrassment. A wide smile showed off his pearly teeth to advantage. She found it difficult to look at him, let alone answer him. Being questioned about Ashcourt caused her blood to roil. It was so secretive, so personal to her.

Brianna cast a murderous glare at her aunt. This conversation was all her fault. Did she put this despicable man up to embarrassing her? Sipping water, she set the goblet down, and settled her attention on twisting the stem and in a sheepish manner defended her emotions, "I feel sorry for the manor."

"Sorry?" His brow scrunched, making him appear stunned

and with a faint sound of humor repeated himself, "You mean as if it were a person *sorry*?"

Slowly her gaze lifted, confronting him with what she harbored deep inside. "And why not? It has been abandoned. Left for ruination. When once it must have been proud and...and magnificent. Happy to have visitors and a family living within its walls." She slapped the linen-covered table, causing the silverware to jingle. "Yes, alluring in another lifetime. Before I ever discovered the place where it was hidden beneath ivy and overgrown sod. Abandoned by careless owners."

Aunt Natty clapped, slowly. "I am invigorated by your passion, my darling. You realize, Sir O'Bannon, she might just be the one to demonstrate to you what Ashcourt could be."

Yesterday's glimpse of the manor proved to him it was nothing more than a near ruin. Exactly as it was painted by this young woman. Though he did wonder if Miss Brianna Walsh had another motive other than rendering it on canvas. He had felt nothing but a sense of old, weathered memories. Some of them hateful if he was honest.

"Have you been inside?" he questioned Brianna.

Aunt Natty gasped. "She wouldn't without permission." Her invigorated countenance now squinted at her niece as if she could be wrong about her. "You wouldn't, would you?"

Brianna's head shook, freeing a curly lock of reddish-brown hair from its pin. She swooshed it with the back of her hand and glared at him. "Not on my life would I trespass."

His eyes twinkled with merriment. "But you do trespass every time you go there with your paints."

"Fiddlesticks." She snapped the napkin from her lap and swiped her fingertips. She had been ready to nitpick with him the moment he entered the parlor. She knew it and so did he. His mere presence set her skin to prickle.

He challenged. "I'm curious as to your appraisal of the interior. And seeing as how you would not trespass if your life depended on it, I withdraw the question."

How dare he put her in the middle of this conversation. Even her aunt goaded her. A faint blush heated her cheeks. "Well, I... the manor has a certain allure. I feel compelled to paint it. I felt badly that it had been allowed to rot. I've peeked in the windows and puttered about the gardens, but I couldn't make myself try the latch."

He drained his goblet. "Would you care to accompany me the next time I go out? You can see the inside to your heart's content. Although I have to assume it's in a dreadful state."

She looked across the table at Aunt Natty, already warranting what she would say. Brianna had put herself in a difficult position. With all her heart she wanted to see the inside. But... but...her embarrassment over her earlier comment caused her to think not. She glanced at her aunt hoping for a way out. "What do you think?"

"I wasn't the one invited, my dear." Aunt Natty forked a chunk of squash into her mouth trying to hide a smirk.

Of course, Brianna yearned to walk about inside the manor since...well, since forever. But she was not sure she wanted to be in his company doing so. He was aloof and challenging and he confused her.

Being with him inside his family residence caused her to consider he might destroy all her dreams of what the home had been, or rather, her vision of what she felt it used to be. It was clear he did not have prideful ownership. He had ridden out to see it and hadn't even taken the time to go inside. She found that disconcerting.

Ashcourt needed love, anyone in their right mind would appreciate that.

"You needn't give me an answer this evening, Miss Walsh. I'll ask again when I'm ready to prowl about the old place." His attention was on cutting another bite of ham.

"Well, I'm glad that is settled," Aunt Natty huffed.

Brianna bristled against Sir O'Bannon's invitation as if he meant to challenge her. She could do little to berate him in front of his admirer. She did not want to upset her aunt, who, it was most apparent, adored him.

Her aunt inquired of her guest, "Do tell, Sir O'Bannon, I hear you've purchased a fine conveyance."

He grinned. "The curse of living in a village. Yes, Mr. Cashel and I have made a bargain." He put his knife down, glancing at Miss Brianna Walsh. "If you decide to accept my invitation, we will drive out in my new buggy."

"My friends said you purchased a phaeton." Her aunt giggled like a school-lass.

Brianna kept from rolling her eyes and quickly spooned a scoop of thick creamy syllabub topped with a sprig of mint and a sweet cherry into her mouth.

Finished with her syllabub and with a break in conversation between her two dinner partners, she announced, after squelching her peevish behavior, "Sir O'Bannon, I would very much enjoy visiting the inside of Ashcourt with you. And as it seems justifiably considerate, please call me Brianna and I shall call you Sir Finbarr."

◈

His green eyes held to hers, as if he wanted to understand her thinking. Did she succumb as a price to pay for seeing the inside of Ashcourt? He presumed yes, but worth the price. "I am pleased you will accompany me, Miss Brianna. Ashcourt needs an artistic eye."

7

Invoking memories of childhood

Brianna knocked on the service entrance to Rockmore Hall. She was delivering an answer to Mrs. Atkinson in response to her request that she and Aunt Natty assist on the day of the garden party celebrating Lord Darnley's 87th birthday.

A kitchen maid opened the door. "Can I help ye?" She eyed Brianna up and down, smiling as she did so.

"Mrs. Atkinson, if she is available, please."

"I'm thinking she is. Come inside and I'll see." She stood aside and closed the door behind Brianna. "Who can I say is askin'?"

"Miss Brianna Walsh."

The last time Brianna stood in this kitchen had been before she left for Dundalk, three years ago. Mrs. Hill had been in charge then. A year or so ago, Aunt Natty had written that Mrs. Bates had taken over as head of the kitchen when Cook Hill had taken ill and died this past winter.

A gutted and plucked pheasant spread out on the planked table, a bowl of onion-bread stuffing ready. The scent of garlicky potatoes stewing in a pot made her realize she hadn't eaten since breakfast.

A kitchen maid rolled out pie dough, several pie plates at her elbow and a bowl filled with cut up apples sprinkled with cinnamon and sugar. If the kitchen maid turned her back for a moment, Brianna could snatch a slice of apple sprinkled with spice.

"She's in her office. Do ye ken the way, then?"

Drawn from the reverie of appeasing her sudden appetite, Brianna nodded to the maid. She crossed the slated floor and entered a corridor to Mrs. Atkinson's office, being the second or third door on the left. She'd figure it out.

The door ajar, Brianna knocked and entered. Mrs. Atkinson stood and came around the desk to hug Brianna, welcoming her back home. She held her at arms' length, her eyes searching her face. "My, my, you have grown into a lovely woman, Brianna."

She flushed with the compliment. "Thank you."

Rockmore Hall's housekeeper returned to her chair, and said, "Take a seat and tell me what it was like teaching a houseful of daughters."

"All six of them were charming and diligent. Especially when it came to learning. I was grateful to be the assistant and not the one in charge. They were also challenging. But I must say, it is good to be back home. I missed my aunt and home."

Mrs. Atkinson said, "We've had need of her service a number of times since you've been gone. I appreciate how she likes to keep busy, and her abilities are put to good use here. I hope both of you are available for his lordship's garden party?"

"Lord and Lady Darnley mean a great deal to us. We would be pleased to help in any capacity." She chuckled, then skimmed the office. Dark stained wainscotting, a window spreading bright sunlight across Mrs. Atkinson's desk and the ledger on which she wrote. Two landscapes on the wall lent a restful feel to the work room. She was comforted to realize nothing changed in all the years since she had come here as a child.

The memory of her sitting at the great table in the kitchen and breathing in the scent of yummy cooking as she drew on her slate made it seem like just a few years ago. Cook Hill was always ready with a scone and a mug of cool milk.

Mrs. Atkinson's voice brought her back to the moment. "Thank you for being available. Your aunt prefers staying in the kitchen. I could use you in the garden organizing and assisting several colleens from the village to stay on task. We will have a tent, possibly two, with tables of food. We expect guests to walk about and fill their plates. Then wander outside to sit at tables that will be scattered about. If you would see that the food doesn't run short and the young lasses keep circulating with fresh trays, that will leave me free to oversee the rest."

She felt comfortable with the position. "Are you sure I can't do more?"

"No, my dear. I appreciate that you are precise and dependable. It relieves my mind that you have agreed to assist. Oh, and no need for a uniform. I would prefer you blend in with guests. You will be back and forth between the food tables in the tent and the guest's tables checking on the maids."

Brianna had no qualms about what Mrs. Atkinson asked of her. It seemed an uncomplicated task one she felt she could handle.

Mrs. Atkinson had been with the Darnley's as long as Brianna could recall. She was a paragon of goodness and a firm hand to keep Rockmore Hall running without incident. Aunt Natty revered the housekeeper as much as anyone she ever talked about.

Mrs. Atkinson wrote something in her ledger. "I expect these two weeks to pass quickly." She set her pen down. "There now, you are noted as my assistant when the day comes. I will expect you about ten, and if you like, bring along your frock and hang it here in my office. You will have time to change within the hour before guests arrive."

A visitor from the past

The bell rang and Natty could hear Mim mumbling to herself as she neared the door. She couldn't place the visitor's cockney lilt.

Her housekeeper thumped into the parlor. "It's a Mrs. Murdock. Says she's your cousin." All stated as a huge question.

Miss Natty's reaction was doltish. She looked at Mim but said nothing as shock slowly coursed through her body and her heart began pounding.

Mim asked, "You look faint?"

Miss Natty whispered, "You said Mrs. Murdock?"

"Yes, it's what she told me. But it is too early for visiting hours. I'll send her on her way, and remind her decent folk aren't about yet."

Miss Natty reached out and grabbed Mim by the arm hissing, "I need a moment. Did you leave her on the doorstep or in the foyer?"

"On the doorstep, Miss Walsh. I didn't like the look of her a'tall."

"Oh dear." Miss Natty slipped a palm over her heart. "Let me think." Her senses were returning. Her mind raced with vexation. She and her cousin had parted company over thirty years ago. The worst time in Natty's life, and all over a young man Natty loved, Niall Murdock.

She let go of Mim's arm. Clearly distraught she said, "Help me stand, and send her in. Do you think we should serve tea and biscuits?"

Mim shook her head. "I'll keep close and if your remarks go well, I'll bring a tray, how is that?"

Miss Natty squared her shoulders and stood as tall as possible against the onslaught of meeting her cousin. Mim stalked to the front door.

Mrs. Dervila Murdock swept into the parlor as if making an entrance from the top of a ballroom staircase. She wore a decent muslin and a shawl of sage green. No hat or gloves. Just like her to run out half dressed. Natty hadn't forgotten how beautiful she used to be. Obviously, the years have been hard on her.

The smile on Dervila's rouged lips and kohl blackened eyes increased Natty's concern. Growing up, Dervila's mother allowed her to smear colors on her face. Little had changed.

"Well, aren't you going to welcome me?"

"I hardly know what to say to you." Natty stood with her hands folded and the unlit fireplace behind her.

Dervila's dark Italian heritage came from her father. Their Irish mothers were sisters. Gray streaked through Dervila's once black curly hair. Her brown flashing eyes had a distinct look of wariness about them, skin sagging beneath, no bright gleam that Natty remembered from their youth. Always a teasing glint in them, over time Natty realized served as motivation to get her way.

"I should think a *how are you* would do nicely after all this time. I've been living in Bristol all these years and returned recently." Her dark eyes scanned the room. Without Natty's offer to sit, she plunked down on the nearest chair.

Natty pushed back a bit of hair that had fallen from her cap and regained the chair she had occupied moments earlier, before this…harbinger of ill swooped in.

"What brings you here?" Her hands folded into a lump in her lap in an attempt to hold herself together.

"It's not as though we are strangers now, is it?"

Natty hoped and prayed this visit would be over quickly. Though she feared not as her cousin adjusted her skirts and made herself comfortable.

Pussycat, curious as always, came into the parlor. She sniffed at the guest's hem, growled, and sat on the floor next to Natty's chair, her cat eyes piercing the new arrival. Natty held a chuckle at the cat's reaction.

"What is it you want? Why are you here?"

"After all these years you snap at me. I've missed you, dear cousin. It's been lonely in Bristol. Can you truthfully say you haven't missed me?"

Natty ignored the question and asked her own. "You have a husband so how is it you are lonely? And a child, too, full grown by now. Is it a lad or a lassie? You never wrote and told me the news."

Natty reflectively lifted her chin and squinted her eyes. Her conniving cousin was after something. She could still read all the signs after three decades.

Dervila had the shame to look away. "There was no child."

Natty bit her lip rather than spout her feelings. Terribly odd after all those years ago, she could still summon devastation and hurt over the ill this woman caused.

She heard a slight shuffle in the corridor thinking Mim held herself in check.

Dervila stood and sashayed to the bay overlooking the back of the house. "You've done quite a lot to this place. Your brother would be proud of your upkeep. You moved in before we left for Bristol. Do you recall?"

Natty kept her silence.

Dervila turned back to face her cousin. "I wanted you to understand that Niall and I have had our troubles. But he's always been able to provide. I begged him to return to Hawthorn. We are in a flat above Maher's, on the Strand."

Upon hearing his name, Natty felt a twinge of sorrow for the loss of his love. "How is he?"

"He's gone most often. You remember, don't you, even as children he would sneak on board a vessel and be gone for weeks at a time."

"But you knew that about him when you quickly married him. I do recall that about you." Her defenses were at the ready. She had been abused and exploited by this woman. And had vowed never again!

"Oh, Natty. I missed you so. I figured you would be glad to see me. I've come all this way because I've wanted to see you."

She picked up a pinch of skirt and let it float back to the floor settling around her in a puddle.

Miss Natty sat a little straighter in her chair. "All this way for me? I'm shocked you would put yourself out so?"

Dervila sniffled. "Of a sudden in the past weeks, Niall has taken ill. I fear he might be dying. If something happens, I will be all alone." She dug for a hanky in her sleeve pulling it out and rubbing her nose.

"What ails him?"

"It's his lungs. His breathing. It happened on our way over from Bristol. And hasn't lightened up."

"Has he seen an apothecary?"

"You know Niall, he wouldn't trust a sawbones."

"It's been many, many years since I've seen either of you. Why would you think I'd know about Niall?"

Dervila ignored her remark. "He's finding it hard to work on the water and hasn't take a job yet."

Miss Natty looked at the woman seated across from her. Try as she might, she couldn't summon an ounce of pity or concern for her. A deft liar, a conniver, Dervila always considered herself above all others. She figured Dervila never gave a thought to the man she married after stealing him from her when they were young. She'd accomplished her goal.

Many years ago, Miss Natty promised herself this woman would never take advantage again. Even though they now live in the same village, she meant to keep that promise.

Dervila's fingers worked the hanky in her hand twisting and turning. Natty couldn't detect one single change for the good.

Her eyes narrowed. Dervila played false all those years ago to get what she wanted. "You lied to your husband about expecting, so he would reject me and marry you." *Oh, my did that feel liberating. She wanted to laugh.*

Dervila tipped her chin down and slanted her gaze at her cousin. "It doesn't matter now."

"You changed my life with that lie." All the years gone by,

and Natty could finally assign blame. She grew breathless with the release of old hurt.

Mim came to the door. "Do you need anything, Miss Walsh?"

Natty's breathing steadied. Her eyes lit on Mim. She wanted to scream at Dervila. Calming herself she said, "No, Mim. Thank you."

The housekeeper harrumphed and left the room. Natty noticed her side glance at the woman sitting opposite her.

Dervila pulled her shawl close as if she had taken a chill. "My problems are real. I didn't come here to complain. I worry about Niall."

Miss Natty quickly stood and favoring her ankle hobbled near the empty fireplace. This woman vexed her to the core. Her thoughts of yesteryear bombarded her. Hurts that she sealed away so many years ago swam to the surface.

Dervila pled, "I only want your kindness. I beg of you. Niall always towered over most others. A big strapping man, and now he is changed. I would never have had time for a child. I couldn't be bothered with one. I'm not that sort."

Dew on Dervila's eyelashes made for a pathetic picture. Natty wished she had the nerve to slap her.

In for a pound now, Miss Natty gathered in all the anger and regret that she had harbored.

Her angst spewed. "I loved him, and he loved me. But you could not stand that I found happiness. That someone could care for me after laying eyes on you. You had to prove to yourself you could get any man you wanted. And you chose the one I was to marry."

Too upset for tears, Miss Natty bit her lip. It had taken forever until she finally finished crying and put Dervila's betrayal behind her. Invigorated to take command of herself, she ordered, "I want you out of my home."

Dervila made quite a display of hurt and despair. Rising from the settee, straightening her skirt, adjusting her shawl, eyes downcast. She started for the corridor and at the parlor's door turned a moment glancing at Natty.

"If it's the lung disease, I'll be so lonely."

Natty held her anger. She wanted to say something like, you made your bed now lie in it. Instead, she turned to the window and clung to the drape waiting for the front door to open and close.

She stood for a time settling her feelings and putting the old hurts back where they belonged.

Mim came in. "Was I right not to bring tea?"

"Yes, thank you for taking care. Oh, and Mim, do not mention this to Brianna. All she knows is that I had a cousin, and I can't abide her fussing over me."

8

Ashcourt Manor

After a good run, Sir Finbarr returned Jupiter to the stable lad, ordering a good rubdown and some oats.

The ride cleared his mind of incidentals. He decided he had waited long enough to open Pandora's Box and sent a note to Miss Brianna Walsh requesting she accompany him to Ashcourt Manor. The messenger would await her reply.

He had been enjoying the early afternoon sun on the porch at Cashel's when Lady Hamerlin happened by and stopped to engage him in conversation.

A moment later a messenger handed him a note. He excused himself for a minute, cracked the seal, and read that Miss Walsh would be available at two. The answer spread his face in a smile.

Lady Hamerlin, obviously curious, asked if she could help with a problem.

"Not in the least, thank you. Now if you will excuse me, I have business to attend." He smiled and turned toward the front desk at Cashel's. "Have my carriage and tiger ready at 1:30."

He could feel Lady Hamerlin's eyes steady upon his departure as he climbed the stairs. He wondered if she came regularly to the inn. This was the second time she had engaged him here.

☙❧

Sir Fin snapped the lines and Miss Walsh put a hand to her bonnet as the buggy took off. "I am surprised you were available on such short notice. I didn't give you much time to decide."

Hardly turning her head, she peeked at him from the side. "It happened that I had returned from the post office and shared a bite to eat with my aunt."

"How is she? I have meant to visit. This past week has the days going by quickly."

"The same as last you saw her when you supped with us. She holds you in high esteem. I hope you protect the image she has of you."

He gave the lines a smart snap. "What about you, Miss Brianna? Do you share your aunt's opinion of me?"

"I barely know you. Except perhaps for the fact that you hardly endure children. And I believe you hold those in your company to a higher standard. You give off an attitude of aloof superiority."

"A woman with opinions. Refreshing. Do you think we will ever have unruffled discourse?"

She didn't try to quell a giggle and took her hand off the rail, which caused her to fall against him with the movement of the phaeton. "Excuse me." She snorted.

Her hilarity captured his interest. She turned so the brim covered her face, but her shoulders were shaking.

"Tell me what is so humorous."

"I find your superiority droll."

His voice held a dismissive edge. "In what way?" The minx was provocative.

She clung to the rail and her bonnet as the dark bays trotted at a good pace. "I must apologize for laughing. But I don't understand you well enough to share my inner notions."

"Come now, Miss Brianna. You had no problem in the coach when you berated me for wanting personal space from two children who hadn't been taught their manners."

She flashed him a grin. "I will remind you they were enthusiastic as children are and cooped up for hours. They had obviously taken a fascination to you. You should have felt complimented by their attention. Children, even in their innocence, are entirely capable of discerning adults. For them to pay any attention to you at all means they felt easy with you."

"I did apologize, if you recall." He rolled out *if you recall* as though she would have a hard time comprehending him.

"Yes. I heard your apology. As if you had just drunk lemon juice then forced your regret from tight lips. Much as you have just now reminded me with your compelling apology."

The turrets of Ashmore Manor were rising in the distance. He pulled in the bays. The woman was incapable of giving him an inch. "Over time I hope to enjoy your advantage."

"I believe we will see little of each other after today, Sir Finbarr. The time or two when we do meet should be burden free. We are adults, after all. And my aunt adores you."

"Much like the children if I understood you correctly." The grin on his face changed his profile. Softened it. He had stooped to an attempt at charm as a last resort.

He brought the phaeton to a stop and tossed the lines to his tiger then helped her from the carriage. "I look forward to hearing what you have to say about the interior."

"I appreciate the opportunity to do so. As my aunt mentioned I've become thoroughly attached to the place."

☙❦❧

When the key didn't fit in the lock, he put his shoulder to the door causing Brianna to wonder when the last person entered. He mentioned he had been away since he turned sixteen, but he had older sisters who might have seen to its upkeep.

After a second shove with his shoulder the door gave an inch. With his next lunge, he stepped aside. Picking up her skirts, she followed him into a tomb-like interior. Filth and cobwebs everywhere and dust an inch thick. She sneezed and quickly shook out a handkerchief covering her nose against the heavy odor of mold. A grayish light sifted from grimy windows where heavy velvet drapes had been left partially open. Dust motes swam in the disturbed air.

The entrance walls were a dark mahogany wainscotting. Amid all the refuse, the impressive staircase, with its carved balusters gracefully elevated and separated to the left and right at the second floor. The newel post seemingly still intact topped off with the likeness of a carved pineapple. A large spider made its way down the banister.

A chandelier of what might possibly be French gold, hung precariously from the scrolled foyer dome. Cobwebs draped the entire double-tiered ornate cage and all its dangling crystals spoke of an elegant and far distant time when life reigned in this home. It would have been a marvelous sight to behold.

Dried animal scat littered the marble floor. Brianna deftly avoided stepping in it as she lifted her skirts and slowly moved around a marble inlaid table. A vase of flowers dried up years ago with bits and pieces of what were most likely petals and leaves scattered on the table and floor. She imagined a family living here and instantly vanishing.

Sir O'Bannon stood in the foyer with a faraway look on his face, as if he had not prepared himself for the interior. Brianna felt a touch of pity for him. His family home, a place where he had lived, she considered it must be horrid to see it in this forlorn condition.

She could almost forgive him his nettlesome manner after so many years away. A part of her was contrite and she felt kindly toward him, glad to share this moment with him. Had he meant to gird himself against facing all this alone? She understood the most arbitrary of men could actually have a sensitive vein.

She cheerfully inquired, "Where would you like to begin the tour?"

He slowly came back from some place far away and his green eyes settled on her in what looked like confusion. "Sorry. My past seemed to come at me like a storm. This wasn't one of my better ideas to bring you here. I apologize."

"On the contrary. This is a thrill beyond my imagination." To prove her point, she asked, "Which way is the dining room?"

She moved toward large double mahogany paneled doors to the right when he called her up. "No. Not there. No one has ever been allowed in that room."

Befuddled, she spurted, "But...how was it cleaned?"

"My father had his idiosyncrasies. The butler, Hutchins, when he was summoned, waited at the door until my father came out."

"Your father has passed, Sir Finbarr, and yet you honor his... well, I would call it a dictatorship?"

This willful woman would have her hands full if his father were alive. He eyed her and wondered how she would react to him. The picture made him smile. "Just be thankful your father would never treat you in like manner."

Her gaze searched his face, looking for something. "All I recall about my parents is from a story my aunt told me of that day. My mother was dying, and my father gave me to Aunt Natty. I didn't even have a name. And he never told Aunt Natty what they were called."

He was taken aback at her frank rendering. And quickly conceded she most likely was done a favor. "From what I grasp of the world and the people in it, you might have been put on a much better path than most."

"I confess, I do ask my aunt about that day now and again. It resembles a lullaby that reminds me to be grateful and to make sure Aunt Natty knows I am."

Sir Fin ran a gloved finger across a table. He drew a squiggly line through the dust in his moment of contemplation. Then he looked at her, all prim and sweet. She had just told him a startling fact of her life and she wasn't the least emotional. Her tone soft and appealing to the ear.

"You are most fortunate in your twist of fate. The reality could have been far worse." He mused about the family who took him in when he was sixteen and he had walked away from Eton to work in the copper mines.

"That's a melancholy thing to say."

He nodded. "Something about this place brings it on."

She spun around and pointed across the foyer. "What is that room?"

"The front parlor. Go ahead and look. My mother's favorite as it has a southern exposure." He opened the door to a ghastly sight. What had once been gorgeous red silk settees and chairs had become small animal nests. Feathers and cotton had been chewed and spread all about. Opening the doors moved the stale air that blew the feathers into the air. Then the particles began to slowly drift to what must have been an original Persian rug.

Brianna took off her glove and stooped down to touch the oriental pattern of reds and golds. "The Reynolds had a similar rug in their front parlor."

Feeling a bit awkward, she stood and put on her glove as she explained herself. "For several years I assisted the governess for a family in Dundalk, and recently returned home. They had lovely rugs. One quite similar to this one."

"That explains your travel on the coach. You were returning home when you seized the opportunity to act as an etiquette marshal?"

"If you care to think about it that way. Yes, your memory serves you well."

He had expected she might roll her eyes at his attempt at levity as he said, "Back to business, Miss Brianna. Tell me of other similarities in decoration that you've spied?"

"The chandelier in the Reynold's foyer appeared similar to the one in this…in your…in Ashcourt's foyer."

He moved away from the doors and stepped further into the parlor. "I've set you in a dither as to what Ashcourt means to me. For the sake of conversation, let us assume I intend to keep it." His hands clasped behind he followed a step after her as she went to the window.

She glanced up at him from beneath the rim of her bonnet with a lovely smile on her face. "She must have enjoyed the view from here."

"My mother would die of sorrow to see Ashcourt now."

"How long ago did she pass?"

"Years ago, I was eight." His gaze quickly came back to her, "Would you mind if I leave you for a minute or two? Browse if you like. I'll wander upstairs."

She turned to a cabinet, glass panels partly ajar, crystal dishes inside. "You don't mind if I get a bit nosy, do you?"

"Would that stop you?" He chortled as he left the parlor then took the stairs.

⚜

Sir Finbarr tramped the west corridor toward his mother's chamber. He opened the door and for a moment reeled back a step. A slight trace of stale lemon floated in the air. Pushing aside the drape, he peered out the window. The material crumbled in his hand as he let in light.

Seeing her bed where she took her last breath made the years fall away and he was eight again. She wiggled her fingers for him to stand close.

The only move he made, he glanced at his father for permission. But his father looked out the window.

He had quickly moved toward her and put his small hand in hers, it was icy to his touch, and he fumbled with the blanket to cover her hand. Her eyes, always warm and comforting were sad. He wanted to crawl into bed and feel her arms about him but if his father saw, there would be anger. He did not want his mother to suffer another of his father's rants.

Almost reverently, Finbarr neared the bed and touched the gold and red damask pillow cover that disintegrated at his touch. He squeezed his eyes shut and tried to fix an image of her smiling at him. When his father was away, his mother laughed easily, the sound rang throughout the manor. He tried to summon the peal of it, and found it too far gone to bring it to memory.

She died that night. His father bundled him off to Eton by week's end in the care of a courier. When he came home for the holidays, he discovered his father had ordered his son's belongings moved to the stables.

Over the years, the kitchen became the only room in the manor that seemed inviting and safe for him to enter. Diarmuid O'Bannon would never bother himself with the working parts of the manor. And as long as he did not have to look at his son, his attitude was reasonable.

Fin heard Miss Brianna call out, "Sir Fin, where are you?"

As if he had done something wrong, he quickly withdrew to the corridor and closed the door to his mother's chamber. A chill swept up his spine. He took a deep breath and chided himself for being ridiculous.

Miss Brianna stood in the middle of the corridor, having just trotted up the stairs, a haze of grayish light about her. "I believe the stairs are solid. Nary a squeak."

He let out a quick breath of relief that his father was not standing in the corridor, a strap in his hand. And shook his head at the nonsense, recovering quickly from the memory. "Have you seen enough to satisfy that artistic mind of yours?"

"If you refuse to let me into your father's study, then the least you can do is take me to your room. I'd like to see the things you collected as a lad."

He laughed outright, mostly over the fact he had been in the house almost an hour and lightening had not struck. He had been right to ask her to accompany him. His absurdities diminished with teasing and laughter. "You expect to see the remains of frogs, and a cricket bat against the wall? I had an unconventional childhood. My room could have been turned into a storeroom."

ॐ

She said, "I think you exaggerate."

"There is one certainty about me, Miss Brianna. I do not exaggerate." He pointed his arm to the left allowing her to go ahead of him. "Go to the end of this corridor and take a left to the end. My room is on the left."

Making her way down the long corridor, they approached his room. He reached around her and opened the door on a stark cave like box. Shades instead of drapes at the two windows, a dresser, a lamp, a chair, and a small bed. Nothing personal to hint of a child's room.

"I would have presumed this was a maid's or a groom's room." He stood behind her. She could almost feel his eyes boring into her.

"Should I give you a fantasy answer to appease your notion of a perfect world, or give you the truth? Neither is all that shattering. As you can see, this room provides for anyone. It's hardly plush, and some would cavil not even comfortable. But it does provide a bed and a roof and light."

"I will quibble the point, sir. You are the son of the manor, after all." She opened a drawer that creaked and noticed a few pieces of clothing neatly folded. Child's clothing.

What graveled her was the parents' treatment of their heir.

They ended the tour and on the return to Hawthorn Village he asked if she would like tea. He happened to have savored the aroma of raspberry pie earlier in the day and assumed Mrs. Cashel would offer it on the menu. One thing he noticed about taking up residence in a small inn, it almost seemed like living in a home with other people.

"I wish I could, but I belong to a book club and it's at a friend's home. There are eight of us who engaged in this activity once a month and today is my turn to read. But thank you. Another time perhaps?" She peeked at him from beneath her bonnet. "I very much enjoyed seeing the interior of Ashcourt. It has many attributes to recommend it. My hope is that you decide to refurbish."

He pulled in the lines and the horses stopped. "I appreciate your accompanying me today. Your artistic eye notices things that most people, including myself, might miss. A talent bestowed on you at birth I warrant."

"You give me far too much credit. But thank you for saying so. I think of myself more as an imitator than an artist."

He teased, "Because you paint Ashcourt?"

"Exactly."

"Then explain the elf in the window. If that's not imaginative, tell me what is."

When she had no response, a light shade of pink bloomed on her cheeks.

※

Finbarr felt the cold slap of leather on his back and tried to twist away. His legs and arms were seized. Sweat bled into his eyes blinding him to his attacker.

The room was black, with only a slit of moon beam. He screamed for his mother. The crack of the leather felt hot on his legs as his attacker kept up the fierce beating. He screamed again and again the stench of his fear real each time the belt struck.

A large man, whose face was hidden moved about in the shadow of his dream. Lurking with the belt in his fist, threatening the child that searched for his mother. A carriage had sped out of the stables, a silky scarf flaying in the wind. The vehicle whooshed by the child and the scarf floated to the ground. He tried to run after the carriage, but the scarf tangled about his feet.

The man in the shadows slapped the belt against his palm as he reached for him once again.

"Sir, sir. It's a dream." Shaken awake Fin's eyes opened. "Sir. It is your dream again. We are at Cashel's Inn. No one but us, sir."

Sir Fin sucked in a breath. Within seconds he quieted and allowed Collins to light a candle then untangle the damp sheets and bed cover. He swiped hair away from his face and glanced about the chamber still a bit disoriented.

"Would you like me to order up milk, sir? Or, we have Jameson in the cabinet?"

Sir Fin lowered his chin almost to his chest. Exhausted, but wary of closing his eyes just yet, he hated the dream, occurring intermittently throughout his life. Like stalking on soft kitten paws, until it pounced like a wild animal, fangs bared when he least expected it.

9

The past rises to the present

A little after noon the next day Brianna returned from work and hung her hat and shawl in the foyer. Aunt Natty called to her and she followed the direction of conversation into the front parlor and handed her a letter. "This came for you in the post."

Aunt Natty's lovely welcoming smile faded as sure as if a black cloud floated overhead.

Concerned, Brianna asked, "What is it?"

Her elder closed her eyes and took a breath. "Oh, I suppose it's of no use to hide this from you. Though it all began an exceptionally long time long ago."

Brianna sat on the stool in front of her aunt and reached for her hand. "It sounds mysterious."

That almost brought a smile to her face. "The woman who sent this betrayed me and forced a dramatic change in my life a long time ago."

Brianna continued to hold her hand, looking at the face of an angel as she did so. A woman she loved dearly.

Aunt Natty swiped a palm over the unopened letter. "This will only bring misery to my life. I'm certain of it."

"Who is the sender?"

"My cousin. Our mothers were sisters. We were best of friends back in the day. Closer than you can imagine."

Brianna leaned away and folded her hands in her lap. "Why haven't I been told of your family? You've only mentioned your brother."

She sighed and glanced at her hands. "We've been out of sorts for many years. My cousin and her husband lived in Bristol up until a week or so ago. We all lived in Tramore growing up. I moved here when I came into my brother's inheritance. But before that when I lived under my parents' roof in Tramore, Dervila and I had a terrible row."

"Will you tell me?" Brianna moved to the settee and taking off her brogues, tucked her legs under her skirts.

"I suppose after all this time it won't matter."

Feeling her aunt's anxiety, she offered, "If it's painful then don't."

"So many years ago, it was put to rest a long time ago. Niall Murdock had asked me to marry him. We hadn't said a word to anyone as yet. Then I made the mistake of confiding in my best friend, Dervila, of my wonderful news. What did she do then? She told Niall she had become pregnant, and..." she shook her head "...he quickly married her."

"He disregarded his declaration to you." Bitter, she practically spat, "The beast."

"He asked me to marry him and all the while he loved her. And then she carried his child..." Nerves had taken over and Aunt Natty's palms cupped her cheeks with the memory.

Brianna's eyelids stung with the humiliation her dear aunt bore and the horrid rejection she must have felt. "How painful for you."

"I never could understand how he so easily deceived me.

Dervila only wanted him because I told her he asked for my hand."

"The child was his, then. He was a faithless man. Is this why you never married?"

Aunt Natty said, "As I look back on it now, I almost believe fate played a role. My brother died leaving me this cottage and a small pension at the same time. And I desperately needed to get away. I packed as quick as a rabbit and turned my back on Dervila and Niall and all the buzzing tattle-mongers." She looked at the unopened letter in her lap. "Tramore is smaller than Hawthorn. My brother gave me more than just a home that day. I got you."

Pussycat stretched from her circle of warmth on the carpet and purred, tail swishing. She glanced at each of them then bounded into the elder's lap. Then immediately taking exception to the letter there, hopped onto Brianna's lap.

"Are you going to open the letter?" Brianna was ready to stand when Aunt Natty had more to say.

"There's a bit more before I open this. It turned out she wasn't pregnant a'tall. It was a ruse to get Niall to marry her." Aunt Natty stirred the air with the letter in front of her face. "My cousin and her new husband moved to Hawthorn as he had gotten a job on a cargo ship. Which meant he would be gone for months at a time. Dervila was thoroughly pleased about that."

"That is the meanest thing I've ever heard. I wonder how her husband reacted realizing he'd been duped."

"You may think I should have turned the other cheek, but I couldn't. As happy as I felt inheriting this cottage, I couldn't get over her perfidy." She picked at a cat hair left by Pussycat. "I told her to never come around me again. And I meant it. Soon after that, they moved to Bristol."

"How many years ago did they leave Hawthorn?" Brianna shooed Pussycat off her lap.

"Late summer in 1817. The only reason I recall because it was the Hawthorn Fair. Nearly upon us at the time, Laura remembered a remark I made about my cousin and suggested I ask her to be on the planning committee."

Brianna brightened. "Can you imagine her on a committee?"

"That is exactly what I feared. I was saved by all that mischief when they upped and moved to Bristol. Apparently, Niall's brother wrote of a grand opportunity on the docks and Niall took advantage of the chance to work with his brother."

Pussycat scratched at the floor where a warm spot of sunlight landed, and then lay down on it.

"Although, she did pay me a visit a bit ago."

"Oh no. She's moved back here, then? Whatever did you do?"

"Let her in. What else could I do?" Shrugging her shoulders her voice tight with annoyance. "Indeed, they've returned to Hawthorn. And, she had the audacity to tell me she is lonely. She thinks Niall is dying. I'm ashamed to say she wanted me to comfort her."

"Oh, Aunt Natty, how awful for you." Brianna uncurled her legs and slipped her feet into her brogues.

"I didn't find it so. I told her to leave and never come back."

"As sad as her situation is, I'm proud of you. Bravo."

"And then I made sure Mim said nothing to you. I wanted to wipe her out of my life forever more."

Brianna bent over her beloved aunt hugging her. "Turning her away was the best thing you could have done for yourself. And when you hurt, I hurt. When something pesters you, please come to me. I am no longer that little colleen you took such care of."

Natty felt so much better telling Brianna all about her cousin and what came between them. Clearing the air was refreshing to say the least.

She threw the unread note from Dervila on the logs for tonight's fire should it get down to where they need to take off the chill.

After Sir Finbarr's memory-invoking tour of Ashcourt last week, he visited the Carrolton Engineering firm in Waterford asking Mr. Carrolton if he would evaluate the manor.

Through Miss Walsh's eyes, he saw the place differently than that of the young lad who lived there. His intuition inviting her to accompany him had been faultless. At her insistence that afternoon, they had continued on to the kitchen with its musty stench and rat droppings. She also wished to see his sisters' bed chambers and the servants' quarters. Finished touring the inside, the woman continued to amaze him by asking to see the stables. But he had drawn the line pointing to the thunderheads off in the distance.

Ashcourt's main structure was developed in the early 1600's by Sir Finbarr's great, great grandsire Kevin O'Bannon, a Roman Catholic. His descendants eventually broke with the Catholic church converting to the Church of Ireland. The family prospered and added on to Ashcourt with east and west wings, enlarging the stables at the same time.

Edmund O'Bannon, a Magistrate and Sir Finbarr's great grandsire, accumulated an enormous fortune out of land transactions in the unsettled period after the Williamite wars in the late 1600s. He died unexpectedly in his early fifties.

Sir Finbarr's grandsire, Robert, increased the family wealth. And Robert's eldest son Diarmuid, Sir Finbarr's father was meanspirited and loved his whiskey. Diarmuid drank away most evenings muttering about the foolish woman he married.

Diarmuid like his great grandsire and grandsire, learned how to invest by instinct. They were brilliant stock and bond market analysts and invested wisely. Ashcourt had been a show piece during its peak. The six hectares of pleasure gardens, parkland, and formal gardens were regarded as one of the grandest in southeastern Ireland. Within the gardens stood a small Norman parish church on an island surrounded by a lake. The surrounding land had returned to its natural state.

As a child, he used to play in the tumbled walls. He loved the feeling of refuge from arguments between Diarmuid and Helen. His sisters were much alike and played quietly like little mice, or so his mother used to say. Younger by enough years, Finbarr grew up as if an only child.

The festive garden party for Lord Darnley's 87th birthday finally arrived. Carriages, one by one, moved slowly up the treelined canopy of green halting in front of Rockmore Hall where liveried footmen assisted invitees. Guests could freshen up inside the Hall and then go to the east park where their hosts waited.

Carriages were directed to the Hall's west side. Their footmen and grooms could take part outside the kitchen area where tables were arranged for idly passing the time.

With plenty of time before the guests arrive, Brianna familiarized herself with the layout of the food tent. Kitchen staff were beginning to bring out platters as the hour was near upon them.

The huge white tent had been set up on the sunny side of the Hall's property where musicians were already tuning their instruments. Six bagpipers, wearing the Darnley tartan, strolled the greens playing soft and sweet tunes. The tent was lined with tables laden with flowers. The meat table boasted platters of chicken, tongue, collared eels, prawns, and trifles.

Another table laden with long thin containers of hot house flowers used as a backdrop for the punch bowls, of which there were four varieties duly marked as to flavor. Although one large ceramic bowl painted in hues of reds and pinks offset with gold, was marked as bubbly champagne, and set in the center of the table and surrounded with etched flutes.

As she inspected each table, her appetite was challenged. However, she refrained from tasting. It wouldn't do for Mrs. Atkinson to catch her.

Encountering the sweet table was another matter. A four-tiered cake, each tier in a different color was spectacular and stood proud in the center with hand carved candles denoting Lord Darnley's 87th birthday. Someone had created a small male doll in black with a cane and top hat, whisps of white hair peeking out. The tiny figure gave the appearance of leaning on the number 7.

Strawberry tarts filled several platters, as did biscuits, pies, and two rum cakes.

Brianna didn't see the maids under the tent, and she decided to hurry back to the kitchen to find them. Mrs. Atkinson had specifically asked her to go over their duties.

Sir Finbarr arrived and tossed the lines to his tiger as he followed other guests toward the sound of music. His long legs stretched out beneath him. It felt good to reacquaint himself with Rockmore Hall and the Darnleys. He recalled from childhood the fun to be had. Now as a man he chuckled at how diminished it appeared compared to his memories of twenty some years ago.

When it was his turn to greet Lord and Lady Darnley, he gave a slight bow to both of them as his card was handed to Lord Darnley.

They looked regal seated on green velvet chairs, a green and white canopy shielding them from the bright sunlight. A soft breeze rippled the Darnley flags on each corner.

Jonathon, Lord Tremaine, and his wife, Mairéad, Lady Tremaine, hosted the garden party for her grandparents, and to honor her grandsire's birthday. Their only child, Lady Fionnuala, stood next to her mother greeting their guests.

Though frail, Lord Darnley clearly owned to a sense of awareness. Adorned with medals and a sash awarded to him by King George III for his involvement in the War of 1778, he looked every bit a gracious nobleman.

His lordship said, "There seems to be a misprint, Sir O'Bannon, your name reads Mister."

Lord Darnley extended his hand and Sir Finbarr gladly shook it. "No misprint, milord. It takes getting used to."

Dainty Lady Darnley seated next to her husband, read the card he passed. "Or just a bit frugal and want to use up your old cards first?"

He bowed to her. "My Lady. It seems you've caught me at my game."

"We are pleased you accepted the invitation. We have read all about your knighthood and baronetcy. You can't fool us with your modesty, you must be pleased to be honored by our young Queen." She stirred the air with her fan as she eyed him. "It's good to see you returned to your homeland. I am curious what your plans are for Ashcourt. Will you dine with us soon?"

"I would be honored, your ladyship."

"Nonsense, call me Lady Adrianna. It will remind me of your dear mother. I'll send a note to you at Cashel's."

His brows pinched.

Her ladyship seemed delighted. "Yes, we've been kept up about you. Your kinswoman is out on the green somewhere, she's informed us." Her dainty-gloved hand waved toward the tents and tables where, no doubt, Nuala, Lady Rutledge wandered. "I'm sure you'll want to find her. It's been far too long since you've lived amongst those who care about you." Her radiant smile made him feel quite welcome.

She turned to the couple standing next to the canopy. "Tremaine, Mairéad allow me to introduce, Sir Finbarr O'Bannon." Speaking directly to Mairéad, she explained, "This gentleman is your mother's cousin, my dear."

He nodded and exchanged a handshake with Tremaine, a man equally as tall as himself. Lady Tremaine was an elegant looking woman. Mother and daughter could almost be sisters.

Lady Tremaine held out her hand. "This is our daughter, Lady Fionnuala. We are pleased to meet you at last, sir." She turned to her daughter. "Sir O'Bannon is a cousin of your grandma'am."

He bowed over the hand Lady Fionnuala presented. "A pleasure to meet you, milady." Though younger and flaxen haired, he immediately noted a resemblance to Miss Brianna Walsh. The smile Lady Fionnuala presented could have been Miss Brianna's.

Lady Tremaine asked, "You are a member of my mother's family, Lady Rutledge?"

"Lady Rutledge's father and mine were brothers."

He stepped aside as another couple moved in behind him, also eager to make acquaintance. "I've been out of the country for an extended time and recently returned to Ireland. And I've yet to greet your mother. She won't recall me."

Lady Tremaine said, "I can't imagine meeting you and not recalling you, sir. Your height alone makes you memorable. And my mother has an uncanny memory. I am sure she will be excited to greet you. She is wandering about in search of lemonade I believe."

He felt the pressure of guests behind him and excused himself. "I'll search her out then." He tipped his hat and moved on.

The food tent spread shade over tables adorned with white tablecloths and decorated with silver platters of buffet offerings that would tempt even the faint-hearted eater.

Several dozen smaller tables dotted about the park were fitted with linen and chairs and lovely bouquets. A number of green and white liveried servers carried trays amongst the growing crowd. The servers offered several different libations to quench thirst on this perfectly balmy sunny afternoon as neighbors and friends mingled.

The scent of ripe-flowering lilacs sifted through the air and mingled with the newly scythed fields. A feeling of being home settled on him though it was strange to be in the company of old friends and relatives. As he moved along the path to the tent and the sound of repartee mingled with music, he wondered why he stayed away so long.

As a lad he had run across this park toward the gazebo any number of times. His sisters in charge of him, but his little legs were quicker. He remembered lots of laughter as they called for him to slow and wait which caused him to run faster. What a difference to feel restful and pleased here at Rockmore. When rambling through Ashcourt, abandonment and gloom seemed to be the prevailing mood.

"Good afternoon, Sir O'Bannon."

Approaching him, Miss Brianna Walsh wore a becoming yellow gown and matching ribbons woven into her upswept hair. He blinked at the vision of her. Her skin glistened in the sunlight. He noted her slight resemblance to Lady Fionnuala proving it wasn't his imagination.

"I thought we were friends. Friendly."

She laughed softly. "You don't like being called Sir O'Bannon? I doubt you will get what you want with this gathering. Seems a friend of yours is busy spreading the news."

"That would be...a busybody?" Irritation grated in his speech.

"For shame, *Sir*. It's Lady Hamerlin."

"Is your aunt with you?"

"You'll find her in the kitchen. I doubt you'll see her unless you go there."

Now, his brow furrowed in question.

She laughed. "Surely you didn't think us guests. We are hired help. We assist when his lordship entertains large groups. My charges are several maids who are new and serving for the first time. I am to keep them at their best. My aunt has worked special occasions in the kitchen with Bates, and before her Cook Hill, for years. She loves the commotion and fun of planning. Most of them are her friends withal."

His gaze roamed over her hair and settled on her face. "You are an unexpected delight without your painting apron and your cheek smudged. Allow me to get us refreshment." He snatched off two stemware glasses of punch from the tray of a passing maid.

"I cannot. I've duties. It is why I referred to you as Sir O'Bannon. It would be unseemly otherwise."

"Waste not want not." He handed her a pink lemonade with a spring of mint and sipped from his.

A woman dressed in a dark shade of blue and a lovely hat

trimmed with a white bird and extra feathers seemed to be heading toward them. He saw her out of the corner of his eye instantly recognizing his cousin, Nuala. Though a lifetime had passed since the last time they saw one another.

He stepped forward. "Nuala. For sure it is you." He took her hand and pressed a kiss.

A little out of breath, she appeared delighted to find him. "I recognized you, too. Just as if Uncle Diarmuid stood here enjoying the day. Though last I saw you, you were less than three feet. I think you've more than doubled that."

Finbarr grinned at her basking in her warm welcome. "Allow me to introduce Miss Brianna Walsh—my cousin, Lady Rutledge, Nuala O'Bannon."

"We are acquainted. As a child, Brianna would come looking for ribbons in my store." She said to Brianna, "You have grown into a lovely woman, my dear. Do I understand you have been away?"

"Yes, your ladyship. I became an assistant governess for a family in Dundalk for several years."

"Ah, and did you like working for the family?"

"They were lovely, but at the end, I missed home."

Sir Finbarr mentioned, "That is how Miss Walsh and I met. We shared the coach coming from the north." His tone softened. "A mother and two young daughters for seven days—in a coach."

Nuala fanned herself. "And you with a low threshold of patience." Her gaze scanned the sky. "Some things one cannot forget." She patted Miss Walsh's hand. "I can imagine the tension coming from him. It must have been a misery for you."

He interrupted, "Seven days of teaching children to sing. Off key."

Nuala smiled at Brianna. "Sir Finbarr and I are meeting after many years apart. We have much to catch up on and plenty of time now that he is making Hawthorn Village his home."

Lady Rutledge asked, "You are lovely, my dear. I think my

granddaughter is near in age with you. And except for the color of your hair, hers is flaxen, you have a similar look."

Brianna's eyes narrowed. "It would seem I should have recognized her. Isn't there a saying we all have a lookalike?"

"She is quite attached to her great grandparents. She won't leave their side.

When the singing begins, I believe they plan to be under the food tent. Perhaps you can catch a glimpse of her then."

"You have just reminded me. I'm not a guest and need to return to my duties. It is a pleasure to see you, Lady Rutledge. If you will excuse me."

"Duties?"

"Yes, for the day I am to watch over several young maids for Mrs. Atkinson. They are new and she has asked me to direct them with their responsibilities."

"Mrs. Atkinson has been housekeeper for decades. She mastered how to keep everyone on task. You had better get on, then."

"It was a pleasure to see you again." She curtsied and swiftly made her way toward the tent where the banners of Ireland waved high in the wind.

☙❧

Sir Finbarr watched as she stepped away. Her posture was that of a woman who is familiar with her own mind. He liked that about her. His cousin's conversation pulled him back from musing.

Nuala said, "I was hoping to see you today. I read that you have been knighted by the Queen. And a baronetcy also. You were amazing and heroic saving all those lives."

He squinted. "Any man would have done the same."

"I am not so certain about that. As a lad, you always stood out when in a group. You seemed to take care of the little ones that stayed back from the crowd. I saw in you an innate caring. Tell me about your plans for Ashcourt. I've taken the buggy out on occasion and noted it is badly in need of repair."

They drifted to a table and made themselves comfortable. "Yes, it's in need of refurbishing. All the years I have been gone it stayed in my mind as the way it was when I left. The reality hit hard seeing it in its present state."

"Your mother would no doubt be quite pleased that you are taking a fancy to the place."

He chortled. "She might be cringing at the idea. My background is in mining, certainly not decorating."

Nuala smiled at him fondly. He felt quite comfortable in her presence.

She said, "I'll not forget the last time I saw you. You were about twelve or thirteen. A gangly lad all feet and arms. Your mother had passed a few years before, and I believe your father was on the brink of some sort of disaster. You were so unhappy. I wanted to whisk you away from Diarmuid but had no authority."

A moment of silence ensued. Fin did not recall the occasion. Besides, he wanted to enjoy the afternoon. "I was introduced to your daughter and granddaughter." He scanned the growing crowd. There had to be near two hundred in attendance.

"I can't recall if you were still in Hawthorn at the time, but surely you would have been too young to take notice. My husband was Garrett II, Viscount Rutledge, Darnley's heir. He died several years after we married. Our twins, Mairéad and Garrett III, were separated at birth."

He pulled her gloved hand into his own and cradled it. "I am sorry you had to endure such heartbreak. I recall Vivian writing to me." A flicker of sorrow flashed in her eyes that he wished he could wipe away.

He released her hand and offered, "Your son is alive in you. In your heart. That must be a comfort."

She shooed a butterfly away from her glass. "Thank you for reminding me. It seems I am relating tragedy as I get you caught up. My son, Rutledge, drowned on his return to England. He was soon to be eighteen. According to other passengers, a fierce storm washed him overboard."

He eased back in the chair, crossed his legs, and clasped both hands on his knee and took notice of his cousin. Except for the flicker in her eyes, she kept her multiple tragedies hidden. Time has a way of healing to some extent. "You were always so kind and pleasant to be around. I'm sorry you've had to suffer such loss."

"There is much to be grateful for, and as you say they are alive in my heart. You have had your share, too. I was aware of Diarmuid's failure as a father and husband. And I see before me a man who shares little more than stature with his sire. It is rather obvious you are of a far different making than my uncle."

Finbarr realized he gaped at her and quickly turned away. Her words sunk in clutching at his insides. With all of their shared history, she had just absolved him from the bewildering fear of being like his male parent. He hadn't shed a tear since childhood and right now felt on the brink of shaming himself. Her words induced a sudden emotional absolution.

In the last few weeks, he seemed to lose control of his emotions. It was highly unusual. Even his dreams had returned. For the moment he allowed the violins eloquent and pure sounds to wash over him and bring a sense of all is well.

He finally asked, "Would you like to stroll the park?"

"I would be delighted. And you can tell me of your plans for Ashcourt."

He placed his now empty crystal on the table. "Always a catch, isn't there?" He flashed her a childish grin.

10

On dits at the post office

This was Brianna's third week at the Post Office. She was busy alphabetically shuffling mail to be delivered and arranging each item in the cubbies ready for pickup when she overheard several ladies commenting on Ashcourt Manor.

"Charlie stopped by the Black Pig last night and it was whispered about that Ashcourt is to be torn down."

"I say good riddance. It's an eyesore."

"Marla, when do you ever traipse across to the east side of Hawthorn Village?"

Brianna glanced over trying to look nonchalant, rather than obviously eavesdropping. She knew Marla, but the woman with the caustic edge to her voice, was a stranger.

Marla said, "I heard the owner has returned. Mayhap to see to its demolition. They say he's a recluse." Marla slanted her friend a look and Brianna quickly turned her attention to the task at hand.

A lump in her throat tightened. How could Sir Fin destroy his charming family residence. Frustrated and feeling the urge to go out to Ashcourt, she glanced at her watch. She had two hours before she could leave.

Done with sorting mail, Brianna took over duty at the window allowing Mrs. Teaberry a break.

Marla stepped away from her friend and came to the window inquiring, "Miss Walsh, what will it cost to mail this up north. It's to my sister."

"Is it your elder sister or the young one in Dublin, then?"

"Meg in Dublin."

She read from a list and said, "That will be 1d."

"Here you go." Marla handed over a coin.

Brianna whispered to her, "Is it true Ashcourt will be torn down?"

"Only what Mick said last night when he came home." She patted Brianna's hand. "You have a fondness for the place, I ken. I've seen you a time or two making your way with your painting kit."

With pursed lips, Brianna nodded.

Marla said good day and with friends following in her wake, left Brianna to fret. She immediately settled on Sir Finbarr demolishing his family home. The day he took her inside Ashcourt, he openly sought suggestions and gave the impression he might likely rebuild.

She had a keen sense that day he was hesitant to explore the place alone. She had had the feeling he actually needed someone with him. As if ghosts from his past would appear out of the woodwork.

Which is absolutely ridiculous!

The man was knighted for bravery beyond anything most men would do, and he received a baronetcy from the Queen for his courageous act. As an owner he worked in the mines, and even she understood how dangerous that was. Also, he has been on his own since the age of sixteen. She scolded herself for thinking he needed someone with him to trek through Ashcourt. But deep down, she knew he had.

Mrs. Teaberry rushed into the work room. "I've lost my ledger. Have you seen it?" She stooped to look on a low shelf and shoved books and files aside.

"Is it black?"

The postmistress turned on her heel. "You've seen it?"

"This morning when I came in. You were working with it at the kitchen table."

Lightning struck "Aha." She poked around the corner. "You are a delight, Brianna. Hiring you was an inspiration."

Always surprised by a compliment from Mrs. Teaberry, Brianna said, "Thank you." But she spoke to the air as the postmistress had already gone down the corridor on her way to the kitchen.

Brianna noted an elderly gentleman fussing at the door. She scooted around the counter. "I'll get it for you, sir." As the door opened, he lost his balance and fell into the foyer all five boxes tumbling to the floor. "Let me help you up, sir."

"I'm not that frail, young lady." Indignation etched in his words, he scrambled to his knees then hefted himself to a standing position by leaning onto a shelf.

She picked up several packages and took them to the counter.

Rubbing his shoulder, he said, "I should have put them in satchels."

"Did you hurt yourself?" She piled up the packages and carried them to the scales.

"It's just me old joints acting up." He stretched out his shoulder and put his chin to his chest as if to prove his nimbleness.

"Give me a minute or two and I'll have the charge figured out." She ascertained the weight of each and their destination. Then looked at the chart on the wall and wrote down the amount. Handing him a piece of paper where she had totaled the cost of 6*d*.

Squinting his eyes, he read the amount and rumbled, "It cost almost double to go to Glasgow than it does Enniscorthy. I don't have enough coin." He dug into his pocket, withdrew a leather pouch, and slowly counted out two halfpence, a thruppence, and dug into his pouch, drawing out another four farthings. "It's me lucky day. This should do it, miss."

He said good day with a nod of satisfaction. She glanced at her watch, an hour, and a half before she could leave.

Stamping each parcel, she put them together for the outgoing post. Lionel would load the coach when it arrived, most days that was promptly at four-thirty.

⚜

Brianna left work and stopped at Cashel's Inn asking after Sir O'Bannon. He apparently left for the day. Firm in her conviction about Ashcourt, she intended to confront him about the tattle she had overheard this morning.

Hoping to find him at the manor, she made her way south. She intended he understand the abandonment Ashcourt suffered through the years. His family home needed care. Certainly not torn apart.

The first time he asked her to tour the inside with him, he seemed quite pleased when she agreed. They had been at supper with Aunt Natty when he invited her to accompany him. Brianna had to force herself to stay calm though she felt like dancing.

Her anticipation kept her awake most of that night. The next day came early enough. She felt giddy riding in the phaeton and tried to appear ladylike. His manner though kind, was aloof, restrained. As if the dead had come to life and would haunt him for walking the corridors.

Stepping inside the manor took her breath away. and with mixed emotions noted the inside was as bad or worse than the outside, but that wasn't her concern. Touching what she assumed was antique wallpaper on the walls and seeing past the dust of ages on the crystal chandeliers, and the graceful flowing staircase with the aged carpet runners fulfilled a dream of long standing.

She had her qualms about Ashcourt. No longer, because everywhere she glanced, she saw opportunity.

Today was different. She was on a mission and strutted a path she had used for many years with her easel strapped over her shoulders and canvas in hand; today, no canvas or easel, she came empty handed, but with a mind filled with criticism.

As she passed through the woods, a chaise and Sir Finbarr's phaeton came into view. He was already here and most likely with the architect. Her pace quickened. She pictured him with a hammer and saw ready to do damage.

The front door was ajar. She stalked up the gravel approach and took a deep breath before stepping inside. From the back of the first floor, conversation could be heard. She retreated to the gravel approach and paced up and down gathering nerve to confront him.

Mustering courage, she once again approached the front step and followed the sounds of talking. Finally, she knocked on woodwork at the entry to the kitchen and both men turned to her.

"Miss Brianna?" Sir Fin's face lit with welcome. "This is Mr. Abernathy, with Abernathy and Son Architect, in Waterford—Miss Walsh."

Nodding acquaintance, she asked of him, "May I speak to you in private?"

Mr. Abernathy offered, "I will start on the inspection, and you can catch up later."

He led the way to the front of the manor and at the door where the air was less oppressive, he turned to her. "Is it about Miss Natty?" a note of concern etched in his voice.

Taken by surprise she assured him, "No. No. It's...I am..." Her arms crossed and she glared at him and plunged right in. "You cannot demolish this home." She stomped her foot for emphasis causing a cloud of dust to billow. "You cannot obliterate this lovely place." Tears bit, mortified, she swiped at her cheeks. A puff of air left her lips as she tried to calm herself and met his steely green eyes. It seemed once begun all her energy and angst wanted to pour out of her.

His brow furrowed. His large hand plowed through his brown wavy hair. "I am at a loss for words. You march in here and tell me I cannot do what I want with my own property?"

Her chin firmed up. He made her sound like a shrew. "I am appealing to you. This home is like a beloved person to me since I was a child. If I had the wealth, I would purchase it from you. Please do not demolish Ashcourt. It doesn't deserve to be torn down. It's been waiting all these years to be tended, to be cared for. To be prettied up and painted as it ought." With her backhand she swiped at another tear.

She continued to stare at him. His lips parted showing white teeth, his eyes preoccupied with notions. As if she had said something *he* never would have considered.

Shaking his head, hands at his waist, he stood so tall it hurt her neck to meet his gaze. "Look here Miss Br—Walsh. I am in the midst of discussion with the architect. We are in the beginning stage of deciding Ashcourt's needs."

Her chest fluttered. Was there hope? She barely breathed and quieted as his eyes scrutinized her. She saw an awareness that he did not share and waited desperate for him to say something to give her faith.

"I don't mind your little paintings of Ashcourt. I think it rather provincial of you dabbing your personal impressions on canvas. Though I have misgivings seeing Ashcourt on canvas in its present state."

Provincial? He considered her paintings, rustic? Her anxiety heightened from concern over the future of Ashcourt, to plummeting into the depths of despair at his disregard for her paintings. She wanted to pound his righteous, puffed-up chest. Instead, she sweetly intoned, "You haven't said what your plans are, sir."

Again, he raked a hand through his dark brown hair. "Even I don't understand what my duty is toward this broken-down domicile. Until several months ago I hadn't stepped foot on this…" he waved an arm about the air "…monstrosity since I was a lad."

She took in a long breath. The plain and simple truth was Ashcourt wasn't hers. Her wrist crammed against her lips. What was on her tongue mustn't come out of her gob. Must not!

He made to return to the manor and obviously thinking of something he faced her. "Even though I've been gone for many years, you do realize this is my home?"

Oh, she wanted to slap his face and curled her hands into fists hoping to quell the urge.

With all his towering superiority he leaned in, "I have a sense you feel proprietorial toward this ruin. Painting it through the years probably allowed you a familiarity that led you to believe it was yours."

He smirked. "You might even feel justified in confronting me with accusations that are patently unfounded. As of this day I have…"

She tore past him and ran down the gravel entrance until her legs could no longer keep up the pace. Faltering, she leaned against an oak, slid to a sitting position on the bramble and succumbed to a good bawl, until her depressed miserable self was depleted of energy.

He was an abomination. Her loathing brought a shiver prickling up her spine. There had to be another way to get him to see the right thing to do with Ashcourt Manor. It would seem she was as provincial as her paintings. Rustic and certainly averse to Sir O'Bannon's world, she couldn't resign herself to complacency. It did quite the opposite, stirring her resolve and love of Ashcourt to new heights.

⚜

Two days later, Abernathy & Son Architects delivered a twelve-paged itemized document, listing problems with Ashcourt's structure and the cost estimate. Finbarr expected Mr. Abernathy's appraisal to be bad as he had pointed out obvious serious structural issues as they walked the premises.

Listed in the estimate were some interesting facts about the manor. The first phase was thought to have been built early in the 1600s, with the foundation above grade level. This much came from family history. By the middle of the 18th century Ashcourt's square footage almost tripled with the addition of both an east and west wing. His grandsire, Robert O'Bannon, had also enlarged the parkland and gardens to six hectars. Tastes in classical architecture had begun to change and with his grandsire's penchant for travel, he returned to Ashcourt filled with ideas from Europe, though most houses continued to be designed in a style changing little from the Regency period.

As he saw it, he had three options. He could tear the manor down and move on; tear the manor down and rebuild; or do a partial tear down with restructuring where needed and repaint and paper while updating the exterior. If he kept the manor, he would add two, perhaps three water closets and update the kitchen to bring it into the 19th Century.

He rode out to the manor after receiving the estimate. None of the options as to cost were a factor in making up his mind. He wanted to assess each option as he passed through the rooms. Mayhap he might come to a decision, particularly now that he had become quite familiar with the structure. Each exploration seemed to peel away the heavy memories he had carried for so many years.

As he approached the manor, an expectation of what Ashcourt might look like with Abernathy's suggestions came to him. Upon opening the front door and stepping inside, he noted a painting in a chair and pushed up against the panels that opened into his father's library. Miss Brianna's style indeed, water colored, depicting the ruin as it was today, a little colleen in the park holding a sign with one word on it HELP painted crimson.

Shaking his head in wonder at the woman who would go to so

much trouble to keep this manor, was puzzling. Somehow, she had attached herself to this place. Beyond his imagination as to why, he decided her emotional flair came from a passionate nature. He recalled the coach ride and her deep feelings for the children and his regrettable taciturn manner toward them.

He decided it was time for him to put the past away and do something he had been forbidden in his younger years—enter his father's library. He was a grown man. A wealthy man. A man whom others accepted as intelligent and hard-working. A man who never disobeyed his father's orders. He wanted to laugh but he balked at frivolity. There were incidents, dreams of being terrorized that still lingered in his mind.

He moved the chair Miss Brianna had shoved up against the entrance to the library then determinedly opened the double doors. A thin line of sunlight burst through a gape in the drapes, and he could see dust motes floating. The room was consumed by dust and cobwebs and animal skat same as throughout the manor.

A massive desk situated in front of two bays dominated the room. An even larger slate fireplace governed the west wall. The skull and antlers of an Irish elk hung above the fireplace. Fin recalled the story that it was the largest deer that ever lived and became extinct thousands of years ago. The remains of this skull were dug out of a bog on Ashcourt's land. He had clear recall of his father's reaction to the find, though his mother had to explain to her son about the bog, which fascinated him.

It was a floating mass of vegetation called sphagnum. His mother had warned him of the danger should he venture to walk on the area, he could sink through and drown, much like the elk did.

Though he heard the story of the elk as a youngster, this was the first he laid eyes on it.

Two maroon settees flanked the fireplace as if they waited for company to sit. Several rugs similar to the one in the parlor that Miss Brianna liked, covered the wooden floor.

The most magnificent feature in the room, aside from the elk's head, were the glassed cabinets filled with hundreds of books and a ladder any bookworm could climb and lose himself in finding the perfect read.

He wiped the dust from a glass door and read a title or two. His O'Bannon family origins encased in books one, two, and three were on the shelf. His eyebrows pinched as he pondered reading them one day. They were his to do with as he pleased.

It amused him to think his father sequestered in this room for most of every day unless leaving his sanctuary when hunting or eating. What would have kept him occupied to the extent he would forsake his wife and children on a consistent basis? What secrets did his father have?

Rather pleased with himself having overcome the fear of entering this inner sanctum, he could come and go as he saw fit. He left the doors wide when he puttered across the foyer and into his beloved mother's parlor.

Miss Brianna had struck again. Laying on the rug he beheld another of her sketches. Bunnies gamboling on the front park. Within the drawing a sign on a pole in the front yard read SAVE. Again, in crimson.

Help and Save? At least she wasn't standing in front of him, with her angry pout demanding he not tear the place down.

Miss Brianna was his first encounter with a determined and fierce member of the gentler sex. Life with her would never be calm and peaceful. The few times they were in each other's company there seemed to be something stirring the air. Bees; paint; her demands on him to be nice to children; to keep Ashcourt in one piece. Her large almond shaped eyes, gray with a black rim, if one looked close enough, could be warm with sympathy or clashing with animosity.

On a whim, he took the stairs two at a time almost as if on a scavenger hunt and raced along the corridor turning left and stopped at his bedchamber door. Would his intuition fail him? He slowly opened the door thinking he would be disappointed if he got it wrong.

But he did not and was not.

A third sketch on the bed was propped by a pillow. This time the watercolor was of the northwest side of Ashcourt. In the drawing, the window to his room flung wide a curtain pulled through the open window and flapping with the wind. At the window, a lad held a sign that read ME. This word in yellow.

Help. Save. Me.

He sat on the bed and reached for the paper. He wanted to be irritated. She'd snuck into his private life, crawling into his head. He wanted to understand how she might discern things about him that she could paint a lad at this particular window with the word ME. The lad's hair hung over his forehead much like his own was wont to do. She was deliberate in her rendering. He couldn't recall ever being the subject of someone's artistic efforts.

After a long spell of sitting on the bed, he put the painting back where she had placed it and palming his knees leaned forward for a minute of contemplation. The bed creaked with his weight. He had missed the comfort of this bed when sent to the stables.

But reluctant to return to the manor and live with the ridicule of his parent.

Before leaving his old room, he glanced at the child she had drawn. Miss Brianna had touched on the three rooms that meant more to him as a child than any other place in his small life. The library because it was forbidden; the summer parlor because it was his mother's favorite; and his bedroom, because of course, it was the only room that had been his.

Or was he reading far too much into her prank?

11

Braving a public rebuke

Aunt Natty's excitement over Sir Finbarr's invitation to dinner at Cashel's Inn took on the importance of a dinner with the Queen. Friday, the 24 of July arrived, and she asked Mim to iron her lavender cotton print and set out a matching light-weight shawl.

Brianna was inclined to refuse the invitation until Aunt Natty made such a fuss, Brianna agreed to go. She was reluctant to explain to her aunt her reason why. She had not heard one word from Sir Finbarr. He had to have been to Ashcourt since she left the signs.

On pins and needles for several days now, she might not be in the right frame of mind to be in public with him. She'd not one word! Drat. Her curiosity over his reaction burned a hole she could not patch. No. He was going to have to give her some kind of response, so she could give him a piece of her mind.

His phaeton arrived to transport them to Cashel's promptly at six. He waited at the entrance to receive them. Tall and undoubtedly the handsomest man in the lobby, Sir Finbarr graciously escorted Aunt Natty into the dining room. Brianna, deliberately, refused his arm, tagged along behind, his broad shoulders cutting any view of the dining room as they approached.

Once seated, he placed his napkin on his lap and treated Brianna with a lovely smile. "How are you this fine evening, Miss Brianna?"

"The air has cooled, making it rather pleasant." She glanced at her aunt. "We enjoyed the ride." Secretly, she was pleased he'd called her by her Christian name. She was afraid after the scene at Ashcourt, he would have reverted back to Walsh.

"My pleasure."

Mrs. Cashel herself waited on them. Tonight's fare was partridge pie or stuffed roast of pork. She also inquired, "Will you be enjoying a wine this evening, sir?"

He glanced at his guests. "Are you interested?"

Aunt Natty perked up. "I would be delighted."

Mrs. Cashel suggested, "Waterford has a vineyard where my son works. I am partial to their white and happen to have a chilled bottle if you would like to try it?"

"Perfect, thank you." He glanced at Miss Natty, whose cheeks pinkened with pleasure.

Brianna shifted her gaze quickly so he couldn't look her in the eye. He was pleasant and accommodating. It was obvious Aunt Natty was in heaven dining with the man who seemed to dote on her.

Mrs. Cashel then asked which meal they preferred, the pie or the roast? Beginning with Miss Natty, who ordered the partridge, Miss Brianna the roast, and Sir Finbarr the roast. Having taken their order, she headed directly to the kitchen.

Brianna could not figure out why his invitation included her, and why he acted as if nothing had come between them. She burst with questions, "Are we celebrating an occasion, Sir Fin?"

He turned his dark green eyes on her, a small tic at the corner of his mouth. Just enough for her to notice. "Both of you were my first acquaintances upon arriving in Hawthorn. I feel as though we have a special bond. The three of us."

Aunt Natty was almost weepy. "You are a rascal," was all she could manage.

Brianna prickled that he amused himself with her aunt's affections. He was up to something, and she hoped to get to the bottom of it. And if he was not going to make mention of their quarrel, why hadn't he mentioned her drawings?

The wine was served, and Sir Fin approved its scent and flavor and the women joined him.

Aunt Natty fussed, "Your mother must have doted on you." She raised her drink, Brianna followed suit and they drank to him.

"Thank you, Miss Natty..." His gaze shifted to her "...and to you, Miss Brianna."

This time the tic at the corner of his mouth grew into a smile that reached his eyes where little crinkles spread. He had a flair about him. It was such a shame he was bent on doing harm to her —er, his Ashcourt. She gulped her wine surprised at how quickly her ire heated.

Aunt Natty tsked.

Sir Fin said, "To respond to your remark about my mother. She was an inward soul. Unusually quiet, I would say. My father ruled our home as if a dictator. My mother let the pieces fall where he wanted them."

"What a horror it must have been for your dear mother." She searched his face for a response. "Do you have siblings?"

"Vivian and Marion. Much older than I. Married and gone by the time I was in trousers. We barely knew one another."

Brianna snatched a hint of misgiving as if he wished he hadn't been so revealing. She could be wrong, but her intuition was usually accurate. She suggested, "You've been out of the country for a long time. Perchance now that you are returned you might renew your relationship. They are your family, after all."

His expressive eyes narrowed. "Family or not, little love is lost between us. And to do so, would also mean an intrusion on their lives. I'm content to leave the situation as it is."

"Come now, Sir Finbarr," Aunt Natty encouraged, "You certainly have the ability to change matters with them. Write a letter, see if it doesn't make a difference." Surprised at her outburst she quickly sipped more wine, then added, "You might be surprised at their reaction."

Aunt Natty took off her gloves and stuffed them in her reticule then glanced at Sir Fin. "I'm being a busybody, aren't I?"

He chuckled, "No you aren't being a busybody. I'm thinking of what I might have to say where I to correspond with Vivian. I wouldn't have any idea how to get in touch with Marion."

Aunt Natty turned her attention to the paintings on the walls.

Sir Fin leaned forward and whispered to Brianna, "Help. Save. Me. I see it as your cry for the future of Ashcourt?" His brow cocked, and he appeared full of himself, puffed up, a smirk at the side of that mouth of his.

Of men she knew little but this one enticed her to be bold. It had all begun in the coach from Dundalk when she chastised him for being rude to a pair of lassies.

Mrs. Cashel returned with steaming plates of food. The scent of roast pork and potatoes, and the partridge pie with hints of rosemary and sage permeated the air.

So, he did notice her watercolors. She dug into her pork and took pains to ignore him without seeming obvious. He had called them a cry for the future of Ashcourt which was certainly true. But she also wondered what else he might feel.

Aunt Natty was so excited about her partridge she closed her eyes and drew in the scent.

Brianna asked, "Is the sage overdone?"

"Oh no, it's divine."

He laughed. A couple at a table down from theirs looked up, smiling as they did so and obviously curious. Brianna had a clear look at them. She pasted a smile on her face for their benefit.

Aunt Natty plunged her fork into the thigh. "I can wait no

longer." The delight on her face as she savored the bite almost made Brianna wish she had ordered the partridge.

Out of the corner of her eye she noted Sir Finbarr. He appeared to enjoy Aunt Natty's enthusiasm for the fowl.

She was impatient for his announcement about Ashcourt. Mayhap, he hadn't made up his mind. Could it be Mr. Abernathy hadn't gotten back with him yet?

Mrs. Cashel returned to their table several times, addressing Sir Finbarr each time, and treating him with great deference. He seems to have made quite an impression on her and Brianna pondered her own feelings toward him, bullheaded and unemotional.

The tasteful dinner finished, with an inch of wine left in the bottle, and raspberry tarts polished off. Aunt Natty reached across the linen and patted Sir Fin's hand. "This was a wonderful treat. Your company and such a grand dinner, I cannot recall when I've had a lovelier time."

Brianna's eyes met his as he dabbed the napkin against his mouth. Her skin prickled when she realized he had been looking at her.

He said, "Nor I, Miss Natty. Your company made all the difference."

"I agree the dinner was lovely, the company also." Even to Brianna's own ears, she sounded a bit prim. This man turned her into knots, and she wished she could understand why.

"As it's early," Aunt Natty suggested, "would I be remiss if I asked to be driven home now. I am growing a bit weary and do not want to take you young ones away from what is a lovely reason for a stroll at dusk."

Brianna looked up sharply at her aunt. "Are you feeling unwell?"

"Absolutely not. I ate too much and would like to get into something that does not bind me." She began putting on her gloves.

Sir Finbarr excused himself.

Brianna hissed at her aunt. "You will leave me with him?"

Her aunt sniffed the air. "I can see that he likes you. The least you can do is chit chat for a fifteen-minute stroll home."

Sir Finbarr returned and spoke to Miss Natty. "The phaeton is waiting for you when you are ready. Miss Brianna, will you be leaving with your aunt?"

His offer took her by surprise, she rather liked the idea of an evening in the fresh air. "I prefer to walk if it's all the same to you."

His smile almost melted her. There were times when he was decent.

"It would be my pleasure to see you home."

The first block was spent in silence. Several carriages had passed, a dog stretched its legs against a tree barking at a cat leisurely cleaning itself on a limb. The moon was rising against the lavender sky streaked with orange and red. The balmy air rustled the leaves in the ash and oaks. It would seem perfect and yet she itched to start a quarrel with him.

Seemingly absurd, Brianna admitted she liked strolling alongside him. Far more than when she and Lionel were about. Sir Finbarr was a complicated man to her thinking. Many layers of intrigue. She liked his smile, which he seemed to offer regularly and his intriguing green eyes that could pierce through to one's soul. She snuck a peek up at him.

"Something's on your mind, I can tell because you are quiet." His low tones fit the intimacy of the evening. As did his leisure ramble and hands clasped behind his back. "Tell me the significance of your three paintings."

That question took some of the starch out of her. At ease, she took a good minute before answering. She wanted to respond. But now that she had the opportunity, her thinking was jumbled.

Finally, she said, "Of course, you've heard how I feel about

Ashcourt, so I shan't go over that again. The watercolors? They were meant to make you think of what you might be losing. And before you badger me, let me explain."

Brianna heard the treble in his throat when he chuckled. His presence next to her felt comfortable. Which was surprising after crying and running off the way she did. She was grateful for the chance to impart her feelings. "You've been away for many years for a reason. I assume it has to do with family…most probably your father.

"I think he must have been the kind of parent that didn't nurture. A child needs love and to understand they are valued. Something of that nature might be the cause of your unhappy memories. Perhaps, why you haven't returned home until recently." She felt compassion for the child he had been but didn't have the nerve to say something that personal.

"Thus, my watercolors, help, save, me. If I am partially right about you, the messages should awaken your inner self to realize that running away is not the answer. As is the destruction of Ashcourt not the answer. Getting even with a dead parent is not a solution."

"Your aunt is correct you do speak your mind."

Her cheeks burned and she was grateful he couldn't detect her embarrassment. They traipsed another block before he spoke again.

"Help Save Me. I must admit I felt the play of your game. But it was not until I got to my old bedchamber and saw ME, that I realized how much you surmised." The sun had fallen behind the horizon coloring the sky with golds and reds. His soft and low baritone was uniquely for her in the darkening eve.

She was taken aback that she *had* warranted his needs. "As secretive as you try to appear, there were a number of signs."

His shoes thudded lightly on the walkway with the weight of him. He certainly was an imposing figure, but not in the least intimidating. More like he would be a safe haven, an unshakable sturdy friend. No matter what, he would be there.

His low voice cut through her musing, "Tell me about the little colleen holding the HELP sign."

"She wants your help to restore Ashcourt to what it once was."

"Why does she want to keep Ashcourt?"

"I've told you the manor needs a family to love it. Some paint and new boards here and there. Horses in the stable would be nice. A fire in the parlor. A cook stirring up delicious meals."

He stopped and turned to her the moon casting a pale light on her face. "Is this about that lass in the painting, or is this about you?"

A lump caught in her throat. "Well, she is a symbol of…of wanting what is right for Ashcourt. Plain and simple."

He reached out and lightly caressed her cheek with his knuckles. His face in shadow with his back to the moon. She could not read what was in his eyes. His feather-like touch riled her blood. Stepping away from the intimate moment was the last thing she wanted to do.

With a sigh, he motioned for them to continue their stroll and after a few minutes said, "I have not made up my mind about Ashcourt. Is it conceivable you might have time after work one day next week to come out? I promise to listen to what you have to say."

They reached the village edge where her home nestled between Stoney Batter and Chadwick Lane. Aunt Natty had left a light burning in the parlor. Brianna was thrilled with the prospect he would listen to her ideas about her beloved manor. "Would you like to come in and say good night?"

"I think not. Your aunt was making herself comfortable, and I would not want to put her at an unease." His voice rippled with the image of Miss Natty in clothing that does not bind her.

"I must apologize."

The streetlamps were lit, and they stood just inside a ring of amber. He appeared bemused. "Because?"

"The other day when I barged in on you and the architect.

Then ran off like a school urchin in an irritating fit. I am sorry. I behaved like a child who was denied a treat." Admitting her own ire lightened her, and as he was entirely the gentleman at dinner, she felt relieved to have owned up to her rotten attitude.

What she got in return for her confession was his smile brightening his serious demeanor. He bit at his lower lip as if to keep from saying something he would regret.

She impulsively threw her arms about his waist and hugged him. For a moment or even less than a moment. And immediately pushed back.

Heat raced up her neck and face. "I can't believe I did that." Her gaze fell to the walkway as she palmed her blushing cheek. His draw of breath was unmistakable. He started to reach out and just as quickly withdrew his arm. As much as he irritated her sometimes, there was something about him that gave her a feeling of completeness, or safety.

The notion was upsetting, and she quickly said, "If it suits, I'll be at Ashcourt on Monday at one to amble through with you." She dashed up the steps and did not look back. He had looked at her with a quirk at the side of his lips as if he baited her, or mayhap he was simply curious. Oh bother! Her impulsive nature needed to be reined in.

12

Anger at the Graveyard

Aunt Natty adjusted the peacock feathers on her bonnet. Using the mirror in the foyer, as she waited for Brianna, she fluffed the pink crepe lining, then donned the French cottage-shaped delight. She wore the bonnet only on special days.

A bit of a breeze refreshed them as they traipsed to St. John's Church for Sunday service. The Stevens, neighbors down the road, all seven of them, hastened and chatted along the way. One of their younger sons asked his mother if Reverend Fulbert intended orating for an hour today.

Brianna put her gloved hand to her face, hiding a smirk at the remark. Aunt Natty tsked and whispered, "For shame. He's a decent and good man."

Brianna whispered back, "He may be, but the child is right, he is long winded."

Aunt Natty pulled on her niece's arm, causing them to fall back a bit from the family. "You wait till you have children, my dear. They repeat what they hear."

"He heard the truth from one of his parents then and spoke the truth. What is the proverb, out of the mouths of babes?"

Aunt Natty looked over the rim of her eyeglasses. "You've been reading St. James Bible again. Good lass."

It was difficult for Brianna to suppress a laugh as they neared the church, bells peeling into the Sunday morning air called the lambs to the shepherd.

They rounded a corner of thick trees that bordered the graveyard. The church set further down the road.

☙❧

Aunt Natty suddenly stopped. She whispered to Brianna. "You go on ahead. I'll be right in. I want a quick word with Mrs. Hawkins."

Natty waited a moment until Brianna crossed the threshold and then she quickly moved toward the graveyard. A woman wrapped in a shawl from head to toe, only her face could be seen, stood next to a tree.

As Natty approached she said, "What are you doing here, acting as if you're hiding."

Dervila spun about. "I remember you always come here on Sunday. Niall is quite ill and refusing to see the doctor. Why didn't you answer my note?"

Natty stepped back. "I told you we are finished. I threw it on the fire."

"Unread?" She dabbed at her cheeks with a filthy handkerchief.

Natty ignored the question and glanced back at the thinning line heading into the vestibule. "If you have something to say, be quick about it."

The thick kohl Dervila had always used bled down her cheeks, mayhap due to the high humidity, although Natty suspected she might have been crying. The look in her eyes mirrored that of a wild woman.

"I don't know what to do." She reached out to Natty, grabbing her arm. "What should I do. I have no one I can call on but you."

What a conundrum. About ready to step into God's Church and all I want to do is run from this woman. Where is my Christianity?

She could hear the choir begin the entrance psalm and felt pulled in two different directions. "I will visit you in a day or two. Where do you live?"

"Today, not tomorrow." Dervila made to crush Natty in an embrace.

Miss Natty quickly put up her hand. "Don't," then argued, "I cannot see you today. And tomorrow I am not sure of. But I will come by when I can, and we can have a chat. You will have to be patient."

Dervila calmed down. "By the wharf, Maher's Pub on the Strand. You'll see a side door and stairs. We are the 2nd flat." She swiped at her eyes, "I can't thank you—"

Natty cut her off. "I don't need your platitudes."

She drew away from her cousin and stepped quickly toward the open doors of St. John's and slipped into the pew next to Brianna hoping her lateness went unnoticed. For once she was grateful Brianna had chosen to sit at the back of the sanctuary, most likely to save her aunt from having to traipse the length of the nave.

Rattled, she drew in a deep breath and rid herself of a growing anxiety.

Brianna shared her hymnal and pointed to where they were on the page. Aunt Natty's hand shook as she reached for her half. She began singing, but Brianna noted it didn't rival her usual gusto.

Reverend Fulbert's sermon did seem to go on and on. Brianna glanced across the aisle where the Stevens family sat. Two children snuggled up to their mother. A lovely sense overcame Brianna with Mrs. Steven allowing her children to sit close. It would appear her young son didn't mind an hour's sermon after all.

Aunt Natty fanned herself with a kerchief. Brianna noted her flushed appearance and wondered what Mrs. Hawkins might have said that caused her aunt's hand to shake and so urgent it couldn't wait until after the service.

After the closing prayer, both women made their way toward the back of St. John's. They had offered to assist with packing up donations for the poor. Aunt Natty had helped two mornings this past week with mending where needed and then sorting.

"Natty, I am so pleased you could spare us an hour or two." Mrs. Hill patted Brianna's hand. "And a pleasure to see you, too. I understand you are working for Mrs. Teaberry."

"Yes, ma'am."

"There is a table near the kitchen where you can leave your bonnets and reticules. Tea will be available after we work a bit. I hope that you are able to stay that long."

Natty assured her, "You help so many in the village who are less fortunate. We are only too happy to assist in the effort of bringing some joy to others."

Mrs. Hill mentioned to Brianna, "You may have noticed a group of young ladies at the table in the back already at work. Perhaps you went to school with most of them?"

Brianna had taken notice. She knew all but one. "I'll go over. Hand me your hat and reticule. I'll put them in the back with mine."

As she approached the table where the young ladies were sorting, Carla squealed. "Brianna. I haven't seen you in ages and ages." The other two, Alma and Diana were just as enthusiastic, though she'd seen Diana in her dress shop. "You probably haven't met Kimberly. Her family moved here a few months ago."

After a short catching up, they settled down to work. Families had been designated with seeing that the committee received lists of children's sizes and items that were needed. The process was to move about the large room from table to table and 'shop' for items on each list. When all done, each family's items were to be wrapped and tied with twine which had been donated by Curley's Butcher Shop.

Brianna worked side by side with Carla and had been fast friends when younger. "I heard you were working near Dublin."

"As an assistant governess in Dundalk for a family of six daughters, can you believe?"

"I've only one sister. No, I can't imagine a home with six."

"Always a lot of fussing and even jealousy between them. Made me glad I was an only child, to be truthful. Mostly though, I'm glad to have had the experience. One I might repeat someday."

Carla reached for a red sweater and glanced at her list. "This should do." She held it up against her. "What do you think? Will it fit a twelve-year-old lass?"

Brianna nodded. "I should think so. With a bit of room to grow."

"Is there anyone special in your life?" She batted her big brown eyes at Brianna.

"No time. And no inclination, either. I've been gone for several years and still settling in."

"Do you remember Joseph? He has a big nose and lots of black hair that doesn't exactly hide his big ears?"

Brianna laughed. "The way you describe him..." she peeked up at Carla "...is he courting you?"

"He is." She practically squealed with delight as she whispered, "And I think him most handsome."

Brianna reached for a pair of black brogues looking them over for holes in the soles. "What have you been doing with yourself since school ended?

"As the eldest, I've taken on the cooking for our family and teaching the young ones. Mother's been quite tired. It began about four years ago after she delivered her last. Father has all he can do to keep the logs split and work full time at the forge."

Brianna chose several pairs of breeches and shirts noted on

the list and wandered to a table laden with under clothing and leggings. She needed three pair of stockings. Carla followed her as she talked of her family.

"How many younger siblings do you have?"

"Nine. There'd be more, but mother lost three that we know of."

Brianna stopped poking through the stockings and looked at Carla. "You're truly needed at home. God blesses you, Carla. You're a dutiful daughter."

Carla's face lit up and her cheeks pinkened. "That's a nice thing to say."

An hour later, Brianna, Carla, Alma, Diane, and Kimberly stood back and looked at their table with twenty-five parcels wrapped and tied. Each person had made a list of wants and that list had been attached to the package with instructions for whom it is meant.

As the women glanced about the corridor, a feeling of immense satisfaction overcame Brianna at the small part she played in fulfilling a need for those less fortunate.

Tea and biscuits were set out at the back of the room. Carla and Brianna headed toward the table. Brianna asked, "Who'll prepare tonight's meal if you don't?"

"I've two younger sisters, twins. Fran and Lily. I've been teaching them. They are quick learners. I told you about Joseph…" She quickly glanced around then whispered, "He asked me to marry him."

Brianna meant to hug her, and Carla quickly put a finger to her lips. "Shush. I have told no one. We can't right now. First, I need to teach my sisters to take over. Until then I'll say nothing."

"I am honored to be the keeper of your secret and thrilled for you, Carla. You certainly deserve a life of your own."

For a moment, her friend's attention drifted to a window. She sighed. "In truth, I'll be exchanging one sink for another. And one roof for another. But Joseph is worth it." She blushed again.

On the way home with Aunt Natty, Brianna asked her, "Have you ever regretted you didn't marry?"

Natty glanced at her rather sharply. "Where does this come from?"

"Just wondering about something Carla said this afternoon. She's cooked for her family since we've been friends, somewhere around eight or nine. She would like to marry someday."

"The Kelly's are a large family, and the mother is sickly. Poor soul, she just gave up trying to take care of her brood. I'm sure she's grateful for her hearty eldest daughter."

It occurred to Brianna that Carla thinks marriage might be her escape. Though she did admit she would be exchanging one sink for another. She asked her aunt again, "Why didn't you marry?"

"I was spoken for once. To a lad I felt sure loved me. In the end, it wasn't meant to be."

"What happened? Did he die?"

"No, he married someone else."

Brianna put her arm about her aunt's shoulders. "You were heart broken, weren't you? Shameful and dishonorable on his part."

A faraway look in her eye, her aunt gave a short nod. "It took a long time to get over him. And the woman he married, well, we had been close. I promised myself I would never allow myself to hurt like that again. And then shortly thereafter a peddler handed me my new life."

Brianna said, "Words can't explain how I feel about you and the life you've provided for me."

Aunt Natty's face melted into happy narrowed eyes. She dabbed where crows' feet spread. "My darling girl, God knew we needed each other."

Beginning with an opinion

Monday afternoon and a lovely day for a good saunter after being in the post office all morning, Brianna headed toward

Ashcourt Manor with excitement. To be asked of one's opinion by someone as worldly as Sir Finbarr, indicated his trust in her judgement. She also harbored a bit of fear that her opinion might be a grave disappointment. She had agreed to meet him at one o'clock.

His phaeton was under the shade of a Hawthorn, the horse nibbled on clover as his tiger rested against the gray trunk of the tree.

Sir Finbarr was standing on the threshold as she arrived. "I hope I haven't asked too much of you. You are an industrious woman."

She stepped up to him. "Ashcourt deserves the attention. I'm happy to oblige."

"Shall we start on the first floor and go room by room?"

She pulled out a notepad and pencil from her satchel. "I hope you were serious about hearing me out?"

His eyes gleamed with teasing. "Absolutely. Our motto, Help Save Me. Remember?"

She cast him a side glance taking exception to *our*. Had he made the decision to save Ashcourt?

His hand placed on her back he drew attention to some of the debris scattered near the door. "Please be careful where you step."

Committed to being of use, she said, "Let's begin with your mother's front parlor then. You said she preferred this room." She went directly through the double-doors and into the cobwebbed parlor.

He blew at the dust on a table and spread out the architect's first-floor drawing. "Mr. Abernathy recommended replacing all windows. He talked of a new way to make glass sheeting rather than individual panes. He also discovered several of the fireplaces need replacing, the rest can be restored."

He stepped to the fireplace. "This one for instance."

Opening a sharp pocketknife, he scraped off the mortar loosening a brick that fell to the pan causing a billow of black dust. Then they heard the distinct sound of flapping wings, followed by a partial nest and two eggs dropped down the chimney where they broke hitting the bricks. He withdrew from the fireplace and turned to her.

Brianna let out a stunned bark of laughter. "Begorrah, if you could see yourself."

He blinked and looked at the hand holding his pocketknife. It was pitch black. He glanced about the parlor, she supposed he looked for a mirror, and quickly dug into her satchel for a handkerchief offering it to him.

With one swipe across his face, he said, "I must resemble a chimneysweep."

She tried not to giggle nodding instead and stepped back a few feet.

He swiped his face several times. "Soot is the worst." He deliberately widened the whites of his eyes. Smiling, his row of white teeth gleamed, framed by the soot on his face. He looked comedic, as enduring as a child.

She laughed. "I wish I had another hanky to offer you." She enjoyed the silly moment, not surprised that he took it in good humor. She liked that about him, a solid enough man to disregard the mishap.

"Is the soot in your eyes?"

"Not that I can tell. Well, shall we finish or call it a day."

His offer to continue surprised her. The upset had not daunted him, treating it as if it were a small incident hardly worthy of notice. She wondered what he might think if he could see his reflection.

"I can imagine how I look." With open palms, he stepped close. "I could use your skirts as a towel."

She shrieked. "Don't you dare."

He chuckled. "A little dirt never hurt anyone." He wiped his hands on her handkerchief. Handsome though he was he took on the appearance of playacting or masquerading. "This is a mere trifle. I looked like this when I began working in the mines, a daily occurrence for all of us."

"The person who will clean your suit won't think it a trifle."

His ridiculously sooty lashes narrowed, "Collins? He's put up with far worse through the years. Now that we have proved this fireplace needs replacing, let's finish with the parlor."

She touched a lovely figurine. "Your mother collected beautiful porcelain."

He nodded as if remembering. "Everything else will have to be replaced."

They continued down the corridor toward the back of the manor.

The dated kitchen layout she guessed to be at least fifty years old. The scullery next to the area where food preparation would take place did not appeal to her. She felt the washing of dishes, pots, and pans should take place elsewhere.

The fireplace consisted of a large opening with several iron hinges on which pots would hang to boil water for cooking and for baths, and stews and such. The size seemed adequate. She counted the number of staff, a butler, kitchen staff of maybe four, a housekeeper, and perhaps three day-maids. But then there would be gardeners and stable hands. She wasn't sure if the kitchen was big enough to feed all. Unless perhaps they ate in shifts.

A slated floor and a long table where servants chopped, cleaned, and otherwise ate their meals would also enhance the space.

"Abernathy says this is to be all torn down and built back up. If you could change this space, what would you do?"

His inquiry humbled her, but he did ask for her opinion. She had guessed at the number of staff needed and hadn't an inkling of his desire for dinner parties.

"Do you have plans to entertain?"

Entertaining never crossed his mind. As a bachelor in Swansea, he had managed a few dinner parties. He certainly enjoyed the company of others and glanced at Miss Brianna.

"I'm not opposed to entertaining. What should concern me about this kitchen?"

"Hmm." She slowly turned about the floor. "It needs a more up-to-date baking oven. It also needs a sink with a drain to the outside. And if the cost is not a consideration, I would have the cobbled floor taken out and slate laid. It is easier to keep clean. The shelving and cupboards are not conveniently located, and badly in need of repair, so I would suggest replacing them. The cook also needs a corner or a room for the scullery. And, depending upon how many staff you employ, you would need a space for their dining."

He teased, "My question was certain to trick you up. How is it you know your way around a kitchen?"

"I lived with a family for several years and became accustomed to tea and biscuits in the kitchen with cook and maids. Besides, why wouldn't I? I'm in and out of our kitchen two three times a day."

He smiled down at her enjoying her enthusiasm. "I didn't think of that. Of course, you would pick up on all the essentials."

Brianna walked about the parameter of the kitchen. He supposed she was thinking of how it would look with the changes she suggested. He leaned against the wall, arms crossed and said, "In the lower classes in Wales, it was normal for lasses to be put to service and rarely educated beyond writing their name."

She admonished. "Most educational experts want to teach women enough to be useful, but not enough that they become ambitious. Not so my employer, Mr. Reynolds. I greatly admired his dedication to fully educate his daughters. He wanted them to learn what interested them."

He gave her the courtesy of his rapt attention. She had a way of expounding on an issue that obviously played on her mind. "It seems a shame your work was finished with the family. Mayhap when the daughters are married and raising children, they will remember your admirable efforts and offer for you again."

She blinked in surprise. "I'm not sure if you mean to be sincere or derisive. What makes you think I would want to continue in service?"

He shrugged. "When you mention the Reynold's family, I sense a certain amount of pride. I took that as affirmation you might continue in that line of work."

"Oh, well, I received praise from the head governess and felt as if I'd achieved a monumental task. It wasn't easy pleasing her. But teaching someone else's children isn't something to which I would dedicate my life."

"Your own then, possibly?" He pushed off from the wall and folded the wide floor-plan papers in half.

"Possibly."

He watched as she glanced about the old walls and dirty cobbles. She hadn't obsessed about marriage and a family like some women he knew. He wondered if living with her aunt and housekeeper, perhaps she never felt the need to lean on a man for support.

He moved the air about waving the floor plan. "Shall we continue? You've not seen the sunroom and library on this floor."

She walked ahead of him and into a room he once said was his mother's favorite. Bright and cheery, it was easy to see how inviting in spite of its present state. "This room needs repapering and new windows. Wouldn't a bay be lovely here? Quite pleasing to the eye, restful and serene. Depending upon how much you are spending, mayhap double glassed doors with a patio beyond." She traced her hand along the sill.

Sir Fin pondered her last suggestion. It shouldn't have surprised him; he already knew her artful imagery.

She added, "As to the formal parlor in the front of the manor, you will no doubt want new furniture. But this room presents why you would want to spend most of your time here. The potential to be at ease is obvious. And once you employ a gardener, it will look lovely. I can see your mother enjoying this and walking out through the double doors onto the slated patio, mayhap sitting on a stone bench under an Oak."

He slowly wandered to the room's far side and glanced at an old painting of a hunt in the woods. Then he looked out the windows facing north as his mother came to mind. A sweet but sad woman who always showed her love for her son.

Brianna turned to a cabinet filled with bone-China figurines. A little lass on ice skates, an elegantly gowned woman, her bonnet dangling by ribbons, a stag with a huge crown of antlers among other small items, and scattered droppings from rodents.

"Why exactly do you care about Ashcourt?" His baritone reached her as he continued to stand at the windows, not bothering to turn about.

His broad-shouldered presence at the window caused her to consider the child that grew up here. He had implied sadness and ruthlessness, his father being a tyrant. And his mother a quiet little mouse. Maybe he wanted to like Ashcourt and needed to see the beauty that could be brought forth. This just might be her chance.

So, she responded to his worsted-clad back. "The first time ever I laid eyes on Ashcourt I was about seven. This home spoke to me almost as if it were a person. I sensed an underlying sadness largely due to neglect. No one loved it, cared for it, or nurtured it.

"As a little colleen, I did think what my life might have been without my aunt. Her love for me was as clear as a sunny day. For some reason, I wished Ashcourt happiness, like my aunt had showered on me."

"I take it that is why you painted this place with someone at a window?"

She nodded. "I meant to spread good fortune on this home. I

see this place as something proud but worn down by time. A place that may have offered sanctuary and love as homes are wont to do. A place where a confused soul could rebirth itself."

He turned from the window facing her with his bandit eyes but said nothing. Mostly looking like she confused him with all her blather.

She offered, "We have different backgrounds. You have a home where generations of your family lived. You probably have two hundred or more years of history here."

His face empty of expression as if carved in stone, he turned back to the window and the landscape beyond.

Was he avoiding the possibility of restoring his family home? What could she say to inspire him to look at Ashcourt with a kind eye, and sympathy?

She said, "You are grieving your past when you could be relishing in a new start."

His hands were at his waist, legs parted as if he sailed a vessel in an emotional storm.

She said, "We only have control over what we do, not what our parents did. And as far as family goes, we have the ability to make our own families. Make them out of friends and lovely people who espouse gratitude and kindness toward others."

When he still did not turn back to her, she sat on the edge of a dusty chair and waited for what she knew not. But considered him in a sad way right now.

He eventually did turn to her, and it shocked her to see a tear running down his blackened cheek. He pulled a chair near her, at the same time wiping his cheek with the filthy handkerchief. "I am a complete mess."

"I think you are overwhelmed with sad memories."

"I feel a burden I can't seem to remedy." His sigh twisted her heart.

"Why did you really come back to Hawthorn Village, if you don't mind my asking."

"To prove something to my father, but I am not sure what that might have been."

"Do you mean, what would you want to prove?"

He took a deep breath. A long minute passed. "I've accomplished quite a bit on my own. And yet I feel as if it's not enough. I came here seeking answers and I end up with more questions."

She leaned over and patted his arm, as if comforting a child. "You have not given yourself enough time to find the answers." She spread her arms. "They are most likely here in this home. Perhaps they will come to you as you work and change this place."

They listened to the patter of a light mist at the windows.

She spoke up. "From what I've perceived about you, I believe you are doing exactly what you should to heal the past and build your future."

His dark face turned to her for the longest moment, when he finally said, "Thank you."

He raised his sooty hand to run it through his hair when Brianna said, "Don't do that."

He saw his filthy palm and laughed. "Collins will have a few words over this." He rubbed his hand with the dirty handkerchief. "I'll replace this for you."

"Mim is a miracle worker with stains. Give her a chance before you purchase anything."

She felt kindly toward him, and at ease. His reactions to her resembled a dance-card. He willingly signed his name giving her allowance to befriend him. "You are angry at your father. And, though I do not intend to pry, let me say that without him, good or bad, you would not have the life you've built for yourself."

He lifted his gaze to her, the whites of his eyes gleaming. The one tear streak down his cheek, now smudged. She felt maternal at the moment. Or whatever it is mother's feel when their children are uneasy over a problem.

He sat back in the chair and asked, "Why aren't you spoken for?"

Her initial reaction was to slap him. But she quickly realized he wasn't disparaging her singleness. "If anyone else asked me this, I would get all huffy. Why is it when you ask me such a personal question, I actually want to answer you?"

He chortled, "Then answer."

"I suppose it's because I've been too busy."

"Maybe you haven't found the right person." His lids half closed peeking through slits.

He made her laugh. "Are you attempting to keep my mind off the real reason we are here?"

"And what is that, pray tell? I've forgotten."

"Your inherited home? *Help Save Me*?" She rolled her eyes.

He laughed and it sounded real, like maybe his sad memories were fading. She enjoyed this man's company far more than the brooding one and said, "My hope is to convince you not to demolish Ashcourt."

He stood up and offered his hand for her to leave the old chair. "I have not made up my mind as yet. And we have not gone through the upstairs. Should we finish another day?"

"I would like to finalize our tour. The more I actually uncover, the more I see it as it could be. There's a wealth of possibility beneath the dust and grime."

As they ascended the stairs, he chuckled. "It is my good fortune you consented to do this with me. I was at a loss how to begin."

An hour later, they were in his carriage. "I discussed water closets with Abernathy. If I keep Ashcourt, I think two or three need to be installed."

"A grand improvement for sure. You might want one off your master for sure."

He glanced at her. One of her hands securing her bonnet, two feathers waving in the breeze. "Thank you for indulging me today. I needed another perspective and knew you would share an honest one."

She smiled at his remark. "You mean I am opinionated."

"I didn't say that." He set his attention to snapping the lines and pointed to the sky. "It looks like rain. That's a thunderhead off to the west."

"Let's hope we get to Cashel's before it begins."

13

Armed for battle

Comfortable in her chair, Pussycat purring on her lap, and Mim in the kitchen attempting to whistle a tune that must be rummaging around in her head, Miss Natty flooded with contentment. Lads and rough men are allowed to whistle, not women. But she recognized it gave Mim pleasure as she went about her chores.

A hard knock at the front door and Mim hustled down the corridor. She immediately turned into the parlor where Miss Natty settled.

"It's her. That woman."

"Take a breath, Mim. What woman?"

"The one who worries you so. *That* woman. She's at the door."

As if on cue the banging began once more.

Miss Natty puffed a breath and closed her eyes. "Oh, no."

"I heard that," came with the front door banging shut, instantly followed by Dervila's dramatic entrance into the parlor.

She flung her reticule on the chair along with a shawl that had seen better days. She waved her hand at Mim. "You can get on with whatever you get on with. I've enough on my mind without your nettlesome chatting."

Her housekeeper sputtered and stood between the mad woman and Miss Natty. "What should I do, ma'am?"

She closed her eyes and shook her head. "Leave us be for the moment." Then whispered, "… stay near."

Dervila plopped into the closest chair to Natty. "Niall is choking up blood constantly. It's gruesome. I can't take it anymore."

"Have you called on Mr. Curran?"

"Niall will have nothing to do with that man. Thinks he kills more than he cures." She rubbed her brow.

"You know that is not true, don't you?"

Thoroughly distraught Dervila swiped at her eyes inadvertently rubbing kohl over her cheeks. "I fear he is dying. He won't help himself. Won't even use the pot unless I help him."

Miss Natty closed her eyes a moment and sighed. "What do you want of me?"

As if on cue, Dervila began sobbing, great heaving sobs, the kohl around her eyes smearing on her hands. "I don't have the strength to take care of him. I need your help. Maybe your housekeeper's help."

Miss Natty heard something drop on the floor in the corridor and knew Mim had overheard. "He is your husband and your duty."

Dervila lifted her frighteningly messy face. Her eyes were cold, devoid of common sense. "It's your Christian duty to help those in distress."

Something again dropped on the hardwood floor in the corridor. Mim must be near hysterics. Miss Natty said, "My first Christian duty is to my household. As is your Christian duty to see to yours. You knew a month ago this day would arrive. What preparations have you made?"

Hysterical, Dervila wailed, "He won't allow that sawbones to touch him."

"If not Mr. Curran, what about an apothecary?"

A growl filled the space between them. "He does as he sees fit. Don't you get it? I am here because he is asking for you. He wants you. Not me. The wife he regularly beat before he left on the boats. I'm no good anymore."

Miss Natty leaned forward. "He beats you?"

She nodded lowering her face into her shaking hands again.

"He has the energy to fight with you?"

A muffled *no* seeped out between her fingers. "His strength is gone now. He beat me before."

Shocked, Natty wondered if Dervila was bereft at his lack of energy to beat her. That simply could not be.

"I've taken to sleeping in a chair. I can't stand to be near him or have him touch me." She blurted, "The sooner he goes, the better for my peace of mind."

Natty could hardly believe her blather. One minute she appeared delusional, the next, bitter. "Do you mean better for your peace of mind if he dies?"

Dervila looked like the devil had taken hold of her. "Yes, when he dies. Good riddance. How can I live till then? How much longer must I suffer? This isn't the life I wanted."

She glared at her cousin. "None of this would have happened if he hadn't wanted me to begin with." She shot up off the chair and paced to the window and back, certainly a nervous reaction to what she had endured—and what would yet transpire.

Pointing a long thin finger at Miss Natty, she shrieked, "You owe me. You practically shoved me at him all those years ago. This is all your fault. If you had not been such a dumpy little drudge, he would have chosen you."

She turned to the window and pushed the curtains aside. Her breathing heavy from her rant. "I can't care for him anymore. I'm finished with him. It's your turn, Miss Natty. It's you he wants now."

Mim came into the room a pie roller in one hand, and a pan in the other. Her eyes round as saucers. She stood in front of Miss Natty. "Give me the word, ma'am."

Pussycat leapt off Natty's lap and ran out of the parlor. Natty pushed her hands downward to designate that Mim should calm.

Miss Natty's firm voice snapped at the uninvited woman, "You have upset me and my household. We've been over this issue regarding your husband before and I told you then to leave and never come back."

Mim stood to the side of Miss Natty and held up the rolling pin acting like she might use it.

Dervila reached for her belongings, placing the shawl about her shoulders. If looks could kill, Mim would be prone on the floor right now, the rolling pin still in hand.

Miss Natty set her chair to rocking. "You have always been theatrical and over dramatic. Most especially when something befalls you. You are not welcome here, Dervila Murdock."

Mim followed her out and locked the door after her, then returned to the parlor.

"Oh, Miss Natty, what's to do? She's bent on mischief."

Miss Natty took a deep shivering breath. "She's no different than years ago. Always got her way, too. No matter who she damaged along the way. I hate to speak of the almost dead, but her husband is not a nice person either. She spoke of him as wanting me. The truth is she does not want to care for him in his hour of need. This visit smacked of manipulation to me."

Shaken by the encounter, Mim asked, "She looks old and used up. Do you know how old she is?"

"A year older than myself, I'm forty-nine."

"Her look says she's had a hard life."

"Of her own choosing, Mim." Miss Natty glanced at Pussycat cleaning herself at the housekeeper's feet, the epitome of an easy life.

"You do so much good. If folks knew what she was up to, they would rally to you."

"We'll keep this incident to ourselves, especially from Brianna. She will worry unnecessarily, and we don't want that."

Mim tucked the rolling pin under her arm and changed hands with the heavy pot. "I haven't said a word about the last time, and certainly won't this time, nor the next should that she-devil visit us again."

As Mim left the parlor mumbling, Miss Natty distinctly heard her vow about not being a next time.

৩৩৩

Relieved of the promise to visit Dervila in a day or two, Miss Natty whispered a prayer of gratitude to see the last of her cousin. In spite of the horrid scene with Dervila, she allowed herself a delightful afternoon with her friends; always laughter and teasing, they got along well these past many years. Each year she volunteered her services for the October end-of-summer-Fair.

Dervila unnerved her and reminded her of what happened in their younger days. Niall and Dervila's dishonesty and lying had been devastating. She had grieved for a long time. She loved Niall then. Right now, she needed to shake off the memories of betrayal and pain that Dervila resurrected with her return to Hawthorn.

Niall had been a lovely young man and in love with her. Though young at 16, she was certain of his honest attention toward her. They spoke of marriage and the future. She was on a cloud in those days. And then Dervila announced she was expecting Niall's child and he quickly married her. Both of them had broken her heart.

And that was the end of her fairytale romance, and the end of her tenuous relationship with her cousin. They had not spoken nor seen each other in all these years. Dervila had told her she suffered a miscarriage shortly after they married. When, in truth, she had not been expecting at all.

Simply put, Dervila wanted him and would do whatever it took to get him. Natty realized a long time ago that Niall's taking of vows with Dervila that quick, he had reason to suspect she carried *his* child.

As she made her way toward the church hall, she was grateful for the sunshine and the brilliant blue sky. And for friends to spend the afternoon with. Grackles soared in playful cloud formation gleefully babbling their song.

Regardless of how this day began, she would make it into something much better. She heard the prattle of her women friends as she opened the door to the large room. Several turned as she stepped into the room. Bonnie indicated they saved a chair for her. She scurried over and sat between Muriel and Bonnie.

"Just in time, we could have given your seat away twice." Bonnie smiled at her.

"At least we haven't begun. Who decided to chair this year?"

"Mrs. Cashel."

"She's too busy to get us organized." Natty shook her head.

Bonnie teased, "There's an old saying, busy is as busy does. Fine for someone else, but I'm done. I won't chair again."

Muriel agreed, and they settled down to listen as Mrs. Cashel stood in front of everyone. "Good afternoon ladies. Seems we have a lovely group. I count twenty. Thank you all for volunteering. And remember your good works will benefit a long desire to build a new school.

"So far, the events for each day are, a man who swallows fire, a ventriloquist, an albino, a dwarf, and a painted Indian from America, bell ringing, and puppet acts, and fireworks for three evenings."

A volunteer raised her hand and asked, "Is there to be an animal tent again this year?"

Mrs. Cashel nodded. "We can't have a Fair without Traton's bird act. The camel and panther are returning. As of yesterday, we'll also have lions, baboons, and a dancing marmoset."

There was some clapping of hands then a question from the same lady. "Have you a list of the musicians?"

"I'm waiting to hear from the hurdy-gurdy player and the

bagpipers. As they were here last year and many have asked for them to return, I'm hopeful. The flutes, trumpet, kettledrum, and fifes will be here. And something new this year, the hornpipe dancers want to join our fair."

More clapping, and a question from a different woman. "I would like to help organize the booths."

There was an undercurrent of whispers from the ladies. Natty found herself thinking of Dervila and closed her eyes a moment.

Bonnie tapped her arm. "Is something wrong?"

Natty opened her eyes. "I was thinking of something that happened this morning."

"Mrs. Cashel is full of herself. She'll go on and on for an hour telling us how hard she's worked."

That brought a much-needed chuckle to Natty who had yet to shake the dreadful effects of her cousin's haunting visit.

A tall woman in the front stood, the feather in her hat giving her even more stature. "You can see me after the meeting. For those of you who signed up for the raffles. I am Mrs. Brown. Thank you for volunteering."

Bonnie leaned in. "She's another one who's all puffed up with importance."

Muriel shushed her. "I can't hear."

Natty began writing down the information she needed. She had worked on Hawthorn's Fair for years with Mrs. Brown and intended to sign up after the meeting. She hoped Brianna would want to display some of her watercolors at a booth.

Mrs. Cashel closed the meeting after reaffirming the dates first through the fourth of October. The gathering hall emptied quickly volunteers scattering. Muriel asked Bonnie and Natty to lunch, but they decided to wander the strand instead which satisfied Natty as she intended to stop at the butcher's before going home. Brianna had been spending time painting lately and planned to return near dinner time.

"Is Brianna settling it? I know how much you missed her."

Miss Natty opened her parasol against the sun. "Our

household is back to normal with her home. She would say her experience was worth it. Now, she works for Mrs. Teaberry three mornings a week. The afternoons are usually filled with painting."

Bonnie said, "I saw you and your niece with that man from Wales, O'Bannon. It looked like you were enjoying a meal at Cashel's."

"It's Sir O'Bannon, and yes, he was kind enough to ask us to dine." Miss Natty felt special being seen on that evening.

Muriel's curiosity got the better of her. "Sir O'Bannon? Has Brianna got a beau then? He would be a real catch. He's handsome and the way he carries himself, like he owns the world."

Miss Natty tried to hide her delight. "Sir O'Bannon lived in Hawthorn when he was quite young. Born here if truth be known."

Muriel, eyes wide with surprise, said, "The O'Bannon's own that old place, Ashcourt. He must be one of them. Does that mean he's come back to live here?"

"I wouldn't know about that." Natty sidestepped Muriel's obvious next question by changing the subject, "Just you wait until the First of October. You'll wish you had run for the hills instead of signing up for a tent full of raffles."

Bonnie laughed. "She's got you there, Muriel. I am already sorry I talked to Mrs. Brown. I could see her writing my name in three different places on her sheet."

They amused one another as they sat a bench on the strand and watched the boats coming and going, and the water birds flying above. It was a beautiful summer day to enjoy friendships of long standing.

Natty wanted to confide in someone about this morning, but decided it was better to leave it be. Both women knew she had a cousin she despised and there had been a serious setback to their relationship, but Natty never mentioned the particulars. So, she was quite surprised when Bonnie brought the subject up.

Bonnie asked, "Did your cousin ever write after she moved away?"

"No."

"Did she move to London?"

"Bristol."

Bonnie rolled her eyes, and Muriel said, "Be thankful for the distance then."

A hollowness in her chest, Natty avoided divulging the truth.

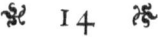

14

Facing childhood fears

Sir Finbarr's fingertips slipped through the panel openings to his father's library. He took a deep breath and pushed them apart. Musty air and a faint whiff of dried grass and vanilla swirled in the air. The scent obviously from the hundreds of old books lining the shelves.

He took two long strides into the room and with hands on his waist surveyed his father's empty leather chair at the desk and slowly turned in a circle taking in the entire room. The desk was laden with a lamp, a blotter, an inkwell, and a pen at the ready. It looked as if Diarmuid had just left the room after working all day, except for the inch of dust.

Sir Finbarr fancied his father's ghost floating about this room. Diarmuid was a formidable parent. Even now, he felt a cautious awareness as if the man lurked in the corners.

Several weeks earlier when Miss Brianna was with him walking about the manor, he had experienced inner conflict about Ashcourt. The effort to hide it from her made him feel like a child.

Now, standing here filled with the memories of that child, he realized how Diarmuid's presence could bring on an overwhelming fear. He always wondered what he had done that was so horrid that his father despised him.

The worries that burdened him when young were almost unthinkable at thirty-three. He had felt unworthy and that he had been sent to Eton as punishment for something he had done. Something unforgiveable.

As if he caused his mother's death.

Brianna said something the night they dined at Cashel's. He had rolled it around in his mind a time or two since then. *I think he must not have been the kind of parent that nurtured you. A child needs love and to know they are valued.*

It surprised him how soothing her words were, as if exonerating him of wrong, imagined or otherwise, and put the blame for his father's lack of parenting squarely on him.

Sir Finbarr breathed in the scent of old books. He had amassed a rather large library of his own over the years, but his books and maps were in crates waiting for him to establish a residence. He knew the vanilla scent was a breakdown of compounds, a common essence from old books. It was a combination of wood-based paper closely related to vanillin that overtime releases into the air.

As if in a trance, he stood at the desk a moment, then sat in his father's chair. No ghosts haunted him. The chair barely creaked. He pushed it back and the wheels hardly squeaked. He planted his long-fingered hands on the desktop and his father did not appear with a belt in hand.

There was some oil in the lamp, and he lit the wick. It flickered and held sending a golden circle over the desktop. His movements broke the solid film of dust, and he blew at it watching it scatter across the old mahogany top, motes floating in the air.

Through the years he feared growing into a man like his father. It was the nightmare of a child who felt cursed. He would wake covered in sweat, and sometimes caught himself pounding his mattress with his fist. And knew instantly it was his father he pounded.

As he sat in this chair and looked around the library, he was amazed to be here. And most importantly that he was nothing like his father.

When had the transformation begun? His time at Eton? Conceivably it was the distance and time away from his parent that allowed him to process his feelings.

What Fin did realize was that his father took his misery out on his mother. He would berate her in front of the servants shouting affronts, belittling her till her features melted in sorrow. He would slap her and throw her plate at the wall and order her to her room.

The first time it happened in front of him he was about seven and allowed to eat with his parents. As his father hit his mother, he jumped from his chair sending it crashing to the floor and ran around the table to protect her. His father grabbed him by the hair and yanked him back to his chair and ordered him to stay put.

After Diarmuid degraded her to his satisfaction, and she inched her way out from under his wrath, his father turned his eyes on him and curled his lip. Fin saw it as a warning—he could be next.

Fin lived with that expectation he would always be next. And when his father banished him to the stables and forbade him the house, Fin experienced a great sense of relief. Late at night he would creep into Ashcourt and attempt to see his mother, softly knocking at her door. Most times she did not answer, but the few times she did, she warned him to be wary lest he anger his father. He was sick in his head and did not mean to be cruel. It was just his way.

She had begged her son not to be foolish and visit her again. By the time he was eight, she died.

The stablemaster, Colby, saw to his meals and helped him set up a cot in the stall next to his own. Without having to explain why he was sleeping in the stables Sir Fin had a sense the stablemaster knew what his father had done.

Eventually, he was bundled off to Eton for schooling. And the person who helped carry his bags to the carriage and strap the trunk onto the back, was Colby. He had ruffled his hair and replaced his cap telling him to learn well and then get on with his life.

The next three years Diarmuid sent a courier to accompany him home.

At first, he hoped his father had changed, but he was quick to discover that was not the reason for bringing him home. Over the several years of back and forth between Ashcourt and school, Fin never quite understood the fuss of returning him other than his father controlling him.

His mother had passed, his sisters avoided Diarmuid, which meant they did not see their young brother either.

At times like this when dwelling on the past, he realized it was leading him to his own personal reformation.

The year he turned sixteen in early December about the same time as Christmas holiday at Eton—which was not an actual holiday, students stayed on campus—he took his future into his own hands. He packed up and left for Wales and Mr. Benford's mine, and never looked back.

In seventeen years from the beginning of his apprenticeship with Mr. Benford until late last year after the dampfire when he decided to put his mines in the hands of an efficient overseer, Fin saved every penny he could and still eat and have a place to sleep.

Along the way, he had been involved in the great changes that took place in mining and safety.

He was fascinated to learn all he could. In the early days, books he had read were filled with ideas of old mining and what the future holds. The growth of mining created the industrial revolution, steam power, mechanized spinning and weaving, iron production, textile production, and much more. He was proud of the small part he played. Mines had been in existence for hundreds of years, but in the last hundred or so advancements had taken place that made mining safer and more industrious.

Eventually he was able to purchase his first shares in a copper mine. It did not take long before he purchased other shares eventually owning considerable percentages in five mines. His persistence and diligence allowed him to step back from mining.

He wrote to his eldest sister, Vivian, telling her a little of what he did for a living. She had dutifully kept in touch once a year and when their father, Diarmuid passed she wrote to her brother. At the solicitor's request, she sent her brother's address to him.

And, after all this time, here he was. Full circle into the present standing in what had always been forbidden, his father's library. He was no longer that fearful child. He was a man, knighted by the Queen and gifted a baronetcy, for saving lives in a mine disaster. A man who had worked hard for what he had today.

He boldly tugged open the center drawer of his father's desk. A letter opener, pens, a pair of cuff links, wax for his father's seal, and the stamp embedded with his initials. He shut the drawer and opened another. It was filled with letters to his father. Fin casually thumbed through them until a familiar name caught his eye, Boyle, whose intent was to enlighten Diarmuid on the merits of designating who should inherit. Fin shook his head over that.

Returning the letters to the drawer, he opened the other side drawer. Accounting ledgers occupied the space. He had no desire to pore over them. Beneath this drawer was another smaller drawer. Several small tins half full of a brown powder, the contents smote him with a faint vinegary scent. He was fairly certain it was morphine and closed the tin. Another tin when opened, released a fruity minty odor he recognized as a liniment for muscular discomfort. He skipped over three other tins but did withdraw letters from the bottom of the drawer.

The seals were broken. The first from Squire Adams regarding the adjoining acreage and inquiring about some fine horse flesh for sale. The letter was dated a year before Diarmuid died. The next letter was from Lady Ophelia, no surname, who inquired about Diarmuid's health and wondered when he would be visiting next. Dated three months prior to Diarmuid's death.

Finbarr was not surprised. His father would have been considered handsome. The next two letters also from Lady Ophelia inquiring about his health and his next visit. Fin assumed his father visited her between each letter that was sent. As they were dated several weeks apart, that would indicate he visited every other week. #80 St. Stephen's Green, Dublin, was imprinted on the upper left corner.

It appeared his father liked women he simply didn't care for his wife.

The last letter was in his father's hand and addressed to Lady Ophelia Kearney, #80 St. Stephens Green, Dublin.

Sir Fin carefully opened the folds where the old paper was torn and separated with age at the creases.

Dear Lady Ophelia,

You can expect me Wednesday—will stay through until Saturday if that suits. I have written to my solic—oblem with Finbarr and expect to take care of the financial and legal situate —hen.

You have been a source of great—tude for me, my dear.

My objective is to have—is in hand by the time I return to Ashcourt on Saturday. But seeing y—ermost to my sanity right now.

I miss you,

Something kept his father from mailing this. He reached in the left-side drawer and drew out the bundle of letters he thumbed through earlier until he found Boyle Solicitors, Blackhall Place, Dublin, on the letterhead.

Fin left the library and took the stairs two at a time then strode the corridor to his father's bed chamber. He didn't know what he would find as he opened drawers and side tables searching for anything that might explain his father, anything that might appease curiosity. Concluding his search, he decided if there was anything at all that could possibly excuse or justify his father, it would be in his library.

So far all he discovered was the name of a woman.

On the ride back to Cashel's it occurred to him Colby might still be alive and living in the Hawthorn area. Stablemasters knew a great deal about the family they worked for, the comings and goings being an integral part of running the stables.

Leaving the chestnut with Paddy Cashel, he returned to his suite. After digging through paperwork, he verified that the solicitor Diarmuid used when transferring the title of Ashcourt ownership to him, was Boyle.

❦

Sir Fin opened the wide oak door of the Black Pig allowing a bright shaft of light to sweep across the room making the customers blink. He sauntered to the bar.

Padhraig wiped a cloth across the bar top and greeted his customer. "You must be Sir O'Bannon."

He held out his hand. "That I am. How about a pint of your best?"

"Coming right up. It's a pleasure to meet you, sir." He set the mug down with a snap causing some of the contents to spill. "Blessed saints, it didn't wet your sleeve, did it?"

"Not a drop." He hoisted the mug eager to quell his thirst. As he set the mug down, he said, "I'd like a word or two if you've the time, though."

He leaned in. "I've a few now."

"I'm trying to locate the old stablemaster for Ashcourt Manor. Colby. Could you help me?"

"He lives out toward Dark Castle about five kilos from Rockmore Hall. He's a right old codger now totally bald and a wee problem with his sight. Ye might not recognize him."

Sir Finbarr laughed. "Oh, I'll know him. The minute he opens his mouth, I'll know him."

Padhraig chuckled. "He does prattle, I'll give ye that. If you don't mind my askin', how is Ashcourt looking to ye?"

"Rough. Needs a lot of work." He pushed his empty mug back and put his hand up when Padhraig meant to refill. "Business calls. Thank you for the info on Colby." He slid a sixpence onto the bar top and left.

৩৯৯

Approaching on horseback, Dark Castle's crumbled turrets and what was left of the mote and edifice of the several hundred-year-old fortress, still looked formidable from what he recalled as a child being frightened of banshees if he got too close. He had no reason to dwell on his childhood, but with memories and digging into the past, he was discovering he had been afraid of a lot of things as a child.

Up ahead etched across the sky in a sort of majestic belligerence was a curl of dark smoke. He meandered through a dense area of tall trees and came out atop a rise where he viewed the landscape. He noticed a hillock of bramble and hawthorn from whence the chimney smoke curled.

Nearing the cone of gray swirl, he saw what he thought was Colby in a rocking chair, smoking a pipe. A whiff of fish frying in the fire reminded him of when he was young. As he got closer, he heard the sizzle of fat.

Colby stood and with one hand on the rocker, he waited for the approach of a visitor.

Tying up Jupiter's rein, Fin spoke, "I've come for a long overdue visit. I don't want to intrude."

The bald-headed man, tam atop, gasped as the pipe slipped from his mouth to the ground. He quickly bent down pawing at the dirt.

"Here, let me get that for you. It's kicked under the rocker."

He straightened, wiped off the pipe and held it out to Colby who stood with his eyes squinting. Sir fin placed the pipe in his hand, folding his fingers over the bowl.

"Is this really you?" Colby's hand sought him, grabbing Fin's forearm. "Yer a man now. A big un."

His eyes glanced downward then up to his face. "A mighty big un."

"So, you think you remember me, then? I've come a small distance to find you."

"Can ye sit, have a bite with me? I've caught some trout in that creek." He nodded toward the rill.

Fin glanced at the sparce meal wishing he had prepared for this visit with something to share, but it never occurred to him. One thing he never forgot was how kind this elder had been to a small, bewildered lad.

"I ate a bit ago. Though I would sure like a bite. I haven't had your fish in all these years, and I'm reminded of the cook you are." He glanced about and took a seat on a log pulled up near the circle of firepit.

"What can I do to get you ready to eat?"

"Nothing. It's all here." Colby smiled as he pushed the rocker and held up a fork. "I'll eat out of the pan if all ye are good for is a bite."

Fin said, "I wasn't sure you would remember me or recognize me."

His gray bushy brows scrunched as he bit into a forkful of trout, chewed, and swallowed. "I don't see too well anymore. Mebbe ye was told so. But ye've a man's timber now for sure, I'd never forget. Ye have a verra slight inflection 'twas like yer ma's."

Colby put another forkful in his mouth and chewed away, pulling out a small bone. A feeling of belonging to someone washed over him. In all these years he hadn't a notion of what his mother was other than sad and listless. And Colby just mentioned that he shared a slight speech inflection with her.

It was like a tiny bright candle flickering in a dark shadow.

"So did ye happen by, or come directly? I've thought of ye often enough over the years, son. I've not come across one hint of ye a'tall." He pushed the pan and fork at him. "'Tis yer's ta finish. I saved ye a bite." A laugh rolled out with his words.

Taking the pan and utensil from Colby, he scooped up the small bit of white meat smothered in the frying juice.

"Well, now, I'm sorry I didn't ask for more. I will have to come back and get my own trout. No sharing next time."

"Ah, I'd like that. Now tell me what this is all about."

Setting the fry pan on the grate, he began, "I do have a reason for seeking you out. You may think it selfish."

A minute passed and Colby cleaned the bowl of his pipe and stuffed it with tobacco. Fin knew he was letting time pass comfortably between them. "I've been at Ashcourt looking about the old place. It is in a ruinous way. The stables have been ransacked. I've had an architect look at it, and it is at a crossroad between demolishing and rehabilitating."

Colby pulled on the pipe stem with his lips, gritting it between his teeth, his graying mustache curled a bit at the ends. He was listening, waiting and Fin continued.

"I've gone through all my father's papers that were left in his desk. I've even been in the library." He gave Colby a side glance. "Yes, the library. Hard to believe."

"Well, well. And did ye have shivers?"

Sir Fin barked out a laugh. "Indeed. Come to think of it."

"Is there more?" Smoke came out his nose sifting through the gray hairs of his mustache.

Fin nodded. "There's so much I never knew. Reading some of his old letters I've come across what I think is a mistress."

"Have ye a name?"

"Lady Ophelia Kearney of Dublin."

"I can't say that she was his mistress, but they were friendly for years. He stayed at her home when he had business in Dublin. Mostly business with his solicitor."

He glanced at Colby. "Did you know he left me Ashcourt?"

"I'd be more interested in if he left ye the means to keep it up."

Sir Fin turned in his chair looking his old friend in the face and would have been affronted if anyone else asked the question. But Colby couldn't stir animosity. He was a man of great kindness and virtue.

"I'll be direct. I regarded the idea of returning to Hawthorn and Ashcourt as much as if I were to face a firing squad. When I found out he willed it to me, but not the finances to restore it, I was greatly pleased."

Colby's watery pale eyes peered at him. How clear he could see Sir Fin was uncertain. But he read the look of something like satisfaction on the man's wizened, leather-creased face.

They were silent in the dusky afternoon light, the fire crackling and friendship renewed, Colby sucked on his pipe stem. Sir Fin felt deeply about the time spent with this kind man as a child. He felt whole.

His elder said, "Ye've taken a sorry lad and made a man of him. A man I'm proud to call me friend."

A knot tightened in his throat. If ever there was a moment in his life for which he should still be alive, surely it was to hear this from a man who knew him better than any other living soul.

☙❧

That night Finbarr fell into a troubled sleep. Someone was trying to kill Colby and Finbarr crept into his father's den and yanked a bloody saber off the wall where several had been displayed. He ran outside trying to get to the stables, but his legs would hardly move, ropes were tied around his ankles, and it was as if he ran in sludge.

"Sir. Sir."

Finbarr tried to fight off his attacker, he flailed his arms, fisting his hands.

"Sir. Wake up. It's a bad dream. Sir."

A fog lifted, Finbarr heard a man's voice and his arms felt heavy.

"Sir. It's another of your dreams. This is Collins, Sir. You are okay."

Finbarr blinked his eyes and became accustomed to the light from the lamp. "Collins?"

"Yes, sir. It's just me."

"What happened?"

"Nothing now. You had another bad dream."

Fin shot up. "Where's Colby?" After a second or two, he fell back against the pillow. "I was dreaming." almost a question, as if he weren't sure about it.

"A dream, sir. Yes."

Collins untangled the linen and asked if he would like anything to drink. Did he intend to go back to sleep or stay up for a bit.

Finbarr swung his legs off the bed and slid his feet into slippers. Collins handed him his robe. "I think I'll sit up for a while."

Collins had his hand on the latch and Finbarr said, "Thank you, Collins. Sorry to have troubled you."

Collins said goodnight and left the bed chamber.

Finbarr sank into a chair and mulled over the dream. Oddly, what seemed to terrorize him during the episode, he can hardly recall. Except a feeling of terror but most of it was fuzzy. Colby played a big part and Fin tried to rescue him from someone or something.

Feeling drained and exhausted, he returned to his bed and slid between the sheets Collins had straightened.

15

A dainty woman with a provocative secret

Sir Fin stepped within the tomb-like foyer of #80, St. Stephen's Square, Dublin. The butler, bushy gray brows, a wide forehead, and an angular chin took his card and closed the door, shutting out the street noises as carriages passed and whistles blew.

Led to a parlor off the foyer, Sir Fin looked out on the square. Across Cuffe Avenue, massive oaks and elms gently swayed in the light breeze, sun streamed through the branches, making patterns on the expanse of green.

The butler returned saying her ladyship would receive him shortly and would he like a refreshment in the meantime. He declined, and the man took his leave. He was eager to get this interview over and wondered if Lady Kearney would be offended with the questions he intended asking. Did she know about him, and the dislike his father felt for him?

He turned toward the sound of light footsteps and swishing satin as the woman entered the parlor. Diminutive in size and lace covering almost every inch of her, she allowed the butler to seat her, as she said, "Please Sir Finbarr, be seated. Would you like tea or coffee?"

It surprised him that she would be generous, but then what was he thinking she would be toward him. "Coffee, thank you." He sat directly across from her, giving up his hat, gloves, and walking stick to the butler. "I appreciate that you agreed to see me, your ladyship. Especially without advanced warning."

"At my age, I hardly stand on formality. I might be gone in my next breath." She shook out her hand allowing a ruffle at her sleeve to lay flat. "I know you have been knighted and received a baronetcy from the Queen. It's a shame your father wasn't alive to appreciate the honor."

"What I know of my parent doesn't allow me to think he would appreciate anything to do with me."

Her face lit with a pixie smile. "Ridiculing a dead person? You have come to ask me about him, have you not, then?"

He was a bit astounded at her acumen. Perceptive enough to grasp his situation, and clever enough to call him out. She was proving to be a lot younger in nature than her actual age would allow.

"I have, my lady."

A maid delivered a tray and poured, handing Lady Kearney's tea to her and coffee to him.

She then instructed the maid to close the parlor door. "Now then, I lost track of you when Diarmuid died. He used to keep me abreast. Although I did read in the *Evening Post* about your honor from the young Queen last May, I believe. Congratulations are in order. When did you return to Ashcourt?"

He was beginning to feel exposed, with her apparent knowledge about him. Her familiarity felt like an intrusion. "Late May."

His cup clinked against the China saucer as he set it down. "The reason I wanted to speak with you has to do with Diarmuid. At the time of his death, decisions needed to be made of which I was unaware until recently when my eldest sister wrote. I left school and traveled to Wales when I was sixteen."

A dainty hand, encased in a lacy half-glove, fluttered in the air. "You left Eton still a lad and without permission as I recall."

She threw him off guard, yet he shouldn't be surprised by what she knew. "With Diarmuid dead I felt no responsibility toward him."

Her pale eyes assessed him. "And so, you left your education unfinished and took up working in the mines."

"Lady Kearney, I didn't come here to discuss my life. I was hoping you could shed light on some decisions my father made."

"If I do, I shall share with you. I believe in being forthright." Her little hands folded on her lap, all the ruffles about her wrists doing likewise.

"As early as memory serves me, my parents loathed one another. My father in particular. Boarding school was a reprieve." His large hands cupped his knees and he leaned forward. "Would you have any idea why my father was so physically and mentally abusive to my mother?"

Her dainty gloved hand lifted a curl that had slipped from her cap. "Diarmuid had a temper. Never showed it directly to me, but I heard the rumors over the years. I suspect his anger came from learning you weren't his progeny. Some men find…"

His chin shot up, the shock instant. "Excuse me!"

"Oh, my. You don't know Diarmuid is not your biological father?" Her little hand patted the fallen curl back into place again.

He gaped, his jaw slack, and shook his head. Memories snapped loose, cascading like a nightmare in his brain. He focused on the woman. She sat all prim and sweet in her satin and lace, sipping from her porcelain cup. As if she had said nothing more than the sky was blue.

Somehow the past years made sense. Though he demanded, "What proof have you of this?"

Setting her cup on the small marble table at her right hand, she tipped her head to the side as if in sympathy. "Diarmuid was suspicious around the second or third year of your birth. And confronted your mother who readily swore to the truth of it. Even told him who your father was.

"I can tell you this much. It does seem rather impossible that fathering a son can be so important to a man. Diarmuid had hounded her to conceive again after his daughters were born... your two sisters. He wanted a son. But she refused him the marriage bed. Locked her door at night against him.

"Then one day she came out of her room, dressed beautifully, as Diarmuid related to me. She was lovely to look at in those days. A rare beauty. She said she would give him a son, but she needed to go away for a few months and rest. She had relatives in Greece, on Crete I believe. That is where she escaped to rest."

Finbarr waited for her to finish, all the while experiencing a sudden loss. He grieved for his dear mother.

Lady Kearney, a smirk in the curve of her lips, appeared satisfied with her revelation.

"How does that prove I'm not Diarmuid's son?" He drew in a breath easing the suspense that had come upon him. Could she be playing a game?

"Your mother made a fool of him. She allowed him her bed one time upon her return. And within weeks said she was carrying. As it turned out, you were born seven months upon your mother's return."

He calculated a live birth at seven months, and knew it wasn't unheard of. Conceivably rare, but certainly not impossible. Lady Kearney also said his mother named the father. He scanned her delicate features. She was delighted with the opportunity to relate this. His mother suffered at Diarmuid's hand for as long as he could recall, and now he learned of a possibility for the abuse.

It would explain why Diarmuid banned him from the manor. When he looked at Fin he was reminded of his wife's affair.

Sir Finbarr glanced at Lady Kearney. "Whom did she name?"

"Oh, my goodness, I cannot possibly recall after all these

years. What are you now…into your thirties I imagine, are you not?" Her dainty little laced hand patted her bosom. "Time gets away from me at my age."

"Why would you be so forthcoming in all matters relating to Diarmuid's and my mother's intimate life and not recall the man she named?" The irony of her statement stuck in his craw.

She batted her eyes as if in wonder. "Perchance there were so many I cannot recall which one was your father."

His blood instantly boiled. If she was a man, she'd be out cold on the floor right now. Something in her eyes told him she understood that. She smiled with her knowing, making it clear she fabricated. A little elder, a liar. Sweet as she appeared, he knew a viper lived beneath her pale skin. She deserved Diarmuid. They were a pair.

He stood. "You were witness to their unhappiness. I read some of the letters you wrote. Diarmuid leaned heavily on your support through those years." What about his mother's suffering knowing she was not her husband's true love, who supported her?

He had rifled through his mother's effects and read all the scraps of paper she left. He could not recall reading the name of a man that gave even the tiniest hint of an affair in her papers.

Taking his leave, he considered Lady Kearney as having a bit of fun with him. There wasn't anyone alive today whom he could question about her declarations. True, the only thing he had in common with Diarmuid was height.

She seemed to take great delight in smearing his mother with unproven gossip. That he knew of, there weren't any O'Connell's of his mother's family alive he could question about those years. Vivian or Marion perhaps, but they were so much older when he was born. If his mother had an affair in Greece, wouldn't he have dark skin, black hair, brown eyes?

The last time he was with her she could barely raise her hand to summon him closer as she lay in her bed. Her whisper of loving him still filled his memory of that day.

❧

Attempting to rid himself of frustration and anger, Fin trekked from St. Stephen's Square toward the Brazen Head. Collins had gone on ahead to secure two rooms for two nights. It took one full day by coach from Dublin, and Sir Fin intended to be back in Hawthorn Village in three-day's time.

The long stretch of evening ahead allowed him to mull over the questions that pestered. Why would she have wanted to go to Greece for a getaway? He may never know the truth, or if Lady Kearney lied about that, too.

❧

Bridge Street swarmed with traffic. The Brazen Head was down a few blocks and all traffic coming off the bridge had to pass the pub. The location was a boon for the business owner.

The pub was dimly lit with dark wood beams and floors. Dark tables, chairs, and benches. Old nooks to while away the day or evening, stone walls probably original to the pub as it stood. Glass paned windows to crowd watch if one was keen on doing so.

A tall, curvy lass wiped her large-calloused—and he had no doubt capable—hands on her apron and asked his pleasure. He ordered a dark dry stout and sat at a corner bench his back up against the stone wall.

What a day.

If Lady Kearney was to be believed, his dear mother may have outwitted her husband, and in so doing changed the trajectory of Fin's life. Her deceit also left his paternal lineage in doubt. It little concerned him. The relief he felt that it was not Diarmuid O'Bannon was uppermost.

He drew on the cool refreshing ale, a slight bitter taste just the way he liked it. The maid asked if he would be eating, and he ordered shepherd's pie. The aroma throughout the pub whetted his appetite.

Collins appeared out of nowhere. "Have you ordered supper, sir?"

Deep into memories, he glanced at Collins a moment and then gestured for him to sit. "Sorry, about that. Lost in the past for a moment. I just ordered a pie. If you're hungry get the server's attention. I also recommend the Guinness stout."

Collins waved the woman over and ordered shepherd's pie, and the dark ale. As soon as she left, he asked, "Did you get the answers you sought?"

He leaned against the back of a leather bench and lifted his arm along the rim. "It's been an interesting day. How about you? Was your aunt at home?"

"She was. I was able to stop her single handedly rearranging the parlor. She was exceptionally happy to see me as I rolled up my shirt sleeves. She reminded me of my mother. They were sisters, barely a year separated them, Irish twins if ever that's true." He sipped the dark ale the waitress brought and smiled. "It was good to see her, reminds me of what I miss about my family."

Early the next morning, Fin stretched his legs trying to clear his muddled brain regarding the facts of his mother's marriage to Diarmuid. He eventually found himself on the boardwalk overlooking the River Liffey as it separated north Dublin from the south.

Upon his return to the Brazen Head, he ordered a generous breakfast of kippers, eggs, bacon, and biscuits. Yesterday, he had sent a messenger to the solicitor's office asking for time this morning. The serving maid brought his breakfast along with a note from Mr. Boyle. The solicitor will receive him at ten this morning. Collins intended to visit a cousin and the two men planned to meet up at the Brazen Head about one.

Boyle stood as Sir Finbarr opened the door to his office. "Sir O'Bannon I take it?"

They shook hands and he took a chair across the desk from the solicitor.

"Thank you for seeing me on short notice."

Boyle smoothed his hair off his brow. "Not a problem, sir. What can I do for you?"

Sir Fin suspected the man knew a great deal about the O'Bannon history. "I am at a disadvantage. I believe you know far more than I about Diarmuid, which is what brought me here today. I met with Lady Kearney yesterday. She informed me of the circumstance of my birth. In light of the possibility, I am not the progeny of Diarmuid, I find it puzzling he left me Ashcourt."

Boyle leaned his elbows on his desk. "Mr. O'Bannon left a letter with me about his feelings regarding your birth and Ashcourt." The solicitor patted a sheaf of papers on his desk. "All this is yours. I would have posted it, but the contents cannot be replaced. It seemed prudent to give it to you in person. I assumed you would return to Ireland at some point."

Fin glanced about the paneled office, black lettering on the windows facing the street. A red patterned rug on a buffed oak floor. File cabinets lined a wall in the adjoining room where the door was ajar.

Boyle's business looked to be prosperous. He was a thin man. His mustache curved upward on his cheeks. His cravat a billowy fluff under his pointed chin. Delicate hands, clean fingers, tapping at the moment, on the papers meant for him. He sized the solicitor up as persnickety almost to the point of being effeminate.

"My sister wrote about Diarmuid's passing and as I was involved with my own business affairs at the time, unable to return to Ireland immediately." He smiled brightly at Boyle who had now cupped his fingers.

"I'll get right to it then. It's an unpleasant topic, but Mr. O'Bannon insisted on my telling you the truth of your birth before handing over the deed to Ashcourt, and other financial contracts having to do with the land surrounding the manor."

With a small shrug of his shoulders, Fin waited.

"Mr. O'Bannon, your only known father, denied his parental obligation to you in a sworn statement. I see no need to go into his precise detail about how he felt. Because you were born during the time your parents were married, it is legally known you are legitimate. Mere accusations hold no authority."

"Is his written denial among the sheaf of papers?"

The solicitor nodded.

"I want it clearly stated he is not my parent."

Surprise widened the solicitor's eyes. "Whatever validation you seek will be in these papers." He cleared his throat. "Another matter of discussion is the documented ownership of Ashcourt.

"It was your mother's legal property, bought and paid for with her own inheritance before you were born. I am sure you are aware it was built by Diarmuid's great, great, grandsire, Kevin, then passed through the next generations, Edmund, then Robert. It came into Diarmuid's hands in 1820. But by that time the manor was in a great need of renovation. Diarmuid married your mother, Helen O'Connell.

"She would not share her sizeable inheritance but did offer to purchase Ashcourt from him. He eventually agreed."

"Why was it so difficult for him to agree, do you know?"

Boyle played with a pen, turning it over and over, when he looked Sir Fin in the eye. "He was a man of little forgiveness, and even less charity when felt wronged. Your mother's actions obviously saved Ashcourt Manor from ruin at that time. Unfortunately, she managed to also crumble his sense of power."

Fin's anxiety fizzled, and he teamed with approval. "There is absolute proof my mother owned Ashcourt Manor?"

"Ironclad, sir. The Seal of Authentication has been imprinted upon these documents."

The pen he toyed with fell to the floor, and he bent over

picking it up. "Aside from your inheritance, other assets of Mr. O'Bannon's have been distributed among his three daughters."

"Three daughters?" His reaction tight with surprise.

"Your two elder sisters, Vivian and Marion. And Diarmuid's daughter with Lady Kearney."

Fin didn't react. But Lady Kearney's revelations earlier fell into a different light. He almost laughed.

Boyle continued, "Lastly, it was stated that any land taxes accumulating over the years were to be paid for by the new owner of Ashcourt Manor. Which, Sir O'Bannon, is you."

He was duly puzzled over Diarmuid's behavior. Critical of his mother because of a possible infidelity, ordering an eight-year-old to take up residence in the stables and carrying on an affair with another woman that produced a child. He was a man of conflicting morality.

Sir Fin drew out a small leather folder from his vest pocket. He opened it and began filling out the blanks in a draft note, putting the day's date, 29, July 1840, on the corner. "How much is owing?" His pen poised above the draft.

Boyle cleared his throat again. "It's a…well, rather staggering amount."

"The figure, if you will."

Sir Fin made out the draft and handed it to him. "Does this conclude our business?"

The solicitor tore his eyes from the draft. His brow wrinkled. "This certainly takes care of our business, Sir O'Bannon." He packaged the sheaf of papers into a brown folder and handed it over and held out his hand to shake.

Sir Finbarr stood, tucked the brown folder under his arm, picked up his walking stick, gloves and hat and left the attractively appointed law office.

16

A naughty man in the parlor

Sir Fin was glad to be back in Hawthorn Village. It appeared Collins was, too. He was humming as he shaved his employer.

"What tune is that?"

"Sir, please don't talk when I'm shaving you." He wiped soapy lather on the towel. "Rising of the Moon. I don't know why I hum it. Something to do with my mother and the loss of her brothers in that battle." He stood back, razor in the bowl of sudsy water. "You may converse now."

Finbarr laughed. "Shaving me is like a battle, then, is it?" He took the towel from Collins and finished wiping his face and neck.

After dressing and a light breakfast, he sat in a makeshift office Collins had repurposed for him with help from Mrs. Cashel. Collins, a dutifully organized valet, had stacked his ledgers and papers in a drawer for easy access.

Since the meeting with the solicitor, and subsequently making a firm decision about Ashcourt, he looked over his finances and concluded a visit to the Bank of Ireland up on Market Street was in order. He needed to have a draft sent from the Bank of England to his account here in Hawthorn.

After a morning spent deciding on the funds needed, he took a leisurely stroll along John's River when he stopped near the crest of a small hill and took in the morning's bustle of carriages, villagers, and street vendors. The scent of turmeric, ginger, and coriander came from a canopy where an Indian stirred up slices of meat, chili peppers, and mushrooms. It reminded him of a business trip when he accompanied a friend to India back in 1833.

Mumbai was overcrowded with food stalls and wares. The scents overpowering at times and living conditions extremely crowded. Funny how a spice could conjure up an old memory.

The stroll cleared his mind of all that happened in the last few days. Most of it in his favor. Miss Brianna Walsh came to mind. It had been almost a week since last they talked. On a circuitous route back to the bank and having taken care of his business, he meandered through the village along the Strand and took a few minutes to watch the vessels bobbing in the tide, sheets furled, masts waving to the rhythm of the water.

Hawthorn Village more than doubled in size in the years since he was a child. A feeling of prosperity abounded. Shop windows displayed wares from Europe, by-passers meandered on graveled streets rather than mud. Children and dogs ran amidst the crowded lanes, ever mindful of the carriages.

He wondered if Brianna was at Ashcourt painting. She would choose such a day with hardly a breeze, and the sun casting warmth on her back. Surprising himself, he turned toward the bakery and picked up a box of raspberry croissants and then knocked on Miss Natty's door.

Mim answered. "Sir O'Bannon, good to see you. Miss Natty is in the parlor." Her eyes were glued to the pastry box.

"It's near teatime. Be sure to save one for yourself and Jane if she is working today." He handed her the box.

"Is that you, Sir Finbarr?"

He entered the parlor and intercepted Miss Natty in her best-loved chair petting Pussycat.

"To what do I owe this visit?" She indicated he take the chair across from her.

"Missing your bright presence and conversation. And as I was about and happened to pass the bakery, I made a decision."

Her face brightened with fun. "I remind you of sweet treats, do I?"

"You will think so when Mim brings in tea."

"What has kept you from our door. Is it a member of the unmarried female gender?"

"Just because a man is of a certain age doesn't mean he is searching to change his living arrangements."

She pursed her lips and raised her gray eyebrows. "Is that what you think?"

He chuckled. "I haven't any interest in complicating my life. Now tell me, how are preparations coming for the Fair. I'm sure you have your fingers deep in the organization."

Mim wheeled in a teacart and Miss Natty craned her neck to see the pastries on the silver platter. She cast him a side glance. "You naughty man."

Brianna returned home from extra duty at the post office and was untying her bonnet when she noticed Sir Fin's hat and cane. Then she heard Aunt Natty call someone a naughty something or other. From the corridor she spoke up. "That's intriguing. We have a naughty man in the parlor. Should I bring in a stick?"

Chuckling from the parlor preceded her arrival.

"Ah, I should have realized it was you. What have you done now?" She tore her eyes off Sir Finbarr and glanced at the tea tray. "We will all suffer if you keep supplying us with treats, sir."

Aunt Natty said, "You are late today. Something came up at the post office?"

"Not really. A number of boxes were delivered on the coach and needed to be dispersed. Lionel wasn't back from his route and Mrs. Teaberry asked if I would deliver them." She took a chair between Aunt Natty and Sir Finbarr.

"She is so worried an official from her majesty's postal system will find an unorganized office. Well, I thought it best to simply take care of it."

"You probably have employment for life if you keep up with your pampering." Sir Finbarr winked at her.

"Well, then I warrant I should throw a tantrum or two and let her see what I'm really like." She glanced at him asking, "Unless you would like to talk to her directly?"

Both Aunt Natty and Sir Fin laughed. Ignoring them, she reached for the tea Mim poured and a frosted croissant. "Hmmm. Raspberry. What inspired this?"

"Nothing more than I suddenly found myself in front of the bakery and that I haven't dropped in on you of late."

Aunt Natty asked, "What has kept you from us?"

After a moment, he said, "Family business in Dublin."

Aunt Natty's pale blue eyes widened with expectation as she bit into the crusty treat.

When Sir Fin didn't follow up with detail, Brianna's curiosity got the better of her. "I hope your business left you some leisure. Dublin has lovely gardens for a stroll. There is lots to do."

He pondered a moment. "I'm sure I've mentioned I have two sisters, Vivian and Marion. Older than I and gone from Hawthorn before I was sent to boarding school. While in Dublin, I discovered I also have a half-sister who lives with her mother."

Aunt Natty wiped her fingers of jam. "And you weren't aware of this younger sister?"

"I may have miss spoke. There is a possibility we aren't related." He seemed to ponder something else and quit talking.

Curious, Brianna dug in. "You found out about her, but didn't introduce yourself?"

He winced, forewarning of an obstacle rather than a pleasant experience. Brianna apologetically said, "Forgive me for prying. I really didn't mean to. I expected you would be delighted meeting a family member."

His chin lowered. She was familiar enough with his moods, he seemed unsure about something. Mayhap the situation in Dublin and learning he had another sibling? The parlor quieted. Aunt Natty's cup clinked when she set it in the saucer.

Pussycat's purring ceased as she jumped to the floor, tail high, and sauntered to the corridor.

Sir Finbarr took in a deep breath and rested his arm on the chair arm. His eyes like chips of emeralds as his attention turned to them. "I don't make it a habit of discussing my personal life. But I have fallen under your friendship and will share some details."

Aunt Natty crossed her arms and gave him her full attention. Brianna drew in a breath. This was so unlike him. His trip to Dublin must have involved an extraordinary discovery.

"My mother died when I was eight and Diarmuid sent me away to school. For several years I returned on holidays. Near sixteen I put school behind me and took on an apprenticeship in Wales at Swansea in the copper mines.

"Eventually I wrote to my eldest sister. She wrote back saying our father had passed. It surprised me to learn his death happened at the same time I left Eton for Wales."

"That's why Ashcourt was all alone for so many years." Brianna's realization was whispery.

He tilted his head gazing fondly at her. "When I saw that painting," he nodded to the wall nearest the doorway to the parlor, "it touched me in such a way I can't explain. I hadn't been out to Ashcourt as yet, but I knew it immediately."

Brianna was overcome, a lump in her throat. She understood his shock.

He shifted in his chair as if cumbrous. "My meeting with the solicitor in Dublin was quite revealing. I learned some things about my parents that I would never have otherwise known."

Aunt Natty was dreadfully quiet, tenderness etched on her features.

Brianna knew he needed to talk and considered Aunt Natty a safe person to whom he could confide. "Would you like me to leave the two of you alone? I would understand perfectly if you wished privacy." She began to gather her skirts and stand.

"Miss Brianna, I know you care about Ashcourt. I found my way here today because I know that. Stay if you wish."

The look on his face fastened to her, and she sat back in her chair.

Aunt Natty asked, "My dear lad, you've come here to sort yourself out, haven't you?"

His features softened into a pleasant contentment. Where on earth could he have gone but here to this parlor with this woman, barely an elder at fifty. She opened her heart to him since the first they met. And in many ways helped him begin to heal.

Aunt Natty cautiously inquired, "When is the last time you spoke with a friend or a loved one?"

A dark brown wave of hair shadowed his brow. He focused on her impish attention. "I don't honestly know if I ever have." Trustworthy Collins came to mind and his rescuing Fin from nightmares over the years, though they seemed to be fading.

"We are here if you choose Sir Finbarr. You have been kind to us. We could do no less than shower you with the same friendship."

Sharing his discovery wouldn't change the shock, but for once in his life, he might feel relieved.

"I'm puzzled as to why my mother lived the way she did with Diarmuid and never reveal our circumstance to me?"

The parlor quieted. Pussycat returned purring and brushing up against his leg. Brianna suggested, "Brush him away, he might leave fur on your stocking."

Miffed, as if the feline understood, she meowed and sprang from the room.

Natty offered, "A mother would find it difficult to share her worries with her child."

He nodded. "My mother was the legal owner of Ashcourt. Her father endowed her with an iron-clad inheritance. She purchased the manor and legally withheld the rest of her wealth from her husband. Essentially, only giving him a purse to live on.

"Diarmuid tried to break it. But lost in court. Ashcourt has been in a trust all these years waiting for me to claim it."

Attentive to his story, Aunt Natty declared, "That must prove to you your mother cared a great deal for you."

He glanced at the pattern on the rug and said, "It might have made my childhood a bit easier."

He took a deep breath. "All this time, I presumed Diarmuid hated me. But now I must consider what might possibly have made him so angry was he could live in the manor, but it belonged to my mother and would pass to me on her death. It would also explain why he sent me to the stable to live when she died. And then probably rethinking that, sent me on to Eton."

He sat back in the chair, crossing his legs, and gained a relaxed posture. "I also learned Diarmuid had a mistress in Dublin, Lady Kearney. They had a child together. So, if Diarmuid wasn't my father, this young lady, couldn't be connected to me. It may sound harsh, but I don't care either way.

"I learned from a visit to Diarmuid's solicitor that unless it was stated otherwise in the settlements or the trust documents, the husband had the right to use the money from the wife's trust as he wished—even to using it to support a mistress and a second family. Which looks like what Diarmuid intended.

"According to law, women had the right to own property and have their own money unless they were married, or legal documents were drawn. Men make the laws and also considered it their due that they have access to their wife's money. Mostly because they must support her and any children. My mother knew the law and knew her rights. And I suspect when her love for

Diarmuid died, she took action to secure the home where I was raised."

Miss Natty kept to herself. Brianna found it difficult to believe the hatred some people have. She sympathized with the childhood Sir Fin lived.

"What a horrid situation your mother found herself in. How do you feel about Diarmuid acting as your father but probably wasn't?"

"Relieved." His fingers dangled over the edge of the chair arm tapping the upholstery.

Aunt Natty was sympathetic. "Your feelings for that lad living with a demon must make you sad. And then to discover he would never get his hands on your mother's wealth the reverse, exhilarating."

"I think it mostly shocking that she stayed with him. She could have gone anywhere. But Ashcourt was hers, so I think I understand. He hated Ashcourt and the moment my mother died, and he knew he'd be without funds, he abandoned it and moved into Lady Kearney's place in Dublin."

"Poor Ashcourt." Brianna's gaze shifted to the picture on the wall. The elf smiled back at her, just as she had intended when she painted it.

He reached over and gently covered her hands. "You should be especially glad to know I am going to refurbish Ashcourt and make it grand as it once was."

"Ah, because Ashcourt wasn't *his* home." She looked so prim and sweet, her hands clasped on her lap, and her gray eyes sparkled with delight.

"Exactly. And seeing Ashcourt through your paintings opens possibilities for restructuring. You helped me see the appeal beneath the ruin."

"I am flattered that you think me capable. But it appears your mother is the real savior regarding Ashcourt."

His head tilted toward her. "As far as I'm concerned, her inheritance can stay in the trust. I've no need of it."

"Even if you rebuild Ashcourt?"

His lips pinched and he briefly nodded.

Brianna considered all the possibilities of renovating Ashcourt. Now she knew why he never balked at anything the architect suggested. She had advocated for a complete makeover of the kitchen never thinking he would actually listen to her.

"Would you be interested in riding out with me the next time I visit Ashcourt? Now that my mind is made, your artist's knowledge would be a further help."

About to take a sip, she lowered her cup. "I would genuinely enjoy that. Thank you for the offer."

Aunt Natty still pondering the previous conversation asked, "Have you given thought to why your mother stayed at Ashcourt under Diarmuid's tyrannical behavior?

"I think in her mind she had an inheritance to fall back on. Diarmuid's great grandsire built the initial structure. It'd been in his family until Diarmuid's financial situation put him in poverty and he had to accept my mother's offer or lose Ashcourt. Either way, he would have lost Ashcourt, but agreeing to sell it to her gave him an income. She may have stayed for the simple reason it was now in her ownership."

He had no intention of sharing the demons and brutality Diarmuid suffered upon his mother. Over time he hoped to reconcile himself to the past. Right now, his gratitude for this day and these two women and the anticipation of Ashcourt coming to life, lightened his heart.

With the decision to renovate Ashcourt firm, Sir Finbarr became free of past familial duties and the gloom that always seemed to hang over him. Awash in newfound determination, the future looked bright.

After leaving Miss Natty's home, he rode out to Colby's

cottage and discovered the old stablemaster down by the creek fishing for his dinner.

Colby turned toward the sound of footsteps plodding through the turf. "Who is it?" he hissed.

"Finbarr."

In a growly manner he barked, "I've got a big un on the line." He tugged on the line pulling in a good-sized trout.

"I can see that. You'll never starve, that's for sure." He reached out a hand. "Can I help you with that?"

"Nay, I've got it. Ye never were good at fishing as a nipper. No patience. Do ye recall?"

Sir Fin chuckled. "Not exactly the way you just described it."

He watched as Colby rolled up the line and unhooked the fish, holding it up close to his face. "Ha, a fat brown."

He dumped it into his bag and slung it over his shoulder, then picked up his walking stick. "What's brought ye out again, so soon?"

"I've a proposition I would like you to consider." They made their way up a small incline toward Colby's cottage. The day began sunny and turned blustery.

"I'm an old man. What good am I ta ye, then?"

"Not so old you can't be stablemaster at Ashcourt, where you'll have stable lads to terrorize."

Colby stopped in his tracks. "So now it's me hearing that's fading?"

"You heard me all right. You will probably demand a cozy space in the corner and eating rights in the kitchen. I'm willing to give you what you want if you will consider overseeing the stables and the cattle."

"Me sights leaving me, ye recall I said so last time we talked?"

Sir Fin palmed Colby's shoulder. "I can think of no one on God's green earth that I would trust my stable to more than you. You see well enough to order around stable lads and take control of what needs to be done. My first plan is to enlarge the stables and you can tell me what your needs are in your own living space."

Colby reached out to Finbarr's arm and squeezed it tight. "You and me, lad. Once again."

He put his hand over the elder man's crusty one. "I like the sound of that."

Colby asked, "Remind me, how many of them lads I'll boss?"

"There you go, finagling a change in the contract. You're going to be difficult to deal with."

⚜

Two days later, Sir Fin delivered a draft to the Architect, Mr. Abernathy, as down payment on the restoration. Ashcourt had now taken over all his free time imbuing him with grand ideas for the sad structure. He invited Brianna to ride out with him tomorrow in the afternoon after she finished at the post office.

When he returned that evening to Cashel's an invitation from Lady Hamerlin awaited, a soiree. He read it twice.

Collins bowed his head rather than have his employer see the smile on his face. Fin barked, "What? A man has to eat?" He dropped the missive on the side table and tossed his hat on a chair.

"Sorry, sir. It is just that you've shown no interest. This is the third the lady has sent."

"I warrant that detail escaped me."

"Do I detect you are softening toward Hawthorn Village and its inhabitants?"

He finished reading the rest of his posts and cast a side glance at his valet. "If I were, would you be of a mind to stay on here, or do you miss home?"

Sir Finbarr could see he struggled to hide a grin as he said, "I would stay on if you will have me, sir. I've taken quite a liking to Hawthorn Village."

"You won't see the world in this place. Wasn't travel your fancy?"

Collins picked up his employer's hat, gloves, and walking stick and put them in their proper place by the door. "It doesn't take more than a few months to perceive if one could live here or not."

"I suppose it doesn't." He picked up the *London Courier* off the sideboard and sank into a cushy upholstered chair with his back to the evening sun as it came through the window.

"Would you like one of your specials, sir?"

Already reading the headline story, he absentmindedly nodded.

17

His mother's gift

"You look fresh as a flower in a summer breeze. However, your frock might suffer as we rummage through the disorder at Ashcourt." Sir Finbarr snapped the lines, coaxing the mare to a faster trot.

"A little dust never stayed my hand. Besides, sir, I am most interested in the changes you wish to make." She grabbed hold as the horse increased its stride. "And thank you for the compliment."

He flashed her a smile, and Brianna's heart softened. He had been through difficulties and obviously overcame them. Mayhap his returning to Hawthorn was a step he was willing to take to unencumber his past.

Both she and Aunt Natty were compassionate of all he had been through. Especially seeing as how he was most eager to restore Ashcourt instead of turning his back. Neither of them would have been the least surprised which path he chose.

"I am excited to see what Mr. Abernathy has done since he began."

He glanced at her, and his face lit with an ease she never

noticed before. "Learning Ashcourt belonged to my mother made all the difference. I can't quite define what brought on the change if not that. I'm looking forward to rebuilding."

He maneuvered the phaeton around a herd of sheep bleating at the intrusion. The herder and his dog egged the sheep off the road and up an incline.

He asked, "Am I intruding if I inquire if you have ever wanted to seek out your parents and family?"

She pondered a moment, then said, "Doing so might break my aunt's heart. And I considered my parent's nomadic existence would make finding them impossible. They are referred to as the *walking people* who roam about Ireland. There was a group a bit ago who stayed in the woods for several weeks before moving on. I did make a friendly inquiry, but felt I was out of place to ask. I noticed almost all the wagons brimmed with children and family. They had absolutely no interest in conversing with me."

She glanced at her hands. "They camped in the same woods where I was found by Aunt Natty. For a moment that day I thought they came looking for me."

"I'm guessing, as happy as you would have been at the discovery, what else might you uncover?" His glance was filled with compassion, not judgment.

She nodded. "I was in a quandary no doubt about it."

Ashcourt loomed in the distance, the small lough in front smooth as stretched silk and reflected a vee of geese honking in the sky. Wherever they headed, they were in a great flapping and noisy hurry.

He asked, "How did it happen that you ended up with Miss Natty?"

"She was returning home and traipsed through the woods coming across a peddler's wagon. Children climbing a tree. The father holding an infant as his wife lay on the grass. Aunt Natty stopped to see if she could do something and the father handed her the bundle in his arms so he could tend his wife.

"Aunt Natty offered to get some milk and bread for them. The father wanted her to keep the infant as she did so, enabling him to tend to his wife.

"When she returned, they were gone. Nary a trace. It seemed an eternity, Aunt Natty's words not mine. It was months and months before she felt I belonged to her. At that point, if they had returned for me, she would have fought them." She peeked at him as she added, "Or, so she's told me numerous times."

He put his gloved hand over hers and squeezed, then continued clutching the lines. "You have no idea where your talent in painting comes from then?"

"It comes from a desire to create."

He barked a laugh. "Or, as I have surmised since we first met at the manor, you have a fondness for seeing the brighter side of life, uplifting one's spirits. You see Ashcourt was abandoned, much like yourself. I dare say, Miss Brianna, you are a wonder of a woman. Compelling and sympathetic. It was my lucky day when I met you."

She glanced away from him, thankful for the bonnet brim, and swiped at a maverick tear sliding down her cheek. Her throat clutched. Receiving a compliment from him warmed her.

Teasingly she said, "I wasn't at my best the first time we met."

He also poked fun. "And once I cracked the shell around you, compassion and delight spilled out."

She looked straight ahead, hoping to hide her feelings, which appeared to run wild at the moment. No one had ever been so frank with her.

As if he read her mind, he noted, "I think it was you holding up the sign that read HELP? You have somehow found yourself synonymous with Ashcourt."

He pulled up in front of the manor, the young tiger jumped out, came around, and took the lines.

Sir Fin assisted her from the conveyance and spoke to the lad. "Mind you water and walk her."

"Aye, sir."

As they strode toward the front door, he said, "I hope my instinct about you isn't out of place?"

"This is a fine time to question yourself. Too late now. I'll give you my opinion whether you want it or not." She tried to hide the grin on her face.

"Ah, now you've got me trembling in my boots."

It pleased her he regarded them as friends. He remarked earlier about friendship. But she had never taken anything for granted in her life and wasn't about to begin now.

After he put his shoulder to the front door, giving it a nudge to open, they began room by room as before, but this time Sir Finbarr took notes for the architect.

With the sun on the downside of noon, each room accounted for, and the placement of water closets solved, they were ready to leave.

On the ride home, he playfully tried to provoke her. "Are you satisfied with the changes I've in store for Ashcourt?"

"Your home will be grand. She will shine in the sunlight and soothe in a storm."

He liked the sound of that. His home, the home his mother left him.

৩২৬

The next week came far too early for Sir Fin. Even less than enthusiastic about attending the soiree than he had been when the invitation arrived, he groused to Collins.

Collins fussed as if his employer was a school lad and hadn't an idea how to properly fit himself out for the occasion. Collins appeared vexed arranging the starched neckcloth, almost making an art form out of knotting the cravat.

"Why are you fretting so over a piece of linen?"

"Lady Hamerlin will be pleased."

"You need her approval?" Fin's face scrunched in fiendish shock.

Collins stepped back to admire his work. "There, sir. Now, you are respectable."

Waistcoat on, jacket on, hat in hand, gloves, and walking stick at the ready,

Collins inquired. "It would be fitting for you to wear your knighthood medal from the Queen."

Sir Fin scowled. "Enjoy your evening."

An hour into the soiree, violins, and a bass, played from a platform. Chitter-chatter swirled throughout the coffered-ceilinged room. He found himself in the midst of discussion with Lords Cosgrave, Dixon, and Longfield regarding the Cricket Club of Hawthorn.

He had played on a league for years in Swansea. His love of the game drew his attention to what the men had to say. Hawthorn boasted two leagues, the *Gaelics*, and the *All-Ireland* team. He had as yet to discover if they could use an extra. At boarding school, he had taken to cricket like a duck to water. Fin was proud to have played on the Keate's league, named after a beloved professor.

Lord Dixon turned his attention to Fin. "I read about you in the *Courier* a while back. You were knighted for saving lives in a dampfire?"

Lord Cosgrove spoke up. "The Queen sweetened the pot with a baronetcy."

Sir Finbarr smiled kindly, hoping both men would change the topic.

"Lady Hamerlin mentioned your bravery. I am pleased to meet you, sir." Lord Dixon held out his hand and they shook.

Sir Fin said, "I take it you play cricket? What league are you on?"

Lord Cosgrove spoke up, obviously enjoying his port. "Dixon plays on *Dante's* a league out of Waterford. You'll want to get involved with one of ours here in Hawthorn."

Fin gave Cosgrove his attention. "And why is that?"

"If you are just now getting interested in the game, you'll

want to brush up on the rules and play a few friendly matches before taking on *Dante's League*."

Fin's humor restored at the reason, he nodded and enjoyed his brandy.

Checking up on all her guests, Lady Hamerlin joined the group of men in a corner of her parlor. "I see you are all acquainted. I invited Sir Finbarr in hopes he would find friendship." She turned a grand smile on him.

Lord Cosgrove belted, "He's interested in cricket, but I've saved him a bit of disgrace with *Dante's League* and stirred him toward one of Hawthorn's. The *Gaelics* would be right for a starter."

Stretching his neck as if checking out Fin he added, "I think you might be a wee bit wet behind the ears." Eliciting a few chuckles, he added, "You could begin by learning to manage the equipment."

Lord Dixon guffawed. "You've stuck your foot in your mouth this time, Cosgrove."

Finishing up his port, Cosgrove eyed his friend. "How's that?"

"This gentleman, whose ears you called wet, happens to be one of Swansea's noted players."

Cosgrove turned his pinkish eyes on Sir Fin looking him up and down. "You aren't *that* O'Bannon?"

He didn't take his eyes off Dixon, as he gave a dismissive nod to Cosgrove, then finished his brandy. He felt quite awkward.

Lady Hamerlin offered a welcome rescue as she asked if she could drag him away from their circle. She wanted to introduce him to Lord and Lady Heath.

She whispered, "Sometimes Lord Cosgrove can be an idiot. But we all love him in spite of his momentary lapses."

"Thank you for rescuing me." He wasn't enjoying the evening and had no real reason for his sense of uneasiness.

"You might wish I hadn't when I introduce you to the Heaths."

After being introduced to her long-time friends, Lady

Hamerlin needed to attend to a small disaster in the kitchen and Sir Fin wandered onto the balcony. The Heaths appeared to fit in with the rest of her friends; wealthy, well-traveled, and enjoying life. He intended to ask her what she meant when she said *he might regret meeting the Heaths*. He found them pleasant and down-to-earth.

The bright moon cast a silvery glow on the gardens. A whippoorwill snapped its *poorwillip* sound over and over.

Out of sorts and unsettled as if he should be doing something, he would like to be elsewhere right now. Could it be listening to people expound and wondering how he fit in? He couldn't fault Lady Hamerlin. She was certainly a charming hostess.

The wind swished through the tips of cedar bordering the garden, sending their fragrance drifting across the loggia.

"There you are. I wondered where you had got to."

He turned away from the pastoral landscape as she approached. "Admiring your garden and wondering if Ashcourt will one day be as estimable."

"I would plow the place down and build something worth my time and trouble." He watched her pluck a bloom off a bush and bring it to her nose. She stifled a sneeze and blinked her eyes.

He had a sense she wasn't a person to enjoy the past and take pleasure in antiques. He said, "I've hired an architect. I intend to refurbish the existing structure."

She glanced at him, half her face in the shadows as she said, "Isn't that a waste of effort? It's a mortification, an embarrassment against your family name."

"It's aged I'll grant you that. I have recently learned my mother owned Ashcourt not Diarmuid." Saying the words out loud gave him a sudden confidence about his parent.

A frown indicated Lady Hamerlin's confusion, she spouted, "Your mother bought Ashcourt from your father when they both lived in it? How absurd, she could have saved her money and lived off him. Whatever was she thinking."

Not surprised by her avarice, he had initially concluded that afternoon on the porch at Cashel's when they first met that Lady Hamerlin wanted something. But what would it be, a gentleman to ferry her about? Surely not him? She could have her pick.

"Hmm," totaled his response to Lady Hamerlin's obvious greed.

18

Revelations and shock waves

Wringing her hands in consternation, Miss Natty cried, "She is my family, after all. Our mothers were sisters. I told her I would see her in a day or two. I must keep my promise?"

Mim paced her arms waving the air. "In the meantime, she badgered her way in here and practically threatened you. I'll worry all the time you're gone."

Mim stopped pacing and stood in front of Natty looking down at her as she sat in her chair. "I should keep my mouth shut, I should. But I can't."

Miss Natty almost rolled her eyes. Mim definitely was as honest a person as she had ever met.

"That woman knows he's at death's door and is trying to get you to take over the last days of his life. Her crying on your shoulder, wanting you to help her, is wrong. She has her nerve blaming you, saying the fault lies with you." She slapped her floured hands on her waist and took a deep breath, gathering more steam.

"Miss Natty, if you go to her, she will burden you and blame her life's trials on you because you didn't make yourself available whenever the wind blew sideways. There must be someone else you could confide in over time about this woman."

Miss Natty's chin snapped up facing Mim. "You promised you wouldn't tell Brianna. She'll worry about me. She's been made aware we are cousins and that Dervila married Niall over a lie. That's enough for any young lady."

"And I have not, nor will I ever. But you have got to make your peace of all this. He married her—good or bad—she's lived with him all these years. She made the bed she laid in *and* told a whopping lie to get him in the first place. You don't owe her an ounce of kindness, nor remorse."

The housekeeper's weary concern tightened her face. Natty rued the day she ever told Mim about Niall and Dervila and what they did to her.

Niall, equally as culpable as his wife, otherwise there wouldn't have been the suspicion she carried his child. He was an offender equally sharing in the offense. Natty sighed. She assumed she'd put it all behind her a long time ago—a lifetime ago.

"Dear Mim, sit next to me, please. I can't have you upset like this. Please sit down and take a breath."

Bewildered and obviously anxious, Mim did as told. Elbows leaning on her knees, shoulders still carrying the burden of disgust. She sighed long and heavy. Her eyes pinkened with near tears.

Natty reached over, gathering up Mim's floured hand, patting it. "You're worried about me. I'm a bit worried, too. Selfishly, I am afraid my cousin will want to lean on me in her bereavement. I've no inclination to renew any kind of relationship. I have this life with you and dear Brianna. I don't want to bring that woman into it."

Mim sighed deeply, she squeezed Miss Natty's hand then let go. "It's just that I've stood in the corridor listening to her. Her kind are capable of real meanness. And you've a heart of gold."

"I'll go to her today and take a basket of kindness from the kitchen. Will you be so good to put something together for me?"

Mim stood and swiped at her apron. Obviously, if she had her way, they would get this unsettled and horrid time behind them. "You trust me to pack a basket for that woman?"

Miss Natty's eyes twinkled. "Leave out the rat poison, else you might end up in the gaol. And we don't want that, now do we."

She huffed. "I'll pack up a basket and go with you. But I won't venture inside, not a chance. I'm likely to say something I'll regret."

Within the hour, the two women strode down Chadwick Lane toward the Strand where Maher's Pub was located. Dervila had mentioned she lived above the pub in a flat. The closer they got to the waterfront the air carried the scent of briny algae. The waterfront teemed with the slurp of waves banging the docks, shouting, fishing boats, and crew gathering up their catch of the day.

As they turned the corner, both women were quite taken by the sight of a flatbed cart hanging by ropes being unloaded from a large ship. They backed away and stood suspended in awe as the ropes lowered the cargo onto a wagon.

Two lads scooping up dung into a small cart appeared unmindful of the unloading of cargo. The odor of raw muck was mighty pungent. The women quickly held handkerchiefs to their faces.

Signs hung from the lintels of shops along the Strand, as Mim and Natty made their way toward Maher's Pub, a frothy mug painted on a swinging shingle drew their attention.

In a hushed manner, Mim said, "I'll likely be accosted waiting out here for you."

Miss Natty stopped in her tracks and glanced at her housekeeper. "Then come up with me. It won't make any difference to Dervila."

The sound of laughter and a concertina spilling out the door of

Maher's and next to that, a stair to the flat. Mim said, "I'll sit at a table near the exit to the pub."

"Have it your way. I want to get this over with as quick as possible." She took the basket from Mim and picking up her skirts began the trek up the stairs as Mim found a vacant bench.

Miss Natty knocked thrice before she heard Dervila growl, "Come in you fool."

She reached for the latch and the moment she opened the door she knew her visit to comfort her cousin would be near impossible. A bed occupied a corner in the flat, her cousin sprawled across the thin mattress naked as a babe. Cheeks rouged, and her breath carried the strong odor of liquor from where Natty stood a few feet away. Or maybe it was the entire room that reeked of drink.

Dervila fought to brace herself up on an elbow. She blinked when her eyes settled on Natty, and muttered, *come in*. Her dark hair hung in straggles about her shoulders. She patted the bed and burped. "Sit."

Natty chided herself. Reaching for the latch, she said. "I'll return when…"

A knock at the door, the latch lifted and in jostled a bearded man bringing with him the essence of the sea.

Dervila laughed uproariously. "Josh, meet my cousin Natty." She sank back into the mattress, having lost the strength of her elbow.

Natty, totally embarrassed, immediately threw a blanket over Dervila and cast Josh a look of disgust.

He pulled off his tam and nodded. "Pleased, ma'am." His gaze swept to the bed. "I'll come back later."

"No," came a screech from the bed.

Natty spoke up. "I'll leave." She glanced about, looking for a place to set the basket.

Josh spoke up. "Ma'am. I'm goin'. You ken stay," and out the door he hustled as if grateful for the opportunity.

Totally bewildered, Natty almost followed him out the door

when Dervila once more braced herself with an elbow. Weaving slightly with the effort. "You came to pay your condolence." She sounded strong, though her speech slurred.

"Yes. I heard Niall died. My housekeeper overheard two women mention his passing at the market earlier today. I wanted to bring you a few things and tell you I am sorry for your loss."

Dervila laughed and laughed until she weakened.

Natty found herself in the presence of a hysterical woman possibly filled with grief. She remained standing, having set the heavy basket on the small table. Devoid of compassion for the woman, and feeling guilty because of it, she wondered how to extricate herself.

Dervila began talking in small tones and Natty moved closer. Her cousin, sodden with drink, rambled. She recognized the behavior because her brother drank too much sometimes. But it occurred to Natty his cheerful singing, and recitation of poetry portrayed him as gentle and happy. Dervila wasn't either—she was in peril. She had lost a man she must have loved. A man she lied to so he would marry her. Maybe her remorse has gotten the worst of her.

Some words were distinguishable as Dervila rambled. Natty heard her slurred whispers, *child, Niall, kill me. Baby* between coughs and gasps. Not making sense of the words, Natty moved to the side of the bed. Dervila's eyes were closed. Long black lashes lay across her rouged cheeks.

Natty whispered, "Why would Niall want to kill you?"

Dervila burped and rolled onto her side exposing her nakedness. Natty pulled the filthy cover up over her long slender legs dotted with old brownish bruises.

She then mumbled and sighed. "If he knew about the child."

"What child?"

"A love child." She softened when she said this. "My love child."

Overcome upon hearing this, Natty wondered if anyone could

believe a drunken person's words. "I know you lied about having a child with Niall."

Dervila drew her long arms about herself and brought her knees up as if giving herself comfort with a giant hug.

Ashamed of herself, Natty acknowledged the curiosity her cousin aroused. Had she given birth to a child, Natty knew it wasn't Niall's. That would explain why he would kill her? Or did she really give birth to Niall's child?

She sank into a wooden chair next to the bed and closed her eyes.

Dervila appeared to have fallen asleep when a low snore escaped her open mouth. Natty glanced about the filthy room. How could anyone live in a place like this?

A knock at the door, the latch lifted and in came that man, Josh. "Not on yer way by now?"

"Have you business with Mrs. Murdock?" Natty asked sternly.

A glint in his eye quickly turned serious. "No, ma'am. Just checking on how she's doin'. Niall bein' a friend of mine and all."

Natty harrumphed. He appeared to be a friend until he had other ideas. She clasped her hands in her lap. "As you can see, my cousin is exhausted. You should leave her be for a time."

"That I'll do, ma'am. Give her my condolences." He backed out closing the door quietly.

What could she do? Poor Mim probably at her wits end sitting outside Maher's.

Dervila moaned and her arm stretched out across the pillow barring her breasts. Natty jerked the cover back in place hoping it would rouse her.

When there was no response, Natty decided to leave and shoved aside the wooden chair.

Her cousin's eyes shot open, her wrist to her mouth, "Don't you touch me." She scrambled to kneel on the bed hovering in the corner yelling at someone, her arms up as if defending herself. "Maggot, damned cockchafer."

Feeling the swift heat of embarrassment, Natty leaned over the bed and grabbed hold of both arms. Dervila appeared surprisingly strong and fought her. "No one is going to hurt you. I am here. You are safe." She repeated herself and noted her cousin calming. Natty loosened her hold and stepped back. Having twisted her wrist in the scuffle, she rubbed it.

Dervila fell to the bed and swiped at her eyes, then looked at Natty a long minute as if seeing her for the first time. Realizing she was naked, she drew the cover over herself and slushed out, "Come to pay your respects to the widow?"

"I brought you a basket of things to eat. I thought you might be overwhelmed with everything you have to see to."

Dervila's doubtful brown eyes scanned the room, settling on the basket. "Making a grand gesture to the widow, are you? How forgiving," she whispered.

Natty detected a hesitation, probably wondering how much or what Natty had seen.

"I'll make myself more presentable if you turn away."

Natty turned to the only window and looked out over the Strand and the boats and all the commotion a port of entry creates.

The bed creaked as Dervila stood and proceeded to cover herself.

Natty said, "You had a visitor. A man named Josh. Said he wanted to check up on you. Making sure you are well."

"I'll bet he did. More like something else on his mind."

Natty was more embarrassed than when she first saw her cousin naked. She kept her sights on the commotion out the window.

A heavy thump, and Natty spun about to see Dervila a lump on the floor. She had managed to tie a sash around her waist holding the dressing gown closed. Natty got down on the floor and rocked Dervila's cheeks back and forth, wondering what had happened. Speaking one minute passed out the next.

A commotion outside the door put a scare into Natty. She tried to lift Dervila onto the bed. The door swooshed open and hit the wall with a bang, and Josh and an Asian woman tumbled into the room.

Josh scrambled to his feet, dragging the woman along with him. She jabbered so fast Natty could make no sense of what she said. Then the woman's gaze fell on Dervila, lying half on Natty's lap and half on the floor. The foreign woman dropped to her knees, running her palms over Dervila's face, talking fast and heavily accented, Natty glanced at Josh.

"What is she saying?"

Josh shrugged. "I think she brought Dervila's stuff."

"Stuff?" Highly agitated, Natty repeated herself. "What *stuff*?" She watched as the Asian mumbled a chant of sorts, her palms running over the limp body as if invoking a higher power. Squatting on the floor, Dervila's head in her lap, Natty glanced at Josh.

"Help me get her to bed?"

Without a word, he scooped the limp figure up and laid her on the bed. Then turned to Natty and helped her to stand. The Asian woman got in bed next to Dervila continuing to chant.

Natty leaned near Josh. "What is going on? She seemed fine one minute and well, deranged the next. Then she passed out."

"It's that medicine she gives her." He nodded toward the Asian.

"Whatever it is, I don't think it's working. I whiffed spirits on her."

"It'd be something from the pub, and maybe mixed with herbs or something this woman brings her. I tried to keep her out when the door opened."

"So, I heard." Natty cast him a side glance. She had summed up what occurred fairly quick and didn't have an answer. She wasn't so naïve she didn't expect her cousin to use something to blot out Niall's passing.

She caught Josh's eye trying to decide if she could trust him. She really didn't have a choice, especially as she did not speak the woman's language. "I take it you've been outside the door all this time?"

"Yes, ma'am. I love Dervila."

She blinked at his firm declaration.

"As far as I know, she's been on this medicine about the time they arrived in Hawthorn, same time as Niall's sickness came on him."

That was the longest sentence to come out of his mouth. Natty was surprised, he'd been quiet typifying a stolid sort. Like someone who stayed in the shadows or corners when others were around.

Natty recalled Dervila's visits and her unpredictable behavior and silently agreed with him about the possibility of an addiction. "We haven't been friendly for years, but she is my cousin. I'm here to see what she needs. You can see she's in no condition to help herself."

"If ye like, ma'am. I'll stay and ye come back tamorra?"

She sighed. "Yes. That might seem best. Thank you, Josh." She picked up her skirts and without acknowledging the Asian woman still soothing Dervila, left the stifling little room.

Dependable Mim waited for her all this time. A frown and squinted eyes alerting Natty to her disposition. "Sorry it took so long. I should have left a while ago, but the commotion in the flat made it impossible."

Mim voiced her concern as she stood. "I saw some of it going up the stairs. How are you?"

"I'll be right as rain as soon as I get my tea." In truth, Dervila's condition overcame her. What dire circumstance might happen next? The ruckus erased the fact Mim waited at the entrance to Maher's. "I'm sorry, Mim. It must have been dreadful to sit outside and wait and hour."

"Only an hour? I assumed it was an eternity."

Natty agreed with her.

19

The Funeral

The next morning, Miss Natty stood at the parlor window with a note from Dervila in hand. Niall's funeral was set for one o'clock. Dervila pleaded with Natty to walk with her behind the casket to the burial yard.

The ache in Miss Natty's chest didn't ease. Would she ever be rid of the hurt from their younger years? Natty crumbled the note into a ball. It was wrong to put herself before the grieving widow, but there had been a lifetime of wrongs and Natty couldn't step beyond them.

She felt the presence of Mim and turned from the parlor window, swiping tears from her cheeks.

"You need some love and the person who could give it to you doesn't even know you are keeping all this from her. For what reason I'll never know." With Mim's firm hands placed on Miss Natty's shoulders, she guided her to her treasured chair. "Sit and I'll bring tea. Let's agree to go to the graveyard, not her flat. And we can leave whenever you give me a say so."

Miss Natty found it hard to sleep last night thinking of yesterday. Frightful and unsettling as it had been, in the deepest recesses of her mind, Natty realized her presence meant nothing to Dervila.

They had lived without each other until several months ago. Why Dervila felt the need to crave Natty's presence through Niall's sickness and burial was too much to absorb. Natty shivered at the word *kill* that Dervila mumbled in her delirium.

Natty wasn't able to shake yesterday out of her head. "Thank you, dear Mim. You give me courage, but I will need you at my side if I'm to go through with his burial."

"Enough said, then. I'll get that tea."

Just as she breathed another sigh of regret, Mim knocked at the parlor door. "Sir O'Bannon would like to see you."

"I'm not fit to see anyone just yet."

Mim reminded her, "He has befriended you and might have come at the right time."

Knowing the truth of it, she said, "Ask him if he would prefer coffee or tea."

Sir Finbarr's footfalls reminded her of her brother. When his step seemed to pound, it always meant he had an idea he intended sharing.

"Good morning, Miss Natty. It's a beautiful day outside, and I suddenly realized how close I was and thought I'd drop in."

"Sit with me. I need your cheery disposition. Did Mim ask after coffee or tea?"

"She did, tea for both of us. And a bakery delight."

"Begorrah, you'll have to change your route. Each time you traipse past Peter's Place isn't good for my figure." Cajoled at her own joke, she chuckled, glad she could take delight in this black time.

"I'm only stopping long enough to drink tea. The architects will be at Ashcourt by noon."

Natty noticed how calm he appeared, more relaxed. "I think Ashcourt has changed you. Refurbishing the manor brings you inner satisfaction. Brianna has kept me up, but that has been almost a week now. What is the latest?"

As he related the current renovations, his voice filled with excitement. She was ever so pleased he appeared at ease. Mim had known, Natty needed his charm.

The housekeeper set the tray down and smiled at Miss Natty as she passed out of the parlor leaving them to their exchange. Natty poured and asked, "I heard you are installing water closets. That is quite modern."

He explained about water flow and pipes in the walls. She had worried about him after his return from Dublin. But time heals. The thought brought her mind back to the gravesite funeral at one, and she sighed without realizing she did so.

Sir Fin leaned toward her. "I'm putting you to sleep, aren't I." He chuckled and stood.

"Heaven's no, sit down young man. I'm not done with my questions just yet." He certainly towered over her as she sat in her chair. His eyes twinkling bringing sunshine to her heart.

"I'm the one who must leave. Give Brianna my regards. I hope she will drive out with me in the next day or two. You are welcome, too, you know. I'll send a note around after I see what's next for Ashcourt."

"Well, then, you are excused. We shall look forward to a tour of your new home."

৯৩৩

Miss Natty and Mim entered the lychgate at St. John's graveyard. The day overcast with dark clouds, though no sign of rain. The temperature dipped to where one felt the need of a shawl and was thankful Mim had insisted she bring one. Natty took note of the small gathering. She recognized Josh and the Asian woman. Four or five folks bunched together in a small group looked rough and dressed like seafarers.

Nowhere to be seen, Natty grew concerned about Dervila. Then a high-toned keening came from behind a large bush to the south of where they stood. A widow's last farewell usually included a loud wailing till her eyes almost fell out of her head and her throat hurt like a cat's claw scratched. For all that it appeared she didn't care for her late husband, her wailing said otherwise.

The priest stood at the head of the burial hole and opened his bible waiting for the widow. A minute or two passed when Dervila leaning heavily on Josh, stepped out from behind the bush. A large cloth held to her eyes as she unsteadily walked toward her husband's coffin.

The tone of her keening softened to a muffled sorrow.

All grew silent as Father waited for the widow to gain a modicum of control before he proceeded with the Rite of Burial.

The Asian woman had stepped up and stroked Dervila's arms and face, speaking in hushed tones. Dervila seemed to gain some control and glanced about, likely realizing everyone waited on her. She dabbed at her face with a cloth and moved to the right side of Father, who then began reading.

The ceremony took less than ten minutes. Mim whispered in Natty's ear, "Ten minutes is an abomination."

Natty whispered back, "I'll give my condolences to Dervila and then we'll leave."

Once Father closed his prayer book and shook the pistol full of holy water on the casket, he stepped back and allowed the four grave diggers straps at the ready who lowered the coffin.

As the widow, Dervila would have been the first to throw dirt on the remains, but she refused, and others did so in her stead. Natty backed away from the group. She couldn't participate either.

Dervila had sunk her face into her gloved hands, sobbing. Josh and the Asian woman took hold of her and slowly drew her from the group into a carriage.

Miss Natty and Mim took that as their invitation to leave and wove their way amongst the headstones to the gravel path.

Natty spoke in a low tone. "I've never wanted anything to get over as quick as I wanted this done."

Arm in arm they strolled toward home and Natty said maybe more to herself than to Mim, "Don't judge her. She is a weak woman who has lost what little strength she had; I am thinking. As to yesterday and how I saw her, I am surprised she could make herself presentable."

Mim mumbled and Natty said, "You needn't worry you'll offend me. Deep down I might be thinking uncharitable thoughts myself."

Brianna was in the parlor when they arrived. "Where have the pair of you been? Pussycat greeted me with a mean growl. She doesn't like an empty home, you know." It was Jane's day off.

Aunt Natty drew off her gloves and Brianna helped her out of her shawl. "How did Mrs. Teaberry seem today? Did she settle the problem with the driver?"

"She stuck her finger in front of his face. I've never seen her go after someone hammer and tongs. She told him in no uncertain terms, he mustn't allow packages to bounce around. She reminded me of a goose protecting little ones."

"I would like to have seen the driver. Perchance he doesn't encounter women with her tenacity," Mim interjected.

Brianna agreed. "I doubt he'll let packages fly loose again. I've noticed him tossing them up top with no regard to the contents." She glanced at her aunt hanging up the shawl. "Where have the two of you been? I don't see any purchases."

"Someone from my early years passed, and we were paying our respects."

"Someone I know?"

"No dear, from a long time ago."

"If you are going to be in the dumps, I'm glad the kettle is on. A cup of tea might be in order," offered Brianna.

"That would be lovely. Thank you. Now, I am going to sit in my chair awhile and possibly doze off. But before I forget, Sir Finbarr came by and asked if we would like to ride out to Ashcourt with him in the next day or two. Apparently, he had already spoken to you several days ago. Business seems to have taken up his time."

"I would enjoy another walk through," said Brianna as she gathered up several books on the table. "I'll be in my chamber if you need me."

⸙

Mid-August was Ireland's loveliest month with bright reds and purples, fuchsia in bloom and spikey vibrant orange montbretia bordering a path that turned this way and that through the garden. Beyond the flowers, creamy white heather gently waved in the breeze for as far as the eye could see.

As always on a clear and bright Sunday morning Mim, Aunt Natty and Brianna enjoyed the stroll to Christ's Church and sat in the fourth pew on the right. Through the years this became their Sunday ritual for as long as Brianna could recall. One she sorely missed when with the Reynolds's family in Dundalk.

After the service, Lionel Murphy asked Brianna if they could walk. Mim and Aunt Natty were already on their way and Brianna agreed. She had been surprised to see him in church as he infrequently attended.

"What are your plans on your one day off?" She asked.

A lanky sort, and much taller than she, he looked down at her, his sober brown eyes reflecting his mood. "I've had it in mind to do something with my life and so am beginning with Sunday service. It seems the post office sucks up all the weekdays."

"I do understand which is why I am content with three mornings a week. I truly don't know how I would manage otherwise."

Mr. Murphy cleared his throat and mentioned, "I've never wanted to think of marriage before now. But I am making changes and finding someone suitable is high on my list. A lady who would understand my circumstance and the hours I have to put in to meet the demands of Her Majesty's Postal Service."

196

His approaching her didn't appear to be happenstance as Brianna had assumed. She picked up her pace as they had fallen a bit behind Aunt Natty and Mim. Was she to assume he indirectly speculated about her? She prayed not.

"Hold on, Miss Walsh. I've more to say to you but not in front of others."

"I'm sorry, Mr. Murphy. My aunt and I have plans for today and I shouldn't hold up our departing."

"Right then." His leathery face reflected understanding. They crossed over Stoney Batter nearing home. Apparently, he intended to see her to her door.

"What is it you're doing today?" he inquired.

"Visiting a friend's home that is being rebuilt."

"That'd be Sir O'Bannon with his old family manor out near St. John's River?"

She glanced up at him, a bit shocked as to how he would have come by that information. "Yes, it would. How do you come to know about it?"

"Seems anyone with eyes would know. He'll toss a lot of quid at it and still have an old home." His hands slid into the pockets on his jacket.

She let the moment pass and then changed the subject. "Mrs. Teaberry certainly gave the coach driver an earful. Were you aware she dressed him down?"

His face opened up with self-satisfaction. "'Twas me what gave her the idea she should do so. I'd of done it, but she has the clout. We'll see how they handle packages going forward, now won't we."

As they turned the corner, her home straight ahead, Sir Fin stood next to his carriage. He and Aunt Natty in conversation as they waited for her. Mr. Murphy showed no sign of leaving her side.

They approached and after introductions, Mr. Murphy gave her a nod and said, "I'll find a time fairly soon to walk out with you again, Miss Walsh. Thank you for this morning." Off he strode back toward the village, whistling as he did so.

"A suitor?" questioned Sir Fin the tone of his shock elevated.

"He's hardly the first. She's had several," Aunt Natty gingerly mentioned. "She's always been too fussy for her own good. She might want to hang on to this one."

"Enough, the both of you." Brianna didn't wait for Sir Fin's hand, she practically jumped into the low-set phaeton and ended up sitting between him and her aunt as they made their way through the countryside toward Ashcourt.

Once inside the manor, Sir Fin explained to Miss Natty about the walls that had been torn down. He drew attention to the messy replastering, and she picked up her skirts as they edged the area. Risers and treads were also being replaced on the stairs.

A heavy cloth covered the chandelier in the foyer protecting it from mayhem.

The pocket doors were gone from the library and Brianna inquired, "What have you planned for this room? Are the doors to be permanently done away with?"

"It will become my office. The doors will be replaced with glass panels to bring in light from the foyer." He eyed the room from this perspective and said, "I want light walls and a cheerful covering for the floor. Something to match the rug in the parlor." He turned to Brianna. "You said it looked similar to one the Reynolds had in their home."

"You are right, it would brighten your office."

They stepped into the room, and she asked, "What have you done with the books? My goodness, there were hundreds."

"All in a warehouse being catalogued by an apprentice. He is a young man of varying interests who aspires to work with books."

Much surprised, she practically gushed, "What a marvelous idea."

Pleased at her interest, he added, "It's made me think about the school's library."

Aunt Natty spoke up. "You'll be perceived as a saint."

Brianna interjected, "You'll encourage learning for sure."

"Then you believe they would be well received?"

Aunt Natty pressed her hands together and looked up at him over the tips of her fingers. "Absolutely. For those who can read, books are most precious. You are a dear lad. And for those who don't read, perhaps it will be an inspiration to learn."

He scowled. "You are on to something there, Miss Natty. I think I'll pay the school master a visit."

Brianna quipped, "You're a nice man, always thinking of ways to better a situation. You have a good heart."

His green eyes slowly fell to her as though he returned from somewhere far away.

"Did I say something wrong?" She looked puzzled.

He took his top hat off and glanced about the great foyer. "No, you didn't say anything wrong. Simply put, receiving a compliment under this roof, is a shock 'tis all. Thank you both."

Entering the kitchen was an awakening. A big blank room cleaned of shelving, furniture, cabinets and seeing a new slate floor and a revitalized huge brick wall gave one the perspective to see what it could become.

Brianna's laugh echoed off the walls as she twirled. "You can make this into a magnificent kitchen. Think of how pleased your cook will be when she prepares all your dinner parties."

Sir Fin mentioned to Miss Natty, "When your niece first saw the kitchen, she suggested ideas for a proper layout. She'd been adamant that used pots and dishes should be carried out away from the actual cooking area. And a proper kitchen also necessitated a bread oven."

Aunt Natty glanced at Brianna who had stepped into the scullery area. As Sir Fin talked, Brianna turned and listened to him repeat her suggestions. It made her feel as though he relied on her. She welcomed the pleasurable thought from a man of his stature.

"Mim taught her well," Aunt Natty said with a distinct prideful tone.

"Shall we move on to the stables." He turned toward the delivery door right off the kitchen. "It's shorter this way."

Aunt Natty declined, saying she would wait in the carriage. She needed to catch her breath.

He was eager to show off the new floor in the stables and Brianna fell into step with him. Glancing from beneath quizzing brows, he asked, "Tell me about your suitor."

She glowered. "Lionel? That he most certainly is *not*. We work at the post office. He usually comes in for the mail and leaves on his route after I'm already gone."

Sir Fin teased, "Methinks the lady doth protest too much."

Her nose in the air, she defended her sensitivity on the subject of marriage. "Think what you want, but I haven't met anyone who's interested me and certainly not Mr. Murphy."

"That is a puzzling statement. Most women of a certain age want marriage, and children. What makes you so different?" His hands were clasped behind his back as they strolled.

"Marriage isn't something I've given thought to. But bringing it up will most likely have it mulling around in my head for days. And I have you to thank for the waste of time."

She picked up her pace putting space between them and affectively curbed his interest on the subject.

They reached the stables and puttered down the center aisle. The scent of fresh air and warmth from the late afternoon sun brightly streamed through the open doors spread across the barren interior. The evidence of painstakingly replacing bricks and mortar flooring, and several stable doors made such a difference to Brianna. The stalls swept clean, were ready for occupancy.

She imagined Sir Fin going to the stables and choosing his mount for a morning's ride. This life would suit him quite well.

"Do you have a time when you might occupy your home?"

"It all depends on Mr. Abernathy. His crew have moved at a

good pace as you can see. Maybe midwinter. I would like to be in before the Christmas season. But that might be pushing him."

On the ride home, the women took great delight in teasing about his enthusiasm over the specifics of Ashcourt's remodel. That he could imagine himself living there, gave him a newfound sense of worth and freedom from the past.

Collins had surprised him just last week when he mentioned how much he was looking forward to making Ashcourt his home. That in itself, added to his conviction he'd made the right decision about the manor.

20

An unbelievable fear

B y the time Sir Finbarr delivered the women home and made his way back to the Inn, he was building an appetite. The scent of parsnips and thyme meant mutton pie, one of Mrs. Cashel's delicious offerings.

He checked in with Collins, who had already dined and had asked for a few hours off this evening. The request set Finbarr to think perhaps Collins endeavored to spark up a social life. He hoped so.

Finished dining himself, the rocker on the porch and the bright moon lured him outside where a pleasant breeze ruffled the treetops. Lamps from inside the hotel spread golden circles onto the porch and its newly painted floorboards.

A cigar and two fingers of Jamison waited for him to spend the rest of the evening. Mrs. Cashel had purchased his favorite after a nudge from Collins.

His moonlight musings drifted to Miss Brianna's reddish-brown hair and how softly it curled against her cheeks. She had marched up the lane with Mr. Murphy in tow as he had waited for both Miss Natty and Miss Brianna after church.

He had misread the situation and became instantly disappointed, thinking her occupied and assumed she would be unable to accompany him to Ashcourt. And then, he felt relief when Mr. Murphy took his leave and walked toward the village.

Surprised she appeared interested in someone, a beastly feeling came over him. Why he hadn't considered her with a beau, occurred to him. Lovely to look at, and quite active, he appreciated her perky presence. He also wondered why it bothered him.

A lovelier and smarter young woman he had yet to meet. Though he cautioned, her tongue was sharp. She enjoyed a number of interests. Opinionated—he blew out a circle of smoke and speculated about life with a pontifical woman. Actually, she was surer of herself than pontifical. A pretty heart-shaped face, full lips. A tendency toward pontification. He chuckled to himself that he brought it up twice now. He also noticed her intelligent gray eyes that turned blue when outside painting Ashcourt, a small slim nose and delicate ears, almost shell like. And, to top it all off, she seemed quite assertive most of the time, though in a nice way.

He chuckled at the thought of her strong will. She was a bold lass when it came to the sensitivities of others. But, when life doles out problems, you would surely want her at your side. He blew out another circle of smoke and contented himself with the memory of when they first met.

Puffing on his cigar, legs crossed, he listened to the cicada's soothing music. The moon cast its light across the evening as it drew long shadows out of the trees. He felt content. Something new to him, especially in this village where he had begun. He toyed with the possibility of residing here. After all, he had engaged the services of a manager for his mining interests.

The next morning, Brianna watched as Aunt Natty pored over a list of items for the Harvest Fair, nearly two months away. "You don't waste a moment. What have you taken on this year?"

"Prizes for the contests. Mrs. Cashel thinks we should have five contests. There were a great many interested last year, and she suspects we will have an increase this year."

"Well, aren't you already adding more raffles? The plowing race, horse race, hasty pudding eating contest and don't forget Georgiana's Best of Rose Contest. Depending upon how many enter, you could need four tables just for that contest alone."

Aunt Natty huffed. "Well, we know who will win this year, don't we? Just like last year and the year before, right? Mrs. Haggarty. I almost think she's in cahoots with the mayor."

Brianna gasped. "Aunt Natty, what a startling condemnation. The mayor is a decent person. He wouldn't deliberately give an undeserved prize." She set a basket on the table and began stacking clothing for the charity box at church and stopped to look hard at her aunt. "Please tell me he wouldn't do such an underhanded thing."

"You're right, I shouldn't think such things. Shame on me."

Brianna briefly glanced at the ceiling. "You had me scared for a moment. I mean, the gentleman is married to my employer. How could I face her knowing her husband deceived her with another woman?"

"It's my imagination, 'tis all. Just you wait and see, someone else will win this year. I'm sure of it."

"I'm thinking about pie-eating contests. But I wonder how the bakers would feel if their creations were finished off in a frenzy of eating. Remember the Robb siblings several years ago? I still can't get the image out of my mind, cherry juice dripping down their hairy chins, picking up crust and shoving it in an overfull mouth. Simply awful."

Brianna nodded as she leafed through the papers her aunt spread over the table. "Tents this year. Where did the committee get the money to pay for them? I remember you wrote to me last year about the huge squabble when the committee simply couldn't afford the expense."

"Well, it seems someone opened up their pockets because this year we've got several tents big enough to hold all the contests, which is why I've got more work to do."

"Tents might mean dancing. What fun." Brianna batted her eyelashes.

Aunt Natty chuckled. "And maybe Mr. Murphy will ask you?"

"I knew I would eventually hear from you about him. I haven't a notion why he walked me home. Somehow I don't see him as a dancer."

"Would that disappoint you?"

"Aunt Natty." Brianna's eyes opened wide, and she squeaked. "Are you thinking I am interested in him?"

She shuffled her papers. "I believe he is interested in you, my dear. Don't get all huffy with me. It's what I saw, not what I think."

"You and Sir Fin. You are a pair with your over imagining. Honestly. Mr. Murphy would test a saint with his old-mannish behavior. And a saint I don't pretend to be." She turned on her heal and left the dining room.

Natty's eyes squinted, and she mumbled, "Sir Finbarr thought the same as I, did he?"

☙❦❧

The bell rang and Mim, covered in flour as she prepared bread for the week, called out if Miss Natty could get the door.

As Miss Natty opened the portal, she faced Dervila's friend, Josh, nervously shifting from one foot to the other and scrunching his tam in crusted fists.

"Miss Walsh. I'm grateful you're at home. It's Dervila, and

she's calling for you. She's in a high state of vexation. Can you come quick?"

With no other decision to be made, Miss Natty hustled alongside Josh, having told Mim about the situation. Mim, of course, wanted to accompany her, but she poo-poohed her leaving the house, what with rising bread and cookies to bake. She assured Mim she would be fine. And Josh, who had the appearance of a calm and steady friend of Dervila's, would be there.

They entered the flat. Dervila sat at the little table near the window, her hand clutching a mug. Her thick, course hair wild about her face and down her back. She lifted her chin when they came through the door, a stubborn expression on her face.

Josh closed the door behind them and, standing against the wall, began shuffling from side to side again, fidgeting. A sinking feeling in her stomach had her regretting she'd come.

She spoke up. "How are you doing? Is it getting any easier for you?"

Dervila held her gaze, a smirk on her mouth, instantly alerting Natty this visit wouldn't be pleasant by any means. "Easy? No money, no man about. I don't know how you manage without a man."

Natty glanced at Josh, who obviously cared about her cousin and her deceased husband. She wondered what he was thinking. "Josh is a good friend to you. I wouldn't discount his assistance were you to need it."

Josh flashed a weak smile.

Dervila drank the contents of her mug and burped as she slammed the empty vessel on the table. "I'm needing another then." She shoved the mug across the table toward Natty.

Josh quickly grabbed it up and said he would return.

Natty sat in the chair across from the new widow. "How are you doing?"

Dervila took her time reacting to the question, then shifted in the chair and glanced out the window. "I'm poor. I need money to live. He left me nothing." She glanced at the ceiling. "The rent is paid through October, 'tis all I've got."

"Be grateful for that. A roof over your head. Surely you can earn a wage doing something. Didn't you tell me you helped out at Maher's? Would they take you on, give you more time? For heaven's sake, Dervila. They know you downstairs, surely they will have compassion for your circumstance."

Dervila snarled. "A simple-minded woman you are. I've greater needs than you. Always have."

Natty tried not to take umbrage of her remark. The woman just lost the love of her life, and Natty needed to remember that. She would try to stir up compassion for her cousin.

Josh returned with two mugs of ale, placing one in front of Natty. The bitter scent turned her off and with fingertips pushed it across the table toward Dervila whose eyes followed the mug.

She said, "Not good enough for you?"

Natty could have laughed. "I've never taken to the taste. Now, tell me why I'm here. You seem to have things under control. What is it you want?"

"I've a way to make money. I've a child who had a rich father. I want to sell the child's whereabouts to the grandparents."

Natty almost tipped back in her chair. "Do you mean the child you lied to Niall about, actually lived?"

Dervila's smirk widened. "In a pig's eye, I never conceived with him. Leave it be, will you?" She slapped her palm on the table spilling some ale. "I'm talking about a child with a dandy man. A man who could get me in the family way. A young buck whose seed took."

Both hands clutched her mug. She focused on the contents as if she could conjure him up in the dark, bitter ale.

Natty's thoughts reeled. Her cousin must have cared a great deal for this man. Sucking in her breath, she said, "Where is the child?"

Dervila lifted her kohl-stained eyelids and stared at her. "With

Niall due back any time, I had to immediately give it up. He would have killed me if he'd known."

"Oh, Dervila."

"He would have done me in without a thought. I kept that whole time a secret like it never happened. I got rid of all traces of it and paid a man to take it away."

"Did the child die?"

"Looked healthy to me. I wouldn't know if it lived, but it squalled, and I feared the neighbors would talk about that and Niall would know."

A thin gauzy curtain flapped at the open window from a breeze off the lough.

Natty's ears buzzed, her stomach riled. Weak with an overwhelming sense she forced the question. "The family you sold your child to, do they live in Hawthorn?"

"I don't think so. They were a peddler and his wife." She snickered. "I think they were one of those who wander all over Ireland, constantly moving."

Icy cold began to engulf Natty. Her heart seemed to stop beating, her breath left her. She felt like she might lose the contents of her stomach.

Done with the first mug, Dervila reached over and drank from the one intended for Natty. She swiped the foam from her upper lip with her wrist. "My biggest problem is finding the peddler and where he might be."

In a weak voice, Natty forced another question, though her heart beat wild like it would burst from her chest. "Is your child a lass, then?"

A crude laugh bubbled. "The father was a young buck able to make a lad." She gulped another swig, then added, "Seems I was wrong."

Miss Natty felt faint, as if she might slide off the chair. While Dervila was in the mood to talk, she needed to get every ounce of information. But she was treading on ground that might open up and devour her.

"I find it hard to believe these grandparents would buy their own granddaughter?"

Dervila lifted a sly look at Natty. "They'd buy her all right. 'Cause the father of my lass was no less than Lord Darnley's grandson. They would pay big. Don't you recall the fuss over Rutledge drowning years ago? We were already in Bristol when that happened, but it made the newsprint. The colleen would be a gift to them. A reminder of him. Don't you get it—his own daughter. They'd set me up nicely to know it."

As weak as she felt, her legs rubbery, Miss Natty stood and carefully made her way to the window. She dared not allow her cousin to see her face, read her emotions. Her knees felt like they would buckle. Her torment nearly caused her to pass out. She took a deep breath, then another, her hands on the sill grounding her. *Dear Mother of God. Give me courage to face this woman and not give myself away.*

Miss Natty remembered that time at Rockmore Hall when the captain of a ship appeared on their doorstep. The Darnley's, grandson, Viscount Rutledge, had sailed on to England and was discovered to have drowned during a horrific storm. That unbelievable information didn't take long to reach the kitchen where Natty was working at the time.

Dervila's adamant declaration pulled Natty's attention from the past.

Her cousin said, "I remember those months with Rutledge as he fought his way out of a foggy addiction. He babbled a lot, mostly about his grandparents, how they had wronged him. I always thought them an odd sort. Family dying, those twins separated. Ye hear a lot of *on dits* living above Maher's."

She continued to address Miss Natty's back. "Those that have, you'd think would share. But no. Rutledge said he'd been forced to leave. Told to get out. As I see it, that might be the only hindrance. Maybe they wouldn't want his child."

Though Natty considered this conversation pure torture, she tried to calm. "How long ago did you go through all this?"

"As I recall, the worst humid July day ever. 1817. Why?"

In as light a voice as Natty could muster, she suggested, "She might have moved on from the peddler if she were older. The lass would be a woman now. Married, most likely with children of her own."

Natty's face burned with her false counsel. She kept at the window rather than face her tormentor. The harbinger of her past and now her future.

"Born on the wrong side of the sheets, she was. Even her father had a rough go of it. I pulled him out of Madame Fornia's opium den, but you wouldn't know anything about that kind of life. He had a fierce vengeance against his grandparents. I believe it's what drove him. I got him clean. It turned out to be a bit of a magical time for me.

"Niall had taken a sail to China. Gone nearly a year. He carried the fault if you think about it. Leaving me, going off for so many months. If it hadn't been for young Rutledge, I might have lost my mind."

The way she swiped her palm over her arm and her eyes closed made Natty think she could feel him.

Miss Natty drew her eyes off her cousin and touched the windowpane. She knew Dervila capable of absolving herself of any culpability. Her lack of empathy toward an infant of her own flesh and blood almost caused Natty to expel her stomach's contents.

Twenty-three years ago, the events in that infant's life over the next few days changed Natty's life forever.

Her cousin droned on, "Under other circumstances, I would have refused. But Niall's brother sent a job offer, and I had a real fear the peddler might return with the baby. I grabbed the chance to get away."

Natty forced herself away from the window. In so doing she noted Josh up against the wall, still as a stone. She wondered if he heard all this before. He didn't appear as though he listened to her confession.

Natty could hardly move, her legs like jelly, her heart pounding. Her darling lass came from the likes of this…this harlot. Miss Natty denied any resemblance between them, however, she might see a likeness with the Darnley family.

She recalled the evening of Lord Darnley's garden party. Brianna had a silly grin when she told Natty someone saw a faint resemblance between herself and Lady Fionnuala.

Mother of God!

Natty almost gagged on a reflexive gasp. She had to get away from this woman. Inhaling to calm herself, she glanced at Josh, then Dervila. A burning question needed an answer. "Do you intend to seek out this daughter?"

Dervila flicked off a bug skittering across the table. "The Darnleys are a thin family and can do with more. Seems likely they'd want her. She'll bring in a fat purse. And they can afford it."

Dervila waved her thin arm about. Natty could tell she was getting tired of the topic. "First, I have to find her." She hit the table with her palm, a resolve settling in. "I'll begin with finding the peddler. Seems it shouldn't be too hard. The wagon painted blue all over. I think some children were about."

She tapped the table with her cracked fingernails and smiled. "I'll put out the word amongst the walkers, word will trickle back to me. Kind of like the tattlers in this village." She seemed to brighten with the idea casting Natty with a sly and clever look.

Brooding fear that the unforeseen was imminent, Miss Natty tried to pull herself together. "It seems you have a plan. And you can live here for the rest of the year and work downstairs. I think you have solved your problem. That must make you feel better."

Natty looked hard at her, eyes smeared, her hair a frightful mess, and wondered if a comb could get through her rat's nest.

As she took her leave of her cousin, she felt a blanket of anxiety slip over her, as if her life were coming to an end. And there wasn't one single thing she could do to stop it.

Miss Natty's step slowed as she descended the stairs. She had a hard time catching her breath. Suddenly, exhaustion blanketed her. Like a finalization; an end to the dream of her life with her darling lass.

Miss Natty recalled being at Rockmore Hall that day so long ago when Rutledge was banished by his grandsire.

Word had filtered down to the kitchen and everyone was on alert because of the Viscount's yelling at his lordship. The worst scandal the family had ever been dealt. Six months later, on a cold wintry February day, the captain of the ship Viscount Rutledge had been on, arrived at Rockmore Hall and delivered the awful news that their grandson and heir had fallen overboard in a storm. It happened nearly on his eighteenth year and on his way to school in London, in his prime.

A death that mirrored his father's, Garrett II, Viscount Rutledge. Whispers were, he wanted to die like his father.

Soon the Darnleys will get the unanswered question of where was he for those six months between banishment and when the ship's captain delivered the horrific news of his death?

With shoulders bent, Natty shuffled slowly. The idea of Dervila birthing her darling girl overwhelmed her. Her breath held, heart hammering in her chest.

She reached out and clutched the top of a picket fence, feeling faint, gasping for air as she slowly fell to the ground.

Brianna, hot tears in her eyes, worried her lower lip trying to keep hold of her fear, hands twisting with the torment her beloved aunt was dying. Stiff as a rod, she sat on a chair in the corner of the room where her aunt lay. Mr. Curran and an aide prodded and poked, tending to the dearest person in her life.

Mr. Curran allowed her to be in the room if she stayed in the chair. Though she found it difficult to keep her hands off her aunt.

Brianna was told a nipper happened to be playing with a hoop in the lane when Aunt Natty had fallen. He ran and got his pa and they put her in their buggy and drove up to the infirmary to Mr. Curran. Brianna felt she could not have been tended to any quicker if the attack happened at home.

Mr. Curran asked Brianna to step into the corridor with him. As soon as the door closed, he said, "At the least, your aunt may have had an anxiety attack. Or it could be worse, spasms of the heart, better known as Angina Pectoris. I won't recognize which one until she revives." His kindly regard swept over her face, and he patted her hands as they twisted and turned the handkerchief.

"She will recover, Miss Walsh. It may take some time. She is heartier than you might imagine. I take it she had gone for a walk. Alone?"

"Mim said she had a visitor, and they both left to visit another friend. That is all I know. Apparently, she fainted on the way home."

"Do you know how long she had been gone?"

Brianna kept her attention on the closed door. She found it difficult not being in the room with her aunt. "No. I don't. If you don't mind me asking, why?"

"I'm attempting to put the pieces of the last few hours together. Attempting to understand if an underlying health issue, or perhaps a bout of anxiety, occurred. I've known her to be in good health. Robust you might say."

His smile meant to calm her. She could tell he did not want to give her any greater concern than she already experienced.

He said, "Sometimes if we experience sudden shock, our whole being is affected. We want the person to be calm, get plenty of rest. I've noted over the years the joy and harmony that family and friends bring does a great deal of good."

Brianna nodded. "Is it all right if I go back in? I don't want her to be alone."

"Yes, certainly. By tomorrow, it will be easier to distinguish the exact treatment. She won't be left alone during the night."

"Thank you, Mr. Curran. She has such faith in you. When she wakes, she will be pleased you have the care of her."

His kind eyes filled with sympathy. "Get something to eat if you plan to stay late. The women in the kitchen usually have extra plates for such as this occasion. We cannot have you fainting, now. Can we? Down the corridor and to the right. I'm sure you'll hear their chatting."

The heavy weight of sinning

"She toppled over right there in front of young Stout who got his da and they put her in their carriage and took her to the infirmary."

"Poor Miss Natty. She's always been robust."

Sir Finbarr overheard the two women while standing in line at the post office. Turning on his heel, he rushed up Stoney Batter, catching Mim at her doorstep. A note had just been delivered and Mim was leaving when Sir O'Bannon arrived. Together, they strode up Forge Street to the infirmary. Sir Fin didn't take time to have the carriage readied. But with Mim's slow walk, he was frustrated. He reminded himself she was older than Miss Natty.

Mr. Curran stepped from his office into the corridor when they arrived. He said, "You are here to see Miss Walsh?"

Out of breath, Mim gushed, "Yes?"

He held out his hand. "Christopher Curran, sir. I presume you are Sir O'Bannon?"

He shook hands as Mr. Curran said, "I believe Miss Natty may have suffered an anxiety attack, or heart spasms. Each present with similar symptoms at first. If it is anxiety, she will come around on her own sooner than later."

He turned to Mim. "Do you know when she left home if someone was with her, or she was along?"

"Well, he's not what I'd call a friend by any stretch, more an errand lad for someone else. He came to fetch her."

"Would that have caused her anxiety?"

Mim fiddled with her reticule, appearing confused.

Sir Fin touched her arm. "Would you like me to leave so you can speak freely?"

"No." She practically shouted. "Sorry. I've made a promise not to speak of it. I can't go back on my word."

"It's becoming clear to me," said Mr. Curran, "her fainting appears to be the result of an anxiety attack. Can you at least say yes or no to that question?"

Almost a whisper, as if speaking low meant she would not break her promise, she admitted, "I would have to say yes."

The doctor glanced at Sir Fin. "I'll keep a close watch on her. If it is anxiety, she could be home tomorrow."

Mim exhaled a long breath. "God bless you, Mr. Curran, sir."

Sir Fin asked, "May we see her? I assume Miss Brianna is with her?"

"Certainly, to both questions. Down the corridor, third door on your right. Your talk should be light and friendly, nothing to cause upset. Her ears work fine." He winked at Mim as he spoke.

Sir Finbarr opened the door. Brianna glanced up as they entered the private room. She sat on the far side of the bed, cupping her aunt's hand.

Mim whispered, "She looks pale." Mim hugged Brianna asking, "Is that a good sign?"

"Her breathing is calm, now. It had been exceedingly jagged and her face a mean red. I see an improvement just since I've been here." She stood, giving Mim the chair, then whispered in the housekeeper's ear. "Something isn't right. She's seemed on edge lately. She's so organized; it cannot be preparations for the Fair. Would you have any—"

Mim put her hand on Brianna's arm. "It's nothing but the Fair." And quickly took her hand off Brianna's arm as if it were a coal burner. "What else could it be?"

"I don't know, I thought you would." Again, Mim denied she knew anything else giving Brianna the suspicion she was hiding something. But this place would not do for a discussion. It is not like Aunt Natty is an old woman. She is not yet fifty. She turned to Sir Finbarr, thinking to ask his opinion.

His stance and the closed look on his strong features bode concern. He looked down on the sleeping figure—her arms tucked inside the covers. "I wish I could do something to ease her."

"Say your prayers."

His dark green eyes scanned her face as if he could find answers. "Will you notify me if anything changes?"

"It would be a relief to count on you, Sir Fin."

The furrows on his brow testified to his concern. "As long as I have your word, I won't take up room. This is a small space."

From across the bed, Mim said, "Thank you, sir. When she wakes, we'll tell her you were here."

As he turned to leave, Brianna followed him out of the room. "You have a strong spirit and a calming way about you."

Hat in hand, he looked down at her. "Your aunt is a lovely woman. And I have never been called *dear lad* in my life. She won me over."

❦

A week passed. Miss Natty spent two nights in the infirmary when Mr. Curran diagnosed her with the lesser of the two initial possibilities—anxiety. He sat bedside and asked if she would be willing to confide in him or a trusted friend. His willingness to help nearly broke her already broken heart. If only she *could* respond to him.

Instead, she committed to a tiny fib, and told him how anxious she had been with preparations for the Fair. She thanked him profusely for allowing her a good rest.

She left the infirmary with a mixture of green tea and passion-flower leaves with the doctor's recommendation to drink the tea twice a day until she felt less apprehension, then once a day until she returned to her normal self.

He told her to return in a week, or sooner, if she worsened.

Once she got past the rigid eye of Mr. Curran, she felt certain she could handle her household.

Knowing Sir Finbarr worried about her, she made attempts to be cheerful on the ride home. They were greeted by the aroma of a fresh baked apple pie to celebrate her return, as if she had been on vacation.

Without making it obvious, Natty scanned Brianna's beautiful features and thankfully decided she saw no resemblance to Dervila.

She forced herself to be cheerful, all the while harboring a secret of immense proportions. A secret that would shake Brianna's world.

Natty's effort was a miraculous display of fakery and tired her out enormously. It seemed her world was on the verge of exploding into smithereens.

She tasted a bite of pie and visited with the three of them a few minutes. But as she agonized over the life-changing secret, all she wanted to do was bury herself beneath the covers of her bed.

Thanking them for a lovely homecoming, she excused herself and retired to her room. Brianna followed and tucked her in, kissing her forehead. "Remember when you always used to do this for me?"

Brianna soothed her brow and left her to sleep. Natty had all she could do to not break into tears.

Sir Finbarr waited in the parlor to have a few words with Brianna before he left.

"She's tired. It is just as well she naps." Though she spoke more to her own concerns than she let on. What would her life be like without her aunt? The sadness squeezed her stomach until she almost shuddered.

"Before I leave, I want your promise to send Jane should the need arise."

Deep in musing of what might come about in the near future, Brianna absentmindedly nodded.

"Will you promise to get a message to me?"

Returning her attention to him, she assured him she would do so, but hopefully, there would be no need.

Left with the quiet of the parlor, Brianna tried to put the pieces of the past week into focus. She felt it might worsen her aunt's anxiety if she asked questions. It all seemed to have to do with a man, Josh, who came to the door and spirited her away. Mim could not, or would not, say anything, leaving Brianna with the option—her aunt. And she would not dare to say or do anything to upset her.

Tucked under the coverlet, all alone with the quiet, Natty's fears billowed. Dervila's shocking revelation wasn't the only thing on her mind. She noticed friendship growing between Sir Finbarr and Brianna. The reality of Dervila's confession would deprive Brianna of any possibility of a future with him.

Who would want a young woman with such a speckled and unsubstantial background, a father disowned by his family, and a mother who committed adultery? A mother who rid herself of her own flesh and blood by paying a peddler to take her.

The door to her bedchamber opened barely inches and

Pussycat jumped on the bed purring as she gently moved over Natty's form in search of a comfortable spot in which to curl. As she nestled in the crook of Natty's legs, Natty sighed into her pillow. Life as she knew it was over, any moment now the sky was going to fall on all of them.

No man worth his dignity would be interested in Brianna once Dervila revealed the truth. This kind of tattle wouldn't remain hidden for long. Reaching for her handkerchief, she sobbed. Natty felt helpless. How could she manage to stop what her evil cousin planned?

The self-centered, immoral devil-woman brought on this case of nerves. Natty must devise a solid plan and calm down, or the doctor will put her back in the infirmary. She reached for the cup of tea Jane was thoughtful to bring up, no matter it had cooled by now.

Dervila's fixation on finding her daughter's whereabouts, made Natty feel like a noose closed around her neck. It was only a matter of time before her cousin finds the peddler in the blue wagon.

And that was half of Dervila's plan. Natty turned the damp pillow over and snuggled her cheek against the fresh side, then fixed on the Hawthorn tree, bending with the blow outside her window. She wished she had the power to rid herself of the heavy dread tightening her chest. Though she was a moral woman, she found herself wishing Dervila gone, as in dead.

Dervila's plan to demand money from Lord Darnley was scandalous. It could result in Natty being banned from working in Rockmore's kitchen. That alone was enough to send her into a delirious fit. She wouldn't blame them one tiny bit.

Natty took another deep breath and sobbed into her pillow all over again.

For the next several days, Aunt Natty stayed to her bed. Deeply concerned about her aunt, Brianna was aware of the used handkerchiefs on her side table. She kept up a cheerful demeanor, attempting to draw her into conversation, but Aunt Natty always appeared to be asleep when she entered the bedchamber.

She refused to eat, other than nibbles. Mim had Jane traipsing up and down the stairs with a bowl of this, or a plate of that. Even Mim's yummy cookies—lemon sugar, wouldn't entice her beyond a nibble.

Sir Finbarr dropped off a bouquet of eyebright mixed with greens and a box of raspberry tarts. Brianna thought his effort might bring her round. Aunt Natty had her back to the door as she lay under the covers. Brianna tiptoed and peeked at her, but her eyes were closed.

Brianna continued to work with the understanding the day maid would get her at the post office if something were to happen. She felt crushed by her aunt's despondency.

That evening, after a minced pork pie, Mr. Murphy came to the door asking if Brianna would like to go for a walk. She shouldn't encourage him, but a good walk would clear her mind of worries. She grabbed her shawl and tied on her bonnet and off they proceeded.

He crooked his neck and shoved his hands in his pockets. "What did you think of the dressing down Mrs. Teaberry gave to the new lass, Miss Simpson?"

Did he ask her to walk out so he could discuss Miss Simpson? She felt a bit odd talking about someone else's problems. Her concern over her aunt was troubling enough.

"She borrowed the *Illustrated London News* and returned it the next day to the right cubby. What's so alarming about that?"

"The Post Office of England recognizes it as property belonging to the person whose name is on the label. I think it'll be prison."

"Did she say why she took it?"

"Apparently she used it to teach her da to read."

"I wonder why she wouldn't have gotten reading material from the library." Brianna shook her head in despair. "Why take what isn't yours when you can borrow what you need?"

His chin jutted with authority. "Mrs. Teaberry threatens to tell the constable. She let her go, you know right then when she discovered her theft. I know the wages she brought home mattered."

His neck crooked as he made eye contact again. "I don't see you as being light fingered."

Did he just pay her a compliment? She wanted to laugh at his disagreeable comment but instead, asked, "How is it you know every farthing mattered, Mr. Murphy."

His smile seemed forced. "We were on good terms you might say. She might have mentioned it."

"But no longer?" Brianna shooed off a beetle that landed on her shawl and cast him a side glance. Did his cheeks pinken?

He appeared flustered by the question. Sizing up what must have happened, she wondered if Mr. Murphy also walked out with Miss Simpson and broke off from her when he discovered what she had done. Honestly, Miss Simpson erred in bad judgement, 'tis all. But Murphy's rejection toward the defenseless woman revealed him as a spineless creature.

Fed up with his folly and with all else going on in her life, Brianna announced, "I'll see myself home, Mr. Murphy. Enjoy the rest of your walk."

৩১৫৩

A steady mizzling kept Sir Fin and ten other men under a tent waiting for it to let up so they could begin the cricket match.

Cosgrove, Dixon, Longfield, and Ranson, whom Sir Fin had met at Lady Hamerlin's soiree in early August, greeted enthusiastically. Dixon introduced him to the remaining two men and mentioned Sir Finbarr's championship in Swansea.

Some cheered, some looked him over as if judging his

capabilities. Sir Fin was reminded of his teammates in Swansea years ago. The majority accepted him, but the rest still needed to see his ability before wanting to shake his hand.

The light rain eased, and the team gathered up their bats and balls. The wickets had been set in place earlier.

The team manager, Mr. Longfield, chose his specialist batsmen, bowlers, one allrounder, and the wicket keeper. Straws were drawn for first, second, and so on. Sir Fin drew third batsman.

It felt good to have a bat in hand. He would have to thank Lady Hamerlin for introducing him to the team. They were a scrub team by Swansea's standards. Cosgrove, with interjections from Ranson, mentioned they were not recognized by anyone other than locals who raked them over at the pub after each match. Heckling and goading between the *Gaelics* and the *Irishmen* characterized their enthusiasm.

Sir Finbarr enjoyed the rousing aftergame. Mugs in hand and undefined keynote ballads accompanied by a concertina embodied the love of the sport. Someone placed a bottle of Guinness on the table and mugs were passed around, directly impacting the loud pitch of singing.

The next morning, Collins swept open the drape allowing a beam of light to spread across the carpet onto the bed. "Good morning, sir. Shall I have breakfast brought up, or will you dine in the cafe?"

The figure in the bed pulled a pillow over his face and groaned. "Go away."

"Enjoyed yourself, did you?"

A decided hint of sarcasm surfaced from the pillow covering his head. Mostly non-distinct words though the tonality sufficient for Collins to distinguish a clear *Get Out*. With a smile on his face, he softly closed the door behind him.

Recovering and A clash of wills

S ir Fin waited a few days before dropping off a book of Wordsworth's poetry to the home on Stoney Batter. It contained two poems that he particularly liked, *Wandering Lonely as a Cloud* and *Tables Turned*. Uncertain of Miss Natty's taste in poetry, he nevertheless hoped it would help pass time while she recuperated.

She received him in the parlor. Bundled up with a cup of tea and seeming quite eager for his presence.

"I have something for you." He handed her the red leather-bound book. "I don't know if you enjoy Wordsworth, but he is one to illustrate feelings and images with his gift."

She looked worn to him as if she was suffering. He sat on the edge of a chair near her. "Dear Natty, I hope you are following doctor's orders. As my first friend when I returned to Hawthorn, you are special to me."

Sighing deeply, she looked at him. "I'll come around. I probably need a dose of fresh air and a reason to be out in it. I've been a lazy thing lately."

He brightened with an idea. "Would you care to see a cricket match?"

"I wouldn't know what to do. I've never been to one." He noted her interest when her eyes brightened.

"I'll send my carriage around if you and Brianna would be interested. My team, the *Gaelics,* play the *Irishmen* next. If you tire, all you need do is tell Collins and he will see you home."

"When do you play?"

"A week from today."

"I'm sure Brianna would be interested. One more week and I should feel more myself."

Mim set tea and biscuits on the sideboard and served.

Settled with the cups and a scone each, he said, "A while ago Brianna told me the story of how you took her in as an infant. It's extraordinary, to say the least. How fortunate for her you happened along. What an unaccountable circumstance."

Miss Natty's cup rattled as she set it on the saucer. Patting her lap for Pussycat to jump up, she said, "Yes, I've often regarded it so. To this day I give thanks to God for her."

"You've never been able to find a shred of information?" He wondered if she had a theory or some inclination.

Pussycat obviously unsettled without Natty's full attention, stood up and waved her bushy orange tail at her before taking flight to the rug. "I did what I could for the first six months or so. Posting it on the wall in the library and the pubs. Nothing ever came of my efforts. And, of course, it would have broken my heart to give her back. Though I would have been bound to do so."

She took up her cup again thinking her nerves had settled, but they had not, and she returned the cup and saucer to the tray.

"I didn't intend to stay this long. I want you well and don't mean to tire you." He stood and took her hand in his. "Take care and hopefully you will find enjoyment in Wordsworth. I'll drop by next week to see if you are still interested in a cricket match. If

I don't run into Miss Brianna, will you extend the invitation for me?"

The sadness in her eyes struck him. He hoped he hadn't tired her out. He thought it worrisome she appeared lethargic. Though he did concede planning for the Autumn Fair wasn't an easy task.

⚜

Mim returned to the parlor when she heard the front door close. "Did you have a nice chat with Sir Finbarr?" She gathered up the bits and pieces of tea.

"He has invited Brianna and me to his match next week. What do you think of that?"

"You don't want to know what I think." Mim stood near the door, her hands clutching the tray of leavings from tea.

Natty gave her a hard look. "Shush. Brianna could return any moment."

"Not likely when they are giving the post office its yearly cleaning and all employees are expected to work overtime."

"Where is Jane then?"

"Sometimes I forget she's in the house, she's so quiet. But gets her jobs done and done well. I go behind her and check and have no fault with her work." Mim gave a quick nod of her head as if to say, *and that is that*.

Natty's shoulders sagged.

Her housekeeper stood across from her, still holding the tea tray. "Miss Natty, you can't hold all this in by yourself. You just can't. I'm surprised Sir O'Bannon didn't notice how lifeless you seem."

"I doubt he did. He's so full of life."

"I've been thinking, something bad happened last time that man, Josh, came and got you. I believe that woman wanted to see you for no good a'tall. Your poor heart nearly shut down."

"Well, dear Mim, I know you care about me, but this time you are wrong. Yes, she wanted to see me, to apologize for her frightful behavior. What happened on the lane has never happened to me before, and Mr. Curran expects if I take care of myself, it will never happen again. He called it...oh, I can't recall... something to do with if my mother had been prone to anxiety, then I could be, too."

Mim looked down her nose. "If you say so, Miss Natty." And marched from the parlor, leaving the impression she didn't believe one word of her excuse.

※

Natty fell asleep in her chair and woke when Brianna returned home from a Fair meeting. Mim could be heard setting the table in the dining room for the evening meal. Aunt Natty woke feeling quite refreshed.

Exhausted, Brianna quickly freshened up. She had built up quite an appetite.

Aunt Natty had excused herself from the meeting. Expecting robust conversations and firm notions of how and what to do in preparation for the Fair. The commotion seemed far more than Natty could handle right now.

Brianna entered the dining room, she made it a point to be cheerful. "You must be feeling better. Your color looks a bit pink. Have you been out in the sun?"

"No, I've had a delightful nap. Sir Fin dropped by with a book of poetry. His own copy of Wordsworth especially for me."

"How nice."

Mim announced dinner and both women sat at the table as Mim presented a platter of cut beef with vegetables, and a dish of mashed potatoes on the table, along with a boat of gravy.

"The committee agreed that you and I could be in charge of the art raffle. Probably due to the fact I'm donating two large oils." Brianna lifted the platter for her aunt to choose what she wanted.

"They hadn't a choice as far as I'm concerned. You worked hard at your painting."

"You're biased. What else did Sir Fin have to say?" She chewed a piece of tender beef, it practically melted in her mouth.

"He invited us to a cricket match next week. He will send his phaeton."

"I hope you agreed?" Brianna cut another piece of tender beef. Covered in Mim's special gravy, she savored the rich herbal sauce.

"I took the liberty of saying yes for both of us. I think you might enjoy watching, and I've never been."

"Really thoughtful, auntie. Thank you. I've also taken a liberty involving you." She bit into the creamy whipped potatoes teasing her aunt for what she had to say.

Aunt Natty laid her fork and knife across the top of her plate, her eyebrows scooted up her brow.

"Mrs. Deanne and Mrs. Turner asked after you today, they wondered if you've begun knitting your share of booties for the Fair."

"Oh, oh. I totally and utterly forgot." She called out with urgency. "Mim, Jane."

Drying her hands, her apron splashed with sudsy water, Mim came running. The day maid, a moment behind her, fireplace ash on her cheek and hands. In unison, they worriedly asked, "What? What!"

"Where are my needles and yarn? The yellow and green skeins, where are they?"

The housekeeper and the maid stared at each other. Mim gasped, "You gave me a fright, Miss Natty. Thanks to God it's just knitting needles and not your health."

Brianna suggested, "Isn't your kit and yarn in the basket in the parlor next to your chair? Right where they've always been?"

A moment of silence, then laughter. A long breath escaped Aunt Natty, her cheeks pink. "Oh dear. I've had my head in a basket, so it seems."

Over the next few days, the occupants of the home on Stoney Batter eased into a calm and more cheerful existence. Each day, Aunt Natty showed signs of putting melancholy behind her. Her bubbly manner setting forth an ease for the household.

They embraced the lighter mood of their mistress, grateful to have her restored.

※

The day of the cricket match arrived. Collins drove Miss Natty and Brianna to the grassy knoll on the outskirts of Hawthorn Village. A misty rain had fallen over the last several days, but this afternoon promised to be as lovely a day as good-old Ireland could offer.

White puffy clouds crawled across the heavens as their carriage pulled up near the playing field. A number of fans already in folding chairs, parasols opened, shielding ladies from the bright sun.

Their driver opened the door and assisted both women to descend. "I'll get the chairs and umbrella and see you well situated. Sir O'Bannon gave me strict orders you were to be under the shade of a tree and along the middle edge of the playing field." He offered Aunt Natty his arm.

She glanced at Brianna, a pleased look on her fair skin. Using her shillelagh to lean on, and holding her head high, Aunt Natty carefully ambled with the valet, leaving Brianna to follow a few steps behind.

Sir Fin's special care, offering opportunities to get out and conveying pastries, flowers, and poetry warmed Brianna's heart.

In return, Aunt Natty adored him and looked forward to watching a game of cricket where she already had elevated him to the level of a star.

Brianna warmed to the gentleman and the heedfulness he showered on her aunt. Ever more so now that she seemed a bit down, obviously not fully recovered from her bout of anxiety.

Settled under the shade of a tree, Aunt Natty, clearly in her element, said, "Do you see Sir Finbarr?" Nodding in his direction.

Brianna felt all fluttery inside and she thought him the most handsome of all the players. He always looked at ease when dressed in his gentleman's clothing. This was the first she'd seen him in a sweater and trousers. Ogling him sent a shiver through her, and it was considerably difficult to pull her eyes away.

Aunt Natty giggled like a child. "He looks so manly in his uniform. We should be able to keep tabs on him with *Gaelics* written on his shirt."

Brianna laid her hand on her aunt's arm. "Each team member has the same sweater."

"But I'd know him anywhere. He's so grand. Taller than most, I'd say."

She smiled in agreement. And remembered an old adage *handsome is as handsome does*. She had realized weeks, maybe months ago, maybe even in the coach that had brought her home, he appeared a worthy man. His gentlemanly manner with her aunt proved her consideration.

The minute she first set eyes on him when entering the coach as she was leaving Dundalk, it had been hard to look away. His brown wavy hair and square jaw framed his thick brows and full lips. Lips that had firmed to a thin indignant line when she snapped at him. His green-as-the-sod Irish eyes had fumed with hostility in the moment she chastised his gruffness toward two little lasses.

Aunt Natty always told her she made her own bumble broth.

Brianna shook off the memory of that first meeting. Over the summer, she and Sir Fin had eased into a friendship. If she allowed herself, she might even say more than mere friends. The small crowd began to roar, and her attention swept to the players standing in groups, *Gaelics* to one side, the *Irishmen* on the other.

There was something unique about Sir Fin that captured her attention. He was basically a quiet man yet engaged in conversation with both she and Aunt Natty quite easily. He always appeared comfortable when in their home.

The crowd's hand clapping charged the air with excitement. The game was about to begin. Batsmen, curved bats at the ready, and a bowler poised to release the ball. Two umpires on the field ready for action.

When the batsman hit the ball, the striker attempted to hinder the catch from the bowler. He missed and the ball directly smashed across the wicket, knocking off the bail as another player tried to place his body in front of it.

Brianna's enthusiasm such at one point, she sprang to her feet yelling that the batsman had used an unusual round-arm bowling delivery, giving him an advantage.

A woman sitting near leaned over, introduced herself as Lady Hamerlin and chortled, "My dear, I don't wish you to cause yourself any embarrassment, but it is extremely unladylike to screech at the actions on the playing field."

Aunt Natty raised a brow, having overheard but kept her silence. With quizzed brow, Brianna reacted. "And what is it a lady does, then?"

"One simply watches and enjoys." The woman smiled, a row of perfect white teeth gleamed, a bit of rouge on her lips and cheeks.

"What if *one* cannot keep from being involved and simply *must* react?" Brianna was stupefied as to what her answer would be.

Lady Hamerlin leaned closer to Brianna. "I suspect she should learn screeching is a childish inability to act properly in society."

A flush of embarrassment crept up her face. Her enthusiasm for the afternoon's entertainment effectively squelched. Throughout the rest of the game, she held her excitement to small remarks whispered to Aunt Natty. Secretly vexed, she felt Lady Hamerlin's presence behind her like a wet blanket. Her feelings bounced between shame and irritation.

At the finish of the game, she and Aunt Natty waited in their chairs for Sir Finbarr. Winning by ten points over the *Irishmen* caused an uproar on the field for the *Gaelics*. The losers turned to their coach for solace and then began packing up to take their leave.

The crowd that sat along the sidelines now milled with the *Gaelics* on the field and Brianna noticed Lady Hamerlin and several other women made their way toward Sir Finbarr's team. Her ladyship headed directly to him. Brianna watched with shock when the woman touched his arm and planted a kiss on his cheek.

Skepticism prickled. Had she been manipulated by that woman? But why would Lady Hamerlin care about her? She would not have had a clue of her identity. Brianna shrugged it off as a queer notion.

At that moment, Collins approached, ready to take the folding chairs and return them to the phaeton. "Sir O'Bannon will be accompanying us."

Towel over his shoulder, and bag in hand the grinning *Gaelic* star approached, a large dark wave of hair fallen across his brow. "Did you enjoy the match?" Collins took the bag from him and returned to the carriage.

Aunt Natty gayly teased, "You were all over the playing field. You must be the most important player. My goodness, how have they gotten along without you?"

Swiping the towel across his brow, he laughed. "Believe me, I'm fairly inconsequential. But thank you for the compliment. I hope I'm not imposing. But I would like to ride with you."

Brianna knew he referred to his playing clothes. She thought him rather dashing in his uniform. "Don't worry on our account. Remember, I've seen you disguised as a highway robber with soot all over your face and hands."

He laughed as he assisted Aunt Natty into her seat and turned to Miss Brianna when Lady Hamerlin yoo-hooed him as she rushed over.

"I wanted to remind you of our dinner party on Thursday. I

am concerned about your busy schedule." She brushed off something on his shoulder and he jerked back as if annoyed.

"Did I not reply?" His dark brows quizzed.

Brianna detected a note of discord and inwardly delighted in his reaction. *That should settle the score with the lady.* With the help of Collins, she stepped into the carriage and left Sir Fin to continue his exchange with Lady Hamerlin.

The woman laid her gloved hand on his vest and glanced upward through long black lashes. "Certainly, you did. But I am trusting you will change your mind."

With a hand on the door of the smart, yellow-wheeled phaeton, Sir Fin assured her, "Nothing has changed on my schedule. I continue to be unavailable."

Brianna could see the pout on her startled face, lashes fanning. Perversely, she enjoyed seeing the woman's discomfort at being turned down in front of others. Brianna tsked herself for such cogitation. Aunt Natty glared at her and shook her head, as if she read her mind.

Sir Finbarr jumped onto his seat, released the brake, snapped the reins, and they proceeded down the road. Brianna dared not indulge herself by glancing back at Lady Hamerlin.

Besides, she already felt like a winner, sitting beside Sir Fin in his cricket uniform. For shame, because it wasn't too terribly long ago, he irritated her.

A tangle of secrets and deceit

A note to be delivered to Miss Natty alerted Mim because she recognized the handwriting and quickly slipped it into the pocket of her apron.

The household turned a corner with Miss Natty's recovery. Mim had no intention of taking a chance that horrid woman sent this. She pegged it filled with rude and hateful words and dreaded hindering Miss Natty's progress with its contents.

All the years she worked for Miss Natty, she never took something that wasn't hers. Mim preferred to characterize keeping the letter from Miss Natty as protecting her.

Secretly, in her room, she tore open what she guessed to be an offensive note.

Natty, good news.

A raggedy man came into the pub last eve. Says he knows the family I'm looking for. It's been twenty-some years, but I believe he's the peddler. I'm desperate for rent money. It's due in November and it's almost October. I'll have nowhere to live.

My only recourse is to tell the Darnleys they have a

granddaughter. You must go with me. You have a relationship with them workin' in the kitchen, as you've always done. I want more money than the ragtag can give me. I want Darnley's money. Set myself up for life is what I want. This is all Niall's fault and yours too. D.

Mim near fainted and fanned herself with the fiendish note. What is *that* horrid woman up to?

Who is the granddaughter that would command such a sum as to keep Dervila in high style? Oh, my, Mim wondered if this is what caused Miss Natty to pass out on the lane and have high anxiety. She must have already discerned Dervila intended more chaos.

Mim frantically fanned herself. Indeed, it made sense now. Dervila must already realize who the granddaughter is, and most likely drew Miss Natty into the intrigue.

Poor Miss Natty. Will she ever be rid of Dervila? Mim fanned faster as heat rushed up her neck and cheeks.

Miss Natty may have lied out of necessity when she told Mim that Dervila apologized; what likely happened is Dervila hinted at getting money from the Darnleys and it sent Natty into a frenzy. Dear Mother of God, what a kettle of fish.

Forced to a decision, Mim fumbled through obvious choices. She could give the note to Miss Natty and have her end up in the infirmary again. Or she could visit Dervila herself.

Mim feared going to Brianna. Natty wanted to keep her ignorant of anything to do with her wicked cousin who was clearly deficit of even one Christian bone in her body.

Fanning herself with great speed, her heart fluttered, and the sound of buzzing bees filled her head. Suddenly, an idea groped its way through the tangle of her distress. Sir O'Bannon was honorable and a worldly man. Surely, he would give her advice in confidence. She kept fanning herself as she considered the possibility. He definitely was a man of integrity. And as an outsider in Hawthorn, he had no reason to be biased about any of the people involved in this mess.

Sitting at Miss Natty's desk, she uncorked the inkwell and noted her hand shaking, and decided sending him a note would not do. She must visit him in person.

With little time to waste, not knowing what Dervila would do, Mim snatched up her bonnet and shawl and strutted toward Cashel's Inn, the letter burning a hole in her satchel. She left word with Jane to keep an eye on Miss Natty because she needed to run to the market.

⚜

Mim asked the man at the desk where she might find Sir O'Bannon and then climbed the stairs to his accommodations and knocked on the door.

A slender man with clear eyes and pale skin that did not seem to match his superior demeanor greeted her. "If Sir O'Bannon is in, would you tell him that Mim, from Miss Walsh's household, needs to speak with him?"

"If you step inside, Miss Mim, I will see if he is receiving."

⚜

Sir Fin strode into the room, a smile stretched on his face that faded within seconds. "What's wrong?"

"Oh, sir. Plenty. I've come to you to help me sort it all out."

"Mim, this is my valet, Collins," as he added, "I think tea." Then he turned to her and said, "Come into the parlor and tell me what has happened to upset you."

As if she had been holding her breath, it gushed out as she sat. "I'm not quite sure how to begin." Her hands grasped her reticule as if she expected it to be torn from her. She was obviously a bundle of nerves.

Mim was as edgy as Miss Natty has been. It seemed

236

preposterous the Autumn Fair would cause such mayhem. He took the chair opposite and gave her his full attention. "Who does the matter concern?"

"Miss Natty Walsh and a cousin of Natty's, Dervila Murdock." Mim's eyes misted and her face heated. "Me, too, sir. But Miss Natty has kept Miss Brianna out of the mess."

She took the letter from her satchel and handed it to him.

As he held the letter, she added, "It was delivered this morning. And let me say, this woman is the reason Miss Natty ended up in the infirmary. She had visited Dervila earlier in the day to sort things." Mim pointed at the folded letter in his hand. "*That* woman is a wily drunken sort."

Tea was served and Sir Fin poured and handed her a cup. "Drink this and take a deep breath. We'll get to the bottom of whatever makes you distraught."

She began explaining, "I did an unforgivable thing opening Miss Natty's letter. It's that I could not take a chance if she became ill again." Tears began, and she swiped at her cheeks with a handkerchief.

He reached across and patted her arm. "Take your time, Mim. Every situation has a path to solution."

Grateful for his certainty, she peeked a small smile at him even though she saw no way out without a lot of damage and fretful upset for Miss Natty.

He unfolded the letter and read its contents without lifting a brow and took a moment when done, his gaze finding Mim's.

"Is Dervila suggesting she has proof of who is Lord Darnley's granddaughter? Because she is clearly suggesting blackmail."

"I don't know, sir. But I think Miss Natty might have proof."

"When did..." he glanced at the letter, "...Dervila begin her blackmailing?"

"Niall is her husband...was her husband. He died recently. Which is why Dervila needs money. As I recall Miss Natty telling me, there was an intrigue between the three of them many years ago when they were young. Oh, my, I'm telling you all kinds of private matters. And I think the world of Miss Natty."

He leaned forward. His elbows on his knees, hands clasped. "Mim, if you aren't comfortable with this, then stop. I do agree with your concern for Miss Natty's health. There must be another way to get at the issue without compromising yourself."

Silence filled the space. She paid attention to her hands, gnarled a bit with years of housework.

He sat back in his chair as Collins inquired if he could be on any use. Sir Finbarr shook his head and Collins left the parlor and closed the door behind him.

Then Sir Fin asked, "Does Miss Brianna share your feelings about Miss Natty's fears?"

"To my knowledge, Miss Brianna is unaware of anything to do with Dervila Murdock. All Miss Natty ever told her was they were cousins who hadn't seen each other in more than twenty years. The letter came this morning after Miss Brianna left for the post office."

Mim shook her head and muttered, "In for a penny, in for a pound."

He heard her mutter because he inquired, "I think the day you and I arrived at the infirmary, you already knew the stress she caused Miss Natty?"

"Yes, sir. The first time Dervila came to our door, Miss Natty asked me to stay in the corridor and come in if needed. I sensed Miss Natty had her hackles up even then." She shifted in the chair.

"The second time *that* woman came to the house, I could tell her presence meant bad news. Believe me, sir. Miss Natty had me keep guard in the corridor with my rolling pin and a heavy pot, ready to do her some mischief. But she stormed out in a rage, and I locked the door after her."

He said, "Did this intrusion come before or after the threat of blackmail?"

"Before. Dervila wanted Miss Natty to care for her sick

husband. But she refused. Dervila was mighty irritated too and put up a case for Miss Natty's duty to help with her sick husband."

He glanced at the offensive letter, then eyed Mim. "I think I'm missing a piece here. Why would Dervila think Miss Natty should care for her husband?"

Her large capable hands twisted in her lap. She appeared hesitant, but finally gave into the wisdom of revealing all. "Years ago, when they all lived in Tramore, Miss Natty and Niall were to marry. But Dervila put a stop to it by telling Niall she was expecting his child and Niall did the decent thing and broke it off with Miss Natty."

"Decent?" He grimaced. "The man committed an offense against his betrothed. To say nothing of her cousin betraying the trust they must have shared."

Mim nodded, agreeing fully. "I've more. After Dervila and Niall married, Dervila told him she lost the child. But they stayed married all the years since."

"Obviously, the child she carried wasn't Miss Brianna?"

"No, Heaven's no." She patted her upper lip with the napkin, then fanned herself.

After a moment of silence, Mim added, "I do believe Dervila must have told Miss Natty she planned to get satisfaction from Lord Darnley and that caused Miss Natty to end up in the infirmary. She is just now acting herself again, getting ready for the Fair. Eating again. I prayed all would right itself. I've been so worried about the dear woman."

She dabbed at her upper lip again.

He asked, "Why would Dervila seek satisfaction from the Darnelys?"

Mim features went blank. "I haven't the slightest thought."

"Perhaps Miss Natty knows?" He swiped his palms on his knees clearly needing more facts.

"I'm at my wits end. I am afraid to let her see this letter. I am afraid she will end up sicker than before. What if she dies?" Mim broke into tears and held the napkin against her eyes.

He leaned near, put a hand to her arm and waited for the emotional storm to abate. "We'll fix this, Mim."

She braved a fluttery smile and sipped her tea. "Am I a foolish old woman?"

"You are within your rights to think the worst of a woman such as she. Lying and evil intent, and who knows what else she's committed to. But I've a sense there's more to this that needs investigating. Dervila has either lost her mind, or she has a good reason for suggesting a granddaughter of the Darnley family even exists."

Mim gave a shuddering breath as she calmed. "I feel much better talking to you, sir."

"Extortion is a serious offense. I wonder if Dervila realizes who she is going to be dealing with? Most likely Lord Darnley's grandson-in-law. Jonathan, Lord Tremaine will step in."

"Do...do you think the family will be harsh with Miss Natty when they discover it's her cousin causing the blackmail?"

He passed the dish of scones to her. "The Darnley's and the Tremaine's are gracious and fair-minded. Hasn't Miss Natty been a part of their household for many years?"

Mim had bitten into her scone, obviously savoring the delicacy. She nodded in affirmation to his question.

"Well, then, I think you can rest assured she will be comforted by their judicious handling of this matter rather than castigate her."

Mim finished with the scone and dabbed at her mouth with the napkin. "Thank you for putting me at ease, sir. Do you think it best I just give the letter to Miss Natty and tell her what I've done?"

He said, "Realizing we are dealing with a devious and cunning woman engaged in criminal activity, and we now have her written statement that she is aware of a granddaughter of whom the Darnley's are unaware. Also, Dervila's mentioning it in this letter, implies that Miss Natty may already know the identity of the granddaughter."

Mim considered what he said.

He suggested, "I think it best Miss Natty be given the note. If you like, I could be with you at that time."

"Would it be possible for you to come with me now? Brianna planned to help Miss Knowles at school with the play after leaving the post office. Miss Natty wants to keep her out of this whole affair." Her glance left the platter of scones, and she looked up at him. "I think she's afraid Brianna might take matters into her own hands and threaten Dervila. I agree, Brianna is capable of doing so. She's a strong sense of family and loves her aunt."

He opened the door and called for his valet. Arriving within seconds, Sir Fin asked, "What is on the calendar for this afternoon?"

"Nothing of consequence, sir. The walls are being plastered at Ashcourt. You had mentioned riding out."

"Ah, I'll be escorting Miss Mim back home. You take the phaeton and tend to that yourself."

As they made their way toward the home on Stoney Batter, Mim began to regret her decision to open the letter.

Sir Finbarr did what he could to reassure her. "It will come to a head soon now. You did what you knew to be best. I sense all will right itself in the end." He reached in front of her and opened the front door on Stoney Batter.

As Mim entered, Miss Natty could be heard. "Mim, is that you?"

"Yes, and Sir O'Bannon also."

He placed his hat on the hook in the corridor and entered the parlor. "It's nice to see you looking rested, Miss Natty."

"It's always a pleasant surprise to see you, Sir Fin. Sit, please and Mim will make us tea." She set her knitting aside and shooed Pussycat off her lap.

"No tea. Thank you. Mim and I are here to discuss a delicate situation."

Mim had stayed in the corridor hanging her hat and shawl. She entered the parlor asking Miss Natty, "When did you return?"

"Not long ago. The committee has decided on the prizes for the drawings. Brianna's paintings are to be the first and second prizes for two drawings."

"Which ones?" he questioned.

"The landscape behind Ashcourt." Miss Natty nodded to him. "And the quay with several boats. You remember the ship with the unicorn. That one."

He smiled. "I must be sure to purchase a number of the tickets in hopes I win the landscape."

⚜

The room grew silent. Miss Natty looked from one to the other. A skittish nerve ran up her arms. "What situation did you refer to?" A frown puckered her brow.

Mim quickly glanced at Sir O'Bannon as he took a chair.

He offered, "I am lending moral support to Mim."

Her pale blue eyes swept to Mim. "Why do you need moral support?"

Mim stepped from one foot to the other, her nerves obviously getting the better of her. "Because I've done something I ought not to have."

Miss Natty's eyebrows lifted. "What, pray tell?"

She pulled the letter from her pocket and handed it to Miss Natty.

"It's addressed to me. I see it's been opened."

Mim confessed, "I've been worried and afraid for you. I recognized the handwriting and knew it would have bad news."

"And does it?"

Sir Finbarr warned, "We think it untoward at the least."

Miss Natty unfolded the letter and read it. You could hear a pin drop. Done reading, she left it open on her lap and sighed deeply, then glanced at them.

He noted more of a resignation from Miss Natty, than anxiety. Which told him she is not surprised of its contents. Further suggesting it was this matter that sent her to the infirmary.

Finally, she said, "After what I have put you through, dear Mim, I forgive you for opening this. I know you did it out of concern for me."

Her weary gaze shifted to Sir Finbarr. "What is it you think?"

"Blackmail is a punishable crime."

Mim slowly sat in a chair as if she did not want to upset the universe.

Miss Natty harrumphed. "How can we stop this villain?" She shook the letter. "I've known her all my life and she is the same today as the hard-hearted lass of years ago."

He asked, "I'm puzzled why she is adamant she has information about a granddaughter of the Darnleys. And that she can sell her whereabouts to them."

Miss Natty twined her fingers and seemed to hold her breath for a long moment. "I'll try to keep it short, but it's a tangle of secrets and deceit. Dervila in her own words, cheated on her husband every time he left for the seas. She mostly met men in Maher's because it's where she worked back then and lived above the pub.

"According to her, Viscount Rutledge, about seventeen years at the time, and living at Rockmore Hall with his grandparents when not at school, was in a bad way at Madame Fornia's."

His lips thinned out. He had been familiar with Madame Fornia's opium den from conversation he overheard between Diarmuid and his mother many years ago. He had also heard wisps of gossip about the trouble Lord Darnley had with his grandson.

Miss Natty continued with her account. "Dervila and Madame Fornia were friendly, and Madame was exceedingly concerned about Viscount Rutledge's obsessions and mad paranoia. Though he apparently was in a room on the third floor in the back, his screams and images of frightful things carried through the drafty walls and down the corridors. She was afraid he would die in her establishment. And more than anything, she feared the wrath of the Darnley family. She begged Dervila to help her with the Viscount.

"Seeing as how Niall had sailed to China at that time, he would never be aware she harbored a young aristocrat in her room.

Natty tapped her chin in thought, then added, "That's how Viscount Rutledge ended up above Maher's pub with Dervila who eventually found herself in the family way. Dervila did help him with his addiction. All of this took place over a period of six months or so. The Viscount finally cleared his head of opium and began to think of a future and declared to Dervila that he would finish up at Eton and go on to university, as his grandsire had always wished. He appeared to have firmed up his resolve to be a better person.

"Mind, everyone at Rockmore worried about where he'd gone the night his grandsire banned him from the Hall the previous summer. The kitchen feared the worst, a huge ta-do as I recall. The servants were frightened of what he might be capable of. No one at Rockmore ever found out where he was all those months. Not a trace. However, the following February, a sea captain arrived at Rockmore with the horrendous news Rutledge had fallen overboard in a storm on his return to Eton."

She took a breath and continued, "I clearly recall young Viscount Rutledge about the Hall. Surly with the maids and on occasion, you could hear him yelling at his grandsire, Lord Darnley.

"Everyone at the Hall worried Lord Darnley would suffer another stroke. His lordship's first stroke already blamed squarely on Viscount Rutledge's behavior. The family feared he might have another. It's all they talked about in the kitchen when the butler wasn't around."

She turned a small smile on them. "If Witham heard them

tattling about any one of the Darnleys, they would be sacked on the spot."

Sir Finbarr brushed his fingers across his forehead as if remembering something. "Nuala informed me of the sad end of her son. I'm sure you knew his father had also drowned. The family has certainly suffered over the years."

He paused a moment before asking, "I'm sure you know Nuala and I are cousins? Our mothers were sisters."

Miss Natty nodded. "Nuala has been a source of calm to them through the years. The Darnleys had already been through so much. I fear that now it will all be dug up again with Dervila's determination to get money for information about a granddaughter they are unaware they have. Though born on the wrong side of the sheets, I am fairly certain they would want to know she exists."

Rubbing his furrowed brow again, he challenged, "They haven't any knowledge of Dervila. Furthermore, why would they take her word about a granddaughter when Dervila is a woman of nefarious reputation."

Miss Natty's brows puckered. Her mouth opened but no words came out and she quickly pursed her lips.

The parlor grew quiet. Natty could tell Sir Finbarr tried to make sense of it all. He shifted in his chair and dropped his hands on his knees.

Then he speculated, "Unless...unless you know who the granddaughter is and Dervila is unaware that you do. Which would explain why she is so free with her decisions because she doesn't realize you actually could inform the Darnleys about her scheme."

Miss Natty raised her eyes and looked at him. His heart seemed to hang on his sleeve as if he knew the burden she was under, the fear she lived with.

He said, "No wonder you fainted in the street. You'd just come from Dervila's apartment carrying the heaviest burden ever to be put on you."

Miss Natty was speechless, as was Mim. Both women looked at him.

He said, "We're talking about Brianna, aren't we?"

Miss Natty's eyes filled with tears as she tried to catch her breath.

Sir Finbarr quickly knelt in front of her and held on to her shoulders. "Take a deep breath, nice and easy, Miss Natty. We'll get through this. Trust me, everything is going to be all right." He stayed by her until she quieted and calmed. He drew back on his haunches, and Mim handed her a handkerchief.

Miss Natty put her palm on his cheek. "Dear lad, I suddenly realize why you are in my life. I will thank God for you till the day I die."

He returned to his chair. "I expect that to be years and years of prayer then."

Mim handed her a glass of water and sat down.

A quiet settled over the parlor until Miss Natty got herself together.

Sir Fin asked, "Brianna isn't aware of her parentage, is she?"

Mim lifted her gaze to him, the most pathetic look on her face, and slowly shook her head. "How does one tell her? You've seen her. She's content, happy. She enjoys a full life. She believes her family lives in a peddler's wagon and moves about Ireland at will."

Miss Natty fanned herself with the formidable letter that held the power to change how Brianna felt about herself should its contents come to light. Not only was her father from a highly regarded noble family, but, paradoxically, her mother lived among the dregs of mankind.

Sir Finn squared his shoulders and frowned.

Natty could almost read his mind. He was thinking about Brianna and this curse of an undeserving twist of fate.

The front door opened and Natty sighed, Mim cupped her mouth, and Sir Fin stood to greet Miss Brianna.

Heart-rending truth

"I'm home." Brianna called out as she hung her bonnet on a hook and stepped into the parlor. Sir Finbarr, Mim, and Aunt Natty, all with dour, humorless faces, eyed her with a melancholy stare.

Aunt Natty spoke up. "How is the play coming?"

Brianna's eyes widened and in a breathy voice said, "I think it's going to be grand. If…and I say this with caution…the students learn their lines." She giggled. "I'll never understand why anyone would agree to be in theater and not think they must learn lines. It's like pulling teeth."

"Ouch," Sir Fin grimaced as he turned his back to the bay windows.

She cast him a fond glance. "How is Ashcourt coming along? I'm surprised you aren't there already. Weren't the walls being plastered today?"

Mim asked, "Should I make tea?" A chorus of yeses and she bustled out of the room.

Sir Fin said, "Collins is holding forth."

"He's a wonder. Saves you some time." She reclined on the settee.

Sir Fin nodded in agreement. Her lovely hand with slender fingers spread out on the cushion. He wanted to take it up and hold it in his own and feel its silky smoothness. She was in for the shock of her life. Strong as she appears, this was beyond just a shock.

Brianna asked, "Something's astir. Are you going to enlighten me, or do I have to wait for the sky to open?"

Mim returned with a tray of sweets, no doubt waiting for the pot to boil, but not wanting to miss anything.

Brianna glanced at each of them. "I'm sensing a distinctly formidable conspiracy thick enough to cut."

Mim sank into a chair.

Sir Finbarr waited for Miss Natty to say something.

Aunt Natty lowered her head, spreading her palm over the letter in her lap.

He saw Brianna taking note of them all as she asked, "Do we have bad news in that letter on your lap?"

Silence ended with the teakettle whistle and Mim almost sprang from the room. "I'll be right back."

Sir Fin said, "If you will excuse me, Miss Natty. Miss Brianna. I think I should ride out to Ashcourt and check the progress myself. Collins is certainly capable. But sometimes I rely on him too much."

Aunt Natty's eyes widened.

"Give my excuses to Mim." He nodded to Brianna and left.

Sir Fin could tell Miss Natty wanted to say *no, do not leave.* However, he felt this family matter did not warrant his intrusion. Brianna would be faced with a difficult truth soon enough. He didn't want to add to the challenges she was about to face.

Upon arriving at Ashcourt Manor, he discovered Collins

already gone. He turned his attention to three crewmen plastering the walls in the foyer. A strong scent of ammonium carbonate would decompose into the air as the walls dried and explained why the doors and windows were open. He gingerly made his way past the scaffolding as the artisan troweled the ceiling.

Another craftsman cut strips of wire mesh, while another worker scooted up the ladder to embed it in the wet plaster in the ceiling. He knew enough to understand the process of building a rosette in the center where a crystal chandelier would hang.

A horizontal band wrapped around the perimeter of the ceiling with a canopy of embellishment that would pull it all together. Then he would follow it up with a brown coat of primer. After which he would set the tracks with the molding to follow.

The walls were out of line in two different places, and he knew Abernathy had his work cut out for him. Beginning to appreciate the transformation, not only in this old home, but in himself, a sense of pride washed over him.

Brianna weighed heavily on his heart. She was at this moment learning of her parentage. He was not cowardly. Leaving as he did, he intended to spare her embarrassment. She is a strong-minded woman, but he also considered this revelation a delicate situation.

He hoped to be by her side and pick up the pieces if she will allow. Right now, all he could do is think of her utterly and completely unnerved and thunderstruck.

Sir Fin buried his cogitations and went in search of Abernathy. He made his way into the kitchen area hearing sounds of industry. "Is Abernathy around today?"

Several of the crew turned to him, one with a red bandanna wrapped around his head answered. "Yes, sir. Ye'll find him in the stable."

Sir Fin found the architect wearing a helmet and clutching a floor plan, looking every inch in charge. "Good day to you, sir. Have you seen the foyer and staircase?"

"Exceedingly impressive. You don't think the molding is too…"

"Georgian in style?"

"Well, yes, though I find I like it."

Abernathy's large hands clutched the plans to his chest, as if he not risk misplacing them. "I've redone a number of residences and must say, your entrance is my ideal."

Hands on his waist as he glanced upward at the crossbars in the roofing, Sir Fin said, "I'm pleased to hear you say that." He stood in the center of the stable, glancing at the row of stalls. "You've made quite a change in here." He stood outside the first stall. The name Jupiter carved into a plaque attached to the lintel above the door.

"A nice touch, thank you."

Abernathy said, "Your welcome, sir. Finding the old plans for the original stables certainly helped with this reconstruction." He pointed to the massive doors leading outside. "When building a new stable, it's important that the horse isn't subject to sudden temperature changes. As you can see, this stable, though first built in the mid-1600s, had been structured with that in mind. Facing south is always best if possible."

He drew Sir Finbarr's attention to the stalls. "A good stall should be ten by twelve feet, so the horse has a reasonable space to move about."

He asked, "Would a copula on the roof increase air flow?"

"Already in the works, sir. We will hoist it up by week's end. Can I show you anything in particular?"

"The stablemaster's quarters."

"Right this way. We also added a bunk area for the extra help, and a water closet between the two rooms."

They walked the few yards to the end and Sir Fin, catching a glimpse of the tack room, veered in. He knew in an instant Colby would feel right at home. He glanced across the large aisle to a closed door. "That must be the stablemaster's quarters?"

"Yes. And the other door has four built-in bunks. The water

closet separates both rooms. I think I saw your vision accurately."
Abernathy set the floor plan on a stack of boxes and gave him a
minute or two to look over the efficient space.

He stepped into Colby's new habitat. The size plenty adequate
for his needs. A bed in the corner, and against the opposite wall, a
sink and countertop with built-in drawers and shelves. A window
overlooked the pastureland where the horses would exercise, and
a stove for warmth when needed. He opened the door to the water
closet and an adjoining door, noting the four bunks and a stove.

Returning to the aisle, he inquired, "When do you think the
work will be done?"

"If all goes as planned, the stable should be finished within
the month. The manor will take us two or more months as the
kitchen isn't near ready."

"The stablemaster will take up residence by next week." He
glanced about the area. "He shouldn't be in your way."

Abernathy's expression turned to a nod. "It won't make a
difference a'tall we'll be done with a few odds and ends and put
the crew entirely on the manor."

They shook hands, and Sir Finbarr left him to his business.

☙❧

An hour later, Sir Fin entered his suite of rooms. Collins met him
in the foyer, taking his hat and gloves. "Come to my office."

Collins followed his employer and waited as Sir Finbarr rifled
through several letters that were delivered. None of them
appeared to be important enough for him to read at the moment.

"Make yourself comfortable. This will take a minute or two. I
have a couple of things on my mind."

Collins sat back straight, ever the gentleman. Sir Fin
considered his valet a bit too rigid at times. However, it
characterized his diligence in keeping his affairs in order.

"I've two situations. Both are delicate but one in particular
involves a woman, Dervila Murdock, recently widowed and a

cousin of Miss Natty Walsh. This unscrupulous woman is planning to blackmail Lord Darnley for money by tempting him with information regarding a young woman he doesn't realize is his granddaughter."

Collins didn't bat an eye. "What is it you wish me to do, sir."

"I need you to represent yourself as a lawyer, briefcase and all, and visit Mrs. Murdock and threaten the living damnation out of her. Tell her you will expose her to the authorities with her attempt to blackmail the Darnleys."

"What if Mrs. Murdock refuses?"

"She's a spiteful and treacherous woman. All she really wants is the money. Since her husband died, she has no income, and the rent is due in another month. I believe her only other source of income is bar tending, at Maher's."

"What about the granddaughter?"

Sir Fin toyed with a paperweight on his desktop. "She doesn't have an inkling about this as yet. But I believe she will be mortified when she learns of the circumstance."

A moment of silence and Collins nodded in agreement. "Anything else, sir?"

"My stipulations are to offer to pay her rent for six months and a monthly stipend to keep her mouth shut. Renewable every six months upon her continued silence. She is never to set foot anywhere near Miss Natty, or Miss Brianna Walsh.

"She is to write a letter to Miss Natty Walsh assuring her she has decided not to contact the Darnleys. Also, you are to make clear to her, she is not to ever discuss these arrangements with anyone.

"If she does not abide by these restrictions, you will see to it she ends up in the Gaol for extortion and never receive another farthing from you. Put together a legal looking document and have her sign that she agrees to these stipulations. And keep my name out of this transaction."

Collins's stiff upper lip spread into a devilish smile. "This might be a bit of fun pretending to be a lawyer. Perchance I've missed my true calling."

"I've another matter that needs your delicate touch. Colby used to be the stablemaster at Ashcourt when I was a lad. Now, he is an elder who literally saved my life back then. I have hired him to run our stables at Ashcourt once again. But his eyes are bad. I want you to make an appointment with an eye doctor in Waterford and take him for a diagnosis."

"I will see to it, sir. But won't he think it odd that you aren't taking him?"

"Not that rascal. You can tell him it would mean a lot to me if he had the examination. He might refuse to go, but you'll work your efficient charm and make it happen." He stood.

Collins quickly followed suit. "I'll do my best, sir. One question. Do you have an amount in mind for Mrs. Murdock?"

"She doesn't deserve generosity. It needs to be a sum that will keep her from further ideas of blackmail. When you see how she lives, you'll have a good number in mind, I've no doubt."

"Yes, sir." Collins left the door open when he exited the den.

Sir Finbarr heard his valet readying himself to leave. A treasure, he never quibbles a point and is supplied with an abundance of common sense. Both attributes are built into the same human. Why cannot everyone be of similar conduct.

৩❀৩

Brianna accepted a cup of tea from Mim and asked, "Did it seem that Sir Finbarr rushed off?"

Mim glanced at Aunt Natty, who fidgeted. Her gaze swept to Brianna.

She asked, "Are you all right, auntie? Your color is ashen."

Aunt Natty took a breath and set her cup down. The opened letter in her lap caused Brianna to wonder if it could be at the root of her odd behavior.

"You must tell me what is going on. The three of you were

whispering when I came in. Sir Fin is gone, and I continue to sense mystery."

"Well, put that way, I warrant it's time to enlighten you to certain facts about your parentage."

"You've learned about my parents?" She set her cup on the tray, then noticed both women appeared to have withered in their chairs.

Aunt Natty's voice wavered. "The first I heard is the day I fainted."

Brianna moved and knelt at her aunt's feet, taking hold of her hands. "Is it that we have a name for the peddler, then?"

Aunt Natty glanced at Mim, and Brianna followed the look. Both of them knew the truth, and she puzzled at their reluctance.

"It's something else? I'm a grown woman. You've raised me well, auntie, and you, too Mim." Brianna squeezed her aunt's hands and returned to her chair.

Mim hesitated a moment, drew a breath and said, "Let her read the letter."

Aunt Natty's hands sprang off the vial paper as if she had forgotten it laid in her lap. "Do you remember me telling you about my cousin, Dervila Murdock?"

"Her husband passed a little over a week ago. You attended his burial?"

"Yes. Well, she's written…" The letter crinkled with the shaking of Aunt Natty's hand. "…she's written this."

As Brianna reached for it, her own hand trembled, her eyes drawn to the scratchy writing. Why would this woman know anything about her parents?

The room was deadly silent as she finished and glanced at her aunt.

"I don't understand. Who is the granddau—" She stopped in mid-sentence, a shocking assumption beginning to penetrate —"Are you saying *I* am the Darnleys granddaughter?"

Her aunt's face paled, as if she saw a banshee. "Dervila is your mother."

Brianna gasped.

Mim's eyes teared up.

Aunt Natty's face paled more so.

Brianna squeaked, "Your cousin? Whom you despise?"

Aunt Natty's hand pressed against her forehead. "Your father is the late Viscount Rutledge, the Darnleys grandson."

Stunned, Brianna lost her voice.

Two more disparate people she could not imagine. And they parented her? She could make no sense of it. The peddler wasn't her father? She didn't have five siblings.

She reread the letter. "Dervila is asking Lord Darnley for money to pay her rent?" Her breath caught in a freakish nightmare of disbelief.

The room fell to silence again. Pussycat no longer purred.

Aunt Natty's voice wavered with concern for this beloved young lady. "She intends to blackmail the Darnleys about who and where you are. Her problem is she needs to find you first. Which is why she is going to send out a word amongst the walkers to keep an eye out for a family who lives in a blue peddler's wagon."

"I am twenty-three years old. Why now? Why not when I was a babe?"

Aunt Natty said, "It didn't suit her lifestyle at the time. And she didn't need an income back then."

Brianna's ire rose with the stupor beginning to vanish. "She has nerve implicating me in a scheme against the Darnleys. How dare she!"

"Bear in mind she hasn't an idea where you live, or who you are."

Again, Mim and Aunt Natty exchanged glances. "Listen to me, all of this is lost in the real facts. The day after the funeral, I dropped in on Dervila to see how she fared. Almost incoherent she looked like a puddle of naked skin on her bed. I think she had been using a potion to calm her grief.

"That's when she told me about Rutledge. He stayed with her, a woman of tarnished reputation, much like himself. He had been banned from Rockmore Hall by his grandsire, who was fed up with his antics and ordered him to leave. When Rutledge left, he stayed with that wicked Madam Fornia and her opium den.

"In time the Madam had her fill and called Dervila to come get him. And under Dervila's care, he eventually recovered from his addictions. Realizing how bad his behavior had been toward his grandsire, Rutledge apparently vowed to make amends and return to Eton to finish school. On his way to England, he drowned in a storm that February as he crossed St. George's Channel. Six months had passed since his banishment from Rockmore Hall. I remember the whole of it all, as I worked up at the Hall frequently.

"Dervila knew she expected a child when he left. Her husband had taken on a year's voyage to China, and she birthed you and gave you to the peddler, paying him to take you before her husband returned. I'm thinking this certainly wasn't the first time she broke her vows to him.

"And strolling through the woods toward home in the lovely warm day, I came upon a family I thought in great need."

Brianna's chin dropped to her chest her palms cupping her cheeks then she slowly wrapped her arms about herself as the truth seeped into her, taking root in her soul.

"Oh, my precious colleen. You are beloved. Do not mistake your beginnings with what and who you are today."

Mim squeaked out, "You were a bright shining light for both of us."

Brianna's head still bowed, her words whispery. "Do you believe Dervila's story?"

"Unfortunately, I do. She is who she is, but it all fits with what I recall from years ago. Being privy to what happened with Viscount Rutledge up at the Hall and the entire house in grave upset over his behavior fits with what Dervila had to say. And her blackmailing the Darnleys is just like her."

A long silence ensued as Brianna slowly allowed these few

minutes to sink in. She lived her life thinking that somewhere in Ireland she had five older siblings, a mother and father.

Not anymore.

In reality, her parents weren't married, one of them was deceased, and the hope she had siblings dashed.

She felt sorry for Aunt Natty, who forced a watery smile. Mim silent, her knobby hands wrestling with each other in her lap. A bitter anger like bile crawled up her throat. How dare that woman bring such torment into their lives.

Brianna's body tensed and she could feel the pounding of her heart. One thing she knew, she would never be able to resolve her parentage.

Taking a deep breath, she forced a smile. "If Dervila is my mother, then you and I *really* are related."

In the moment of suspended angst, both Aunt Natty and Mim released their pent-up tension. Aunt Natty said, "Leave it to you to find a silver lining, sweet."

Silence fell over the parlor as each retreated into their thoughts. Astounded with the discovery of her parents, she realized it mattered little in the life she led. And then she gasped.

"Are you certain Dervila doesn't have knowledge of me?"

Aunt Natty's attention turned on her as she blinked her eyes. "No. How would she unless I told her, and I haven't."

"If it's up to me, I'd rather she wasn't told." An awkward sense of revulsion crept over her.

Mim cried out, "If she gets to Lord Darnley, he'll surely investigate."

Aunt Natty spoke up. "All of that will take time. Dervila has to find the peddler before she can learn anything about her daughter's whereabouts. And the peddler might lie, else he would fear she'd want her money back."

Brianna said, "That gives me time to think this through."

Mim nodded. "Thank heavens for time."

Brianna asked, "I'm assuming Sir Finbarr is aware of all that has transpired?"

Both mobcaps nodded.

"He left shortly after I arrived. It's unlike him to bolt in times of trouble."

Aunt Natty implored. "He knew what you were going to discover. I believe he felt it best if you were told without his intrusion."

Brianna declared, "I'll think better of him then. He is thoughtful in that respect. Worried I'd feel awkward is just like him."

They were quiet another moment, absorbing the issue of Dervila when Brianna said, "I don't want our lives to change. I love you both and we are family and that is that."

Yet, she felt off balance, wobbly inside, and a false sense of holding the moment together did not help. If she had to pinpoint a time when her life seemed normal, she regarded the time just before she left the Reynolds family in Dundalk.

Since then, her life seemed in a state of confusion. Befuddled disorder, like a chicken coop after the fox's visit.

☙❧

Collins entered the apartment and, noting Sir Finbarr's hat on the shelf, went in search of him.

He stood in front of the grate, fixed on the flames as they sparkled and spit.

"Can I get you anything, sir?"

"I assume you've been out taking care of Mrs. Murdock and maybe found time to see to Colby."

"Both, sir. The bank is readying the papers for Mrs. Murdock to sign. She is most eager to take advantage of *someone's* largesse. She didn't even ask after the name of her benefactor. I am to return to the bank tomorrow and then deliver the papers to the woman along with an amount that will be forthcoming each month until she breaks the contract."

"Did she try to wiggle you for more money?"

"Strangely, no. I had expected she might. However, she did mention she might move and how could she reach me to give me her new address. She has the name of the vice-president of the Bank of Waterford. He will get in touch with me if a problem occurs. I had anticipated this and had already talked to Mr. Stricker regarding the possibility."

"Well, glad that's taken care of. What of Colby?" He stretched his long legs out in front of him, enjoying the heat from the grate. It turned out to be a damp rainy evening, rather gloomy outside.

"Colby saw the doctor you suggested in Waterford. A most interesting man, I might add. It seems your new stablemaster has a slow form of degeneration of the eye. In fact, it may be the worst it will ever be right now. Mr. Fisher also suggested a salt and water rinse each day and demonstrated for Colby how to do it. The doctor fitted him for optics that should increase his sight."

"How did Colby take the news?"

"He whistles. He whistled all the way from Waterford. I think every single tune that has ever been composed, he whistled."

Sir Fin chuckled. "Good work. Thank you for seeing to both."

"I ordered dinner to be brought up, giving you a night off the dining room. Unless you would like me to tell the kitchen you'll dine downstairs?"

"I am a bit weary. I'll dine up here."

Collins left, and Sir Fin eased back in the comfortable chair and mused about the last two days. Beginning with leaving Natty and Mim to handle the sorry news of Brianna's background.

Brianna didn't need him to hear what Miss Natty and Mim had to say to her. He wished to spare her dignity. If she wanted to talk to him about Dervila, she would have to begin the conversation.

Grateful Colby's eyesight was not as bad as he had considered, Sir Fin intended Colby live out his years doing the one thing he always loved, tending horses.

Taking matters into her own hands

As the *Gaelics* waited for Manager Fergus to arrive and begin their match, several players shared remarks with Sir Finbarr regarding the *Waterford Vikings*.

"You must be new to Hawthorn? By the by, my name is Keith, me chums are Damon, and Mike."

He extended his hand to each. "Finbarr's the name." He did not wait for a response as he mentioned to Keith, "You had several spectacular shots in the match against the *Irishmen*."

As they shook hands, Keith responded, "We can always use strong batters. Especially playing the *Vikings*. You'll want to watch out for the red-haired bowler they use. He's a cussed fellow."

Mike, skeptically humorous, said, "He's known for his runs."

Manager Fergus approached the group. "Nothing better to do, eh? Gabbing like a gaggle of lassies. You should be warming up."

The rest of the morning, the team strengthened their strategy in preparation for the First of October's match against their dreaded rival.

Brianna slipped out of the house after announcing the need for a new brush and some paints. She was not proud of lying, particularly to Aunt Natty and Mim, but considering her mission, she could not tell the truth.

She arrived at her destination after a brisk tramp along the quay. Rapping on the door of the flat above Maher's Pub she heard shuffling and a curse, then padding of steps.

"Josh, is that you?" A voice from within, as if waking from a deep sleep.

Brianna answered, "No." And heard a grunt and movements about the bed and then footsteps on the floor.

The door unlatched and a woman about the same height as Brianna stood in the open space. The black hair that framed her face was slashed with a streak of gray above the right forehead. Heavily lashed brown eyes squinted in question. Her work-worn hands and long thin fingers grasped the door frame as if ready to slam the door in her face.

Wrapped in a colorful silk robe that floated about her, she struck Brianna as being of Italian descent. And absolutely nothing like what she expected. Which made her think she had knocked on the wrong door.

"What do you want?"

Flustered, Brianna stepped back and looked down the short corridor. There were no other doors. She stepped up to the slightly ajar door and said, "Are you Dervila Murdock?"

The woman's eyes narrowed. "Who's asking?"

"I believe you've been looking for me."

Her eyes widened with skepticism.

Brianna hardened her chin. "Think back twenty-three years ago to an infant you gave to a peddler."

Her cold eyes swept the length of her. "*You,*" she almost spat.

She opened the door enough for Brianna to step inside, then closed it and tightly knotted the sash on her robe.

Brianna got right to the point. "I heard you were looking for a peddler in a blue wagon with flowers painted on the side. You paid him a goodly sum years ago to take an infant off your hands. Did you not?"

Her lips parted in surprise. "Sit. I can't talk with you towering over me?"

"I prefer not to sit." She wrapped her hands about her reticule.

"Was it the peddler sent you here?" She adjusted the sagging upper part of her robe.

Avoiding the question, Brianna challenged, "I'm curious after all this time why you would want to contact me?"

"Scrappy, aren't you? Well, let's say it involves a business transaction."

"Is that what you call blackmail, a business transaction?"

"I've got needs. A dead husband can't pay the bills, now, can he?" Her throaty laugh stung. "You're not made of milk and water I'll give you that."

Having read Dervila's letter, and the subsequent story of what really transpired between the two who sired her, Brianna presumed she would be prepared to meet this hardened woman. But she wasn't. Dervila was a viper with a sting.

Through the years, the most she hoped for was that fate might allow her to meet a brother or a sister. This cold-blooded woman was like none other she had ever met. It sunk in her heart she shouldn't have come here. This woman wasn't worth any effort.

Aunt Natty had said this woman was hard, lacking empathy and civility unless she wants something. Brianna felt her chilling dark eyes as they raked a daughter she gave away.

Brianna was struck at meeting a woman like none other she had ever met. She took a moment to assess the dingy room circling back to Dervila, who was striking in a wild, earthy way surrounded by the scent of mold and dirt and the salt breeze blowing in off the lough. Brianna had no words to describe her. Perhaps *bawdy,* but she was not sure it was the right adjective.

Dervila challenged in her throaty voice, "Where did you get the notion, I'm paying for information about you?"

Ignoring her question, Brianna said, "I came here to make it clear I will alert the authorities if you attempt to blackmail the Darnley family." She whisked off imaginary dirt on her skirts.

The woman's thin gnarled fingers slid to her exposed skin above the loose robe. "Don't you threaten me. You owe me something. There are other ways to rid oneself of a child, you ken?"

Brianna looked her in the eye. She felt proud of herself for not falling apart. There was no emotional attachment a'tall. Lord and Lady Darnley, to whom she felt protective, were the reason she was here.

"Hadn't thought of that, huh? Banging on my door with all your fury at being tossed aside." Dervila appeared nervous, fingernails scratching at the skin on her upper chest. Her dark eyes darting about.

Black kohl ringed her lower lids. For whatever reason Brianna recalled the day Sir Finbarr stuck his face up the fireplace and loosened soot.

Strangely, the image calmed her. She had a confident and caring friend in him. She bent over, slapping her palms on the table, and with as vicious a voice as she could manage, said, "You keep your distance from the Darnleys, or you will live to regret your actions."

She stepped to the door and unlatched it. "Mark my warning."

Dervila jeered, "You look like him. Same eyes and forehead. Pity, too, if you're marked for tragedy like him."

Brianna closed the door on Dervila's guttural laugh. She leaned against the wall and tried to calm herself. Her mouth felt dry. Her stomach tightened as she tried to diffuse the shock of meeting her...mother.

Being told she resembled her father was overwhelming. It was the only pinch of light to come from this whole gruesome affair. Out on the lane, she breathed fresh air, loosening the fear in her stomach and without a backward glance strode toward the post office. She glanced at her watch—exactly seven minutes until Mrs. Teaberry opened to the public.

The piteous filthy one room where Dervila lived was shocking. Brianna had not known what to expect. But certainly, some sense of cleanliness. She prayed Aunt Natty would never get wind of this encounter.

She reminded herself the woman hadn't a clue where she lives. And it suddenly dawned on her, Dervila hadn't even asked her name.

Brianna found it unbelievable that she had just been with her mother. She needed the day ahead to be filled with normalcy and trembled to think a decision made so many years ago could shake her to the core. She would pray that Dervila never found out Aunt Natty raised her. God alone knows what she might be capable of. And then, perhaps she wouldn't care a'tall. That would be best for everyone.

Arriving at work, Brianna quickly hung her bonnet on a peg and donned an apron and sleeves with a few minutes to spare and followed the sound of chatter from the kitchen.

Mrs. Teaberry was in mid-sentence when she entered.

"Sorry for interrupting," Brianna sheepishly glanced at everyone.

Mrs. Teaberry did not skip a beat. "The Postmaster General at Westminster has written. The Earl of Lichfield, Thomas Anson, will be paying us a visit." She folded her arms and looked over the top of her spectacles.

Lionel asked, "When they raised the flat postage last January and the Uniform Penny Post started with prepaid letters, weren't we to receive a raise? Maybe he will tell us?"

"When the flat rate of postage came into effect," caviled Mrs. Teaberry using her superior demeanor, "It was not intended to increase your wages. The penny post costs the Postmaster General. It was more likely so clerks would not have to handle money."

Lionel was about to object when Mrs. Teaberry raised her hand, shushing him. "Within the next few months, I expect we will be receiving The Penny Black stamp with the image of our young Queen. You mark my word; this stamp will be remembered as the first of its kind."

She slapped her hands. "Time to work. Shoo to your stations please."

Brianna used her few free minutes mid-morning to request a moment with Mrs. Teaberry. She was at her kitchen table, working on her ledger. "Yes, Miss Walsh, speak quickly you've only a few minutes and I'm rather busy."

"Right." She kept her hands at her side. "I want to register my feelings about the way Miss Simpson was let go over an incident that I see as her poor judgement, not a criminal act."

Mrs. Teaberry set her pen aside and sat back in her chair. "I'm listening."

"She was teaching her father to read. I see that as helping someone better themselves. And she fully intended to return the paper, which she did the very next day. Her intention was not to thieve but to assist her father with the gift of reading so he might better himself."

Mrs. Teaberry wagged her finger at Brianne. "She used poor judgement. We agree on that count."

"Yes, ma'am. But she's a hard worker and respects everything you've done to make this post office efficient and well organized. She mentioned a week ago how easy it is to learn when the postmistress keeps us all on our toes."

Mrs. Teaberry's brows slightly rose.

Brianna added, "If she is to go to prison for theft, that will make two people who will never rise above the squalor of a life without work."

"Your time is up, Miss Walsh. From this moment on, you may keep your opinions to yourself."

Brianna gave a nod and exited the kitchen, her face burning with frustration.

Four busy hours later, Lionel insisted on seeing Brianna home during his lunch hour. It was a cool September day. Geese honked their way through the gathering clouds above River Suir.

He groused as they strolled along Sister's Lane. "I looked forward to that raise. Mrs. Teaberry is disappointing when she says a penny a post won't see its way to my pocket." Lionel settled his cap more firmly on his head as a wind came up.

Brianna teased, "Whatever do you need more money for. A bachelor on his own should not have to worry about funds. You've no babes to feed."

"Mebbe that's to change soon." He shoved his hands into his pockets, casting her a side glance.

Of a sudden, Brianna had a freaky idea that agitated her. She quickly changed the subject. "My Aunt and Mim are knitting up a storm for the Fair. Do you enjoy such things?"

"Mebbe, we'll see when the time comes. I do like to watch the sheering contests." She cringed at his humorless comments and reminded herself he appeared an honest and good man. Though he'd wronged poor Miss Simpson. All Briana could do was keep her mouth shut and see if Mrs. Teaberry would rethink her actions.

They had reached her doorstep, and she thanked him for the company. He touched the brim of his hat and turned about, lumbering his way back to the post office.

Brianna hung her bonnet on the peg and peeked into the parlor. Aunt Natty was not in her chair. She meandered into the kitchen. Busy washing dishes, Jane looked up as she approached. "Do you know where I can find Aunt Natty?"

'She's in the kitchen garden snipping parsley."

Brianna moved along the corridor that housed two storage rooms and out the kitchen door that led to a patio area and the kitchen garden. Aunt Natty sat on a bench, her face raised to the sun's warmth.

"You've found yourself a patch of sunshine just like Pussycat."

Aunt Natty smiled, "How did your morning go?"

"I'd say one of my better beginnings."

A soft cooing turned Brianna's attention to the arbor where Aunt Natty sat. A pair of collared doves perched on a branch. They were almost hidden by a thick web of pink bougainvillea. That has to be an omen of good things to come.

"Have you been listening to them?"

Her aunt nodded. "It's a lovely sound."

Brianna snuggled closer to her aunt as they sat on the bench, noticing a handful of parsley in her clutch. "So, what have you been up to this morning?"

"I've grand news." Aunt Natty drew out a letter and handed it to her. "This should make a difference."

Brianna recognized the penmanship with its telltale scratchy lines. Dervila. She quickly scanned the message. Then glanced at her aunt and reread the two sentences. "I'm sorry to be such a pessimist. Can you believe this? What do you think?"

"Maybe she's seen the light."

Brianna huffed. "You think everyone has a loving heart because that's how you see the world. I don't share your opinion of that woman."

Aunt Natty patted her hand. "Oh, my dear, this business has hardened your heart. Dervila can only abuse you if you allow it."

Brianna reread the two lines. Dervila wrote that she would not inform the Darnleys that she had given birth to Rutledge's child. Simple and direct. Brianna had no reason to think this woman suddenly felt compassion for the upheaval she caused others.

"Who delivered the letter?"

"Her friend, Josh."

"Did he have anything to say?"

"Jane received it and by the time she gave it to me, he was gone." Aunt Natty squeezed Brianna's hand. "I've been waiting for the sky to fall and crush us all. Her letter lightened my fear. Blew it away."

Brianna mustered a sour glance at her aunt.

She would like to think her visit with Dervila this morning had scared the woman into doing the decent thing. Still and all, Sir Finbarr came to mind.

His care taking of Aunt Natty, and innate compassion, made it easy for her to envision him warning Dervila. The thought made so much sense to her she chewed her lip over the notion, and it was a moment before she realized her aunt was speaking to her.

"Bonnie and Muriel stopped by and picked up the booties. They seemed rather concerned about the stage act thinking Romeo and Juliet should be played as a comedy because the two principal players haven't an ounce of talent."

"I couldn't get any of the players to be serious enough to settled down. They are right to be concerned. Perchance the target audience should be children?" Brianna suggested.

Aunt Natty shrugged. "Poor Bonnie. It's her daughter playing Juliette."

A nipper approached through the side gate. "A maid at the front door told me to come around back. I'm to deliver this to a Miss Brianna Walsh and wait for an answer."

Brianna read the short note and informed her aunt Sir Finbarr invited them to ride out to Ashcourt and check on the work this afternoon.

Aunt Natty sighed. "You go, dear. I think I need a rest after all the intrigue about the Fair." She shook the letter in her lap. "And the mess to do with this woman. You can tell me about it when you return, and I have refreshed myself."

An hour later, Brianna and Sir Finbarr were on their way to the manor.

Being her forthright self, Brianna asked, "Did you warn Dervila not to approach the Darnley's?"

They were bumping over a rough patch of ground where sheep grazed, and he slowed the roan. "I wouldn't know her if I saw her."

Brianna looked at him from beneath the brim of her bonnet. Their eyes met as he maneuvered their transport.

He said, "What? You don't believe me?"

"It's not that. I met with her this morning."

He glanced at her again, his brow scrunched in disbelief. "You what?"

"I asked her why she looked for me. I touched a nerve. She immediately asked if the peddler had talked to me. I warned her I would make trouble for her if she so much as stepped near the Darnleys."

"I'm impressed. What was her reaction?" His arm brushed against hers as he maneuvered the lines.

His clean, soapy scent mingled with the fresh air and for a brief moment, she wanted to rest against him and feel his arm about her. She breathed in and said, "She called me a milk and water woman, a namby-pamby. I asked her why she would demand money from the Darnleys after all these years, when she freely sold her infant. She said it was a business matter."

Brianna's breath snagged, and she whispered, *a business matter* as if it just now sank into her heart.

Sir Fin pulled over, tied the lines about the break stick, and turned to her. His arm slid over the back cushion and touched her chin, drawing her attention to him.

"Confronting that woman was brave of you." His green eyes held her attention just before she tumbled into his embrace. She needed to feel special and cared for, and knew she'd find that in his arms.

He spoke low and comforting. "I don't know many who could face the perpetrator of such misery. You remind me of a determined woman I met on a coach who berated me for ignoring a pair of colleens."

He drew away just enough to look into her tearful eyes. "I'm proud of you, Brianna. Not that you need my approval. Because I believe you confronted that woman for your aunt and her relationship with the Darnleys. Not for yourself."

A tear trickled down her cheek and he removed his arm from the bench and handed her a handkerchief. For the next few minutes Brianna tried to calm herself from the angst that just now fastened on her.

"You are a good..." she sighed "... friend."

His thumb dabbed at a tear on her cheek. "As you are to me. If ever I should need help, I would want you by my side. Ne'er a care for yourself, you take on the woes of others."

He waited patiently until her distress subsided. "Are you still interested in seeing the manor, or should I take you home?"

A tremulous smile accompanied her decision. "If I don't look a fright, I'd really like to see what's been accomplished these last weeks. I've missed Ashcourt. Since I began at the post office, I don't seem to have a lot of extra time."

The muscles on his face tightened. He inhaled deeply and nodded. "I'm pleased you have time for me." He chuckled. "Or should I have said Ashcourt?"

The Autumn Fair and confusion

S ir Finbarr drew up under a triangle of gently rattling Aspen and helped Brianna down. They made their way toward the manor.

Ashcourt's picturesque view through the Aspen, Oak and Hawthorn with the bubbling brook running alongside was like unwrapping a gift. Two workmen pushed hand carts gathering up debris from the storm last night.

"Why didn't you tell me you had the front windows bowed. It lends a whole new appearance. Quite inviting. And the sash bars sparkle in the sunlight."

Her enthusiasm kindled his as he said, "If new windows sparked your interest, I can't wait to see your reaction about the inside."

His delight was infectious as they stepped into the foyer, and immediately began explaining how the artistic moldings came about. He then pointed out a large plaster rosette in the center of the ceiling that showcased a gorgeous pendant chandelier. The prisms glistening in the sunlight from the windows.

She specifically asked, "What is it about Ashcourt that turned you around?"

He obviously enjoyed the question as he opened his arms, much unlike him, and turned about. "All of it. I'm not partial. Abernathy created what I did not have the words to describe. Like he read my—"

"Your heart. Your big heart is what he read. You are kind and generous. You put people at ease when they are troubled. I am glad he created a space for you to feel at home. Perhaps you are where you belong?" Her brow rose as she looked at him.

For the second time, she noted the muscles on his face tighten. He inhaled deeply. She knew he would not boast of himself. She wondered if he suffered conflict with a touch of pride in ownership and reluctant to admit that he created all this.

She might feel the same if all this beauty belonged to her. The bewilderment of having created something so unique and yet ancient with the years of O'Bannon ownership should allow him pride in his accomplishments.

His hands stuffed in his pockets, he cocked his head backward to see the ceiling and the chandelier that hung from it. Though a grown man, she saw a child with something he never knew he could have and was just now realizing it.

She drew his attention to the fireplace where he had dropped soot all over his face and hands. "The marble surrounding the chimneypiece is elegant. Look at the center. The string of rosettes carved out of the marble perfectly match the centerpiece of the ceiling." She ran her fingertips over the carvings.

He had not changed position as he continued to stare at the ceiling. "What do you think?"

"It's beautiful."

Canvas covered the floor, as workmen were not done. She could see enough black and white marble flooring to deem it quite handsome, indeed.

He motioned her to follow him to the parlor off the foyer. Papered with a design of Chinamen using long poles to maneuver boats, cherry trees ripe with red berries, roses, and golden bridges, all rather pleasing to the eye.

"I think my mother would have approved."

"Who is your decorator?"

"No one. Though I'm sure I will need one." With a wolfish gleam in his eye, he grinned at her.

"Oh, no. I'm not capable. No." He nodded *yes* each time she said "No."

"You don't believe in your talent, but I've seen what you can do."

"Canvas perhaps. But this?" She swept her arm in the air.

He cocked his head and looked her in the eye. "I have faith in your talent. Please." He looked like a little puppy begging.

She laughed and pushed at his chest. "Really? Entreating?"

He wiggled his brows, and she couldn't help but giggle. "I'll need to see all the rooms to understand the scope. Even the chamber you will be using."

"It's just a sleeping chamber. Wouldn't you rather see the water closets newly installed, or the kitchen?"

She could tell he teased. "I want to see if you are attentive enough of yourself, since you are no longer at the end of a long corridor in a one window bedchamber." Off she marched toward the stairs, holding her skirts so she would not trip.

"You have a habit of putting your nose in where it might not be wanted, Miss Walsh."

"I'll remind you I am here at *your* request, sir." His footfall on the steps to the second floor assured her he followed. At the top, she went to the left and halfway down the corridor then opened the door to his father's chamber.

She laughed. "Tried to trick me, didn't you? I am much pleased that you have chosen this room for yourself. It is fitting. Apropos. You are, after all, knighted by the Queen and a Baronet. No back stair room for you."

For some reason, he seemed to want her approval. At the realization, she thrilled. "Your choice of soft green for the moldings and doors are an inviting compliment to the warm Wych-Elm floors."

"I take it this chamber has your approval?"

She half expected him to roll his eyes. "Pish posh. You don't need my approval for anything. Knowing what I do about your beginnings, this gives me pleasure that you've stepped beyond Diarmuid's hostilities."

He had been preoccupied with the view from the windows and glanced at her. An odd expression on his face, as if memories bombarded him. He twirled his beaver hat, fidgeting.

"Forgive me. I should not have mentioned him."

His vision narrowed. "You're fine. You do have a way of getting to the heart of the matter."

"I certainly didn't mean to upset you."

He took her hand and bowed slightly. "I should not have responded as I did. Though I'm not intending it as an excuse, sometimes odd memories still pop up."

She put her hand on his arm. "I wish I could help you with those. You do realize, life is what we make of it. And look at all you accomplished already. I think you have a splendid future ahead of you."

His eyes narrowed as he listened to her. She reached for the door on the opposite wall, and walked past closets, into a room with a washbasin, and a large round tub for bathing.

He caught up with her and offered, "This is the water closet. Water is supplied by a cistern on the roof. One only need turn a knob and water flows through tubing into the basin, or the tub."

She took note of a chair with a hole in it, assuming the drawer beneath held the chamber pot. As if mentioning Diarmuid was not embarrassment enough, now she felt really uncomfortable and quickly sashayed back toward the bedchamber and stood at the door to the corridor.

Following her out, hat in hand, he said, "I'd like your opinion about the kitchen."

"I am not short on those, as you well know."

He chuckled as they returned to the stairs and the first floor. They entered his mother's parlor. The floor appeared to be Elm. Brianna loved that he had opened the wall and put in doors to an outdoor patio. Work was continuing on the patio.

He had mentioned his mother preferred this room as it faced the gardens in back. Brianna knew it might just be her most-liked, too.

They made their way to the kitchen at the back of the manor. As they entered, she smiled at what he had done, knowing he had actually taken her ideas and incorporated them.

The kitchen sink was outfitted with running water and the old pump was no more. The fireplace now provided built-in ovens, one for baking and a separate roasting pit. Several large potholders on a central post allowed the pots to swing out, then swing back over the fire. He had spared no expense for modernization.

Though gloomy clouds were moving in, a bay of windows over the sink area and at the door leading outside allowed a great deal of light to brighten the whole room. On a sunny day, it would prove to be one of the best kitchens she had ever seen.

The table at least ten feet in length with benches on one side and chairs on the other. The original floor of cobbled stone gone, and slate installed. Cabinets lined one wall, and shelving lined another, painted in a cream color.

Sir Finbarr touched this and that as she wandered about. He seemed enthralled with the makings, maybe wondering at his own determination to turn it into all its glory, conceivably as his mother would have wished.

"You should be proud of yourself. This is why you returned to Hawthorn. It is your dream, and you made it come true."

He glanced over at her, a calm but distant look in his eyes as if distracted. Something appeared to be going on inside his head. She knew he kept a lot to himself and would like to help him but considered he might deem it an intrusion if she were to inquire.

He tipped his head. "It's gratifying to see Ashcourt through your eyes. Though your love of the place might bias your feelings."

"I will treasure seeing this home almost completed. You have turned your dreams into reality. I'm happy for you."

"Will you paint Ashcourt?"

"You mean like I used to?" Surprised he asked, she interpreted his question to mean that he intended letting go of the past and warming to the future? For his sake, she hoped she was right.

"Like it is now, refurbished."

She trailed a gloved finger over the window sash overlooking the back of Ashcourt and the forest of green beyond.

How odd their opposite feelings for Ashcourt were? He could accept it because it was made anew. Her heart was in the past when she loved to come here and paint the abandoned home.

They returned to the front of the manor, and she leisurely strolled once more through his mother's parlor, lingering on the expanse of park beyond the new doors. "Have you considered that the renovation changes everything now. Ashcourt is in its glory. It has you to take care of it and live here in comfort if you so choose."

He came near. She breathed in his fresh, soapy scent and felt his breath on her cheek. He stated, "As long as you are comparing, I see no likeness between what this house was and you. None whatsoever."

She turned her glance up at him. "Then you weren't looking in the shadows."

His jaw tightened as his gaze captured her. "You could marry me?"

She gasped and looked him in the face. His dark brows, the seriousness of his gaze, and his strong jaw, left her breathless, "But we…we are friends."

He brushed her cheek with his knuckle. "Do you know how badly I've wanted to kiss you?"

Her gray eyes darkened. "But…we are—"

His lips lightly brushed hers before she could say *friends*.

He drew away just enough to whisper, "I want us to be more. Since we first met on the coach, you've put a spell on me. You do recall the dressing down you gave me? By rights, I should have been irritated. Instead, I was totally enthralled. And each time I am with you, I learn more about your mystery that lures me to you."

His warm breath softly caressed her face. Barely inches apart, she wondered if he would kiss her again.

He said, "Soon after I discovered you painting a likeness of Ashcourt I could not believe my good fortune." His brows lifted as he chortled. "You ordered me from my own property, if you recall?"

"For shame." She warmed to his retelling of her inner shrew.

"You've brought me back to life, Brianna. I've spent years building a kingdom of sorts, and since that day in the coach, I'm finally alive."

"Stop."

❦

"Stop what?" He eyed her with difficulty, as her voice had taken an edge.

"I can't marry you. We come from vastly different backgrounds. And if I have learned anything these last few days, it's that contrariety matters."

He reached out.

And she stepped back. "No. It's folly. We do not match. You know we don't. You have heard where I come from, who my parents are."

He appealed to her, "Who they are, has nothing to do with how I feel about you."

"It will matter in time." Her head shook decisively, her voice like ice. "NO."

A moment passed with him breathing heavily, as if punched. "What can I do to sweep away this folly of yours."

She marched to the front door. "I want to leave."

How on earth did his suggesting they marry turn into a recrimination of her parents' begetting her? "Brianna, be reasonable."

She stopped at the door. Her soft green skirts twirled as she turned to him. Her bonnet and lovely dark hair framed her distraught face. He ached to hold her in his arms. He had been playing the friend for as long as he could hold himself in check. This woman would be the death of him. He had made up his mind to begin the conversation with her today about the two of them and a future together.

Receiving a resounding *NO* was not a surprise. Her reasoning was. *They are not the same?* Poppycock!

He had never met anyone more his match than this stubborn, beautiful, willful, and soft-hearted woman standing in front of him, fully determined to walk out of his life.

Slamming his hat on, he reached for the doorknob, opened it, and followed the determined swish of her skirts as she headed for the carriage. He remained silent the entire ride, baffled by her definitive *NO*.

With little ceremony and not one word exchanged during the ride to Stoney Batter, he dropped her off, leaving her at the door.

Then he veered toward Colby's shack northwest of Hawthorn, not too far from dark castle, near River Suir. A curl of black smoke pinpointed where he would find his stablemaster.

His boots scrunched acorns as he crossed the rough ground toward the fire. It looked as if Colby just finished his fish dinner.

"Colby, it's me, Fin."

"I see ye."

"I like your glasses. Must be your eyesight has improved, then?"

"Surely, as the day ye were born, it does. And I've yet to thank ye for it. That fella, Collins, said he had orders to take me to a doctor."

Sir Fin turned an old barrel on its end and sat on it. "I'm glad you didn't put up a fuss. It seems as if he did you some good if your eyes are better."

"I know who 'twas got the ball rollin'. Thanks to ye, Fin." He chewed on his pipe and smiled at the same time.

"It's about time we looked at some cattle and maybe sheep, too."

"That would suit me. What else have ye got in mind?"

"Would you be ready to move to Ashcourt? It's ready for you. I'll give you authority to act as caretaker until the house is finished and I move in. You can fish out of St. John's River and your private quarters has a kitchen of sorts. I intend purchasing a horse and cart, unless you prefer a donkey. You can move in when you're ready."

Colby swiped the end of his sleeve across his face and stuck a pipe stem between his teeth. "I don't know, Fin. I'm kind a stuck on this place."

A knot tightened in his throat as he considered Brianna's phrase, *we are not a match*. It must have shown on his face because Colby started guffawing.

"Yer kiddin' me. Of course, I want out of here. I can't leave quick enough. I'm just getting even after all the sass ye gave me in yer early years."

Sir Fin shook his head. "You had me fooled, old man."

"And, since we're talking about me moving. I'd like a donkey, one of those feisty ones that Napoleon left here."

Two weeks later

Opening day of the Autumn Hawthorn Fair Mim stacked two baskets of orange marmalade scones on the floor by the door. Miss Natty called out to her to put the three satchels full of knitted items by the front door, too.

Pussycat trotted back and forth from the kitchen to the parlor, tail in the air, probably wondering whose lap, she could claim with so much activity.

Brianna patted a stray lock before securing her green silk hat adorned with small peacock feathers. She picked up the two paintings to be donated to the contest and set them against the wall near the front door.

Jane had been given the day off to enjoy the festivities. One would have thought she was attending a wedding the way she fussed over which dress to wear. Holding up two, she asked for Mim's suggestion.

Under her breath, Mim groused about the young and how they fretted over the oddest particulars. "If you are clean and neat, it isn't going to matter a whit, lass." But when Jane held up a light blue frock, and then a dark green one, Mim declared, "Well, your eyes sparkle with the blue."

Jane brightened and hugged her, then ran to quickly change.

Aware the household on Stoney Batter had a number of items to deliver to the fairgrounds, Sir O'Bannon had previously arranged for Collins to transport the ladies, as he had to be at the cricket yard for an early setup before their match against the *Waterford Vikings*.

Collins, with his take-charge acumen, had foreseen the probable need for more room and asked Paddy Cashel for the use of a larger carriage. All four women and their paraphernalia would not fit in the phaeton.

Mrs. Cashel had baked two dozen cupcakes for the bakery table and asked Collins if he would convey them to the proper tent. Jane held the basket with the cakes on her lap as she and Brianna sat in the back with the parcels and paintings. Aunt Natty and Mim squeezed in next to Collins. Brianna noticed the valet appeared to be enjoying himself immensely. His sense of organization carting four women and their paraphernalia didn't appear to be a problem in the least.

White tents flagged with Ireland's silver-stringed gold *cláirseach* harp banners proudly waving from center poles. This year's Autumn Fair might just prove to be the best, surely essential because all profits were to benefit the building of a new school.

Collins drew the carriage up nearest to the bazaar tent. Aunt Natty fussed with excitement as he helped her down and she reached for her satchel, Mim taking her share intended Jane help, but the lass had already left for the bakery table with Mrs. Cashel's cupcakes. Brianna lifted her paintings out of the carriage.

She mentioned to Collins, "Aunt Natty and I plan to watch as much of the match as we can before we need to be at the raffle tent. Will you be there?"

"Yes. I have Sir O'Bannon's change of clothing as he intends to wander the fairgrounds after his match is over."

Brianna felt awkward and sad the way she left things with him. He clearly did not see the problem, the disparity in their backgrounds. They simply were not suited. Though she had not slept well these past two weeks and tried to blame it on Dervila, she knew better. Deep down she knew how she truly felt about him. Feelings she could, nor would ever share with anyone. Least of all him. It was going to be difficult to sit through a match.

A large caravan of caged animals pulled up near Collins's borrowed carriage where they were unloading. The wild and frightening animals up close were exciting to watch. In separate cages, a black panther turned in circles in the small space, as did a lion. Three baboons sat on their haunches watching the goings on as if today was normal. Thank goodness they were caged.

Another caravan drew up with a number of colorful birds in cages. A crew of ten men hauled the cages to their tent in preparation for showing. The caged birds made a huge racket, and either the panther or the lion roared—she wasn't quite sure which. Once all the cages were distributed, an earthy scent lingered.

Not until Collins smiled did, she realize how rare it was for him to exhibit any kind of emotion. He said, "Though it's closed to the public, Sir O'Bannon enjoyed a Royal tour of London's Zoo after the knighting ceremony. As his valet, I had the good fortune to accompany him, and I must say these animals remind me of that tour."

"Mrs. Cashel is quite proud to have the exhibit." Brianna said, "I'll mention to her Sir Finbarr's experience. She would want to know that."

At that moment, a painted Indian, several dwarfs, and an albino swaggered past and engaged in laughter and loud ruckus. A dwarf dressed in a clown outfit came up to Brianna and bowed, handing her a paper flower that popped up in his hand.

"Thank you." She gave him a pert curtsy, and the clown waddled off to catch up with his cohorts.

She mused, "It is a wonder how they all survive four days of entertaining."

Collins said, "When a lad, our village held a Fair. I have never forgotten the pleasure. I understand the money raised will go toward a new school?"

"The charity school has long surpassed its prime. And thank you for driving us. My aunt and Mim are especially grateful not to have to lug everything."

Brianna wondered if he had family. She also wondered how his wife could endure his absence. In the end, she decided he could not possibly be married. She warranted he must be close in age to Sir Finbarr.

"My pleasure, miss."

The ladies had gone on ahead, leaving Collins and herself to carry the last boxes into the cooler tent. Unpacking and setting out the numerous items they had brought, Brianna noted Jane in her blue dress halfway down the first aisle. She was pleased to see the girl take charge, as it looked like she was explaining to several men that they needed the long planks set on the barrels and covered with clothes.

Mrs. Cashel, who just arrived and was in charge of raffles, asked Brianna if her cupcakes had been delivered intact to the bakery tent. As she had noted Jane going off with them, Brianna assured her they were delivered.

Brianna held out her donation. "Here are the two paintings. Can I help you with anything?"

Mrs. Cashel instantly began pinning red bows to the cloth overhang. She held the pins between her lips and pointed to an easel indicating where Brianna should hang them.

Brianna glanced at her watch, noting Sir Fin's game was to begin in half an hour. She warred with her feelings. Two weeks had passed since he asked her to marry him. Or, rather, suggested they marry. *You could marry me*–is what he actually said. She will never, ever forget that moment.

Her heart had flip-flopped; it soared and then crashed upon the reality of a marriage between them.

She believed he meant what he said, though a preposterous notion. They may seem to get along and undoubtedly did enjoy each other's company. But marriage would never be possible. As much as she hated to think it, Lady Hamerlin would be a far better choice.

All these musings of Sir Finbarr and with their friendship most likely coming to an end, Brianna looked forward to watching him play cricket one last time. She told herself it was more for the team as a whole, not just *him*. Her heart wouldn't harden against him. As much as she tried to not think of him, he entered her thoughts constantly. It would take a great deal of effort to accomplish her decision.

27

A sunny day and a slap in the face

Collins set up two chairs for Aunt Natty and herself, strategically placed so they would not miss the action. They were in an area where many others were seated. Aunt Natty, caught up in the excitement, nudged Brianna with her elbow. "Isn't that the lovely Lady Hamerlin talking to Sir Finbarr?"

A bitter longing stabbed her. "It is." Her eyes feasted on his animation as he conversed with her. A strange feeling came over her. Lady Hamerlin irritated her, and for what reason? For that matter, Sir Finbarr also irritated her. She was of a mind to stomp back to the raffle tent when realization hit her.

She begrudged Lady Hamerlin the closeness with Sir Fin. Her hand on his chest, her flashy smile. Urged by some unexplainable feeling of *possession* as if he belonged to her, Brianna cringed at the thought.

What was happening to her? Even from across the field she noted Sir Fin turned away from Lady Hamerlin and greeted several men who had approached. They stole his attention and Brianna watched with intrigue as her ladyship went unnoticed.

Brianna had never felt such glee as she did right now. Shame on her. She pinched her lips and forced herself to look away as her face melted into a grin.

A chalk line had been drawn on the grass in a huge oval and the wickets set up. She knew if the ball goes outside the playing area but has touched the ground prior to leaving, the batting side earns four runs. If the ball does not touch the ground, the opposition earns six runs.

More and more chairs were set up as the match would begin in minutes. Lady Hamerlin gained Sir Finbarr's attention once again and fussed with his bat when the captain yelled for the players to gather round. She then perched on the balls of her slippers to likely give him a kiss on the cheek, but he smiled at her as he held her arm, stopping her intent, then joined his teammates.

Brianna cursed herself for looking across the field again. The pangs of jealousy were like needle points poking her.

A whistle blew, and all players took their places. Aunt Natty's excitement got the better of her and she clapped her hands. "Begorrah, such fun."

Collins opened a parasol for them as the late morning sun promised to blister. He then retreated somewhere behind them.

"Collins is amazing. He seems to know what is needed at any given moment." Aunt Natty cheerfully noted as she clutched the handle of her white linen sunshade.

ॐ

All onlookers clapped hard as the players got into formation on the field. Excitement stirred. When it was his turn to bat, Sir Fin batted a perfect hit, sending the leather ball *over* and the crowd went wild yelling "*SHOT!*"

Brianna thrilled for him and clapped wildly along with the crowd. The score would be immediately recorded on a chalkboard set up on the far side of the field.

The next player was definitely out, yet the bowler shouted, "*Howzat*?!"

Aunt Natty had trouble keeping the bowlers and the fielders straight. Brianna couldn't help her understand the fine points of cricket and they both ended up laughing when the bowler shouted, "*Howzat*?! again.

The game was a one-day match, with a limited *over* of twenty-five per side.

Not sure how long her aunt was willing to be in the harsh sun, Brianna suggested they leave half-way through.

At that moment, she noted Lady Hamerlin approaching and wished she could simply disappear. "Good morning, ladies. Isn't this a beautiful day for cricket?"

Aunt Natty moved her parasol enough to glance upward at the sound of a lady's voice. "We agree, don't we Brianna?"

She did not want to be drawn into conversation with the woman, and shading her eyes with her hand, glanced at Lady Hamerlin painting a smile on her face. "Good morning to you."

Lady Hamerlin asked, "Are you enjoying the match?"

"Indeed." Brianna puffed.

Her ladyship's lacey half-glove hand drifted to her cheek. "Sir Finbarr has changed my habits rather positively. I would never have thought cricket a lady's entertainment, but he determined I should watch a match. And now I thoroughly enjoy the sport."

Brianna felt forced to be agreeable when first she spoke, then fiddled with her parasol to otherwise ignore her ladyship. A mean streak had signs of popping out in a rush of discontent—that she readily admitted she brought on herself.

Lady Hamerlin said, "Miss Brianna, how long have you been a cricket fan?"

She wanted to blurt, *since Sir Fin brought me to a game*. Her churlishness, however, quickly doused with Aunt Natty's rule number one: be kinder than necessary.

"Only a few months. And it's such a lovely day to enjoy the sunshine and outdoors. Will you also take in the Fair?" She prattled. Drat Aunt Natty's rule that kept her from spite, again reminding herself she caused her own misery.

With her handkerchief, Lady Hamerlin shooed off a bug flying close. "Sir Fin and I are in charge of the auction." She waved her handkerchief in the air, dainty like. Brianna perceived it as a helpless gesture and Lady Hamerlin certainly was not helpless.

Her ladyship added, "A man's deep voice is much better calling at an action. You must come by and see if we are auctioning anything that might interest you."

Brianna tried to contain her emotions. She felt her insides tighter than a knot.

Lady Hamerlin summed up her little display. "I must get on. I wanted to say hello when I spotted you." Her lovely round dress with a half-high bodice and drapery folds in a light blue, swished as she made her way across the grassy park toward the tent area.

At this moment, Brianna felt...oh, she could not name what she felt. Sad. Empty. Her gaze slid to the slender figure, a woman of privilege. And as quick as a rabbit, Dervila flashed in Brianna's mind. She wasn't a woman of privilege, but certainly as wily and cunning as Lady Hamerlin.

She had absolutely no intention of watching her ladyship fawn over Sir Finbarr as he played the auctioneer.

Collins approached them near the game's end. "Will you be staying until the Fair closes for the night?"

Brianna lowered her sunscreen and said, "The raffle is finished about four o'clock." She glanced at her aunt, who clearly showed signs of fatigue. "Would you rather Collins take you home now?"

Fanning herself, Aunt Natty implored, "I know you manage well, but it takes at least two of us to handle the raffle."

"Bonnie and Muriel have offered their services. If you are fatigued, auntie, please take advantage of Collin's offer."

"I don't want to miss the excitement. But I am tired."

Collin's offered, "I could return you at one or two, after you've refreshed yourself?"

Brianna smiled. "You are kind Collins, thank you. A perfect solution, don't you think, auntie?"

She nodded, and Brianna saw the tiredness in her eyes. A nap would do her good, as the sun does take its toll.

৩ﾟ৯

Early afternoon Brianna, Bonnie, and Muriel had sold almost one hundred raffle tickets, and they still had three hours before the drawing. The school coffers were mounting, and they hoped the other raffle tables were doing as well. It would be wonderful to discover the school not only could expand, but mayhap with enough raffle money the committee could purchase new desks.

Lionel stopped by to say hello as if he wanted to purchase a ticket. Instead, he suggested they return to the village together now.

Unabashedly surprised at his lack of understanding, she explained, "I am committed to work all afternoon. Perhaps another time."

His wide brimmed felt hat, worn no doubt to shield from the sun, further shadowed his deep-set eyes. He glanced at the table and the wire box where the ballots were piling up, and then back to her. "Some other time then." He tipped his hat and plodded off without making a purchase.

Bonnie and Muriel stifled giggles. Bonnie said, "Of all the gall. Asking you to go about with him, but not even purchase a ticket."

Muriel leaned near, "A beau?"

"He works at the post office. Though I suspect he's looking for someone special."

"Seems it won't be you. Such a strange thing, Brianna. You are of an age when marriage should be on your mind."

"Well, it's not. Strangely or otherwise. And certainly not with Mr. Murphy."

Muriel snapped. "You mean you've fooled yourself into believing you're happy. There's a big difference."

Brianna scoffed at her aunt's friends, and thankfully was saved by further comment when several Fair goers stepped up to purchase raffle tickets and talk about the new school. They were the parents of three and had done quite a lot to enrich the coffers for the school already.

Much to Brianna's surprise, Miss Simpson approached her. A big smile on her face, and an elderly man walking close by her side. "Miss Walsh. I hoped to find you here. I want to thank you so much for defending me to Mrs. Teaberry."

Genuinely surprised, Brianna harrowed her eyes, "I don't know…"

"Yes, you do. You spoke up for me and 'Twas enough to make the postmistress change her mind about sending me off to the Gaol. Though I'm on a…a…"

"Probation?"

Miss Simpson lit up. "That's it. Probation period to see how I can be trusted not to take anything again."

"I think it's admirable you want to teach your father to read. The library has any number of books you can take home for a length of time and then return. The librarian is a friend of mine. Ask for Miss Browne. And let her know you are teaching your father…" Brianna nodded at the gentleman standing at her side. "…she will loan you lots of appropriate information."

Miss Simpson hugged her. "You saved our lives. I was so worried about how we'd get on. It's just the two of us, you know. And I'll be right as rain from now on." She took her father's hand and as an afterthought added, "My beau left me over what I did."

Brianna leaned in. "If I were you, I wouldn't trust him as a beau. You are too fine a young lady to walk out with him."

Her eyes grew large at Brianna's pronouncement. "I'll trust you, Miss Walsh. And thank you."

Sir Finbarr arrived at the raffle booth mid-afternoon. He had changed from his uniform into his regular clothing.

Bonnie edged Brianna out of the way and asked, "Are you interested in purchasing a ticket, Sir O'Bannon?"

He nodded to Brianna, who stood off to the side, then glanced at both Bonnie and Muriel. "That depends. How many have you sold?"

Muriel answered as Bonnie clearly swooned over the handsome gentleman. "I think nearly one hundred and fifty so far. You were one of the *Gaelics*. I watched for a few minutes earlier."

With an assertive smirk on his handsome face, he glanced at Brianna and winked. "I'll take two hundred. And, yes, did you enjoy the match?"

Bonnie shook herself from daydreaming and squawked, "Two hundred?"

"Is there a rule says I may not?" He loomed over the woman and her eyes widened.

Muriel edged Bonnie away and said, 'No, sir. You may purchase as many as you wish. It's for the new school."

Bonnie elbowed her way back to stand in front of Sir O'Bannon. "You are a very good player, sir."

"Thank you, miss. I'll take two hundred tickets." He drew out a leather purse and handed her the bills.

Sir Finbarr asked if he could return to pick up the stubs later in the day. Muriel quickly assured him that would be fine.

Brianna, having watched and listened to the exchange, suddenly realized what he was doing, attempting to make sure he would win her landscape of Ashcourt.

A flush came over her as pleasure soared. With Bonnie and Muriel occupied writing his name on the tickets, Sir Fin stepped close to Brianna. "Thank you for coming to the game. It meant a lot."

"You saw us?"

"Collins said you would be there. But I also kept my eye on

you both. Two lovely ladies under their sun shields patiently waiting for a big moment in the play. I hope you weren't disappointed."

All of Brianna's hurtful feelings melted away. It mattered to him they had taken the time to watch him. Even though she refused his offer of marriage, he still cared. "My aunt could not bear missing your game. And Collins accommodated her."

"I heard your dulcet tones spurring us on." He teased with a side grin and a twinkle.

She felt heat crawl up her neck and wanted to deny screaming, which didn't deserve the flattery of dulcet, but decided to ignore his remark. "I certainly did, and congratulations on a spectacular play. It's obvious you enjoy the sport. You've been playing for a long time?"

His eyes twinkled with merriment. "I'd have to admit, yes, since Eton actually."

"Well, I think you are invaluable to your teammates."

"As long as I do well, they'll want me. A man is only as good as his last game."

Their eyes met, and Brianna sensed his competitive nature. She was also mercifully happy that he didn't seem to hold any animosity toward her for not only turning him down but for making a fool out of herself shouting.

She changed the subject. "We are grateful for your purchase of two hundred tickets. It's a grand amount. I hope you are still able to put food on the table."

He chuckled. "It helps the budget that Collins is a valet of little demands."

She glanced over at Bonnie and Muriel, who continued to write his name on the stubs, "I assume you recall that I intended to paint a picture of your new Ashcourt. You needn't have gone to this expense."

"I appreciate your concern about my spending habits." He chuckled, seeming to enjoy their conversation.

She blustered and drew in a breath.

"The odds are I may win nothing, but it's a chance I'm willing to take. Especially considering the new school. The expense is well worth the gamble."

He pulled out his fob and took note of the time.

Realizing he might be in a crunch, after all, Lady Hamerlin did make it a point to mention the auction, she saucily said, "You don't want to be late attending Lady Hamerlin. She will expect you to be on time for the auction. I believe it begins shortly."

With the bearing of a gentleman, he would not gape, but Brianna enjoyed watching him recover from her flippant remark. She found his reaction worthy of note.

His green flinty eyes narrowed. She waited for him to gather his wit. Instead, he returned his fob, lifted his hat in polite departure and said, "I enjoyed hearing you spur us on today. You needn't have been embarrassed." He turned and left.

Muriel and Bonnie had a fine time guessing his reason for purchasing so many. Brianna, cheeks burning with her social indiscretion, said nothing as she assisted with writing his name on the stubs and the tickets, in between selling more tickets.

At three o'clock, Collins returned with Aunt Natty and escorted her to the tent, along with a chair for her to use if she grew fatigued. Bonnie continued gushing about Sir O'Bannon's purchase.

Best of Rose Garden contest

Aunt Natty reminded Brianna, "We must go to the garden tent if we are to see who will win this year's Best of Rose contest."

Brianna turned to Bonnie and Muriel. "Do you mind if we leave you for a while? We should return well before the raffle."

With encouragement from both, Brianna and Aunt Natty made their way across a short field, dodging hordes of others at play and strolling about.

Aunt Natty commented, "We would have some time after the

Rose Garden contest to stop by the auctioneer's tent. Might you like to watch the bidding awhile?"

Brianna knew her aunt was digging. "I think not. We don't need anything in the way of furniture, and I believe that's all they are selling."

"If, you're sure."

As they stepped within the fragrant tent, Aunt Natty whispered to Brianna, "Do you see how many entries we have? There must be fifteen."

She paused a minute counting. "How does nineteen sound? This should be interesting."

Aunt Natty muttered, "Look at Mrs. Haggerty sashaying back and forth. And that bustle!" She smothered a laugh with her gloved hand. "I feel it in my bones he is going to choose her flower again. Mind my words." Her gaze shifted to Mrs. Haggerty and at that moment, she glanced at Aunt Natty and had the impudence to wink at her.

Her aunt's cheeks were as red as the flowers on display. Brianna whispered, "What's wrong?"

Whispering again, Aunt Natty said, "She winked at me. She's well aware of what I've said about her."

Brianna tried not to react to her aunt's distress. But it was a ticklish moment to be found talking about someone and having them catch you at it.

The former Mayor, Mr. Teaberry, paced back and forth between the tables of entries. He bent over, looking at the petals, and poked his finger into the loam, drawing in the scent of each rose, then ran his fingers along the leaves and thorns. He made notes on a pad and moved on to the next pot.

All aflutter, Mrs. Haggerty leaned against the wall next to the table where she had placed her flowerpot. Flanked by two friends who conspired to keep her spirits up, a good amount of giggling and side glances at Mr. Teaberry were noticed.

Brianna would not have believed it if she had not been told about the flirtation between the former mayor and Mrs. Haggerty.

Seeing them together conversing was an unmistakable sign the rumor might be true. It was the look in their eyes that gave them away.

She felt sorry for Mrs. Teaberry and wondered if her employer had any idea. Leave it to Aunt Natty and her friends to notice. Unless you were not expecting to see such, you would probably not consider the possibility. But it did explain why Mrs. Haggerty has won the coveted ribbons for the last several years.

Brianna watched as Mr. Teaberry inspected each pot. She would like to see his notes, because at least half these blooms were stunning in color and health. A chart on the wall detailed the point-scoring system, and she had taken the time to read it. Form, color, substance, the stem and foliage, and the balance and proportion all received points. The flower with the most points wins. Form being the most important factor in the judging process it comprised the unfurled spiral from the point in the center of the bloom.

Aunt Natty elbowed Brianna and whispered, "Psst, look who just arrived."

Mrs. Teaberry entered, and spotting her husband, she moved directly to his side. Aunt Natty noticed his face paled, though he managed a smile.

"Me thinks the pot is going to boil. And I don't mean stewpot. Right now, I'd not put a hand full of shillings on Mrs. Haggerty's win." An elated Aunt Natty prophesied.

Brianna considered it as if watching one of Shakespeare's dramas rather than a flower contest.

Finished with his judging, Mr. Teaberry looked a bit peaked. His wife whispered something to him, and he picked up a pot with a beautiful red rose, then called out *Number Twelve.*

Mrs. Haggerty screamed and fainted.

An elderly woman with pure white hair stood, and using a cane, gingerly made her way toward the front.

"Congratulations, Mrs. Sweeney." Mr. Teaberry handed her the flower in its pot and turned her around to face the crowd. Her pale cheeks pinkened and her face broke into a lovely smile. Tears slid down her cheeks as she tried to announce her thankfulness.

Aunt Natty got in line to give Mrs. Sweeney her congratulations. Brianna greeted Mrs. Teaberry. "How nice for Mrs. Sweeney."

"She's been deserving for the last three years. It's about time. Did you happen to notice who screamed? What a retched sound. Made my skin crawl."

"I'm not sure, ma'am. It might have come from outside the tent. All the clapping made it hard to distinguish. If you'll excuse me, we have to return to the raffle tent. My aunt and I are in charge."

Brianna noted Mrs. Teaberry eyed her husband as they conversed. Brianna had all she could do to stay focused on her employer, who appeared preoccupied though she managed to say, "See you Monday morning."

Raffle drawing benefiting the new school

Nearing the hour of the raffle drawing, Sir Finbarr reappeared. Collins stood in the back of a growing crowd. Brianna decided after Sir Finbarr's support for the new school, the least she could do is paint the picture he wants if his ticket is not drawn. She had no scruples about Lady Hamerlin's intensions toward Sir Finbarr. But she was not painting for her ladyship.

Ten-year-old Dean, Muriel's nephew, had been chosen to dig in the barrel and pull out the winning stubs. All the tickets, well over five hundred, Bonnie said, had been dumped into the barrel.

The first draw set off clapping and hooting for the Dunne's as their name was withdrawn and luckily, they happened to be in the audience winning a dinner at Cashel's Inn. The second draw created the same response and happened to be a neighbor of Bonnie's, the Clever's. They won a cake at Nolan and Brady's Bakery.

The third draw, good for a horse shoeing at The Forge, was

quite popular if loud praise meant anything. Won by Molly who quickly assured everyone her father would be pleased. The fourth drawing, a length of ribbon at Daley's Milliner, did not exhibit the same response as the horse shoeing. Sir Fin's name was called, followed by laughter from those who knew he was a bachelor.

A little drum roll announced the fifth and sixth prizes, two paintings by Miss Brianna Walsh, the local artist.

Dean dug so far into the barrel his aunt had to hang onto his breeches to pull him out. The landscape winner was Michael Flaherty. He accepted it to a round of applause.

Dean dug into the barrel again and gave a ticket to his aunt. The winner of the painting of the Quay with boats, Sir Finbarr O'Bannon. He, too, received a round of applause.

Once the crowd began to scatter, Brianna stepped over to where her aunt and Sir Finbarr conversed. Collins was standing off to the side, watching the crowd as it thinned.

She saw a flicker of strain on Sir Fin's furrowed brow. And wondered if it was because the picture he wanted, another gentleman had won. She whispered, "I'll paint you another."

Mr. Flaherty, the winner of the landscape, addressed Sir Finbarr. "I say. How would you feel about trading paintings? I had my heart set on the Quay. The ship, you see, happens to be mine." He pointed to the Unicorn.

Sir Finbarr introduced Brianna. "This is the artist, Miss Brianna Walsh."

She gave him a slight curtsy. "I hope you do not mind that I painted your ship. It was so lovely bobbing in the wind that day. Shadows coming and going from the clouds. I couldn't resist."

Sir Finbarr held up her rendering of the ship and the men exchanged their winnings.

Mr. Flaherty, Unicorn painting in hand, pronounced, "I preferred this one all along. Miss Brianna, I assure you this lovely oil will have a home on the wall in my parlor."

Flaherty held out his hand, and the men shook. "We are both content, then. Thank you, Sir O'Bannon."

When Flaherty left, Sit Finbarr searched out Brianna. "Does the offer of another painting still hold?"

She chortled. "If that is what you want. Though I'm confused as to why you would want two of the same?"

"If you would paint the front of Ashcourt as it is now and include the bunnies and a face peeking out the window upstairs, I would be a happy man."

"You once took umbrage at the one in my aunt's parlor."

He led her by the elbow and faced them away from the others. "I've had a change of heart."

"Because—?" She eyed him skeptically.

He took her hand and placed it on his arm. "Come outside with me for a minute or two."

He scanned the area for a patch of privacy. They stood beneath an Elm, and he rested his eyes on her. "I'm not going anywhere, Brianna. I declared myself to you. And I am a patient man where you are concerned. There is no one else for me but you."

Tears instantly stung her eyes. She was beside herself with a tangle of uncertainty and embarrassment at what she was thinking earlier during the cricket match. She also wanted to kiss him and hug him, the relief she felt overwhelmed her.

Two men with sticks leading a group of pigs wearing tutus passed in front of them. A riot of coughing from the swine meant they were annoyed, probably because they knew they had a performance to complete before feeding time. But the sight caused Brianna to giggle. Pigs waddling in tutus.

Sir Finbarr had a hard time remaining serious, but pigs in tutus was too much considering they trotted past in the midst of an extraordinarily serious question he put to Brianna.

He waited until the pigs passed, and asked, "Where was I?"

Brianna could not help herself and continued to chuckle at the strange sight. "I am so sorry. Forgive me. But…" she giggled again "…those fat little pink pigs all dressed up for the ballet is too much."

Sir Fin shook his head and brought her hand to his lips. "They were quite funny. I will have the image in my mind's eye for quite some time."

She finally composed herself and touched his cheek with the palm of her hand. "Please continue what you wanted to say."

He gripped her hand, rubbing his thumb over its surface. "I acted in haste with my offer of marriage. I realize you aren't ready, *mauverneen*. I don't want you to back away from me. I will wait."

He called her my darling and her urge to kiss him bloomed. What was wrong with her? She withdrew her hand from his. "I feel you are a true friend and want what you think best. But there are other considerations that have merit. One important element is my family background."

Which reminded her of Dervila, and her eyes narrowed with suspicion. "You didn't perchance offer money to Dervila if she would write a letter to Aunt Natty, insisting she would not reveal the whereabouts of a granddaughter?"

"And, what if I said yes?" He stood tall, his beaver hat at a rakish angle, but the smile was gone.

"Can you not understand how demeaning it might seem to me that you have to offer Dervila money to make her do what is right." She wasn't able to hide her dissatisfaction.

He glanced at the sky, as if studying the passing clouds. Then he glanced down at her set features. "I meant for you and Miss Natty to be free of her crude assault on the Darnley's. I sensed how it would impact you both. I had hoped to alleviate the pressure Dervila caused. She was going to get money from somewhere, and I can afford it."

He took a deep breath. "She could bring shame to all parties concerned. *THAT,* I could not abide. You did nothing wrong, nor did Miss Natty. And believe me when I say, the Darnley family would never have laid this at your door. They would have immediately realized the woman was blackmailing them. She will not be so foolish with information that isn't entirely hers to reveal, again."

The heavy dread in her heart seemed to lighten with his words. She wiped a handkerchief under her nose. "Who does it belong to?"

Stupefied, she had to ask. He said, "*You,* for starters. And I would add Miss Natty, and the Darnleys for certain. You, my dear, are a direct link to their deceased grandson. You share a likeness to their other great granddaughter. And what about their granddaughter, Mairéad, Lady Tremaine. She was your father's twin. Which makes her your aunt."

He shrugged his shoulders. "I simply cut to the chase with Dervila. And she will not bother any of you again. You can take my word for it."

Brianna gaped at him her lovely eyes wide with unspoken shock. Eventually, she asked, "You've explained you paid her to be quiet, but why did you?"

His finger touched the soft skin of her cheek, his eyes narrowed on her questioning gaze. "I'm a selfish man. I want you content. My feelings for you are more than mere whimsy, my darling Brianna."

※

He pushed his top hat back from his forehead.

Her gray eyes sparkled. "I'm nonplussed that you care enough to go to such trouble."

"Do you mind if we sit a moment?" He motioned to a bench located under the branches of Elm. They enjoyed the cooler spot while Brianna sifted through the whole of Sir Fin's recitation. She concluded he meant well. And whether or not his generosity toward Dervila will keep her silent, only the future can tell.

Off in the distance, a large tent housed circus acts. Howls of laughter drifted on the slight breeze. The pigs were probably performing.

She asked, "Do you know the Darnley's and the Tremaine's?"

"Somewhat, I do. My memories come from when I was young. My parents visited at Rockmore Hall. Tremaine and I have met a time or two since being formally introduced the day of Lord Darnley's birthday. They have a daughter, Lady Fionnuala. She is a year or so younger than you."

Brianna puzzled over this. "The day of Lord Darnley's birthday party, Lady Rutledge mentioned that her granddaughter and I shared similar features. Do you recall her saying such?"

He nodded.

"I never did meet her that day and simply forgot until now."

"It shouldn't come as a surprise. After all, you are cousins, your parents were twins."

She avoided his searching gaze and shook her head. "I will mean nothing to her. Why should I?"

"With an attitude like yours, you are right. Why should she?" A bland look shadowed his handsome features. Glancing at his watch, he added, "I promised to assist at the auction tent. Will you be attending we can walk together?"

With the tiniest fraction of a pout, she hastened, "No. There is nothing I would want to bid on. Thank you."

৩৵৹

The next afternoon, Sir Finbarr drove a mule-led cart out to Colby's little patch of home. Colby knew to be packed up and ready to move to the stables. After unloading, they had plans to attend the cattle sale at the Fair.

Colby ran a hand over the silky mane of the animal. "Is this one of Napoleon's mules?"

"You got what you wanted. Her name's Jose."

Colby laughed. "Could she be named after Napoleon's first wife?"

Sir Fin shook his head. "Only you would ask." It meant a great deal to him that the elder stablemaster consented to live at

Ashcourt.

Together, they filled the cart with everything Colby owned. Strapped in tight, Colby snapped the lines encouraging the donkey to move along and asked Sir Fin, "What kind of cattle are ye looking for?"

"I spent an hour plodding through the stalls at the Fair. What do you think of two milchers, maybe the old native Irish stock? I saw several at the Fair. Do you remember hearing the name John Mitchell?"

"They lived past the Forge out in the countryside?"

"Yes, well, they brought in several milchers. He's also got some black-faced sheep. Long hairy fleece, horns. He swears by the delicacy of the flavor."

Colby snapped the lines again. The donkey was slowing as they passed a creek where fish were jumping at flies. "Have ye heeded pigs a'tall?"

"I have." And as he couldn't help himself, he added, "I know where we might get some wearing tutus."

Colby took his eyes off the donkey long enough to see if Sir Finbarr had lost his mind.

He chuckled, "Never mind. It was a bad idea. You'll need a lad to come help during the day if we get too many cattle before the household is up and running. Do you know of anyone?"

"Now that I've got a way to get around, why not let me figure it out. You just tell me how many and I'll see what I can do."

He could not help but smile. "It's in your capable hands, Colby. I'll think no more on it."

"Can't thank ye enough, Sir Fin. I'm as excited as the verra first time ye plucked some trout. Do ye recall that day? Ye fell in, trying to keep him on the line. The funniest thing I'd ever seen."

Scorn dripping over his answer, Sir Fin growled, "No one ever told me to bring the fish up on shore. All you did was laugh so hard you almost fell in yourself."

"You had to be the dumbest five-year-old ever born. Ye didn't even know how to swim. I had to jump in and haul ye out by your skinny little behind. Ye were spouting out water like a whale. Then I had to go back in and get the rod. At least the fish hadn't gotten away." He poked Sir Fin with his elbow. "We fixed all that over time. Got ye all ready to tackle the world and then some, didn't we?"

He shook his head at the fond memory of learning to swim at Colby's insistence. "If I ever marry and father a son, he'll have the benefit of all you've taught me, Colby. You can bet on it. I might even name him after you. How's that for thanks?"

Colby chuckled. "If ye teach him how to swim, I'll be proud he's got me name."

They kicked up a lot of dust with the laden cart as they traveled to Ashcourt. When they reached the stable, Colby pulled back on the lines and the donkey brayed loud and clear. "I'll be stumped, sounds like she knows she's home."

Collins called out to the arrivals as he carried a box into the stables. He had spent most of the morning purchasing items Colby would need. Staples for the larder, several lanterns and a mattress and bedding that had been ordered and was ready for pickup at the general store.

"Looks like Collins is ready for us."

The day after the Autumn Fair, all the animals were caged and on their way to the next village to entertain.

Relieved that everything was fairly wrapped up as far as accounting for raffle donations and funding for the new school now in the hands of the Fair committee, Miss Natty Walsh could relax.

She paced her steps toward Rockmore Hall, fussing to herself over what she planned. She had not said a word to Brianna fairly certain her niece would not be in favor of her endeavor.

Mrs. Atkinson was at her desk when she arrived. "This is a

surprise. What brings you to Rockmore?" The housekeeper stood up and came around the other side of her desk.

Natty and Mrs. Atkinson had been friendly through the years. If anyone Natty could talk plainly to at the Hall, it was this woman. They sat facing each other, and Natty began.

"What I've to say is going to bring up sad memories, but I need to tell you. It has to do with Rutledge, III and all those months unaccounted for between the time Lord Darnley banished him, and the sea captain announced he'd washed overboard."

Mrs. Atkinson's eyes widened. She leaned toward Natty and gripped her arm. "Why, Natty, that has to be more than twenty-some years ago. How is it you remember something about that time?"

"More than recall, the source is iron clad. And, as I said, it's going to shock you."

The housekeeper closed the door to her office and sat in a chair next to Natty, nodding for her to continue.

"When Rutledge left here, he took up residence at Madam Fornia's opium den. After weeks of him at her establishment, the madam got in touch with Dervila Murdock and told her to come get him. She didn't want him dying knowing her business would be shut down."

"I've heard whisps over the years about that horrid place. But who is Dervila Murdock?"

"I'm sorry to say, she is my estranged cousin."

Mrs. Atkinson gasped. "I am grateful his lordship never knew any of this. It might have killed him."

"Indeed. It's why I came to you. I'm not sure what to do with this information."

Mrs. Atkinson stood up. "I would like you to tell this to Lord and Lady Tremaine. They are receiving today. Would you mind going up with me?"

Natty felt uncertain facing them. Reminding herself of the lives this would impact, but she did not trek up the hill to gainsay her firm conviction. With a deep breath, she agreed. "I will."

"Come with me." The two women climbed the stairs to the upper floor and crossed a beautiful marble floor, down a corridor, and into the front of the manor. As many times as she had been inside Rockmore Hall, today would be her first to traipse upstairs.

Mrs. Atkinson knocked on a closed door and then opened it, asking Natty to wait in the corridor. Several minutes later, she opened the door and asked her to step inside.

"This is Miss Natty Walsh. She and her niece, Brianna Walsh, have helped at Rockmore on a number of occasions. Most recently Lord Darnley's birthday party."

Lady Tremaine, a woman in her late thirties, Natty warranted, appeared like a flower in her light-patterned flounce dress. Busy with needlework as her husband, Lord Tremaine, worked at his desk. Both looked at her with somewhat of a skeptical interest.

She gave a small curtsy and stood in the center of the room as Mrs. Atkinson directed.

Lord Tremaine came from behind his desk asking, "Mrs. Atkinson says you have information regarding the late Garrett III, Viscount Rutledge?"

She nodded and tried not to twist her fingers. He towered over her most forbiddingly. Yet, she knew him to be a fair and kind nobleman.

"How did you come by this information?"

"My cousin, Dervila Murdock, whom I have not had a relationship with for many years, informed me several days ago. She nursed the young Viscount Rutledge from the effects of his illness."

Tremaine stated, "We learned that he fell overboard on his way to school. He died within six months of leaving this home."

Lady Tremaine's voice stilted with resolve, "However, we never discovered where he was…from July 1816…" her eyes closed… "until we learned of his death Feb. 1817."

A silence hovered over them as each drifted back to that time.

Lady Tremaine appeared shocked. "Are you saying you know where he lived all that time?"

"Yes, milady. I am. I learned of it recently from Mrs. Dervila Murdock."

"Please make yourself comfortable and tell us everything."

By this time, Natty's knees felt like jelly. She gladly sat and glanced across the room at Mrs. Atkinson, who encouraged her with a nod. "I can soften the news or tell it exactly the way I heard it."

Tremaine said, "The truth is what we want, all of it, Miss Natty. Please."

She began with the opium den and Madam Fornia. Following up with Dervila taking him in, and his recovery. Then Rutledge's decision to become the man his grandsire wanted him to be, so he made plans to leave for his school near London.

She glanced at her superiors, wondering how they were taking it in, but could see no sign of acceptance or rejection, perhaps more like shock.

Then she added, "Dervila discovered herself expecting a child about the same time Viscount Rutledge left but said not a word to him because she knew he needed to finish his schooling. She also had another problem. Her husband, Niall Murdock, had always been a...well a rough and tumble sort. She expected him to return from China in a month or so. So, without telling anyone, Dervila delivered the child and paid a peddler to take the infant.

"If I am to tell the truth, I'll also say she did not want to keep the child. Her lifestyle such that motherhood would be a curse she did not want."

Tremaine coughed into his fist and turned to the window. Lady Tremaine set her needlework aside and looked at Natty as if she wanted to ask more, but her apprehension overruled the asking.

From the window, Lord Tremaine inquired, "Are you knowledgeable about the child? Where it might be? What the sex is?"

"Yes, milord. I named her Brianna Walsh, and she is a lovely young woman of twenty-three."

Both Lord and Lady Tremaine looked at her as if she had grown horns.

"You raised her?" They said in unison.

"Yes, and all these years with no grasp of her identity, until Dervila told me three days ago. Dervila is unaware I raised the daughter she bore."

Lord Tremaine's forehead knit with suspicion. "How did that transpire?"

She related the story about arriving at the woods and helping to ease the peddler's worry over his wife by holding the infant. And then waiting for months and months for him to come back and claim the infant.

"I always told Brianna the story of what I assumed was her family. The peddler, his wife, and five siblings. That is what I saw in the forest that day. That is what Brianna has always believed her family to be."

"Has Brianna been informed of any of this?" Tremaine's words edged with caution.

"All of it. That her real mother paid the peddler to take her when she was barely several days old. And she is a child begotten on the wrong side of the sheets by the late Viscount Rutledge and a woman of wicked nonsense who cheated on her husband."

Lady Tremaine's delicate hand covered her lips, her, *ooh*, nonetheless heard by all.

After several minutes of uncomfortable silence, Tremaine offered a hand to Miss Natty. "You must have speculated as to how we might regard this rather shocking situation?"

"I did, milord. Telling you brings me relief."

"Lady Tremaine and I will discuss the matter and communicate with you in the near future. You must realize my wife would be the young lady's aunt?"

"Yes, milord. I am well aware."

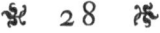

28

Handling the future and then some

Sir Finbarr entered his accommodations and maneuvered his way into his office, his arms full of architectural drawings. Collins on his heels. "You have a letter, sir."

"Who is it from?" grunted Sir Fin as he dropped the drawings on a table.

"The handwriting resembles Lady Hamerlin's." said Collins.

"Open it and tell me what she has to say." He stooped to pick up two drawings that rolled onto the floor. "I'm getting to the point where my patience is wearing thin. I hope we are able to move in within another month or so."

Collins read. "The lady has issued you an invitation to a musical on Wednesday next at five, with dinner following."

Several more drawings rolled off the table, and Collins bent to pick them up. "Does she say where the musical is to be held?"

"No."

"What does the calendar look like?" He added the ones that had rolled off, causing the rest to fall to the floor. He glanced at the mess and drew an exasperated breath.

307

"Let me take care of these." Collins handed Sir Finbarr the message and added, "You are free on Wednesday evening."

For a week now, Finbarr had been involved with Abernathy and the finishing details of Ashcourt. Exhilarated to see his childhood home returned to its former glory and then some, he wanted Brianna's reaction. She had held him off for one reason and another until he decided he would let her come to him. He knew she would because her curiosity always got the better of her.

৩৫৬

The day of Lady Hamerlin's musical party came earlier than he would have expected, as he dropped the brass unicorn head against the knocker on her door.

The butler opened the door. "Lady Hamerlin is in the parlor, sir."

Sir Finbarr handed over his beaver hat, gloves, and cane and strode into the parlor. Aware of his late arrival, he fully expected Lady Hamerlin to be annoyed.

She turned about at the sound of his footsteps on the marble floor. "What is amiss that makes you late?" She had not been able to disguise her displeasure, and he knew the evening ahead would be frosty. "I plead being carried away with the drawings of Ashcourt Manor."

"Collins didn't remind you?" She held a long-stemmed goblet of something pink in her hand. As she sashayed across the room, he might guess it to be a third or fourth glass of wine.

"I'd given him the night off."

Gowned in a dark bluish color that sparkled as if alive, she knew how to stride toward him to make the frock shimmer. Elegant and secure within, she exuded sureness of a life she controlled, an existence she presided over.

Sliding her palm over his waistcoat, resting it against his shoulder, she glimmered with feminine wile. Batting her lashes, she drew close enough for him to breathe in her lavender scent. He covered her hand in his and placed a kiss on her knuckles. "A beautiful woman, a lovely dress. The world is waiting for your sparkle and wit, madam. My carriage awaits."

Lord and Lady Thornton hosted the musical in their regency mansion. Sir Fin met the middle-aged couple earlier at a soiree about the same time he met Lady Hamerlin. He scooped up a glass of what he assumed was Jamison off a passing tray and backed into a corner. Lady Hamerlin maneuvered the throng, waving, smiling, and talking, reminding him of a butterfly flitting from flower to flower.

"You find crowds a bother, do you?"

He glanced at one of his cricket mates, Eddie Winthrow. "Unless it's on the playing field."

"I say, let the women do their darndest to stir things up. I'll take a wall at the back anytime."

Sir Fin barked a laugh, causing several who stood near to ogle both he and Eddie. The men nodded and turned back to continue with their discussion.

"This isn't my sort of thing."

Eddie asked, "Then why are you here?"

He sipped his drink, ignoring Eddie's question, and asked his own, "Thornton brought out his best tonight. He must be trying to impress someone."

"Ah, so you came for the liquor." Eddie finished off his libation.

Sir Finbarr eyed his teammate. "That's a good question. Why am I here?"

Eddie said, "You have the most beautiful woman in the room on your arm when you arrived."

"I did, didn't I. That must be why I'm here."

They both reached for a drink when a starched, black-suited

servant passed the tray. Clinking their glasses, they leaned back against the wall and watched the room fill with luster and frivolous laughter.

Sir Fin did not feel out of place—he felt restless. The musicians tuned their instruments, and the butler announced it was time to find a seat. He glanced around for Lady Hamerlin, discovering she had claimed two chairs in the middle in the second row. Mrs. Thornton, with an elderly guest in hand, said something to Lady Hamerlin and then the elderly woman sat in the chair meant for him.

For some obscure reason, Sir Finbarr felt relieved and nodded from his position against the wall when she turned to look at him. He was familiar with her forced smile and attention to etiquette.

Thornton had gone to a great deal of planning for this evening to be successful. He had a special dais built in the middle of the large room for three musicians—a flute, piano, and violin. The domed area made sense with regard to sound transmission. Sir Fin wondered how often the Thornton's offered musical entertainments to go to so much trouble.

The vaulted room grew silent with Mozart's harmonies on the flute and violin. He noticed unconscious toe-tapping as a sprightly number followed. Overall, the simplicity and balance in the melodies seemed to calm him. Sir Fin had not realized how tense he had become.

At one point, he slipped from the room and wandered into the foyer as the sound of music curled in the air. Moonlight shafts filtered through windows high above. He mused about the nearly completed Ashcourt when soft footsteps approached, and for a moment when he turned, he hoped to see Brianna breezing toward him.

"The musicians are taking a break and I wondered where you were." Lady Hamerlin came up next to him. He focused on the upper windows and the beams of moonlight. She trailed a finger up his arm and tightened her hand around the muscular upper arm.

"This is where you belong, beside me, and in good company. I worried Miss Walsh would be an enticement. But I can see you came to your senses. You must have grown tired of her shall I say, childish innocence?"

He almost choked on his drink. He had been thinking the same thing only in reverse; he was not good enough for her. He fell into the worldly and hardened group.

She said, "Our friends worried something was wrong."

His brow quizzed at this. "I beg your pardon?"

"You said nothing about wandering off. I've assumed we are more than mere acquaintances, considering all my valuable time that is taken up by you. My friends think of us in tandem when filling out their guest lists." As if she was talking to a dolt, she added, "They are concerned about your absence from their company."

He stepped around her and set his empty drink on a highly polished mahogany side table about ready to return to the music room when she continued.

She leaned in. "Miss Walsh is without family. She was discovered in a field abandoned as an infant. She is not even Miss Walsh's niece?"

He was about to take her elbow but pulled back in surprise. "I recall Miss Brianna telling me about her remarkable beginning. As her background is of no consequence, I simply shrugged it off. Why do you find *on dits* about her worthy of mention?"

Her brilliant smile almost matched the shine of moonbeams landing on her gown, but her eyes were cold. "We should return lest anyone consider our absence is due to mischief."

She smoothed her palm over his waistcoat and glanced up at him through her long, dark lashes. Her white teeth gleamed through the red of her lips as they parted.

Sir Fin circled her wrist with his fingers and removed her hand from his chest. "This might be inconvenient, but I am leaving and wonder if you would mind terribly finding a ride with one of your friends?"

Stunned, she managed to sound agreeable. "Certainly, I don't think that is a problem. Are you of a sudden ill?"

"Not a'tall. I have never felt better in my life. And it is my pleasure to relieve you of the tedious objective of being a couple, milady."

The butler must have overheard their exchange as he stood at the door with Sir Finbarr's hat and cane.

※

A knock at the door on Stoney Batter was most unusual at the evening hour. Mim already had a net over her hair as she answered the door.

"Sir. Good evening. Come in, please."

"Is Miss Natty in? And receiving visitors at this hour?"

"You can ask her yourself. She is in the parlor. I'm certain she's privy to the conversation thus far."

He took off his hat, and placed it on the chair, along with his cane and gloves.

As he entered the parlor, her twinkling bright eyes greeted him. "This is an unexpected visit. Would you like a libation? I am enjoying a raspberry port."

He glanced at Mim, waiting at the passageway. "If you have a brandy?"

She nodded and went off down the corridor.

Miss Natty asked. "My, you look like you've been to a gala affair. And here you are traipsing past our door. What brings you here at this hour, dear lad?"

As usual, he smiled at the moniker. "I need you to convince your niece to marry me."

Aunt Natty's mouth literally dropped. Her eyes appeared to almost fall out of her head. She reached for her port downing it in one gulp, then coughed and said, "I should have warranted it was something special as you are gussied up in your blacks and patent leather slippers."

He sheepishly admitted, "I attended a musical, and it came upon me as I stood watching the moon that you could help. She has refused me once and—"

"She has *not!*" Her hands clapped in shock.

He nodded. "I need you to champion my cause."

"What is her reasoning? Blast her. Does she not know *I* want you for a nephew?"

His heart eased, and a chuckle burbled from his lips. "She says we do not match."

"Ah, the poor thing. She's hurting because of learning about Dervila. And much affected with embarrassment at how the Darnley's were drawn into the mess. She makes excuses not to talk. At this moment, she has set up her easel to paint the sunset. Something she turns to when troubled."

"Where?"

"Out toward St. John's River. She loves the view. It's on the east side of the bridge; you will most likely see her on the rise. She has a preferred view, looking west back over the river and catches the sunset. I think it is her next favorite after Ashcourt."

ॐ

It took him ten minutes in the phaeton to approach the upper bridge over the river. He saw her standing at the easel intent on the sunset with a handful of minutes until it reached the horizon. Not wanting to startle her, he waited on the bridge, hoping she would look his way.

Sheep rustled about, nibbling on the grasses as herd dogs stood watch. A light wind rustled the treetops and sent ripples over the river. A lovely pastoral scene with Brianna in silhouette against the reds and oranges in the sky.

He waited until it looked like she was beginning to wipe her brushes, then advanced toward her, whistling as he did so.

She heard him and looked his way, then smiled and waved as he neared.

He reached for her hand and pressed his lips on her knuckles. "May I see you home?"

"A knight errant wandering in search of a chivalrous deed. I would not want you to get paint on your velvets."

He gathered up her easel, folding the legs, and wrapped the strap that held the pieces together. "Collins is wizardly at cleaning."

He reached for her box of paints and together they made their way across the heather toward the bridge the carriage in the hands of his tiger. Sheep scattered as they approached.

"I attended a musical and decided I needed fresh air." He grinned down at her.

"My fortune then. Juggling all this is tedious."

"Seems a wagon of some sort would make it easier to cart your paraphernalia about the hills."

"Did you come all this way to talk about a wagon?"

"No. I'm here because I want to be with you."

The brim of her hat got in the way of looking at him, and with her arms full, she could not push it back, grateful her blush would not be noticed.

❦

Early the next afternoon, Mim answered the door and nearly crumbled to see Mairéad, Lady Tremaine, asking if Miss Brianna Walsh was at home.

Curtsying, Mim explained. "We expect her from work soon. Would you care to wait? Miss Natty is in."

Lady Tremaine stepped over the threshold. "Thank you."

Ushering her into the parlor, Mim inquired, "Would you like tea, milady?"

"That won't be necessary. If Miss Natty is not occupied elsewhere, could she spare a moment?"

Mim curtsied and left. Within moments, having heard the

exchange in the foyer, Miss Natty was already on her way to the parlor.

"This is a pleasant surprise, milady. What can I do for you?" Lady Tremaine was gowned in dusty pink trimmed in a creamy lace about the cuffs and neck. Pearl buttons dotted the front. Miss Natty recognized the resemblance to Brianna but kept her pondering to herself. She had been too flustered yesterday when she repeated the conversation with Dervila, to her ladyship and had not taken notice then.

The eyes and wide brow, delicate ears, and slim shape of the nose were obviously the same. The hair color was off, though. Brianna being much darker. Probably the influence of her mother. Natty shuddered, thinking of Dervila.

"Did Mim offer tea?" Her ladyship, though appearing calm, seemed a bit unsettled.

"She did. I ah, I want to meet with your niece, talk with her if I may. We were introduced the day of my grandsire's birthday gathering, but it was such a crush, I can't recall her."

"She works at the post office three mornings a week helping Mrs. Teaberry out. I expect her any time now."

"Yesterday, when you came to the Hall and told us about Rutledge, I imagined you must have been fraught with concern."

Miss Natty took her time answering. "I realized you had no reason to believe anything I had to say. I admit my concern is Brianna."

The front door opened, Brianna called out, "I'm home," as was her usual greeting, to the rustling sounds of hanging her bonnet on a peg.

"We have company, dear. In the parlor," called out Aunt Natty.

Brianna entered the room smiling. When she recognized Lady Tremaine, her eyes darted to her aunt and back to her ladyship. She stopped mid-stride and curtsied. "Good afternoon, your ladyship."

"I understand you are returning from work at the post office?"

"Yes, milady."

"A job you must enjoy?"

Brianna sat in the chair across from both women, wondering why Lady Tremaine would be gracing them with a visit. Had she caught wind of Dervila's intentions? "Very much. Though Mrs. Teaberry can be a taskmaster at times."

Her ladyship's eyes brightened. "In my early years, I was under the influence of a task mistress. In the end, we became the best of friends. She has passed on now. Her title, Abbess of the Sacred Heart of Jesus Convent, didn't begin to describe her."

Miss Natty said, "My niece does not know I visited you yesterday. I can see she is graveled at your presence."

Lady Tremaine glanced at Brianna. "Let me tell you a little story first. Before we go on to the reason for my visit. As an infant and left on Sacred Heart's doorstep, the Abbess raised me, and I believe loved me. She taught me as a mother would have taught her daughter.

"Lord Darnley discovered an old letter and a marriage certificate of his deceased son that mentioned *an infant named Mairéad was taken to the convent.* His lordship hied to the only convent with many miles of Hawthorn Village, the Sacred Heart of Jesus. The convent where I lived as a postulant. I was seventeen at the time. He believed me to be his son's daughter but said nothing to anyone, not even to me, lest his family be hurt with misinformation."

Tears streamed down Aunt Natty's cheeks. and she dabbed them with her handkerchief, obviously remembering that emotional time so long ago.

Lady Tremaine continued, "As I had been taught to illuminate manuscripts, Lord Darnley brought me to Rockmore Hall to work on a book about his ancestors. I was to stay for the summer. That's how he cleverly explained my presence in the household.

"Mother Abbess allowed me the summer away from the convent to do this. So, even I did not realize his motive. The butler, Witham, tried to quell the tattle below stairs. Over time, servants and landed gentry alike were kind and helpful. One person seemed to have trouble with my presence. Garrett John Wallington, III, Viscount Rutledge, my twin brother. Neither of us knew our history. But Lord Darnley had rightfully guessed and told no one, not even Lady Darnley."

Bewildered, Brianna could not take her eyes off the poised and lovely woman. Her hands folded in her lap as if she waited for her portrait to be painted. Brianna wondered at the strength within that allowed her ladyship to reveal this personal story about herself. Tension gripped Brianna's body. She drew her arms close as if she might fall apart.

After all, this was a story about her own father and her aunt.

Aunt Natty was silent. Her watery eyes glanced between the two.

Lady Tremaine continued. "The purpose in telling you all this is to draw a comparison for you. Finding out about your story goes much deeper than the possibility you are my niece. When Lord Darnley discovered my true identity, he told me I had a mother, a twin brother, and a grandma'am.

"Your resemblance to my daughter is remarkable. That alone warms my heart. I have grieved for Rutledge over the years and feel like I have a part of him returned to me in you, Brianna.

"You see, when he was banished from Rockmore, we had not yet discovered my mother delivered twins. We did not find out until after Rutledge's death that I had a twin brother."

Aunt Natty dabbled at her tears, her lips wobbling between a smile and sorrow.

Lady Tremaine had not changed her posture.

Brianna breathed in slowly, her mind a jumble of what Lady Tremaine was possibly getting at. "How sad, milady. All the years, and all the missed opportunities."

"And your remarkable story, Brianna. If not for your aunt in the woods that day, where might you be now?"

Brianna reached over and squeezed her aunt's hand. "We've pondered the same question over the years."

Aunt Natty dabbed at her eyes once more. "Milady, we are honored to have you visit and tell us of your own beginning. I know it has brought me a sense of Brianna's own wellbeing with her knowledge of who were her parents.

"Please take our word we will not make it known to others. This will be our secret. Your presence has relieved me greatly, it is the least of which we can assure you."

Her ladyship's gloved hand stroked her throat, her brow knitted. "I think you have misunderstood my intentions, Miss Natty, Brianna." She glanced from one to the other.

"I fully intend to claim Brianna as my niece at a dinner in our home, Friday next, if you will agree to attend."

Aunt Natty gasped and began dabbing at her eyes all over again. "But she can never be recognized. Her parents weren't married."

"Fiddle DeeDee. Her family will recognize her. Tremaine left it up to me to make the decision. My eyes tell me all I need to know. She is practically a copy of my own daughter, Lady Fionnuala. I recall the resemblance was remarked upon at Lord Darnley's party by several who were in attendance."

Shocked, Brianna's mind whirled. She was speechless.

"I intend to be your aunt, Brianna. In so doing, maybe I can give some glory to my brother, whom I miss with all my heart. The time we had together was far too short. And not the least pleasant. Presumedly, I am able to make up for those wrongs by doing what's right for his daughter. So, you will need to get used to me." She stood and shook out the skirt of her pink day dress.

Brianna and Aunt Natty stood, as Lady Tremaine said, "We will invite family and close friends. I also intend to invite Reverend Gaskill. If you would like to invite anyone, inform me and I'll send them an invitation."

Still recovering from Lady Tremaine's generous invitation, Brianna managed to say, "I would be pleased to have Sir Finbarr O'Bannon invited, milady."

"How nice. Tremaine will be delighted. They are friends.

Now I must return home. Your great-grandma'am, Adrianna, intends to surprise you next Friday. She is waiting to find out if our meeting today has *borne fruit*. As she says."

When Lady Tremaine hugged her goodbye, Brianna was left with the scent of fresh linen and sunshine. She stood a moment in the corridor and gathered in all that had transpired in the last hour. Aunt Natty came up behind her and she fell into her arms, sobbing away the pent-up anguish that had resided in her heart.

❦ 29 ❦

Raindrops on Ashcourt Manor

Tuesday morning Brianna snuggled in the cozy comfort of her bed and woke with the desire to paint Ashcourt, as if she had a great thirst and needed to quench it. Sir Finbarr would be pleased.

She also wanted to begin the day with less severe musings of Dervila—after all, the woman was her mother. Perchance she could kindle empathy, some sort of sensitivity toward her.

Tossing the covers aside, she began her morning ablutions, dressing in a simple cotton frock permanently splattered with paint. Then she tucked up her hair as best she could and donned her wide-brimmed bonnet to ward off the sun.

Entering the dining room, she kissed Aunt Natty on the cheek and grabbed an apple and a piece of buttered toast left on the plate.

Aunt Natty's request filtered in the air, "If possible, try to be home mid-afternoon."

"I'll do my best." Brianna worked her way through the kitchen, where she kept her supplies, and drew the easel's strap over her shoulder. She pocketed her apple, juggled her toast, snatched up a three-legged stool, her box of paints, and left through the kitchen door.

No one loved a purpose more than Brianna. Lady Tremaine had given her just that when she visited yesterday. Brianna allowed the entire visit and every heart-felt word to sink in. Her insides shimmered with the wonder of understanding her background.

Before she fell asleep last night, she pondered Lady Tremaine's overwhelming revelations. If this grand, newly identified aunt could open her heart, surely Brianna could find room in hers for Dervila.

Right now, more than anything, she wanted to paint Ashcourt. Filled with a sense of contentment, she planned to embellish the canvas as her dearest friend, Sir Finbarr, had asked.

Thick mist blanketed the park in a dusty white. As the sun came up, as the mist cleared, tiny bell-shaped flowers on the heather began to unfold. A cock crowed off in the distance. Trudging along the path, she felt the weight of her hem dampened with moisture. A hawk took flight, soaring from a perch high up in a treetop, probably in search of breakfast.

A glorious day. She whispered to herself, thank you God for the gift of family.

Inspired by a break in the clouds, the sun spilling through, she set up her easel on the south side of the manor facing St. John's River.

The morning dew had already left the bushes and grass on the approach to Ashcourt. She opened her box of oils. Setting the tubes of various colors within reach, she watched the sun bounce off a window, bringing Ashcourt to life.

Sir Finbarr's move-in date was close. Both happy and bewildered, his offer of marriage seemed an awkward moment in the past. Much had changed since that afternoon. The knowledge of who she was now—and who she was not, allowed her to feel comfortable with herself.

The warring within receded though a few scars remained. She

had not an inkling if she had been gotten by lovers or just two lonely people. Nevertheless, her gratitude abounded that her male parent had a sister who wanted a relationship with her.

It was all too new, and cobwebs lingered.

Glancing upward, Ashcourt's windows glimmered. On the first floor, the front door was graced by bowed windows on each side, allowing sunlight to stream in. Brianna could envision Sir Finbarr living here. The façade stripped of ivy, a newly painted front door, and a large brass knocker depicting the head of a lion made a welcoming difference.

Would he marry? Might he marry Lady Hamerlin? Brianna took in a deep breath, feeling rather sure milady would be his choice.

Shaking her head of it all, Brianna sighed and looked at the exterior. *You have been here all my years and offered me solace, been my silent friend.*

Mawkishly sentimental, she trudged here with the idea of painting a likeness of the front of Ashcourt. Instead, she sat on her stool glancing at the canvas and recalled Aunt Natty's story of the cleric in Co. Waterford who Baptized Brianna in St. John's baptistry as orphaned Brianna Walsh.

She had been nearly a year old at the time. Before Aunt Natty registered her, she waited through that year for the peddler to return and reclaim his child.

Two small bunnies scampered across the dewy park, bringing a smile. She took their gamboling as an omen of good things to come.

She prepared the canvas using a blend of white pigment and marble dust that would modify paint absorbency. Focusing on the reason she was here this morning, she chose a thin stick of charcoal to outline the major points of the painting, and scale them to size accordingly, the manor, St. John's River, and the landscape.

The sun was halfway to noon when Brianna suddenly realized she had been sketching for several hours. Completely absorbed in her artistic efforts, she could not believe how fast the time passed. The manor, the landscape, and a slice of St. John's River cutting through pasture acreage completed her initial rendering.

She stretched and shook out her hand. Reaching for the apple tucked in her satchel, she sauntered up the park to the manor as she bit into her snack. A patch of strawberries, edible yet she knew to be tasteless because of their color, were growing under a large section of pointed evergreens. Returning to the front, she practically stumbled upon clusters of bell-shaped purple and pink flowers that probably would not last much longer. This time of year, the Irish were lucky to get bright sun five or six hours a day. The rest, if not mizzling, was usually dampish and gray.

The canvas waited for her, and the light would be good for maybe two more hours. As she approached her easel, her critical eye scanned the canvas. She favored Ashcourt, but had not done justice to the surrounding land, an easy fix.

Settling on the stool, she began mixing a paint color to match the stone façade, a light gray would do perfectly as she mixed black with a touch of white until producing the exact tint she wanted.

As time passed, she found herself squinting, a few hours past noon she noticed clouds rolling in. Quickly wiping off brushes, she hurried because the rain was coming. A plop of water, then another, she grabbed the canvas and ran to the front door taking shelter beneath the overhang.

The rain quickly advanced and she turned the latch on the door delighted to find it unlocked. With a breath of ease, she stepped inside to wait out the squall.

Leaning the canvas against the wall, she sat on the marble stair treads and took off her bonnet.

From the back of the manor, she heard a loud ruckus, pounding and yelling. She scooted through to the kitchen, shocked to see Sir Finbarr beating his fist against the door. Quickly unlocking the door, he stepped inside, wringing wet, and shook off his soaked beaver hat. Then he stripped off his cape and laid it on the newly installed counter.

Sweeping his hand through wet hair, he grinned. "Sorry if I frightened you, but I wasn't sure you could hear me otherwise. How did you gain entry?"

"Through the front door. Fortunately, it was unlocked."

"Lucky for me, too. When I rode up, I saw your easel and paints as I came through the woods. I hoped you had gotten to cover."

She suggested, "Shall we sit on the stairs until it abates?"

He nodded and followed her to the front of the manor. Folding his cape inside out, he placed it on the step for her to sit.

Brianna warned, "It will be ruined."

"I have the world's cleverest valet. Remember?"

"In that case, thank you."

A silence built up. She had so much she wanted to say to him. Just sitting near with the sound of his breathing and the energy that emanating from him comforted her. This could be her life if she would allow herself to accept his offer.

He promised her the world, and all she saw was a painted blue wagon filled with family that transformed into an immoral adulteress who would pay someone to take her infant.

His hands clasped between his knees his thumbs twiddled. "I'm surprised to see you here. You told me you would not paint Ashcourt until the renovation completed. It's not entirely there yet, but here you are." His lovely smile brightened the gloom of the hall where they sat.

They were sitting on the same step and she scootched back against the banister to better see him. "When I woke this morning, I had a sense of freedom, as if I could accomplish anything. Wonderful really and I owe it to Lady Tremaine."

He grinned, the one where his eyes squinted and glistened with mischief. "You've spoken with Lady Tremaine since Friday?"

"She came to the house and told us all about her earlier life and how Lord Darnley discovered her true identity. I think she wanted to put me at ease about my parentage."

Reaching for her hand, he warmed it with his palms. "And you were inspired to begin my painting?"

He noted a canvas against the wall near the door. "May I see it?"

"Oh, no. There is nothing to look at. It's hardly begun. Then the storm came. Lucky for me I could bring it inside."

Water dripped off his black Wellingtons and seemed to catch his attention as he finished warming her hand. "I am pleased you care enough to paint Ashcourt again." He tipped his head. She was caught staring at him.

Flustered, she muttered, "Why wouldn't I want to paint Ashcourt? It's meant so much to me through the years. It's been my mainstay."

"You aren't that old to need an anchor." He chortled. "I recall you saying you would paint it one last time when the renovation completed withal. As if you were never painting again."

Silent a long minute, she took in a deep breath as if she were going to dive underwater. And maybe she was. "How are you and Lady Hamerlin getting along?"

He eyed her again, not so pleasantly this time. "Where does that come from?" he said, his hands spread on his knees and fingertips tapping against the worsted. "Why do you ask?"

Drat. She shook a wasp's nest. "Because I'm nosy?"

Rather than respond, he said, "You've gone to the trouble to save a wounded man some time ago and give him purpose and promise. HELP… SAVE…ME literally returned my sanity. And then you refused my offer of marriage. Your pert little nose is no longer allowed to satisfy its snooping."

She gaped at him before catching herself, then quickly tried to recoup her dignity. "I misspoke. She is a good friend of yours and it isn't any of my business."

He leaned back against the opposite banister and looked

directly at her. "It could be your business if you decide we are a match." His lip twitched as if he tried to stifle a grin.

Mayhap Lady Hamerlin is not important to him. Her emotions warred. She considered him the most confusing man she had ever met. She was in a tangle and for some reason, Lady Hamerlin stood at the center.

He unclasped his hands and rubbed them against his buckskins. "Why do you think I've visited your household all these months?"

"Because you rescued Aunt Natty when she fell. And you came to like her?"

"Yes, certainly true. But there is another reason far more compelling." He reached over and tucked a stray curl behind her ear.

"I am in love with you. I want to make a life with you. Who your parents are or are not is of no consequence to me. You opened my world and brought me back to life. I feel out of sorts when I'm not near you. Strange as it might seem, I've lived thirty-three years in a solitary kind of mindset. You are a breath of fresh air that I want to breathe for the rest of my life."

A long minute passed as their eyes held. Maybe it was the acceptance Lady Tremaine gave to her. Crinkles at the corners of his eyes sharpened her yearning, and she scooted over, placing her palms on his cheeks, and kissed him, as he had once kissed her, with a light brushing of her lips against his.

When she drew back, his arms circled her, drawing her onto his lap as they sat on the steps, and he introduced her to a different kiss…at length…until he pulled away and looked into her eyes. She rested her head against his arm and felt warm and safe and loved.

Lady Hamerlin's imagined presence faded away. Nor did Dervila loom disastrously into her thoughts. Her fingers played along his jawline and traced his nose, then his lips.

"Will you ask me again to marry you, please?" As her head rested against his arm, her eyes were on his lips.

"Not if you are going to say *no, we aren't a match*."

"I shouldn't have said that, but at the time I considered I had no right to assume otherwise."

He swept his palm across his chin and looked down at her, cradled against the nook of his arm, a tender look in his eyes. "My darling Brianna. How am I to get on with living if you are not by my side?" His finger traced the outline of her ear. His breath was warm against her cheek.

Brianna began to explain herself just in case he wondered about a few things. "Lady Tremaine shared a story about herself that helped me think differently about my odd parentage. And I cannot stand the picture of you kissing your lady friend. Also, Ashcourt is going to need me in the years to come."

His eyelids slipped halfway over his eyes, the side of his mouth curled, "Please stop this nonsense and give me your answer."

Crinkles spread from his emerald eyes, and she snuggled close and slid her arms about him, her face resting against his paisley waistcoat as she sniffled. "Yes, yes, yes, I will marry you."

"I'm glad we've got that settled." He hugged her tightly and whispered, "I love you more than you will ever know. But Collins will be upset if your tears stain."

Pure joy filled the fibers of her being. "He is clever with stains."

He kept her close within his embrace. His large hand cradled the back of her head and rocked them both, taking immense pleasure in the feel of her against him.

"Speaking of Collins, he will be most pleased. I've been a canker for weeks."

Marrying Finbarr was sinking in, and a loving warmth centered on her, like the sun inhabiting her heart. "Oh, I almost forgot, Lord and Lady Tremaine are inviting you to dinner next Friday."

"What is the occasion?"

"Lady Tremaine wants to introduce me to her family and friends. She inquired if I had anyone I would like to invite. Naturally, I mentioned you." It felt so right to be in his arms, content and safe and loved. She loved him, had been falling in love with him for a long time. Her fear of rejection had held her in check.

He rested his chin on the top of her head and continued to hold her close. "If you agree, that would be a perfect time to make our own announcement."

She whispered, "I agree," as she tipped her head back and reached for his kiss.

The Friday dinner

Sir Finbarr arrived at Stoney Batter to escort Brianna and Miss Natty to Rockmore Hall. October's chill and gray sky notably upon them as the carriage he hired drew to a stop in front of the Stoney Batter cottage. As the weather had changed considerably these last few days, his phaeton would not have staved off the wind and possible rain.

Mim promptly answered the door, her eyes wide with excitement. "I'll tell the ladies you are here, Sir O'Bannon. The parlor if you will."

A feeling of wellbeing swept through him. He chuckled as Mim quickly made her way up the stairs.

Tonight, will be a turning point for him, too. Grateful Lord Darnley's family intended to embrace Brianna as one of their own, filled Sir Fin with gratitude. Legally Brianna could not claim herself to be a family member, nor would she care to.

His wife-to-be would not insert herself into the Darnley fold. The knowledge there was much more to her than being Dervila's daughter is what mattered.

Sir Fin stood at the bay window looking out over the misty rolling hills, a vee of geese honking their complaints on the way north. He waited for the two women who were instrumental in changing his outlook on life.

He had come back to Hawthorn Village with the intention of ridding himself of his family home and then return to Swansea.

Fortune snuck up on him in the guise of a woman on a coach who berated him for his scowls—that drew his attention.

The ensuing weeks and months allowed him to discover her outlook on life. Her exuberance and vitality and regard made him realize his life would be meaningless if he could not have her as his own.

Without any awareness of doing so, she had thrown off the black pall that enveloped Ashcourt. No longer the sad place filled with silence or his mother's weeping. An odd sensation had taken root in his heart, and something he would never put to words, but he felt the walls were happy. A place where a family could grow. He had Brianna to thank for that, seeing Ashcourt through her eyes…and heart.

He turned toward the patter of leather shoes on the floorboards.

Miss Natty, gowned in black sateen with a beaded top, and fan to match, entered the parlor, two feathers, one pink the other white, waving from her hair done up atop her head.

She offered her hand, and he made a short bow. "You look lovely, Miss Natty."

"Thank you for the compliment. It has been far too long since I have been in full dress. Have you made yourself a drink? I think Brianna will be another minute or two."

"What would you like?"

"Not just yet. I will save myself for the party. Otherwise, I might be on a slant." She eyed him with a delightful smile. "You look ever the prosperous gentleman with far too many opportunities for delightful parties at your fingertips."

He chuckled. "Not so many. But one must be prepared."

"Did you move in high society in Swansea?"

"Occasionally. I dedicated my time to the running of the

mines. And contacts are an important asset." He raised his drink to her before taking a sip.

Brianna's footsteps on the stairs turned his attention to the parlor entrance and his mouth slacked, which he quickly mended.

With each step, her gown changed from lavender to lilac as if sun and shadow blinked over her. Her dark auburn hair sparkled with inset pearls; curly side ringlets dangled over her ears. Her face was bright with excitement.

As he stilled at the sight of her, Aunt Natty chirped, "You look lovely. The color of your gown is perfect with your hair."

Shaking himself out of a stupor, he said, "I will be the envy of every man, escorting the both of you." He finished his drink and put it on the sideboard. "Shall we be on our way?"

Aunt Natty giggled like a young lass. "I'm ready."

Brianna blushed. "I am excited and nervous at the same time."

Sir Fin reached for her hand and drew it to his lips. "Lady Tremaine would not have pulled this night together if she did not already have faith it would be an enchanting evening welcoming you into the fold." He glimpsed at Miss Natty. "Right? You can vouch for the family well enough. What do you think?"

"I agree." She tapped Brianna with her fan. "You, my dear, have come into your own and it's high time you found your place."

Mim had their capes on her arm as they gathered in the foyer. Sir Fin placed them about each lady's shoulders. Filled with excitement for Brianna, Mim's face glowed. "Bless you. And take care tonight to enjoy all. I'll want to hear about your grand evening at breakfast."

Family and other look-a-likes

As the carriage neared Rockmore Hall, Sir Fin and his passengers enjoyed the many windows aglow with light. Flickering sconces were lit on the sides of the carved double doors. The carriage drove up the lengthy lime-bowered approach past a lough with a fountain spouting to the heavens.

A pair of swans majestically glided on the water amidst lily pods, three cygnets following in their wake.

A stable lad scrambled to take the lines from Sir Fin as he stepped down from the driver's seat and instructed his tiger to follow the stable lad who was already filling his tiger with visions of eating in the kitchen once they took care of the carriage and horse.

The butler standing at the open door greeted the party of three. And a liveried servant directed them inside, where another servant took their accouterments.

The butler led them to the largest parlor Brianna had ever entered, and introduced them to everyone at once. A reception of hand clapping and welcome greeted them.

Aunt Natty whispered, "I knew you would be astounded."

Lord and Lady Darnley were the first to greet them. Brianna was overwhelmed by Lord Darnley's reception. "You take me back many years, my dear. To a time when your Aunt Mairéad, Lady Tremaine, came to Rockwell for the very first time."

"She told me the story of you finding her from information found in a letter."

His gnarled hand reached out to her, and she leaned down. "I am deeply thankful for the chance to meet you, Lord Darnley."

Lady Darnley stepped next to his lordship's chair, and Brianna curtsied.

"We welcome you with all our hearts, dear Brianna. Finding you gives us a chance to think of our son and grandson with much appreciation. If it weren't for them, we would not have you."

Lady Tremaine approached and nodded to Sir O'Bannon and Miss Natty Walsh, then reached for Brianna's hand as she spoke to Lady Darnley. "Grandma'am, do you mind if I take Brianna for a few minutes? We will return before dinner is served."

Lord Darnley barked, "See that you don't dawdle. I've quite an appetite."

"We won't, grandpapa." She grinned at Brianna as they turned to leave. "He's always hungry."

Sir O'Bannon and Miss Natty Walsh stepped toward Lord and Lady Darnley as Brianna was on her way with Lady Tremaine.

As they were leaving the room, Brianna quickly glanced at the exquisitely lit front parlor with colored glass shaded lamps. Settees flanked a huge fireplace crackling with burning apple wood. The scent permeated the room. Many paintings of fox hunting, family portraits, and landscapes of the area surrounding the village, and the grand River Suir adorned the walls.

Lady Tremaine whispered, "If we hurry, they won't even realize we've left by the time we return." As they headed down the corridor, the strains of a fiddle, harp, and concertina rippled through the air from a corner of the parlor.

Servers offered refreshments, as Lady Tremaine explained to

Aunt Natty, "We will return in a minute or two. Please make yourself comfortable."

Lady Tremaine hurried Brianna as they traversed the carpeted corridor. "Tremaine is building us a home more inland from here. My grandparents have given us a suite of rooms in which to live until our new home is completed. I do love this place and shall miss it. It is where I came to live when I left the convent. It will be grand to have our own home, however."

Brianna stopped Lady Tremaine, who turned to her and said, "Is something wrong, my dear?"

Brianna asked, "I... I'm unsure. What is it you want of me, ma'am? What do you expect of me?"

Lady Tremaine smiled and cupped Brianna's cheek. "It's what I expect of my family, not you. I refuse to see you as anything other than one of our own. You are my brother's daughter. No one can take that from us. I intend to prove something to you, should you be in doubt."

Brianna felt her anxiety slip away. She took a deep breath, hopefully warding off tearing up. They approached a smaller parlor and Lady Tremaine closed the doors behind them. "I want to privately introduce you to my daughter, Lady Fionnuala."

Brianna had not noticed at first, but a slight figure turned from the shadows and slowly emerged into the light. The closer the figure came, the more Brianna's breath caught. It was like looking in a mirror.

Brianna bowed. A tremulous smile flirted with her lips. Nervous behavior overcame her.

Lady Tremain spoke to her daughter. "Brianna is the daughter of my late brother, Rutledge. Miss Brianna Walsh, your cousin, Lady Fionnuala."

Lady Fionnuala bowed. "It is a pleasure to make your acquaintance, Miss Walsh."

Lady Fionnuala's gray eyes and beautiful golden hair, ringlets about her crown and ears, stunned in a white lacy gown, even though she frowned.

Brianna wondered if the young lady found her difficult to accept. "I hope our meeting is not uncomfortable for you. I have just recently discovered my parentage. Like you must be, I, too, am surprised."

The younger woman nodded as if she agreed, then she peeked at her mother. For assurance? Brianna wished to make friends with her. She could hardly fathom a look-alike and tried not to stare. What must Lady Fionnuala be thinking? She acted as though she had just met someone who did not measure up.

"Well, then," offered Lady Tremaine, "I wanted the two of you to meet before your family crushes you to talk to them."

She smiled at her daughter and turned to Brianna. "We are mostly family tonight with the exception of Mr. and Mrs. Curran, and Reverend Gaskill, who are dear friends, and your aunt. My own dear mother, Nuala, Lady Rutledge, who is your grandma'am, is also part of our dinner."

As they returned to the parlor, Brianna considered the years without knowledge of family and said to Lady Fionnuala. "You are fortunate to have always known who you are."

The young lady could not be more than a year or two younger and appeared withdrawn. It took her a moment to respond. "Were you discontent until you were made aware of your connections?"

"Heavens no. I love my aunt dearly. I probably should have said, how wonderful for you to have been raised within the fold of a mother and a father."

Appearing hesitant, Lady Fionnuala faltered in her speech. "You have experienced...shall I say...an early life similar to my own mother." She maintained an even tone as she offered an obviously forced smile.

The last thing Brianna wanted to do was give cause for Lady Fionnuala to dislike her. "Your mother graciously shared information about my father. In so doing, I realized how fortunate a person you are to be loved by her."

As they entered the parlor, chatter came to a stop. Kindly eyes fell to Lady Fionnuala and herself. Sounds of delight came forth and then clapping began.

Lady Fionnuala stepped away from Brianna, leaving her to be the recipient of goodwill. However, what her action caused was for Brianna to doubt a friendship would be possible with her newly discovered cousin.

Nuala, Lady Rutledge, immediately came toward her. "Do you recall, at Lord Darnley's birthday party, when we first met, that I saw a resemblance between you and Lady Fionnuala?"

"I'd forgotten. But yes, now that you mention it, I do remember."

"I would never have dreamt of meeting my son's child. You have no idea how thankful I am for this moment, dear Brianna. God has surprised me once again with a gift of enormous love." She kissed Brianna on both cheeks and turned to Lady Fionnuala, taking up her hand. "Now I have two of you to hold in my heart."

Sir Finbarr, in conversation with Lord Tremaine, winked at her as their eyes met. His broad smile warmed her heart. She would need him in the days and years to come for his support and love.

A hush came over the small group and Lady Rutledge said, "Look at my darling granddaughters. Are they not the most beautiful to behold?"

Aunt Natty and Lady Darnley both pulled out handkerchiefs, dabbing their eyes.

Lord Tremaine steered Lord Darnley's wheeled chair directly toward Nuala and her two granddaughters. Lady Darnley came forward at the same time.

Emotion overcame Brianna, and Aunt Natty stuffed her kerchief into Brianna's hand. Through the minutes that followed, she intermittently teared up and surged with elation.

Family. Glorious family.

They were her family. She looked for Lady Fionnuala, finding her in the corner alone and staring at her, a curious look on her face that Brianna could not define.

The butler announced dinner and Lord Darnley designated Brianna to stay beside him as a servant rolled him into the dining room. The rest of the family followed, pairing off accordingly.

The dining room walls were papered in an embossed deep blue, drapes of gold hung from the ceiling and puddled on the dark floor. It was the most striking setting Brianna had ever seen. Mirrors framed in gold flanked the walls and made the chandeliers shimmer with light.

The table was laid with China, stemware and silver flatware all embossed with the family crest. She balked at the six knives and forks at her place and several others she had no idea what their use would be. Serviettes were folded to look like swans with a bread roll on the swan's back. Thankfully, she sat across from Lady Tremaine and would follow her example.

Mr. Curran sat to her left. "Your aunt looks exceptionally well. No doubt being able to know your background has helped put the mystery behind you."

"Who my parents were, of course. But now there are other factors to consider. It's a bit overwhelming. I don't think I've fully absorbed it all."

"Well, Miss Brianna, if there is anything I can do, please don't hesitate to stop in. If nothing else, I am a good listener."

"I will remember your kindness and appreciate your offering."

Lord Darnley tapped the edge of a knife against his water crystal. "Reverend Gaskill has offered to lead us in prayer."

As the dining room quieted, the Reverend began. "In your goodness, God, you have seen fit to bestow upon us a new member of the Darnley family. We give thanks for Miss Brianna Walsh, and we also give thanks for the generosity of Lord and Lady Darnley in their great pleasure to recognize Miss Brianna as a member the family. Amen."

A short mantle of silence followed until servants entered the room carrying silver platters filled with the first course, oysters, and clear mock turtle soup.

A second course of turbot, horseradish sauce, and smelts

followed at the same time the normal sound of conversation began to rise. Listening to the swelling rise of camaraderie from her new family relaxed Brianna.

Lady Darnley clanked her utensil against the crystal, and stillness reined as she began, "I have a gift for my new great granddaughter." She spoke to a servant standing against the wall, asking him to bring in a picture from the corridor.

Two servants carried it in, holding it high.

"This is an oil rendering of my son, your grandsire. Garrett John Wallington, II, Viscount Rutledge. He loved to paint, just as I understand you also love to paint. He is twenty years of age in the painting. Of course, none of us knew it at the time, but he only had a little time left. He painted himself from his mirror image. I think it quite fitting to gift it to you, my dear."

Brianna put Aunt Natty's handkerchief to good use and attempted to steady her voice. "I am at a loss for words as to how to thank you for such a marvelous and generous gift. I shall treasure it all my days, ma'am."

"I prefer grandma'am. And in this instance, it is great grandma'am." She blew a kiss to Brianna who sat at the other end of the mahogany table.

Brianna bowed her head in acceptance and dabbed at her eyes as emotion overcame her.

The third course began with chicken, minced veal and bechamel sauce. Brianna ate tiny bites. Her insides roiling with the anticipation and now the reality of this evening and all it symbolled.

Sir Finbarr engaged in lively conversation with his cousin, Nuala, who sat across from him. They were laughing at something Nuala had told him. Brianna could also see Lady Fionnuala's plate. She had hardly touched her food. Brianna hoped it was not because of her and that she had taken personal offense. Perhaps it is just her nature.

After finger bowls were put out and raspberry tarts, vanilla cream, and cheese straws were delivered, everyone seemed to calm with conversations more like murmurs.

Aunt Natty's lilting laughter came to Brianna's attention several times. Her seat partners were Mrs. Curran and Lady Fionnuala. Though the latter had little, if anything, to say. Mrs. Curran, a lovely dark-haired woman, was born in Portugal. Someone had mentioned it was her mother's birth country. She was the wife of Aunt Natty's doctor. She kept up a lively repartee.

Brianna could see that Sir Finbarr thoroughly enjoyed himself. He was next to Mrs. Curran, on one side, and Lady Darnley at the head of the table. He had been entertaining them, as they both were quite attentive toward him.

A moment later, he stood and tapped his eating utensil against a stemware for attention. "I wish to make a toast."

Brianna held her breath. She knew what he was about to announce and hoped she would not shed one more tear. Her life had not changed a'tall until she met him. And now, after Lady Tremaine's lavish acceptance of Brianna, she would forever be someone else.

A hush calmed over the table of diners when he began, "I am prompted to share this with you because of what you all mean to Brianna. She has consented to become my wife. And we intend to make Ashcourt Manor our home."

A round of cheers and drinks raised as heartfelt congratulations were offered.

Sir Fin interjected, "I am presuming, but I suspect my future wife will want to put the painting of her grandsire in the foyer above the fireplace."

Lord Darnley took exception. "That's all well and good, Sir O'Bannon. But don't think for a moment that you can get away without an interview with Miss Brianna's living protector? As the eldest male in this family, I have say over my great granddaughter's future. We need spend time discussing the matter of your marriage proposal."

For a moment, the dining room stilled. Lord Darnley beamed.

"I haven't commanded anyone's attention all evening until now. As to you, O'Bannon..." He chuckled... "Why don't you stop by tomorrow late morning when I'm at my best. We'll discuss the matter then."

"I would be honored, your lordship. Tomorrow at eleven."

Lady Darnley stood and her granddaughter, Lady Tremaine, followed suit. "Shall we retire to the library and leave the men to their nonsense?"

Titters followed the *nonsense,* as the women knew cigars would be brought out and a strong port would be offered.

Lady Darnley tucked her hand on Brianna's arm and beckoned for her other great granddaughter to join them. Lady Fionnuala appeared hesitant to do so, if her slow shuffle accounted for her lack of enthusiasm.

"Finny, is something bothering you tonight? Did you dislike the minced veal?"

"No, Great Grandma'am. I'm not feeling up to sorts is all."

"How is your writing? Have you finished your latest story... wasn't it about a horse and a young lad?"

"Yes, and I am almost done with it. I've trouble with the end. I'm not sure if I should be dramatic or carefree."

Surprised to hear she penned a novel, Brianna asked, "What a wonderful endeavor. How long have you been writing?"

Narrowing her eyes at her great grandma'am, she asked, "Has it been six years?"

Lady Darnley said, "That sounds about right, you started off with a small tale for lasses, *Mimi's Pony.*"

Brianna expressed delight. "I assume you are published."

Lady Fionnuala, on the other side of their great grandma'am from Brianna, spied her and nodded.

Her great grandma'am stated firmly, "She won't tell you this, but she writes under a pseudonym because publishers state they cannot sell books written by the weaker sex. So, if you happen to go to the book sellers, you might look up Garrett Rutledge."

Brianna laughed outright and stopped in her tracks. She held

Lady Fionnuala's eye. "How wonderful for you. I am certainly sorry about you being a member of the weaker sex, which we as women, discern as a fallacy. The idea is to create what you please and having your work displayed in the window of a store. How marvelous of you."

Lady Fionnuala's reserved manner brightened. "Do you really think so?"

"It's a step into the future of what you endeavor to achieve. Next to come will be when you challenge that book seller to either put your given name on the book, or you will take your business elsewhere. Believe me, he won't want to lose the income you bring in."

Their great grandma'am said, "Well now, I do believe the two of you have much to talk about, and I want to chat with Miss Natty." She withdrew, leaving both young women near the table set with scones and punch.

Brianna asked of her cousin, "Would you mind telling how you approached the publisher. I am rather curious how you got him to take you on."

Lady Fionnuala smiled with a roll of her eyes. "Let's get some punch and sit in that corner." She nodded toward the bays that overlooked the garden. "You might be surprised at what I said to him."

Brianna dipped the ladle into the punch bowl and followed her cousin to the chairs she had indicated. Shyness had been the problem, and Brianna's anxiety eased with the surety they could have a relationship after all.

A fairy tale ending

The first to say good night was Lord and Lady Darnley. Brianna and Sir Finbarr accompanied them to the bottom of the grand staircase.

Lord Darnley, though a smile on his elderly features, looked tired. He really enjoyed sharing a few stories with Brianna.

He said, "Meeting you reminds me of the first time I set eyes on your Aunt Mairéad illuminating books in the convent, paint on her fingertips. It took her a long time to accept the change in her life, but family won out over the convent in the end. I am just as grateful you have been found, my dear."

She bent low and whispered *me too* in his ear, then kissed his cheek.

His craggy features brightened as two very capable servants were about to lift his wheelchair. "I need another minute with my great granddaughter." The servants backed away, and Brianna leaned over to face him. "My dear, don't let my little drama at the table worry you. It is an honorable tradition I uphold with my female family that I meet with the gentleman who wishes to marry them."

She kissed him on the cheek. "Thank you, your lordship. I'm overwhelmed that you would put me in company with your family."

"That's what we are, my dear. And we take care of each other."

He waved for the servants to return and lift his wheelchair and began the trek to his bedchamber.

Sir Finbarr and Brianna offered their appreciation to Lady Darnley for the wonderful family evening. Brianna could tell it had been a long day for her great grandma'am. She gently hugged and kissed the sweet woman, promising to see her again soon. They watched as she made her way up the stairs, a maid at her side.

Returning to the parlor, Lady Fionnuala sought out Brianna. "I took up most of our time talking about my writing this evening. Great grandma'am mentioned you paint. Is there a time I could visit and see your work?"

Brianna wanted to raise her eyes to the heavens in thanks. She worried about her cousin's approval. "I work in the morning on Monday, Wednesday and Friday at the post office. Afternoons are best."

Lady Fionnuala spontaneously hugged her. "You can expect me sometime this week." She blushed furiously, as if her overture had taken every ounce of initiative in her slender frame. "If that's alright with you."

Overwhelmed by Lady Fionnuala's interest, Brianna said, "I would cherish time with you. Let me know when."

Sir Finbarr, finished with his goodbyes, neared Brianna as she said goodnight to Lady Fionnuala. "I will look forward to your visit." She felt a ruffle in her heart. All these people were her family. As he reached for her hand, she knew he would be hers forever too. She was blest and fortunate beyond anything she had ever dreamed.

He whispered, "Miss Natty is succumbing to too much rich food and the lateness of the hour. I left her in a chair, fighting to keep her eyes open."

"In the small parlor?"

He nodded. "I think the others are readying to depart, also."

"Then let us say our goodbyes and gather her up."

The fresh air roused Aunt Natty as Sir Finbarr drove them home. "What a grand evening. The Darnleys are gracious and loving. And my *dear lad* did not disappoint. He stood bold as could be and announced his intentions to marry my dear Brianna."

A fairly good chuckle rumbled out of him. "Lord Darnley brought me up short. But he is within his rights to want an audience."

Brianna said, "You think so?"

"Lord Darnley is assuming a paternal role over you, my dear. You will always have his protection, even when we marry. I won't be the least bit surprised if, on our wedding day, he endows you with a purse you can be proud."

Aunt Natty proudly announced, "Lady Darnley asked if Brianna would honor them by choosing to be married at Rockmore Hall."

Tears spilled down Brianna's cheeks.

He reached over, handing her a handkerchief, then squeezed her gloved hand. "Are you alright, my love?"

At the moment he glimpsed her, a shaft of moonlight found her soft pink lips framed by a brilliant smile. "Dearest Fin, my heart is so full of love."

In the blue October evening, as the moon rose over Ashcourt Manor, a window twinkled in the moonlight.

THANK YOU FOR READING

❧

Don't miss out on your next favorite book!

❧

Did you enjoy this book?

We invite you to leave a review at your favorite book site, such as Goodreads, Amazon, Barnes & Noble, etc.

DID YOU KNOW THAT LEAVING A REVIEW…

- Helps other readers find books they may enjoy.
- Gives you a chance to let your voice be heard.
- Gives authors recognition for their hard work.
- Doesn't have to be long. A sentence or two about why you liked the book will do.

ABOUT THE AUTHOR

Karen Dean Benson gained a love of history from travels that took her into many different cultures around the world. A voracious reader from an early age, she loves research, history, and tales of complicated lives. Her stories, woven against the backdrop of a by-gone era, present numerous plot twists.

Her first series, *Ladies of Mischief,* is about women who find themselves enmeshed in mischief and mayhem spiced with charm in the 18th and 19th Centuries.

Her second series, *Prickly Hawthorn Village:* Southwest Ireland in the early 1800's where the inhabitants of Hawthorn Village's lush emerald hills and breathless azure heavens find adversity and acceptance along the banks of the ancient River Suir.

She lives with her husband Charlie in Florida on a golf course.

www.karendeanbenson.com
http://freshfiction.com/author.php?id=40966

facebook.com/Author-page-for-Karen-Dean-Benson-1415121542104941

goodreads.com/karendeanbenson

bookbub.com/authors/karen-dean-benson

amazon.com/Karen-Dean-Benson/e/B016PMAZRE